D0492601

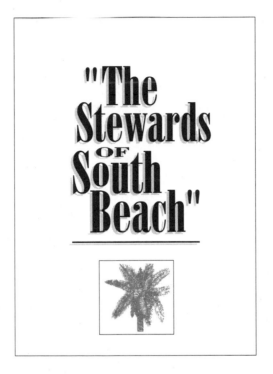

"The
Stewards
OF
South
Beach"

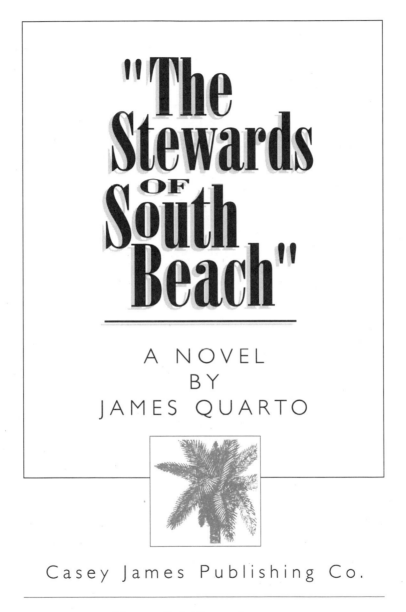

"The Stewards of South Beach"

A NOVEL
BY
JAMES QUARTO

Casey James Publishing Co.

jimq56@aol.com

Edited by Chris Roerden

First Edition.

ISBN 0-966-8975-0-1

Many thanks to: Andy, Bill O., Bill S., Charles, Edith, Eva, Katie,
                  Jack, John, Mary Ann, and Mike

I will always be indebted to JESSE, whose wisdom and encouragement
were invaluable in assisting this first time novelist.

My sincere gratitude to CHRIS, for her guidance and editing.

And especially to PAT, for her endurance and patience.

WHAT INSPIRES ONE TO WRITE A NOVEL?

IN MY CASE IT WAS EASY -- MY BEST BUDDY, CASEY.

TO HIM AND TO ALL MY OTHER GRANDCHILDREN:

CORI

NYKOLE

SAM

I DEDICATE THIS BOOK TO YOU.

ONE

Two days of fog had brought Kennedy Airport to its knees. Thousands of frustrated travelers pleaded with airline employees for information about their flights.

This was his first flight. In fact, he had never been to an airport before. As he walked through the maze of stranded travelers, he thought, I wish something could be done to assist these weary people in reaching their destinations. Perhaps I could intervene? After considering the idea for a few seconds, he shook his head, realizing its inadvisability.

Look at that young mother chasing her brood around. Those three children sure are cute, especially the little red-headed girl. Looks to me like she's about four years old. I wonder how many hours they've been waiting?

Come to think of it, I hope my flight is on schedule. He continued to the Delta ticket counter, weaving a path through hundreds of disheartened travelers sitting on their luggage and sneaking an occasional peek at the monitors to see if there was any change in the status of their flights. He grinned at the thought that perhaps his first flight might also be delayed and then jokingly reconsidered his need to intervene on his own behalf.

The roped-off line was filled with impatient, complaining passengers. As he listened to them, he thought of the monumental mission ahead of him. Father has once again given me a demanding assignment. I trust this group which is about to convene in South Beach will be as dedicated as the followers I assembled in Israel. We have so many more people to reach out to than the first time I was here. I wonder if they'll be up to the task? Such a difficult assignment and so little time to implement it. Before this weekend is over I'll know one way or the other.

"Next please," the ticket agent said. She couldn't help noticing the unusual garment bag strapped over his left shoulder -- navy blue, with a unique emblem on it of what appeared to be a silver chalice. Thinking he was probably a priest or clergyman of some denomination, she greeted him with her customary corporate greeting.

"Hello, sir. On your way to Florida?"

As he handed her his ticket he replied, "Yes, Miami."

"You're fortunate. I believe the Miami flight is just a few minutes behind schedule. More than I can say about most of our departures today."

"That's fine, Linda. By the way, how are the boys?"

"They're just wonderful, thank you." Wondering how he knew about her two children, she asked, "Do I know you?"

"I believe so."

"My apologies. I don't seem to recall who you are. Were you a friend of my husband's?"

"Why, yes. Jack and I are good friends."

"You mean you **were** good friends. I guess no one informed you Jack died in a fire last year."

"Oh, yes. I know."

"Are you a fireman, too?"

"No, just a good friend."

Linda's face flushed, nearly matching the bright red jacket she wore, as goose bumps glazed her milky white skin. She handed him a boarding pass and watched as he turned and walked toward the escalator. Her eyes followed him until he was out of view. I wonder how he knows about Jack and the kids. He said he was a friend of Jack's, but it seemed to me he was speaking in the present tense. Either he's some kind of a nut or.... What seemed uncanny was that this man had left the counter only a few seconds ago, but she had trouble remembering what he looked like. Linda couldn't even recall the color of his eyes, only that they appeared warm and sensitive.

Scanning his reservation once again, Linda was certain she didn't recognize the name: "Brother." I don't know any Brother, she thought, but said to herself over and over again, this is no ordinary man.

If only she knew.

TWO

The *Queen Elizabeth II* was on its way to Miami, Florida, an unusual port of call for her. She had been at sea for six days, departing from her home base, Southampton, England, on the eleventh of December. Normally, New York would be her destination; but the North Atlantic had been exceptionally rough the last few months. Three ships had already been lost in the traditional northern shipping lanes of the Atlantic. The Carnival/Cunard management, owners of this majestic vessel, had decided safety was paramount and had changed the ship's course to a southern port. Those inconvenienced would be airlifted to New York, of course, at the shipping line's expense.

Sipping his drink, Charles Montgomery, the captain of the *Queen Elizabeth II*, looked around the table at those passengers privileged to be dining with him, and predicted, "No storms in the forecast."

"Jolly good news," replied one of the captain's dinner guests, James Thompson.

"I do hope you enjoyed the brandy."

"Yes, I find a shot of the nectar relaxing. Helps me sleep like a babe in a pram, steered by an experienced nanny," responded James.

The Captain continued, "I believe this Remy Martin is perhaps the finest of all the cognacs."

"You see, in spite of their reputation, the French can do some wonderful things at times. Let me take this opportunity to thank you for your hospitality."

The captain nodded. "Is this a vacation or business trip?"

"Well, it's mostly business. We will manage to find some time to relax, I trust."

"What kind of business, may I ask?"

"My brother, John, and I are investment bankers. We invest in, and occasionally acquire small companies in the computer-related industry. As a matter of fact, the company we are looking at happens to be in Miami, so going there directly instead of New York is a stroke of luck."

The captain agreed, and asked how long the brothers would be staying in Miami.

"Two weeks, which will give us time to mix a little business and pleasure. Perhaps a round or two of golf." James sipped his drink. "I understand the South Beach area of Miami is quite European. Have you ever been there, Captain Montgomery?"

Before he could reply, one of the captain's executive officers approached the table. After a brief conversation with his subordinate, the captain said, "Have to go to the bridge." Shrugging his shoulders, he added, "Something to do with sailing this ship they want my opinion on." Apologizing, he wished James and the others a good evening.

While James was engrossed in conversation at the captain's table, John Thompson, the younger of the two financiers, was enjoying himself on the dance floor in the lounge. At twenty-nine, he was four years his brother's junior, but appropriately regarded by those in the London financial community as the more gifted of the two. At the age of twenty-two it had been his idea to purchase a computer chip company. The Thompsons had paid ten million pounds for the fledgling company, a price its previous owners thought far above its worth. Four years later, the brothers had resold the company to an American firm wishing to expand their operations in Europe. They received three times what they had paid.

Life had been more than kind to the two brothers, both financially and in matters of health. What else was there? Well, neither was married, and though John had all the social skills required to meet and entertain the beautiful women of London, he had yet to find the girl of his dreams. James, on the other hand, was more reserved than his charming younger brother, and had devoted most of his life outside of business to helping the less fortunate. An active member of the Evangelical Church in England, he served on a variety of fund-raising committees. In addition, he worked with various religious charitable groups, regardless of their beliefs. He did not evaluate the recipients on any specified criteria, so long as the money he donated was spent wisely. Because the donations were substantial, James did ask with whom and how the funds were -- as he liked to say -- invested.

They would be in Miami tomorrow, thought James as he tried to track down his brother to have a last review of some paper work. The late night bar and lounge was surely where he would be found. James immediately picked him out. John was dancing with a good-looking blonde in a blue sequined dress. Watching their precision-like footwork James thought of Fred Astaire and Ginger Rogers in *Top Hat*. The blonde's turns were performed with flair, as John extemporaneously choreographed the act, deftly collecting her back into his arms.

The two dancers could just as well have been part of the *Q E II*'s entertainment staff. The music stopped and John strutted over to introduce this lovely lady.

"James, this is Mary, Mary Dellany. She lives in Fort Lauderdale, not too far from Miami."

How convenient, thought James. Still mesmerized by their performance on the dance floor, he said, "Pleased to meet you, Ginger -- I mean Mary."

Mary smiled at her new acquaintance. Amused, she replied "Just following Fred around the dance floor."

"I believe we have found a wonderful tour guide when we reach land tomorrow," said John.

"Great." But do you think you might spare a few moments with me tonight to review some documents?"

"Of course," John said, not happy, but responsible enough to know that his brother was always right about these things.

As gracefully as she had danced, Mary sized up the conversation between the two brothers, faked a yawn, and turned to John. "The evening was delightful, but I must get my eight hours of sleep. Perhaps we can have breakfast tomorrow, before we reach port?"

"Sounds wonderful to me," said her dance partner. "Good night, fair lady."

"Yes, good night, Mary. It was indeed a pleasure meeting you," said James.

THREE

Philip Silva had arrived in Miami on December third, a little more than a week earlier. Anna, his wife of four years, remained home in their high-rise apartment in Santiago, Chili. Philip, a brilliant and successful engineer, had come to Florida for a job interview. He wasn't concerned about his fluency in English, since it had been his second language in both high school and at the University of Santiago. He was currently employed by a firm that was responsible for the design work and implementation of Santiago's Metro system, one of the most sophisticated and functional subway systems in South America.

Although his family had the best of everything in Chile, Philip wanted his young son, Philip Jr., to grow up in America. Thus, he had applied for a work permit in the United States. His long-term desire was to become a U. S. citizen, but it was even more important to him that his son become one. The unstable economy and the political situation in Chile were the two primary reasons for this desire to relocate. In addition, air pollution in Santiago was out of control. Smog in that beautiful South American city was so dangerous that health alerts were issued almost every day. Travelers familiar with both American continents referred to Santiago as the Los Angeles of the southern hemisphere.

For about two months, Philip had been communicating by telephone and letter with MRM Corporation, one of the greater Miami area's five largest electrical contractors. The company was owned and operated by Josè Diaz, a Cuban immigrant, who employed many Spanish-speaking people. Diaz's company needed qualified engineers to cope with the substantial growth in the South Florida area. An ability to speak both languages enhanced the candidates' qualifications.

The interview process had gone smoothly, so smoothly in fact that at their second meeting Diaz offered Philip a position. Philip accepted a salary of sixty thousand dollars a year to start, with a review in six months. The manager of the human resources department informed Philip that the firm would rather he settled into new living quarters before he began work. Philip telephoned his wife, informed her of the good news, and told her to prepare to move. The couple agreed that she and Philip Jr. should bring only a few clothes and only the most cherished of their personal belongings, such as pictures and other family mementos. Philip would stay in Miami and begin the search for a place to live.

It took two days to find an apartment that fit the Silvas' needs, a modestly priced high-rise. Philip measured the rooms so he could purchase new furniture. Added to the ordeal of finding a job and apartment hunting, shopping for furniture was taking its toll, and the man from Chile was as tired as he could ever remember being in his life. But nothing -- not even the lack of furniture -- was going to prevent him from moving into his new home that very night. He picked up his luggage, stopped off for a six-pack of beer and an order of rice and beans, and went to the apartment. He enjoyed his simple dinner in the bare kitchen and slept on the carpeted floor of the living room. In the morning he called Anna from his new office and told her about their beautiful apartment near the ocean. He emphasized its location in a Spanish-speaking neighborhood, with many shops and a good school for their son. He had only to wait for their arrival. He hoped they would be with him for Christmas.

The overwhelming applause was a pleasant surprise to the traveling band of troubadours, as they liked to call themselves. Classical musicians, they had just finished the tenth and last concert on their tour of the United States, playing in front of a strange multi-ethnic audience under an enchanting Miami moon. What an experience for this group of exceptional artists from Germany, who had dedicated their lives to music. Bart Kessler, a thirty-seven-year-old pianist from one of the most picturesque cities in all of Europe, Heidelberg, was eager to tell his wife, Elsa, of this unusual mixture of people, but he would wait until morning before calling her at home. He could not recall if the time difference was five or six hours, but in any event, did not want to waken Elsa or his two children in the middle of the night.

Born Bartholomew Johann Kessler in 1962, he was named after his distinguished great-uncle Johann Bartholomew, himself a classical musician. Musicians had been in the Kessler family line for many generations. As deeply devoted as Bart's ancestors were to music, they were equally as irreverent when it came to belief in God. The Kessler family had been atheists for hundreds of years. Family records traced the root of this disdain for God back to the sixteenth century, coinciding, interestingly, with Martin Luther's split with the Catholic church. Although Bart wore the atheist label, he was one of the first in the Kessler clan to keep an open mind on this profound subject.

Bart was a worldly person, having spent most of the last six years on the concert circuit, with engagements all over the globe. Still, he thought as he sat in the hotel coffee shop, nothing he had seen was quite like this city called Miami. Its beautiful sandy beaches dotted by swaying palm trees were enchanting. The blend of different cultures in this vast melting pot warmed by the constant sunshine made this one of the most fascinating cities he'd ever been to. And if that wasn't enough, outdoor cafes serving ethnic dishes from faraway lands were within walking distance of the hotel in South Beach where he was staying, complementing this entertaining area.

Last night's performance had marked the end of the current tour. No concert or rehearsals for the next two weeks. He was going to take life easy, perhaps visit some of the sights of South Florida. But for today, Bart just wanted to spend a leisurely day at the beach. No better way to unwind, he thought, than to let the sun tan your body and read a good book. In less than a week, his wife would join him without the children for a second honeymoon. With his demanding schedule, their marriage had been anything but stable for the last few years. Since the birth of their two children, Elsa's time had been dedicated to them, and Bart's to his career.

He hoped a week alone with Elsa in this exciting city would help to ease the tension and perhaps warm up their relationship. He wanted her vacation to be perfect, and he had planned each day's itinerary with care, so each meal and all the sightseeing would be designed for two lovers on a romantic getaway. Fresh flowers in their hotel room each morning. A chauffeur-driven limousine, to allow the couple to see the sights of Miami one night. That's stretching my budget, he thought, but what the heck, this is going to be a memorable experience for us.

FOUR

The weather in Miami was unusually warm for December. Tourists flocked to the beaches enjoying the sunshine, tanning their bodies and tiptoeing around the man o' wars as they waded in the warm salt water. The hotels were at or near capacity, with bookings for the balance of 1999 and the millennium, far above normal. Restaurants flourished. Wait time for dinner in most cases was an hour or more on a weekday night. Natives who were accustomed to relaxing evenings at the numerous outdoor cafes at this time of year had to pull strings to get a table.

Thomas Olson from Malmo, Sweden, was enjoying himself by watching all the characters as they walked in front of his table at Siani's, one of the art deco district's busiest eateries. Young girls dressed in the most attractive beach cover-ups pranced up and down the street while the young men flexed their muscles, pretending not to notice them. What a strange game these Americans play with each other, he thought.

Thomas was in Florida on business; he hoped to get his foot in the door with some elegant designer fashions from Sweden. His partner, back home in Malmo, was a well known designer respected throughout Europe for his exquisite cocktail dresses, catering to the elite of most of the continent, even Paris. Two weeks and several meetings with buyers from prominent dress shops in Miami had brought a ray of hope, but no sales as yet. Patience and persistence will pay off, he thought, but that could wait, for tonight he would enjoy some of the sights and sounds of the city.

As with most of the restaurants in South Beach, Siani's enabled one to dine al fresco. The majority of patrons enjoyed the entertainment that passed by as they sipped their cocktails at the streetside cafe. The beautiful people of South Beach, as well as the pretenders, paraded by in brightly colored outfits.

None were more fascinating than the Hare Krishnas, chanting their spiritual verses in front of the cafes. Standing on the sidewalk, occasionally jostled by the beautiful people walking by and squeezed in between those sipping their cocktails, and a pair of red Ferraris parked at curbside, they sang their simple religious songs accompanied by brethren jingling tambourines. The delighted and inquisitive international travelers watched these young people recite transcendental sounds, while garbed in Spartan attire of white strips of cloth with multi-colored sashes and red and blue beads.

Tom Olson was no exception. He, too, enjoyed the procession of interesting characters parading by. Single, handsome, modestly wealthy, and impeccably dressed, Tom was the envy of all his friends back home. This was Miami, though, and most of the men at the in places here appeared to have similar qualities. What he did not know was that four out of ten of these guys, attired in five-hundred-dollar sports jackets or eight-hundred-dollar suits, were in hock up to their ears. Another twenty percent were married and cheating on their wives, and as far as their looks were concerned, the Florida sunshine can do wonders in that department.

Dinner was excellent, even better than the first night. As recommended by his waiter, Tom ordered an eggplant appetizer, veal marsala, and a tomato and onion salad. A 1983 bottle of Bolla Chianti Reserve complemented the meal. The waiter's recommendation was excellent, and Tom thanked him for his selections. A double espresso ended dinner. He loved music, especially jazz, and recalled it was only a short walk to a lounge with a great band he had heard his first night in Miami. Perhaps those interesting Americans he'd met over the weekend would be there, and that surely would make for an entertaining evening.

Entering the dimly lit lounge, Tom ordered a vodka on the rocks from the slinky waitress. Glancing around, he spotted the two Americans with whom he had enjoyed cocktails the previous week. Hoping to get their attention, he tried a casual if not wishful wave. One of them spotted him and began to sidestep some of the beautiful people to make his way to Tom's table.

"Hello, Tom. Sell any dresses today?"

"Not yet, Pete. Sell any fish?"

They laughed, and their heads turned to follow a small blonde as she sashayed by. Peter Albano and his older brother, Andrew, were in Miami attending a commercial fisherman's convention. Both Albano men were single and in their late twenties, sons and grandsons of fishermen born and reared in San Francisco. Andy had gotten married at eighteen to Ellen, also eighteen -- the girl next door. They had a beautiful daughter, Diana, after one year of marriage. But Ellen and Diana had been killed in a horrible traffic accident two years later, yet the drunk driver had survived the crash. The Albanos' fishing boat and the hard work of maintaining it had become his great therapy, helping him through the difficult period following this tragedy. Although his loved ones had been gone almost six years now, Andy's thoughts were with his wife and child, each and every day.

Like his younger brother, Andy was rough around the edges, strong and gutsy. His muscular arms and chest stretched his white dress shirt to the limits. He found his way to Tom's table, commenting, "Did you see that little...?"

"Yeah, yeah, yeah,"interrupted Pete. "You were always the second one to see things as a kid, Andy, and nothing has changed in twenty years."

Thomas, in an attempt to play the game, offered, "No, no, guys, I saw her first."

The three of them enjoyed a harmonizing chuckle while they listened to the music. The piano player, accompanied by a trombonist, an alto saxophone and a bass, began playing an arrangement of *"April in Paris."* Toes tapped and fingers snapped to the catchy arrangement of the great Count Basie's version of this classic.

"All right, settle down boys, and might I ask how was your day?"

"To be honest with you, Tom, the fishing convention has been over for two days, so Pete and I thought a few days of beach time in the Florida sunshine would be a great way to relax before we get back on the boat."

"Do you mind company? I could use a little sunshine myself."

"Okay,"responded Andy. "Let's meet for breakfast at ten. You're staying at the Ocean Hotel, if I didn't have too much to drink the other night, isn't that right, Tom?"

"As usual, fisherman, you are correct. See you in the hotel coffee shop at ten."

They exchanged good nights outside the lounge, and called it a day.

FIVE

The Sand Pebble Hotel is located on Washington Avenue, one block west of Ocean Drive. Its tangerine-painted dining room is small but it was adequate for the sixty or so guests staying there. Matthew Singer had checked into the Sand Pebble the night before, flying in from New York. Matt, a thirty-five-year-old native New Yorker, lived and worked in Manhattan. Employed by *Time* magazine, he was in Miami to do a story on an Australian who had sailed, solo, halfway around the world in a twenty-four-foot homemade boat.

"How many in your party, Mr. Singer?" the hostess asked.

He raised two fingers and she proceeded to seat him at a table near the window. The reporter informed her he was having breakfast with an Australian by the name of Jim Albright. Matt welcomed the opportunity to come to Miami just to see the sun once again, as New York had been depressingly gray for the last few weeks. The story he was assigned to was a dud, as far as he was concerned, but the Florida sunshine made the trip worthwhile.

A complimentary *Miami Herald* lay on the table and Matt began reading immediately, as the waitress poured his coffee from a floral pitcher. The headlines seemed similar to those in the New York papers. Crime in the streets, trouble in the Middle East, and the presidential race, coming next November, dominated the front page. Scanning through the business and sports sections in less than two minutes, he eyeballed the stock market, which was up again, and took delight that his favorite hockey team, the New York Rangers, had won last night's game against Montreal.

Matt attacked the crossword puzzle with a vengeance. He considered the puzzle to be his first major battle of each morning. Ten minutes and the puzzle was history, each blank filled correctly he hoped. He checked his Rolex, poured his third cup of coffee before the waitress could get to it, and began to wonder about the man from down under who should have been there half an hour ago. After all, Albright was staying in the hotel, so getting caught in traffic could not possibly be his problem.

"I finally found him, Mr. Singer," said the hostess.

"Thanks for your efforts. Did you require the assistance of the police or fire department, or the maid rousing him from bed?"

The hostess escorted the newcomer to the table and left the two men, a big grin on her face, having seen this scenario many times before.

"Hello, Mr. Singer. Thanks for the offer of police assistance; however, the maid was more than up to the task. Sorry for the tardiness." Pointing to his watch he added, "But I don't believe I've paid too much attention to time since my voyage."

The men smiled at each other, shook hands, and sat across from one another. The newcomer wore a blue striped shirt and a pair of faded jeans. Without question, the most striking feature about this world sailor was a long red beard covering a good portion of his weather-beaten face.

"A pretty sharp hostess, don't you agree Mr. Albright?"

"Jim is the name. Yes, she sure is. Matt, if I may, how did you get assigned to do this story? Did you lose the office pool?"

"Yes, I think I did,"replied the reporter. "The editor's son is a fourteen-year-old sailing enthusiast who is intrigued by your great adventure."

"But this is not current news, for gosh sakes. I've been here a month,"said the bearded one. "What's more, a number of articles have been written about my voyage already."

"Well put, my Australian friend, but I have been commissioned to come up with a new angle. Perhaps *Time* will offer you a bunch of money to sail back to Australia."

"No thank you. I have no intentions of setting foot on any boat for a long, long time. If you would join me, I'd consider going,"joked Jim.

"Thanks, but no thanks." The reporter grimaced and emphasized his no with a wave of both hands.

The two men breakfasted on juice, coffee, eggs, and English muffins, while Matt attempted to find out more about the sailor. "I know why and how you made your voyage, Jim, but what I'm looking for is somewhat more profound. I mean, when you were faced with that fierce storm you referred to, did your sailing skills pull you through or did you seek and receive guidance from somewhere else?"

"You mean something spiritual?"

"Why yes? This is what I'd like to explore with you. Is that okay, Jim?"

"Sure, Matt. Sounds interesting. But first I must tell you that I'm to be at the Australian embassy at eleven. Something to do with my passport. It's ten-fifteen now, which doesn't leave me with too much time. Can we continue this tonight at dinner? I'll buy."

"That would be fine. I'll make a reservation and meet you at the bar at the White Sand Hotel at seven. All right with you, Jim?"

"Thanks for your patience, Matt. See you at seven."

As the Australian sailor neared the hostess station, Matt called across the room, "Jim, the magazine will gladly pick up dinner, but only if you are on time."

The hostess offered to provide a police escort to assure Jim's punctuality at dinner, and the sailor reveled at her comment. Matt signed the bill to his room, left a generous tip for the hostess, and headed for the beach. Work can wait, he thought, as he walked toward the beach, taking pleasure from every ray of the penetrating sun.

S I X

The *Queen* docked at precisely eight on the morning of December seventeenth. One would not expect less than efficiency from this magnificent lady. The bells chimed, and one of the ship's officers informed the passengers of the debarking procedures. He told the new arrivals to keep their passports handy for going through United States Customs. Luggage, which had been placed outside each passenger's room the night before, could be retrieved at the color-coded section on the docking area. John and James Thompson were used to this drill, and were amused at the tone of voice of the ship's officer.

"This must be his first time on the public address system,"remarked John.

Holding his hands over his ears, James took it one step further, saying, "Based on his piercing voice I hope it will be his last."

The brothers' conversation was interrupted by the chimes again, announcing open seating for breakfast.

"Shall we go?"

James grinned at his younger brother and said, "Only if you want me to see how Ginger Rogers looks the day after."

Mary was already on her second cup of coffee when John and James arrived. "Welcome to the colonies,"she said, looking ravishing despite last night's workout on the dance floor.

James greeted her with a big smile and a warm hello. John offered the same warm hello, but couldn't resist giving her a peck on the cheek. A red blush appeared on that stunning face as she voiced how hungry she was. The last meal aboard ship was spent with one brother trying to converse with this attractive American woman about her day-to-day life in Florida, while the other brother was trying to become part of it.

"Like all good things that must come to an end, so must this delightful voyage,"said James, as he got to his feet and bowed to their beautiful breakfast companion. "Goodbye, Mary. Without question, you are the most attractive dining partner we've had on the entire cruise. I'll leave you two alone, as I need to review some documents before tomorrow's meeting."

Without hesitation, Mary walked over to James and gave him a warm hug and kiss. He blushed and informed his brother, in a joking manner, that the ship had actually reached port and that he would have to get off eventually. John, as witty as usual, asked his older brother if they had truly reached port, for he felt the ship was still rocking. James grinned, but reserved any additional comments and returned to his suite.

John and Mary, in an effort to extend their cruise and strengthen an already warm relationship, decided to take a stroll on the boat deck prior to debarking. After a bit of small talk about the different types of people one meets aboard ships, John asked, "Are you free for dinner tonight?"

"Tonight is out of the question, but tomorrow would be fine." Mary gave him a telephone number and told him that if he did not call, she would contact him. John thought that straightforward, a trait he was not used to with women, but charming. He turned Mary toward him and embraced her, his knees weak and his heart seeming to skip a beat. I'm really falling for this girl, he said to himself.

Mary kissed John and told him she wished they could stow away back to England. What she didn't tell her new suitor was the story of her checkered past. A life of abuse, hardship and five years as a high-priced call girl. The getaway to Europe was in a sense her graduation from that life and the beginning of a new one. She pondered telling him, before the relationship went any further. The chimes rang, interrupting Mary's opportunity to speak up.

Holding back tears of mixed emotions, Mary said, "Until tomorrow." She turned and walked rapidly to her cabin.

John waved to her, unaware of the change of direction his life and that of his brother, James, would take before tomorrow.

The Thompson brothers hired a limousine to take them to the White Sand Hotel, where they had booked the penthouse suite for their two-week stay in Miami. During the brief ride, the main topic of conversation was Mary. It was apparent to James that his younger brother had fallen for this beautiful, interesting woman.

After checking in, John asked the concierge for a restaurant recommendation. The seafood restaurant called The Coral Reef, in the hotel, was the concierge's number one choice.

"That will be just fine,"said John. "Could you make the reservation for two, at 8:00 p.m.?"

"It will be my pleasure,"responded the dutiful concierge.

Philip Silva whistled as he walked through his new apartment. The doorbell rang, and Philip rushed to the door expecting the delivery man from Burdines department store with the furniture he had ordered. Instead, the man standing at the doorway welcomed him in Spanish, stating that he was his neighbor from across the hall.

"Hello, my friend. My name is Rudy Romero. Welcome to Miami."

Philip paused and then graciously said, "Please come in, but I must first warn you that there is no place to sit as yet."

"I don't mind at all. I just wanted to know if I could be of any assistance to you, my new friend from Chile. Don't ask me how I know you are from Chile. Just let's say this is a very small community, filled with Latinos trying to help each other."

After telling this new neighbor his name, Philip offered his apologies for not having anything to drink in the apartment.

"Don't worry. I have some Cuban coffee brewing and will bring it over in a few minutes. By the way, Philip, do you have any cups?"

"Yes I do. I just bought some, and you and I will be the first to use them."

"Any sugar?"

"I'm sorry, my new neighbor, I didn't think of sugar or any other...."

"That's okay,"interrupted Rudy. "I'll bring some when I come back and we will christen your new apartment."

The furniture delivery occurred without a problem, on time, and without a scratch. Philip gazed around his apartment, proud of his new purchases, and confident Anna would like his taste in colors and designs. The pieces all fit, and appeared to be custom-made for the apartment.

A knock on the door, and there was Rudy once again, this time with coffee and pastry. "Sorry for the delay, one of my clients called and.... Well look at this,"remarked Rudy. "A place to sit and enjoy your first meal in your beautiful home."

Philip said, "Smells great,"as the aroma of fresh coffee filled the room. "Here let's sit down in the living room...."

"What do you do for a living?"inquired Philip.

"I'm an attorney. I'm originally from Mexico, but have been in Miami for three years."

"How about you?"

"I'm an engineer. And, I have a wife and son back in Santiago. Are you married, Rudy?"

"No, but I have a beautiful girlfriend."

"What kind of law do you practice?"

"I usually represent individuals accused of minor infractions of the law, such as traffic violations and petty theft. Occasionally I defend clients who are accused of possession of narcotics, but I rarely get involved with drug smugglers or street dealers. Just those poor souls who are caught with small amounts of drugs in their possession."

"I take it that most of your clients are from the community?"

"Yes. But every once in a while I do get people traveling through the Miami area who have had a run-in with the law." Rudy's tone was more serious when he added, "You will find out the longer you live in this area, the police treat the Spanish-speaking immigrants like second-class citizens. Always seeking to blame the Latinos for all the ills of the community."

Philip was a very trusting individual; though drug trafficking being what it was in Florida, turned on the warning light as far as this attorney was concerned. That aside, Philip enjoyed the brief time he spent with this protector of the misfortunate and defender of those in trouble with the law. Be neighborly, he thought, but keep the relationship at arm's length.

"The coffee hit the spot. I do appreciate your generosity. Also, may I add, let's hope my family is never in need of your professional services." Rudy was amused at his new friend's comment as the two of them sipped some more coffee.

"I have a great idea, Philip. What are you doing this afternoon?"

"Actually, nothing. I had planned to spend the entire day at the apartment, waiting for the delivery of the furniture. But as you can see, it has arrived."

"Then, why don't we go to the beach?"

"Sounds terrific. But unfortunately I have no swim suit."

"That's okay, you can wear one of mine. I have many to choose from. Have you been to South Beach since you arrived in Miami?"

"Not as yet."

"Good, we will go to South Beach. I think you will like the sights and the sounds of it."

SEVEN

Simon English was an aristocrat born in South Africa. For the most part, he had lived his entire life in Johannesburg. As usual, he spent the month of December at his condominium on Fisher Island, vacationing with a group of friends, all of whom were as rich as he. Simon's family had a significant interest in a diamond mine, and the family fortune was --- well, too much to count. As a child he had lived in various places in South Africa, following his mother and father around from one estate to another, depending on the time of year.

Sixteen years ago, when he was twenty-two, he had married his childhood sweetheart Victoria, who divorced him after five years. A boy, Richard, now thirteen, was the only positive product of the failed relationship. Simon made every effort to see his son, and he even maintained a civil relationship with his ex-wife. He saw to it that Richard and his mother had everything they wanted, including an extended vacation to any destination of their choice once a year. His son had everything, except a father whom he could talk to on a daily basis.

Never having had to work, Simon spent most of his time playing or practicing polo, and traveling from continent to continent to see every Formula One race. Golf, tennis, and deep sea fishing completed the portfolio of activities of this well-to-do South African. He played golf at the most prestigious clubs around the globe and fished all the oceans for exotic species. An avid sportsman, he might even have been called a fanatic by some.

Although he always stayed at his condominium, a trip to West Palm Polo Club was ordinarily part of his Florida itinerary. From time to time Simon would play polo or, at the very least, practice with some of the highly ranked players who lived in the area. His passion to compete against the best-rated players often ended with an injury to his thirty-eight-year-old body. Simon had usually been able to shrug off most of the bumps and bruises he'd received through the years, but the knee injury he had suffered in a fall from a horse a year ago had left him with a noticeable limp. Still, he loved to ride these regal animals as fast as they would take him. Possessing a good eye for horses, he was always in the market to purchase a good-looking steed with little regard of the cost.

Today, for a change of pace, Simon preferred a day away from his wealthy friends and all the exciting things money could buy. A simple day at the beach in a faded pair of cut-off jeans.

EIGHT

Three young men met at the Ocean Hotel coffee shop and began joking immediately about the night before.

"Another beautiful day in Miami, just like Malmo,"chuckled Pete.

"Here we go again. This is like a tennis match, you serve, now I must return a barb. "Let's see...."

"Hold it, Tom, you have no chance trying to compete with two fishermen,"said Andy. "What do you think we do all day on the boat? Besides, your accent precludes you from saying anything remotely funny."

"All right, I give in. Fishermen one, dress salesman nothing. But the game isn't over. This is just the first set."

The fun and games began again as the waiter delivered breakfast.

Pete asked, "A kaiser roll and coffee. You call that breakfast?"

As the badgering began again, Tom replied, "Let's see, what have you got there? I recognize eggs, ham, biscuits, an orange, toast, potatoes, and, oh yes, sausage. Yes, you were hiding the links of sausage under the toast. How many people are eating off your plate?"

"Round two to the dress salesman,"said Andy, sounding like a sports broadcaster.

The light-hearted conversation continued throughout breakfast, as the bonds of friendship grew tighter.

After breakfast, Pete shouted out, "Let's go to the beach."

The three men walked across Ocean Drive to the beach, settling in about twenty yards from the inviting cool water of the Atlantic. Eleven thirty, and it was already eighty degrees.

Tom said, "Let's get an umbrella. We want sun but don't want to bake."

"Good idea. With your fair skin you'll be red as a beet before noon." Andy was concerned for his new Swedish friend, for he had seen many of his crew on The Amalfi, the family fishing boat in San Francisco, suffer severe burns after a few hours of sun.

The sand was too hot to stand on without sandals, so the guys made a quick dash for the salty, warm water of the Atlantic. Pete jogged to the temperate water's edge and dove in, coming up for air about twenty yards from where Andy and Tom stood wading. An excellent swimmer, with both strength and stamina, Pete had been a life guard before his father made him an offer he couldn't refuse: the boat or get out!

"He sure can swim,"remarked Tom.

"Always could. Actually won a few medals as a kid,"replied Pete's brother, Andy.

Tom and Andy returned to the towels now partially shaded by the orange and white umbrella they had rented for five dollars. They looked back toward the ocean and admired Pete slicing through the water like a graceful porpoise.

"Oh the good life,"said Tom.

"Yes, it sure is,"replied Andy.

The two young men had dozed off for about a half hour when Andy was awakened by a gust of wind and asked Tom, "Do you see my brother?"

"I do, and it looks like he's made a new friend."

"Male or female?"

"I know you're not going to believe it, but it's another guy."

As Pete and his new acquaintance walked toward the umbrella and towels, Andy felt a strange sensation. Even with eighty-degree temperatures, a chill went through his entire body. Sitting up, he reached for his Amalfi Fishing Co. sweatshirt, pulled it on and turned around, making eye contact with a distinguished-looking man wearing a straw hat about five yards away. Although the man's facial features were shrouded by his hat, Andy sensed an aura of nobility about him. The elder Albano brother gestured to him as if to say hello, and received a friendly greeting in return. He wished to know more about this man, however, Pete's boisterous voice diverted Andy's attention.

"Guys, this is Tad,"said Pete. "He's from Detroit and sells cars for a living. Tad, this is my brother Andy, and the Swede over there is Tom. He's from Malmo. Andy and I have kind of adopted him so he doesn't get into any trouble while he's here in Miami. Oh, by the way, Tad, Tom sells fancy gowns to rich Europeans. Now he wants to peddle his dresses to well-to-do Americans. Are you in the market for one? Please say yes. I get a piece of the action."

They all laughed as Andy turned to see if the man in the straw hat overheard his talkative, as well as comical, brother.

"Tad, welcome to our little square of Miami Beach. Sit down and tell us about those great American automobiles,"said Tom.

"Well, first of all I don't sell cars. I work for...." Pete, in an amusing but charming manner, interrupted. "Tad, tell these guys your real name."

Tad looked at him, shook his head, and said, "How do you put up with this joker? He knows me for all of an hour at most and already teases me about my name."

"Come on, tell them your name."

In a voice resembling a television quiz show host, Tad announced, "I'd like to introduce Thaddeus Jackson, African-American, thirty-two years old, born in Detroit, Michigan, engineering degree, played football, second team defensive end at the University of Michigan. Go Blue!" He took a deep breath and continued, "Automotive engineer, divorced, two children, six-figure income, half of which goes to my kids and ex-wife. Do you need any additional information, gentlemen?"

Andy smirked and asked Tad, "Are you finished?" He poked his kid brother in the ribs, while turning to see if there was any reaction from their neighbor. This guy had a sense of humor at least, thought Andy, for the man in the straw hat was also grinning. He, too, found the show under the umbrella both entertaining and amusing.

"Okay, let's talk about cars,"Tom said.

"All right,"Tad responded. "You want to compare that box your countrymen manufacture to our new high performance...."

Again Pete interrupted. "Who wants a beer?"

All four raised their hands. As Pete got up to head for the restaurant across the street, Andy said, "Wait a minute Pete, I'll help you." When he arose from the sandy beach towel, he looked in the direction of the man sitting next to them. As he walked by, Andy stopped and offered, "Would you care for a beer?"

"Thanks for asking. I'd love one. How much is...."

Before he could go any further, Andy said, "That's okay, the first one's on me."

"Thank you very much,"came from the lips of this impressive individual.

Pete and Andy made their way to the edge of the sandy beach. Andy looked back over his shoulder, scrutinizing this man more closely and noticing that, besides the hat, he was dressed in lightweight white pants. He shook his head, unable to get his mind off of this figure on the beach who unquestionably had captured his attention.

As the brothers waited for the traffic light to turn green, Andy asked Pete, "Did you see that guy next to us?"

"No."

"Something about him; I can't explain it. When we get back I'm going to ask him to join us."

"Okay, pretty soon we'll have half the beach on our towels. Hey, I got an idea, Andy. Let's charge everybody five dollars for sitting under our umbrella. We'll make a fortune."The brothers kidded as they entered the restaurant, taking time out to notice the pretty waitress serving lunch.

The hot sun was responsible for the Blue Crab's crowded bar. Two bartenders were pouring beer from a variety of taps, offering a selection of regular, light, and lager. An occasional piña colada, or other tropical drinks, was prepared in advance by these experienced and entertaining bartenders to meet the demands of the thirsty tourists. Andy and Pete waited to get into an ordering position at the bar, dodging those who were attempting to make their way back to the beach with hands full of drinks in plastic cups. The entire process required persistence. A juggling background helped.

Returning to the beach, the brothers noticed another umbrella had been placed next to the one they had rented, and more people had gathered. Pete said to Andy, "Gee, I wonder if Tom is selling any dresses?"

Andy's reaction to Pete's comments was restrained, for he sensed that the unusual man sitting next to them had something to do with this.

"Get your beer, guys,"offered Pete. "I'm glad I got extras."

Tom, seeming somewhat dazed, took over at this point, making all the introductions. "Pete and Andy Albano, this is Matthew Singer from New York, Simon English from Johannesburg, South Africa, and...." Tom paused, almost unable to get the words out of his mouth. "And, this is **JESUS OF NAZARETH**."

Andy stared at Tom, trying not to make eye contact with any of the three newcomers, almost dropping the beer. Shocked, but attempting to gain his composure, he proceeded to offer the beer to this increasingly larger group of men. Handshakes and hellos were exchanged with Matthew and Simon, but Andy was perplexed as to how to approach *Him*! Not to worry about that, as this man calling himself Jesus smiled and offered his hand to Pete and Andy. The brothers each took their turn, shaking this man's hand, this man who had referred to himself as the religious leader of Christians.

Andy, still mystified, sipped his beverage and looked for guidance from the others. None was forthcoming. He grabbed Tom's arm and walked away from the group. He needed desperately to get the

Swede's perspective on this strange individual calling himself Jesus. "Come on Tom, what gives? Is this one of Pete's capers?"

"I don't know, but I must admit there is something about this man that sure is odd. And I don't think Pete had anything to do with it."

"I agree. Do you remember when I got that chill earlier? It sure as heck wasn't the temperature. Up and down my spine, an eerie feeling, unexplainable. Let's be careful, he could be unstable, and with Pete around, well ... let's be careful."

"Perhaps it's best if we call it a day."

"All right. I'll get Pete and we'll walk with you back to the hotel."

Although not well educated, Pete had street smarts, which enabled him to size up people and situations as quickly as any military field general facing battle. He had never considered himself a very religious man, but he did make an effort to go to church each Sunday. Raised as a Roman Catholic, he had served as an altar boy with his older brother when they were kids. He believed in what he had been taught in grade school at Saint Mary's in San Francisco. The nuns were very strict but extremely good educators. He learned his lessons well, never forgetting the miracles and sacrifices of Jesus.

Thinking about his newfound friends, Pete tried to evaluate the chain of events that had occurred today and the men he had met, especially the man who called himself Jesus. This guy is probably a phony, he thought, but check out the names of all the other men here. The names! All the names fit. Could it be a coincidence? I must speak to him. I have to know more about him.

Bewildered, Pete nevertheless managed to maintain his composure as he sat down next to this man calling himself Jesus, and in his own sagacious way, asked him, "Where are the other six?"

Without hesitation, the man responded. "Quite perceptive, Peter. You will meet them in due time. Before the day is through, the other six will join you."

Pete, still perplexed, looked around expecting the rest of the group to be sitting somewhere close by, but this was not the case. I guess they will appear when he wants them to, he thought.

Jesus reached over to Pete, put his hands on the fisherman's shoulders, looked deeply into his eyes and said, "Peter, **I am who you think I am**. I know it is understandably difficult for you to believe me, for it requires great faith and vision to accept the fact that I have returned."

Pete, still confused, but for some unexplicable reason now more believing, asked, "Why us?" Without waiting for a response, he continued, "I can only speak for my brother Andy and to some degree,

Tom, and tell you that we are just common people who have little, if any, influence. I do not know the other three gentlemen, but they appear to be average guys too. Why have you not made your presence known to the Pope, or to any of the other religious leaders?"

"You have many questions, Peter, and I'm sure the others have some too. I will explain why I am here and why these men were chosen when the rest of the group arrives."

"What is it you want us to do?"

"For now, remain calm and instruct those who are here to do the same. Our time spent together here on South Beach will be short; therefore, I need your complete support and leadership to accomplish our mission. And, please, do not be in awe of me, for that will serve no purpose. Instead, treat me as you would your brother, with respect and love."

As the man spoke, Pete looked for signs of the brutal wounds the Romans had inflicted on Jesus when they'd crucified him. Trying not to stare, Pete examined him to see if any tell tale marks or scars were present on his hands, feet, and forehead, but he could find nothing that resembled any old injury caused by nails or a crown of thorns. He paused, while trying to formulate his next question, but before he could ask, Jesus said to him that he would not see any traces of those wounds.

"I do not wish to reveal any unnecessary evidence of man's transgressions in the past. Also, all of you must maintain your composure and make every effort not to excite those outside the group at this point. Believe me, there will be plenty of commotion around here in a day or two."

Looking back at those under the umbrella, Pete wondered, what is going through their minds, especially Andy's? He is going to think this is another one of my pranks. Pete's mind began racing with all kinds of confusing thoughts. He was almost convinced this was actually happening. This man was indeed Jesus, who had died on the cross some two thousand years ago, sacrificing his life for all of mankind. But who would believe me? I don't know why I'm accepting this so calmly. For God's sake -- OOPs, I better watch what I say and think. Why am I able to talk to him as easily as I would Andy or Tom?

It was then Jesus said, "I realize how overwhelmed you and the others must be. If you wish, tell them of your feelings and of our conversation. All will be explained to you tonight. We shall meet this evening at eight o'clock for dinner at the White Sand Hotel. I have made a reservation under your name for thirteen in a private dinning room."

As Jesus arose from the warm sand, Pete looked up and couldn't help but ask, "Do I call you Jesus? I mean...."

"You can call me Jesus, but to avoid a commotion, please refer to me as Brother when we are around outsiders. They might not understand. Referring to me as Brother will help you avoid explaining yourself for the next three days."

Pete's first thought was, They might not understand! What about me? I can't quite grasp this either! Stabilizing his thoughts, finally, Pete asked, "How shall I know the other six?"

"Have patience, Peter. They will appear before dinner tonight."

"Shall I remain here at the beach to wait for them?"

"Do what you think is appropriate, but, believe me, you will meet them before dinner. I must leave you now, Peter." Without waiting for Pete to respond, he began walking northward on the beach. Pete watched him, where the surf deposited its white foamy waves, as this king amongst men took each graceful stride. Pete kept looking until he could no longer see him, which did not take long because of the mass of humanity on the beach. He wondered if this man who wished to be called Brother would talk to other people as he had spoken to him. But he discounted that idea immediately, for only twelve men were to be seated at dinner with Brother tonight.

Twelve men whose names were identical to the apostles who shared the last supper with Jesus two thousand years ago. What other similarities did these men have, other than their names? Keep an open mind, Pete, he said to himself, for Jesus will explain everything tonight. Curiosity forced him to look for footprints, but he was not surprised when none appeared. It truly is him, Jesus Christ.

Pete had great difficulty remembering any of the man's facial features. This he found intriguing, for the two of them had spoken no more than five minutes ago. But there was one characteristic he could recall -- his eyes. Yes, his penetrating eyes. Not the color -- just their ability to burn a hole through you, it seemed, and at the same time be warm and loving. I do remember what he said, but I cannot for the love of me recall what his voice sounded like. He asked me to tell the others to join him for dinner. Let's see. How do I tell them this? I have to convince the others this is truly happening -- at the very least, persuade them to join me for dinner tonight. Yes, yes, that's the proper tactic. The group of us will have a relaxing dinner tonight and exchange ideas concerning what happened today and . . . forget it! They are going to think I'm nuts.

Andy and Tom observed Pete conversing with this seemingly unstable man and wondered what they talked about. The ten minutes Pete and this man spoke seemed like an hour. They were pleased if not relieved to see the intruder depart. Pete remained standing by himself, thinking of the group now assembled, consisting of the six men from all parts of the globe, and he wondered where the other six were from and when he would meet them. His mind racing like a greyhound chasing a rabbit, he continued to think about how he was going to explain his conversation with Jesus to his brother, to Tom and to the other four.

At least those that were here saw him, even if they did not speak to him, as I was fortunate enough to do. What about the other six men? They did not even see him. Why should they believe me? I'll just tell them the truth. Sure, I'll tell them that I was sitting on the beach with my brother and it just so happened that I ran into Jesus. You know, the savior of humankind. We bought him a beer, had a brief conversation with him, and oh, by the way, he'd like to break bread with you tonight. How can I even attempt to explain this to them? That Jesus honestly wants to talk to them. He wants to discuss the reason he has come back. And, get this, Jesus has a mission for us, too. He wants us to have some patience, for all of this will be discussed in detail later. He hoped that we would be free tonight, for he made a dinner reservation for thirteen in a private room at the White Sand Hotel. You know, the thirteen of us!

When they ask me who I am, I'll tell them that I'm just a fisherman from California who was asked to invite all of them to have dinner with Jesus. Of course, that's who I am, just a fisherman.

Pete was finally able to gather his thoughts, sit the group of six down under the umbrellas, and tell them of his conversation with Jesus. Andy supported his brother's unbelievable account of the afternoon's chain of events. He also added his own feelings and observations about this man calling himself Jesus. Pete thanked his brother for believing in him, and asked the others to keep an open mind. He tried to be as accurate as he could, describing each and every element of this event which seemed beyond belief. He explained that Jesus has some kind of a task for the group. Then he told the group about the other six men who would be joining them for dinner, making sure to emphasize the exact number who would be there.

"Thirteen, that's right guys, there will be thirteen of us for dinner tonight. Are you beginning to get the idea? "He added, "I have a good idea what the names are of the six gentlemen we have yet to meet.

Let's see how good those nuns were in teaching me religion in grade school. Please chime in, if you have any thoughts. Well, we are missing Philip, James and John. He paused for a few seconds, okay help me someone."

"I had an uncle Bartholomew,"added Simon."I'm sure he's one of them."

"Good going,"said Andy, "That's a tough one."

"I believe there were two called James,"said Tad.

Pete thanked Tad for his input, thinking of the performance earlier in which Tad described his background to Andy and Tom.

After a delay of two to three minutes, Matt supplied a missing name. "I believe we must include the traitor, Judas."

"Very good gentlemen,"said Pete. "Now I suggest that we get to know one another better, for I feel the next few days will be the most interesting days of our entire life."

Matt was the first to offer his background, that of a middle class, hard-working journalist, on assignment in Miami. Andy gave his and Pete's biography, followed by Tom and Tad. Simon was the last to speak about his upbringing, and it became apparent almost immediately that he was the only one of the six with considerable wealth. Simon was also inquisitive, and asked if each man would make known his religious background. He began with his own, stating that his upbringing was in the Dutch Reformed Church, but he made it clear he was not a very religious man. Yes, he believed in a supreme being; although going to church -- well he just did not attend. Tad offered that he was a Baptist, believed in God, but also was not a churchgoer. He did add that even though he and his ex-wife were divorced, he tried to make sure his children went to church and attended religious classes.

Tom said, "Guess you could say I was raised as a Lutheran, but other than weddings and funerals, I've not been in a church for more than ten years. "Lifting his hands in the air he continued, "It's true I believe someone created all of this and have even read the *Bible* from time to time, but I have no strong convictions regarding the subject of religion. Sure, I'm aware of the story of a man who was reputed to be the messiah, but that was two thousand years ago. "He paused and then raising his voice asked, "Anyway, what's this got to do with me? I don't consider myself religious."

As a result, he had great difficulty believing anything he had seen or heard today. Tom let it be known that he did not put much credence in Pete's comments, nor did he accept this man they called Jesus. At minimum, he thought this mysterious individual was eccentric, but his gut feeling was that he was some kind of charlatan. Nevertheless, he liked his two fishermen friends, and if this is what they considered to be true, he was willing to back their point of view. He turned toward Andy and Pete and smiled at them in an attempt to show his support, and decided that if this stranger returned, he'd create an excuse of some kind and leave.

Andy spoke for Pete and himself. "We are Roman Catholic, churchgoers, but not what you would call very religious. I am not sure what very religious means, and perhaps more important, who sets the standards."

Matt said, "I'm confused as to why he chose me to be with this select group of Christians, for I am from a Jewish family. What's more, I'm not religious at all." Much to the dismay of his parents, it might be added, who were true believers in their faith. He continued. "Perhaps I should leave, since I do not appear to belong in this group."

Andy told Matt, "I am as bewildered as you, my friend, and don't honestly believe that one's religious background is an important criterion. Moreover, your name is Matthew, and by heavens, we certainly need a Matthew."

Pete took all this in and asked the others, "Do you understand how all of this might change your life? I mean, if he truly is Jesus.... How could any of us possibly comprehend the significance of today's events and what is to occur from this day forward?"

The six men looked at each other, perplexed by the position which they had been placed in. Simon suggested, "Let's try to absorb what has transpired by separating for ten or twenty minutes. This might help each of us formulate some questions about how to proceed."

Andy agreed, and so moments later the group scattered. Tad and Simon decided to wade in the water just beyond where the blue and white waves had crested. Simon thought this would serve two purposes. One, to give him some time to think and, two, perhaps the salt water would help ease the pain in his knee. Tad also had two motives. He wished to spend some time away from the group and use his engineering logic to attempt to understand what was happening. Trying to understand why he was chosen to be included in this group. In spite of this historic event facing them, he also had a burning desire to spend some time with the South African to discuss what was going on in his country. Race relations and the state of the black-run government were questions that he hoped Simon would be open and honest about. The two men discussed the changes in South Africa, the good and the not so good, as Simon, trying to be diplomatic, referred to them. The men also found a common bond; both were athletes, and each had a banged-up left knee. A lull in the conversation gave both Tad and Simon some time to reflect on the day's events. The two men stood in the tepid Atlantic, trying to determine if all of this was indeed true.

Tad asked, "And if so, why, oh my God, why did you pick me? Why did my mother give me this name in the first place? She could have just as well named me Carlton, after my father. But no, she had to call me Thaddaeus, which was her grandfather's name." Thaddaeus thought he might get a humorous response from Simon, but none appeared. Instead, he noticed a look of concern on Simon's face, creating no doubt that this entire episode had left the South African suspicious. He was not convinced himself, but, unlike his companion, wanted to believe this was all really happening. "Simon do you have any thoughts about the others who have not yet appeared?"

"To be honest with you Tad, I'm not totally convinced."

"Who is?"

"I mean, who in their right mind would believe this strange man is actually Jesus? Anyway, I think it's time to rejoin the group."

As they returned, Tad realized that he was in the presence of a skeptic who needed more proof before he would become a believer.

Andy, Matt, and Pete had already returned to their headquarters on the beach under the umbrellas. Andy took roll call like a marine drill sergeant and determined that the fishermen, writer, engineer, and, for lack of a better term, international sportsman were present. The only one who had not returned was the Swedish dress salesman.

Pete said, "I believe Tom will probably need more time to think about things, but I am sure he will return."

NINE

The crowd at the Blue Crab thinned out as the afternoon sun drifted to the west side of the pastel-colored buildings. Most of the sun worshipers went back to their hotel rooms to get ready for dinner or, in some cases, to attempt to find relief for their burning bodies. The waitresses also went home to catch a break before the dinner crowd came in. Bart Kessler found a spot at one end of the bar and ordered a Beck's beer. The bartender took notice of his German accent and did not even bother asking Bart if he wanted a regular or light, for anyone from the Fatherland would never order a light beer.

The bartender placed a coaster on the bar and poured the beer into a ice-glazed glass, chilled in the freezer.

"Do you always get a perfect head on the brew?" inquired Bart.

"Yes, thank you,"responded the bartender. "We sure get enough practice. On vacation?"

"I am working in Miami on a concert tour."

"No kidding. What kind of music do you play?"

"I am with a symphony orchestra from Heidelberg, Germany, and for the most part we play classical music," answered Bart proudly.

"Cool. You mean like Mozart and Bach and the rest of those guys?"

"I guess you could put it that way,"replied the amused musician.

"So, how long are you in town for? And when is the next concert?"

"Well, the tour has been completed, but my wife is coming here from Germany to meet me. We will be in Florida for another ten days."

"Sounds great, and since you're going to be here for a few days, I guess we should get to know each other,"said the bartender. "My name is Bill Murphy, but my pals call me Speed. Why, you ask? Because I can mix and serve cocktails faster than anyone else on the beach. What's yours?"

"Bartholomew Kessler, and I wish my friends had a unique nickname for me, but you will have to settle for Bart."

"What instrument do you play?"

"The piano."

Speed poured another beer for his musical friend and turned toward the other end of the bar, where a new patron was trying to get

his attention. Tom Olson had slipped into the bar, needing some solitude. Tom felt detached from the men on the beach, surmising that he
was the only one who did not believe the significance of what had
occurred on the beach. Most of it was obviously a coincidence. As far
as the man calling himself Jesus, well.... Tom's thoughts were interrupted by the bartender.

"What can I get you?"

"I'll have a cold beer and some chips or pretzels, if you have any."

"Beck's okay?"

"Fine."

Speed grinned, fantasizing that he was in Europe, for upon hearing Tom's Swedish accent, it dawned on him that he was the only
American at the bar. Speed asked the newcomer where he was from.
Tom put a twenty on the bar, took a sip of beer, and told him. Speed
slid a bag of potato chips to his new customer and asked his name.

"Tom, Tom Olson."

Speed shook his hand and announced, chortling, "Well, you guys
sure have me outnumbered. Utilizing all the skills he had learned
through the years to enhance his tip value, Speed continued, "Sweden,
meet Germany. Tom, say hello to Bart. He's from Germany."

Bart waved toward the man at the other end of the bar, greeting his
fellow European and drinking companion. But Tom, on hearing the
German fellow's name, almost choked on his beer, coughing the brew
embarrassingly through his nose. Either this was the most unusual
coincidence the world has ever seen, or perhaps the man on the beach
was indeed who he claimed to be. Maybe, just maybe, he thought, this
could be one of Pete's master con jobs. And all of it at his expense. He
pondered over his last thoughts for a few seconds and only then did
he come to the realization that even Pete wasn't theatrical enough to
stage this plot. Therefore, any doubts in his mind about this incredible
episode on the white sand of South Beach were dismissed -- for now.

The fisherman wasn't kidding, this really is happening, Tom
thought while squirming on the bar stool like a slippery eel. I must
return to the beach as soon as possible, to tell him and the others about
this new entry into the group. But first I should attempt to explain to
Bart what occurred today, and then, try to convince him that there's a
good chance he also fits into this bizarre plot. Perhaps I should have
Pete explain what is going on. Without question, he could do a much
better job than I.

It was at that point in this phenomenal saga that Thomas Olson,
dress manufacturer from Malmo, Sweden, bought into the entire pro-

gram. No, I'll do this myself, at least try. If Bart needs more convincing, then I'll have Andy and Pete talk to him.

"Pardon me, do you speak English?"

A nod of the head from the musician from Heidelberg affirmed his language capabilities.

Tom proceeded to say hello, once again, to the German. He asked, "Is your name Bartholomew?"

"Yes it is. Why are you so inquisitive? I mean regarding my name." *

Tom walked to the other end of the bar, shook Bart's hand, and asked, "Could I speak with you for a few minutes?"

"I would be most happy. How can I help you?"

Tom turned and noticed the nosy bartender looking their way. "Could we sit at a table, since what I have to talk to you about is a bit sensitive?"

Bart was confused, but in an effort to be cordial agreed. Speed, on the other hand, was a little taken aback because all discussions at the bar, which was his domain, included him. Tom sensed Speed's feelings and offered a brief "Sorry." Speed shook his head as if to assure Tom that it wasn't a problem. Tom knew his feelings were hurt, nevertheless, and decided on a generous tip to ease the pain. He ordered two more beers and joined Bart at a nearby table.

Tom began by asking, "Bart, are you a religious person? And, if so, do you believe in Jesus Christ?"

"Not really. In most religious circles I would be considered an atheist. I've read a great deal about Christianity and other religions as well, and came to the conclusion they are full of trouble and pitfalls. Therefore, I prefer not to discuss religion with anyone."

Since Bart had some pretty striking views on the subject, Tom sensed his task would be more difficult. He hoped, some soft-hearted persuasion could open the German's mind. Tom looked directly in Bart's eyes. "I realize this is difficult for you, but please hear me out."

Bart took another sip of beer, nodded his head and returned the eye contact with the Malmo native.

"I don't quite know how to continue, but I'll try to explain to you what transpired today." After going through most of the events of the day and attempting to recall each minute detail, Tom looked for a reaction from his German companion. He got one all right, for Bart's head snapped back a few times in disbelief. When he mentioned meeting Jesus, Bart got up from his chair, shook his head, and began to walk toward the exit."Please hear me out," Tom pleaded.

The musician, trying to maintain a moderate tempo with the Swede, returned to the table and said, "Do you realize what it is that you are asking me to believe? You are asking me to believe that you met Jesus Christ, who, by the way, I don't believe in in the first place! In addition, you are expecting me to comprehend that he wants me, an atheist, to have dinner with him tonight."

Speed's head spun around as if on a swivel when he heard the commotion. As things cooled down between the two men, his expression saddened, for he wanted so much to be part of the conversation.

"Please,"begged Tom, "you must understand that I, too, am skeptical. This entire day has been a complete enigma to me. You say that you are not a very religious man,"continued Tom. "Well, neither am I. All I can tell you is that there are five other men on the beach who have seen him, and some of them I'm sure, like you, have doubts that all of this is actually happening. Meeting you, Bartholomew, was no coincidence. He planned it this way. Meeting you is what it took to convince me that he is Jesus."

Bart attempted to digest this unimaginable tale from a man he had just met in a strange country full of unusual people. For almost five minutes he remained speechless, a conflict brewing in his head. One side of his brain, argumentative and contentious, completely distrusted Tom, wanting to know if he had been chosen the pigeon of the day. For some inexplicable reason, the other side of his brain sincerely wished to believe what Tom had told him was true.

Bart carefully selected his words. "You know, Tom, I'm a pretty fair and logical individual. Also, you must understand that I am not a believer in Jesus, his life as described in the *Bible* or its teachings regarding Christianity. But, strange as it may seem, there is nothing more I'd rather do than to meet him. That is, if there really was a Jesus. Before we go any further, would you mind if we review today's events once again, this time in chronological order."

"Sounds reasonable,"said Tom. "But first, how about another beer?" Instead of calling out to Speed for another round of Beck's, Tom decided to go to the bar and get the beer himself. This would keep the inquisitive bartender away from the table.

Tom began reconstructing the day, starting at breakfast with Andy and Pete and ending with Pete's recap of his conversation with Jesus. "Do you have any questions?" he asked the musician.

"You must be kidding! I now understand why you choked on your beer when I told you my name. I guess the same thing would have happened to me if I were in your situation. I don't disbelieve what you have told me, although I would like to meet with the others as soon as possible before making up my mind."

Tom was relieved, as if a tremendous burden had been lifted from his shoulders. "Sounds fine to me. Let's drink up and go to the beach."

"I have a better idea." "Let's drink up, get one to go, and then head for the beach."

"Spoken like a true German,"remarked Tom.

Before they left the Blue Crab, Tom gave Speed a generous tip and thanked him for introducing him to Bart. The fastest bartender on the beach was appreciative, but somewhat disappointed at being left out of the conversation.

It was after five when Tom and Bart arrived at the beach. The air was much cooler since the sun had disappeared behind the buildings on the other side of Ocean Drive. The umbrella man had performed his daily function of picking up all the rentals. It almost appeared that the beach was naked without the brightly colored sun shields, but the five men still sitting on the beach hardly noticed. All of them were now dressed in sweatshirts and pants or shorts, to fight off the chill. They were engrossed in profound conversation, trying to determine where all of this would lead. As Tom neared the group, he detected the more serious tone in their voices accentuated by the solemn look on each face, especially Pete's, who was somehow either self-appointed or chosen to act as their leader.

Tom greeted Pete and told him about meeting the musician at the Blue Crab. Pete welcomed Bart and introduced him to the rest of the group. Bartholomew, yes, that's one of the tougher names, Pete thought.

"Five to go,"commented Andy. "And they best show up soon, as dinner is in three hours."

A look at his watch and Simon echoed Andy's observation. He also suggested that perhaps the men should return to their respective hotels and get cleaned and dressed for dinner.

"Any thoughts on what to wear tonight?"inquired Tad.

Pete responded, "I was told by Jesus to try to act as normal as possible, so I guess the same goes for our dress. I recommend a sports jacket and slacks. That should do the trick. I don't think a tie will be necessary."

"That does not address the issue of the other five," said Matt. "Don't you think someone should wait here to see if they show up?"

"Yes, that's a good idea," added Andy. "Perhaps one or two of us should wait here, until, let's say, six o'clock."

Pete suggested that Andy and he wait until six; the others should go on ahead. "Before you leave," he continued, "if any of you have second thoughts about coming to dinner tonight, please call me at the White Sand Hotel. Furthermore, I think it's in our best interests not to discuss what happened with any outsiders. That includes wives and girlfriends. Andy and I will be at the cocktail lounge at the White Sand at seven o'clock. If you have any problem getting there on time, I would appreciate a call."

"What if we should happen to meet someone who seems to fit into the group?" asked Tom. You know, like I ran into Bart."

Pete replied, "That's a very good point, my Swedish friend, and I wish there was a definitive answer. All I can say is, use your own judgment."

Andy noted a serious tone to his brother's voice, one he had not heard since the death of their mother. His demeanor reflected an attitude of authority. The usual jovial and sometimes impish Pete whom he loved, and who was also his best friend, was in total control of the men selected to have dinner with Jesus. Amazing, simply amazing, thought Andy.

T E N

Bart, Matt, Tad, and Tom departed for their respective hotels, and Simon to his condo, each of them in his own silent, private thoughts, trying to digest what was happening. More important, what would happen tonight. A dinner with a man calling himself Jesus Christ, and twelve men from around the globe, gathering to discuss a mission that he expected these twelve men to carry out.

Many questions raced through their heads. The first and most puzzling -- why us? What will he ask us to do? Is he expecting us to dedicate the rest of our lives to this? Each of the men's minds were working overtime in an effort to sort out how this was to affect their lives. Although they all had to walk in the same general direction to reach their hotels, the lack of conversation reflected a sense of self-examination each man was quietly going through.

Bart's thoughts were directed at his wife and children and how this evening's dinner could perhaps alter their lives. Elsa, the dedicated mother of Erica and Martin, would be here next week. He had spoken to his family on the telephone just this morning. Should he call back and tell Elsa what had happened this afternoon? Pete said not to, but Bart feared that after tonight's dinner he might not get a chance to.

What surprised him the most was the metamorphosis he had gone through in just two hours -- from an atheist to an agnostic -- considering the possibility that God truly existed. How could I have made this radical conversion, he wondered. He went so far as to speculate that perhaps Jesus had returned to proclaim the end of the world was near. That possibility was chilling, for if that were the case, it was likely he would not see his family ever again.

As he sat in the wicker chair in his hotel room, Matt's first thoughts were directed at Jim Albright. How could I possibly forget, he thought, he's the reason I'm in Miami. Perhaps I should tell Pete about Jim? No, I'll wait till we meet later and explain to the Australian what had happened today. We were scheduled to meet at the White Sand, on any account. Now Matt wondered if Jim was indeed the other James who fit into this complex puzzle. It makes sense, Matt rationalized, Jim Albright has to be one of the others. Why else would he sail halfway around the world? If not, then I'll make different arrangements to have someone else conduct the interview. In any event, I'll get there early to resolve the matter. Deep down he hoped the Australian was the second James.

Matt still sensed that he was an outsider, based on his religious background. His parents would probably disown him if they found out he was involved in a religious scheme with a bunch of Christians, an atheist and an agnostic. He could envision his mother racing to the synagogue to tell the rabbi what had occurred. After an hour or so of bending the holy man's ear, his mother would coerce the rabbi to call her son, to try to give him spiritual guidance. She would also get on the first plane to Miami to save him from this band of religious fanatics. No, he would not call home, he laughed to himself, because he really liked the rabbi too much to put him in a situation such as this with his mother.

I'll go to dinner tonight, be polite, and see what happens. As far as believing, well I'll leave that up to the rabbis and priests. On the other hand, if only ten percent of this is factual, he thought, then his journalistic career could reach a plateau reserved only for a few privileged writers. He had always thought that being a good writer wasn't enough -- you had to be at the right place at the right time.

And was he ever!

Simon found solace at his spacious condominium. Although he appeared to go along with the others, inwardly the South African was still a skeptic. In addition, he surmised that he also had the most to lose. Selfishly, he concluded all the others were working people and so had little to sacrifice. He was quite sure that his estate surpassed the total net worth of the rest of the group. Could it be a con game to bilk him out of some money? He discounted that thought, for these men appeared to be honest and sincere, but that's exactly how con men would act. Then again, if this man is truly Jesus, money won't mean a thing. Simon, Simon, he said to himself, you are normally so much in control! What are you going to do? Perhaps a cold shower and a glass of vodka on the rocks will assist you in making up your mind.

Tad was searching his memory, trying to recollect any lesson he had learned at Sunday school that would guide him through this evening. He, like the Albano brothers Andy and Pete, did not require any additional evidence. This man positively was Jesus of Nazareth. He was as sure as one could be. He also realized there would be a few skeptics in the group, and the two fishermen would most likely need assistance in keeping the flock together. Tad decided to get to the restaurant early in order to deal with any dissenters who might attempt to undermine tonight's activities. That's the least I can do. How he wished the good Pastor Robinson, who was responsible for teaching a much younger Tad religion at the First Baptist Church in Detroit, was here to tutor him. Perhaps this time he would listen more intently. The *Bible* -- yes, there is one in the hotel room, he thought. I don't know what good it will do me, but reading a few passages, especially those regarding the last supper, might help refresh my memory. I don't know about the others, but this engineer is really looking forward to dinner.

As Tom neared the Ocean Hotel, his thoughts focused on his cavalier attitude toward religion over the years and why he might have been selected to be part of this group. He shook his head, shrugged his shoulders, and said to himself, what a way to get reintroduced to religion. Meeting the man himself! Tom tried to rationalize how he could have possibly reversed his position on the subject in such a short span of time. His feelings about the day's events had done a one-hundred-and-eighty degree turn. From a position of complete doubt to a stand of absolute belief. He thought, at first I went along with this charade only because of my friendship with Andy and Pete.

Although Tom had known the fishermen for only a short period of time, he had no question about their honesty and integrity. In spite of his good feelings about the two brothers, he had been very close to returning to his hotel in the afternoon and leaving this supernatural theater to the fishermen and the interloper posing as the leader of the Christian faith. Meeting Bart in the Blue Crab had changed his mind completely. Had it not been for this extraordinary encounter at a friendly drinking establishment -- a nosy bartender by the name of Speed and a casual introduction to a pianist from Germany -- he might still be a doubting Thomas.

It was now quite dark at the beach. The sun had set and the moon, in its first quarter was visible in the southeastern sky. Andy and Pete waited until six fifteen, but no one showed up.

"Let's get ready for dinner," suggested Pete. "It's getting late."

"Where were the others?" complained a disappointed Andy as the two began walking back to their hotel. "I thought they would have introduced themselves to us by now."

Pete did not share his brother's concerns about meeting the other five men. "Dinner is not until eight,"he said. "There is still time for them to appear."

Pete was in complete control, thought Andy, not only over the others, but over his own emotions as well. He has complete faith and trust in Jesus and what will happen tonight. I must also maintain my composure, even if my beliefs are not as profound as my brother's. Andy shook his head in awe of his brother's transformation. He was happy for him, but nonetheless mystified by how quick and sweeping the changes had been. They completed the short walk back to the hotel deep in thought.

ELEVEN

Philip and Rudy's day at the beach was pleasant, but uneventful. Their afternoon was spent tanning their already brown bodies while conversing about family and friends. They also talked a great deal about their careers. In addition, Rudy was proud to reflect on the impact the Latinos had made on the Miami area.

The Chilean was amused by his new friend. He had many fine qualities, Philip thought -- intelligence, charm, and a great passion to enjoy life to its fullest. Rudy knew many people in Miami and offered to introduce Philip around. His general knowledge of the South Florida area would also be most beneficial.

How fortunate I am to have met someone like Rudy and so soon, Philip thought. Still, he felt there might be a dark side to this man. He couldn't put his finger on it, but Philip sensed that perhaps Rudy was not being completely honest with him about his past. His association with drug users, or maybe even dealers of narcotics, could have possibly positioned the attorney on the wrong side of the law. Why, with all that money changing hands, the temptation might have been too great! For the moment, Philip decided to put aside these negative thoughts regarding his new friend.

The afternoon was fading into evening when Rudy suggested that they have dinner together. His girlfriend, Connie, was a waitress at a very fine restaurant, and he wanted his new friend to meet her. Rudy described his girlfriend as beautiful beyond words. At twenty-six, she was ten years younger than Rudy and, yes, she was gorgeous. Divorced, as so many waitresses seemed to be, Connie Lopez, her married name, had a two-year-old girl named Rosa. Her precious Rosa was cared for by Connie's mother, who lived with them, while Connie strived to make ends meet. Her ex-husband had been on the run since their divorce and child support was neither paid or expected.

Philip learned that the restaurant where Connie worked was in one of the newly renovated hotels in South Beach called the White Sand. Although not a pretentious facility, the hotel was known for its upscale accommodations. Its dining room was rated as one of the finest in Miami Beach, with its intimate decor and fine selection of seafood. Its biggest attraction for the locals was the entertainment in its cocktail lounge. Not that there were big name stars appearing there, just that the beautiful people of South Beach considered the hotel one of their preferred watering holes. Thus, people-watching was the main event.

In his usual persuasive manner, Rudy convinced Philip to join him for dinner. Philip needed little coercing and was delighted to have company at dinner for a change. The new friends decided to meet at Philip's apartment at six-thirty and drive to the restaurant in Rudy's car.

TWELVE

The lounge at the White Sand Hotel consisted of a dozen or so cocktail tables and a large circular bar, accommodating twenty. Green carpeting clashed with magenta-colored bar stools and chair cushions. In a separate piano bar, another eight to ten patrons could enjoy listening to and singing a medley of time-tested ballads. By eight o'clock Wednesday through Sunday, every bar stool and chair would be occupied. Standing room only five nights a week -- and tonight would be no exception. The staff, both cocktail waitresses and bartenders, were all experienced and exceptionally good looking.

When Matthew Singer arrived at six forty-five, there were only a handful of people in the lounge. He scanned the bar and saw a beer mug working its way through an opening in a red beard. As he looked closer, he was happy to see that the beard belonged to the Australian sailor.

"You are actually early, Jim," teased Matt. "Are you trying to make up for this morning's tardiness?"

"That's a fact, Matt. I just wanted to make sure your magazine would pay for dinner."

The writer sat down at the bar next to his assignment, and the two men smiled and shook hands.

"Did you take care of your passport at the embassy?"

"Sure did. The ambassador's secretary was most helpful. How was your day? It looks like you got a little sun this afternoon, so I'm guessing pretty good."

"Yes, I got some sun, but the rest of afternoon was, well, let's say interesting."

"What do you mean by that?"

"First I need a drink. A vodka martini on the rocks for me and another beer for my friend here," Matt told the bartender.

Jim saw the expression on the writer's face and knew he was about to hear one heck of a story. When the drinks arrived, Matt suggested that they move to one of the cocktail tables, because in the ten minutes since Matt had arrived, the bar had gone from a handful of people to standing room only. And since this was for Jim's ears only, he wanted to be as far away from the other patrons as possible. The intensity in the writer's voice was apparent. This was not the same smooth and relaxing tone Jim had heard that morning. Obediently, he got up from the bar stool and sought out a table in a corner of the lounge.

When they found a suitable location, Jim said, "Okay, let's hear it. Why did I have to move to the corner of the room to listen to your story?"

"Patience, have some patience, my sailor friend."

No sooner had the two men sat down than the cocktail waitress came over to see if their drinks needed refreshing. Matt thanked the attractive woman and asked if she could return in a few minutes. When she left the table, both men commented on her striking beauty.

"Jim, you are going to need both vision and imagination, for what I am going to tell you requires both."

Being an excellent reporter, Matt found it remarkably easy to describe what had happened at the beach. Like anyone attempting to tell a fantastic story, especially one of this magnitude, Matt looked for and got a reaction of disbelief -- his listener's head snapping back, eyeballs looking up to the ceiling, and hands holding the chilled glass of beer as if trying to crush it.

Jim shook his head, finding it difficult to comprehend what the writer was telling him.

"And, furthermore," added Matt, "I think you are one of the men invited to dinner. There were two apostles named James, and we don't have either one of them in the group as yet. You see, I don't believe our meeting was a coincidence. On the contrary, I think this entire event was planned by . . . well, you know who. I know this is hard to believe, but it did happen, just the way I told you."

Jim could feel the tension in his arms contracting his biceps. His concealed jaw tightened under its red beard, for the thought of him being selected to meet with Jesus was bone chilling. A few minutes passed in silence as Jim tried to digest this incredible saga.

"Wow! That's quite a story, but for some incredible reason that I cannot put my finger on, I find it believable. I'm not suggesting that I believe you met with Jesus, mind you. It's just that I sense you did have an encounter on the beach with someone who appears to be very religious and that you have accepted him as such."

In spite of Jim's hedged comments, Matt was relieved at his reaction but tried not to show any emotion.

"Before we go any further, Matt, I have a question for you. I'd like to know if you are a religious man."

The response was a definite no. In addition, Matt informed the Australian he was not even a Christian, but the son of two wonderful parents who were Jewish. They were religious; but much to their regret, he was not.

"How about you Jim? How religious are you?"

Jim played with his beard, stroking it rapidly, reflecting some nervousness on his part. "Matt, I must tell you, when I was a young lad my parents sent me to a Catholic seminary with the hopes of my becoming a priest. I spent two and a half years at the seminary and was well on my way to becoming a man of the cloth."

"What happened?"

"My dad got ill. He had a stroke, so I left the seminary to be the breadwinner for my mom and two younger sisters. You see, Matt, I am a very religious individual. How else would I have managed to sail through that storm in the Pacific? There were times out on that big pond when all I did was pray. Nothing would thrill me more than to meet with Jesus. But what you have told me is one fantastic tale."

Matt sensed he wasn't convincing Jim. This was understandable, but how could he persuade him it was true.

He felt more secure when Jim asked, "When will I meet the other men? Not that I don't believe you, but...."

At that very moment, Matt saw Tad enter the lounge. He could use a little reinforcement in convincing Jim. He called Tad over to the table and introduced him to Jim Albright. "He's the sailor from Australia I told you guys about. You know, the reason the magazine sent me to Miami. My story."

"Nice to meet you mate."

As Tad reached to shake Jim's hand, he looked at Matt and asked, "Is this the James...?" But before going any further, he thought perhaps Matt and he should speak privately.

Without hesitation, Matt told Tad that he had very strong feelings that this man, Jim Albright, was indeed one of the group.

"Welcome aboard Jim. This should be a very interesting evening. Yes indeed sir, a very interesting evening. I need a beer. Anybody else thirsty?"

"And your full name I take it is Thaddeus?"inquired Jim.

"Good guess."

"Well, the name certainly fits into the scheme of things, since there was a Thaddeus at the last supper."

"You know the good book well,"added Tad. "I must admit I was not aware of that fact myself until I returned to the hotel room this afternoon and looked it up in the *Bible*."

Matt mentioned that Jim had studied for the priesthood and, there-fore, must be well versed in the *Bible*. The sailor acknowledged his host's compliment, but made them aware that many years had passed since then. He wanted to know more about the events that had occurred during the day, especially where the rest of the group come from and what their individual religious beliefs were.

Matt noted that all the men were average guys, from different countries, with a wide assortment of faiths and convictions, from very religious to not at all. Satisfied about that point, Jim paused, had a sip of beer, and tried to collect his thoughts for the next series of questions.

"If I understand things correctly, you gentlemen just met for the first time today on the beach?"

"That's right,"replied Tad. "I might add, we are all as flabbergast-ed as you are."

"What did he look like?"

"You know, that's one of the mind-boggling things we've had to deal with. None of us can recall."said Tad. "In fact, Pete, who spent the most time with him, went so far as to say he cannot even remem-ber what his voice sounded like. But he has no difficulty recalling what Jesus said."

"I'm not saying what you have told me is true, although you sure have my curiosity switch turned on,"commented Jim.

"So, you will join us for dinner?"asked Matt.

"Why not? You know I'm an adventurer, and besides, Matt, you owe me a dinner anyway. What time is it?"

"A quarter after seven. I thought the others would be here by now."

"I think that's Andy at the far end of the bar,"said Tad.

"Matt asked, "I wonder where Pete is?

"If Andy is here then I assure you Pete can't be too far behind,"replied Tad. "Well, there's two more -- Bart and Tom just walked in."

"That still leaves Simon. Do you see him, Tad?"

"No I don't, and it wouldn't surprise me if he didn't show."

"Why do you say that?"asked Matt.

Tad responded that he was a pretty good judge of character, and it was apparent to him that Simon was sitting on the fence. As far as Tad was concerned, Simon showing up was a fifty-fifty proposition.

Bart and Tom made their way through the crowded lounge, located some hard-to-find chairs, and joined the three men sitting at the table. Jim was introduced, and when they told him where they were from, he couldn't resist telling them how small the planet had gotten.

He added, "Perhaps even smaller, gentlemen, in view of what has happened today."

"I get the feeling somehow we are at the center of the universe," added Tom.

Bart echoed the Swede's statement. "I believe you are correct. At the present time, South Beach could very well be the religious capital of the entire universe."

Neither Matt nor Tad wanted the discussion to get too profound and suggested that each man tell the group a humorous story about his past.

"Drinks, who needs one?" asked Bart.

All wanted refills; unfortunately, the cocktail waitress seemed to have disappeared. The conversation at the table continued to be light, with each man containing his inner emotions about what might possibly happen at dinner.

THIRTEEN

Rudy's 1999 red Corvette pulled into the parking lot of the White Sand Hotel at seven-thirty. The hotel's valet jumped to attention, as he had been waiting for an opportunity to drive a hot number such as this around back to the reserved area. But Rudy would have none of that. He gave the young man a ten-dollar bill and told him he was going to park the red chariot himself in front of the Coral Reef restaurant, which was situated to the left of the hotel's main entrance. He had often parked his car in this spot, which was reserved for the hotel's assistant manager. Connie had let Rudy know that this space was usually vacant after six o'clock.

Philip was impressed by his friend's ability to maneuver people and get what he wanted. "Interesting custom you have in America."

"You'd be surprised what ten dollars will get people to do for you. Also, you'd be shocked at what it does to their vision."

Philip smirked. "If his eyes get so blurred by the money, how does he drive the cars?"

Rudy enjoyed his new friend's sense of humor. He parked in the reserved space at the front of the parking lot, and Philip teasingly asked, "Is this as close as you can get?"

As they walked toward the lounge, Rudy overheard a conversation taking place behind a large ficus tree situated to the left of the restaurant's entrance. He stopped in his tracks at the sound of the familiar voice of his girlfriend. He did not recognize the voice of the man she was talking with, but from the tone of their conversation it was obvious the man was someone she knew. Rudy didn't think it was the manager or anyone from the Coral Reef, since he would have recognized their voices.

As jealous as he was, Rudy had to find out what was going on between this strange man and his beautiful Connie. Not wanting to embarrass himself in front of his new friend, he told Philip he had left a gift for his special girl in the car and would Philip mind waiting for him in the lounge. Philip agreed, entered the lounge, and went directly to the bar.

#

The bar was crowded as usual, with thirsty guests waiting to get the bartender's attention. Philip managed to find a spot and ordered a glass of chardonnay. As he attempted to maneuver his full glass of wine in the crush of people, a few drops of wine fell on the back of one of the men next to him. Politely, the Chilean tapped the man in the lightweight brown suit on the back and apologized for the mishap.

The man turned around, grinned, and said, "I appreciate your candor. "In his elegant English accent he introduced himself, "I'm John Thompson, and this is my brother, James. I'm sure my brother and I have been guilty of spilling our share of wine in the past. And, I may add, not all of it was reported."

This brought a smile to Philip's face as he introduced himself. "Are you here on business or vacation?"he inquired.

James replied, "I guess you could say both."

Philip told the two brothers that he had spent his first day on the beach today and that they should not miss the opportunity. He made no mention of Rudy, who still had not entered the lounge, as far as he could tell. He had no idea what was happening in the parking lot.

After fifteen minutes of conversation, James asked, "Would you care to join us for dinner?"

But before Philip could respond, a man sitting next to the two brothers at the bar interrupted the conversation and introduced himself. He said he was a fisherman from California. "Name's Andy Albano."

Having overheard the three men introduce themselves, Andy was certain that each of them fit into the group. Already believing in what had happened at the beach, Andy's running into these men reinforced his convictions. But he realized that because of all the people around them, it would be impossible to inform the three gentlemen of what happened without risking a scene. In addition, time was becoming a major factor, since it was approaching eight o'clock. He decided he had to invent a tall tale in order to get them to have dinner with the group in the private dining room. Andy knew this would take quite a selling job, and he dare not overdo it for fear of turning the three men off.

James commented on how friendly -- perhaps he'd even go so far as to say zany -- the atmosphere and the people were in American pubs. "Let's see,"he added, "an engineer from Chile, a fisherman from California, and two investors from England. This is truly America, and as big as it is, everybody wants to be in the same confined places."

John agreed about the friendliness, but was careful not to expand on the craziness of the people his brother had alluded to, even though he believed it to be true.

Philip said, "This reminds me of the lounges in Santiago." What he didn't say was, perhaps the Englishmen might be a bit stuffy. Philip's body language led John to think his brother's strait-laced comments were offered from a very narrow perspective. He tried to lighten up the conversation by saying, "What do you expect from people living on such a small island?"

This brought laughter to the group of men, followed by James, the elder of the Thompson brothers offering a toast to the two men from the Americas.

Andy recognized his task would be more difficult than he had first thought. He had to tell his white lie now and it had better be believable. "Gentlemen," he began, "I have an unusual proposition for you. I am a charter member of The Two Oceans Gourmet Club, and tonight we are celebrating our tenth anniversary. We meet every year and dine on the finest seafood available, prepared by some of the most prestigious chefs in America. The dinner is held on the west coast of the United States on even numbered years and the east coast on odd numbers. One of the characteristics of the club is unique. You see, we get to invite new acquaintances to have dinner with us. And, as luck would have it, we are having dinner tonight right here in this hotel in a private dining room. I would be most pleased if you joined me as my guests. I can assure you the evening will be most entertaining, and I dare to say quite memorable.

The elder Thompson brother, who was usually extremely cautious, pondered this interesting invitation for a moment. His prospective host appeared an honest individual, but what if he weren't? What could the man possibly gain by having us as his guests for dinner?

Andy sensed the uncertainty, looked at the three gentlemen one by one, and tried to assure them his proposal was above board.

James cleared his throat and said, "I would be most delighted to join Andy at dinner." He looked at his brother, who was totally amused by it all, to get confirmation from him. John was pleasantly surprised at his very conservative brother's response and gladly seconded. "However, on one condition," he added. "Only if my new friend from Chile agrees to attend."

Philip, still not sure where Rudy was, appeared reluctant and stated, "I'd be happy to, but I'm supposed to meet one of my new neighbors at the lounge tonight."

Andy hesitated before responding. "What's his name?"

"Rudy. Rudy Romero."

Andy didn't want to chance the three men declining his invitation, but dare he risk an outsider attending dinner? Some person with a name that didn't fit. He sensed his options were limited and said, "If he shows up, he can join us too."

"Well, since you put it that way, how can I refuse?"

"What time does the affair begin?" asked John.

"Eight o'clock." Andy looked at his watch. "It's about five to eight now. What do you say, shall we go?"

The men stopped at the hostess station and asked the hostess for directions to the private dining room. She told them the room was just outside the lounge and to the right." She added, "I believe Mister Albano, your host, is already there."

Andy was greatly relieved that his brother was where he was supposed to be. Philip informed the hostess he was expecting a friend named Rudy Romero, and would she direct him to the private dining room.

The hostess knew that Rudy was Connie's boyfriend, but though she looked for them, she could not find either Rudy or the beautiful waitress.

FOURTEEN

The billboard in front of the double doors read:
PRIVATE PARTY
PETER ALBANO
& FRIENDS

Pete was in awe of his name's appearing at the top of the placard. He really expects me to lead this group of men! Why me? I certainly don't have the credentials to preside over this group. The questions continued to fill the humble fisherman's already-clouded head. What is this mission he has spoken about? And what if we don't succeed?

He sat down at the table thoroughly consumed by the possibility of being placed in the role of leader of the group. He went so far as to wish his mother had reversed the names of her children. It took several minutes until he finally reconciled his mind to accepting the fact that Jesus had selected him. That thought behind him, Pete determined it would be appropriate to deliver some opening remarks. He thought this approach would serve two purposes. One, it would give those individuals who had not been on the beach earlier an opportunity to meet him and the others. Two, it would get everyone up to date on what he and Jesus had spoken about.

Quite sensitive regarding his leadership role, Pete wanted to assure the men he was only the spokesman for the group. He did not wish to be considered anything other than their equal. Coming off as a pompous orator would only add to the skeptics' arsenal. When speaking to the group I must appear to be calm and in control of my delivery, he concluded. A scary thought crossed his mind. Suppose Brother gets detained? He shuddered at the thought. How am I going to deal with the disbelievers? There is no question there will be a few of them. And that does not take into account the new members of the group, who did not see him on the beach this afternoon. What if they decide to leave before he gets here? Control yourself Pete, he will be here! Have faith! He will be here!

Pete next directed his attention to dinner. He thought the menu should be limited to two or three entrees, which would keep the ordering process as simple and short as possible. He also considered order ing six bottles of wine, three white and three red, and, he guessed, a case of beer. As far as the waiters were concerned, Pete would inform the maitre d' that the meeting was very confidential and under no circumstances was to be interrupted. Someone would call for a waiter when service was required. Yes, he thought, that eliminates anyone from the outside entering the room without notice.

Pete picked up the house phone in the private dining room to inform the maitre d' of his instructions for serving. The voice on the other end of the phone informed Pete that the menu for dinner, wine and beer included, as well as instructions on serving it, had already been conveyed to the staff. Need I ask if he ordered Beck's, Pete thought. "Thank you,"he said, asking that the drinks be delivered as soon as possible. As he hung up the phone he smiled. Jesus, you are way ahead of me. Oh, yes, I must remember to call him Brother, as he suggested. And I must remember to tell the others in my opening comments to do the same.

One of Pete's first observations on entering the dining room was the layout of the table and chairs. Not that he expected a replica of Leonardo da Vinci's *The Last Supper*, with all thirteen men sitting on the same side of a long table. No, that arrangement did not seem practical, he thought, since it had obviously been fabricated for the convenience of the artist. I guess I expected Brother to be sitting alone at a head table, enabling him to view each of us and to make it easier for him to speak to the group. But why should I think he wants to be anywhere but close to us? He wants to interact and have dinner with the group and enjoy some wine. Although I know he liked the beer Andy bought for him this afternoon. The last thought brought a grin to the face of the fisherman, as he tried to make sure all the particulars regarding the dinner were covered.

"This must be the place,"said Tom as he knocked on the closed doors. "Peter Albano's friends are here."

The doors opened and a smiling Pete welcomed the first arrivals. Matt introduced Jim Albright, making fun at the fact that both the Australian sailor and the fisherman earned their living on the ocean. Matt went on to say that Jim was a Catholic and had attended a seminary for two years.

"You gentlemen have had quite an interesting day,"said Jim.

"That's an understatement if I ever heard one,"said Pete.

"Do you really believe the man on the beach was truly Jesus?"asked Jim.

Pete didn't respond at first, so impressed by the sailor's long red beard that his mind toyed with the thought of how long it had taken Jim to grow it. "My dear friend, there is no doubt in my mind he was there at the beach this afternoon, and I believe with all my heart that he will be here tonight. I realize you must think we're a bunch of lunatics, but have patience and you will meet him too."Trying to change the subject to release some of the tension, Pete added, "By the way, dinner will be served as soon as the others arrive. Wine and beer have already been ordered and should be here shortly."He added playfully, "Don't worry Tom, I ordered a case of Beck's especially for you."

Tom returned the barb. "What, no vodka?"

"Sorry, my Swedish friend, no vodka."Pete added in a serious tone, "Tom, please see that the doors remain closed."

This did not require an answer from Tom, who noted the transformation in Pete's voice. He checked the doors.

"Jim, we are pleased you have joined us,"added Pete. "And with your religious background, I'm sure you can assist me with a project I've undertaken. Since this afternoon many questions have been bouncing around inside my head. Questions I intend to ask Brother -- that's what he's asked us to call him."

Matt interrupted. "Sorry, I completely forgot to inform Jim."

"That's okay Matt. Just make sure you tell the others. As I was saying, I have written down a few questions regarding what Brother expects from us. I am quite certain that similar thoughts must be on the minds of the entire group. Additionally, I've taken the liberty of asking some of those basic religious questions that you think of even as a youngster. Such as, is there a heaven and hell? What about the end of the world? I'm sure you understand, Jim. I would appreciate it if you would spend some time and put your thoughts together. Please take a look at the questions I've written and let me know if you would approach any of these points from a different angle."

Jim scanned the list and said, "I see where you are coming from. You wouldn't mind if I delve a bit more into the depths of religion? I mean questions that have been on my mind for many years regarding the contents of some of the passages from the *Bible*."

"Your knowledge of the good book far outweighs mine,"said Pete, approvingly. "Write down any of those thoughts on which you are looking for answers."

Jim was now certain that these men had seen someone today who had an enormous amount of spiritual power. So much so, that this man calling himself Brother had the entire group, even those who had not seen him, spellbound. Whether or not he is truly Jesus, this is a man I must meet. Feeling he had nothing to lose, he said, "Pete, I accept the challenge. Is there a *Bible* handy?"

"I brought one from my hotel room. Of course, I have every intention of returning it when the night is over." Pete turned to Matt and asked, "Would you mind assisting Jim in compiling the list of questions? Your journalistic skills would be most valuable to the group. Also, Matt, because you are the writer in the group, I would like to ask you to take notes during the meeting with Brother to make sure all that is spoken about is documented."

The writer's shining eyes revealed his answer without his speaking. Pete walked with Jim and Matt to the table where the good book and the pad containing the draft of the questions lay. Pete commented, "I'm not totally sure Brother will answer any of the questions, but I guess we'll just have to wait and see."

Jim agreed, and without any further reservations the two men went to work.

Another knock on the door, and Tom looked at Pete for approval to open it. Pete nodded and Tom opened the door, expecting the rest of the group to appear. But as it turned out, it was the waiter wheeling a cart holding a plate of assorted appetizers -- shrimp and crab legs complementing the wine and beer. The waiter set up bottles of white and red wine and began to open them with his corkscrew. Pete thanked him for the prompt delivery and asked him to leave the opener, saying that they would take care of themselves. The surprised but obedient waiter did as Pete asked and left the room, closing the door behind him. "Gentlemen help yourselves," offered Pete.

Again a rap on the door, and this time it was Andy and three new members of the group. Andy rushed over to talk to his brother, barely acknowledging Tom's hello. The conversation between the brothers covered the chicanery Andy had used to get the newcomers to attend the dinner. In the meantime, John and James Thompson and Philip Silva introduced themselves to the others, whom they believed to be members of a prestigious dining club.

Pete asked each of the men to help themselves to a drink and appetizers, and to please be seated at the table. It was now a quarter after eight, and Brother was nowhere in sight. Time for my opening remarks, he thought, but first I must make sure everyone is introduced to each member of the group. I'll ask each to give a short autobiography. This might be an effective stalling tactic, which apparently is going to be necessary until Brother arrives. As far as The Two Oceans Gourmet Club is concerned, I'll address that charade as soon as possible.

One by one, the men proceeded to give the group an idea of where they were from and their occupations. The many different accents manifested an interesting international atmosphere featuring various strains of English, from pure to hybrid. If that wasn't enough, those for whom English was a second language added a touch of Swedish, of German, and of a Chilean version of Spanish. One had to concentrate to capture what was being said.

When Tad stood to speak, Pete looked at Tom and the two men chuckled, remembering a lighter moment on the beach earlier that afternoon. The diverse backgrounds of the men impressed even the conservative James Thompson. Not because of their wealth or the lack of it, since money was obviously not a criterion for membership. But the gathering of these men to have dinner once a year dazzled him. John, of course, like James and Philip, still did not know the meaning of the dinner, although the younger Thompson brother was beginning to have his suspicions. John could not believe that some of these individuals could afford to be members of any gourmet club, let alone one that required them to travel halfway around the globe once a year. With a skeptical tone to his voice, he asked, "Pete, how many members are in the club?"

Tom turned to Andy. "What club is he referring to?"

His question was stated loudly enough for all to hear. Soon all heads were turning in different directions, looking for answers. Eventually, all eyes focused on Pete.

It was apparent to Pete the time had come to level with the three newcomers to the group. He stood and begged forgiveness for his brother's tall tale in the lounge, but quickly added, "Andy's intentions were not only moral, but righteous, as well."

James and John, feeling they were being hoodwinked, excused themselves and raced toward the door. Philip was not far behind. Pete dashed after them and hooked onto the arm of James, turning him around. His strength froze the elder Thompson brother in his tracks. John lunged at the powerful fisherman in an attempt to free his older brother from the man's vice-like grasp.

"Please, John, please hear me out," Pete pleaded, shrugging off the Englishman's attempt to rid his brother from the stranger's grip. "Just give me ten minutes to explain what's going on. We mean no harm to you or your brother. We do have a fascinating story to tell you. As you can now surmise, the subject matter is so incredible, Andy had no choice but to tell you a lie in order to get you to come meet with us."

Still holding James tightly, Pete continued to appeal his case. "Please stay and hear what we have to say. I promise after you hear what we have to tell you, the three of you will be free to leave."

John noticed that all the men at the table had gotten to their feet, but that none of them seemed intent on harming him or his brother. None of them even advanced to participate in the struggle going on. Still enraged, he looked at his older brother, seeking guidance on what to do next. James shrugged as if to say, what options do we have?

Pete read James's body language and proceeded to release his hold. James, still full of contempt for his pursuer, stared at Pete to see what kind of reaction he'd find. Pete's eyes reflected not hate or rage, but warmth and concern for the potential anguish he might have caused.

This man did not choose to harm me, James sensed, but his method of getting my attention was surely underhanded. "Sir, I will listen to your story, but I promise you, we will leave as soon as you are finished."

"Thanks for your patience,"responded Pete. "As I said, after hearing this extraordinary saga of today's events, the three of you can leave if you so choose. Please be seated, gentlemen, and keep an open mind as to what you are about to hear. I'm sure after you have listened to what we have to tell you, the reasons for Andy's devious method of getting you in here will be understood."

Pete began the convoluted task of explaining what had occurred on the beach earlier that day. Without any hesitation, the others who had been there and actually seen the man who called himself Jesus, attested to his presence and added their own observations. Even those who had not been on the beach chimed in to describe how they had become part of the group, inspiring the thought that it defied all odds that the meeting today of these men could be just a coincidence. Pete indicated to the newcomers how Simon was introduced to the group, but quickly added he had no knowledge of the South African's whereabouts.

The three newcomers looked at one another repeatedly, trying to read each other's minds. Stunned at the possibility of what was happening, but attentive in an attempt to hear and absorb every word and phrase, they continued listening without saying a word. What they heard and what reinforced all of their views was the fact that their names, with the exception of just one not accounted for at present, matched those of the apostles at the last supper.

"Just to refresh your memories,"cited Jim Albright, "they were...." He then proceeded to name the twelve followers of Jesus as recorded in the *Bible.*

Of course, when Jim mentioned the names John, Philip, and then a second James, all eyes at the table focused on the three newcomers. Still in awe of what Pete and the others had said, all James could do was nod his head, reflecting a sign of understanding and perhaps a gesture of belonging. On the other hand, John Thompson scanned the room in an effort to conduct a head count. He remarked that only ten men were present.

"That's correct,"said James. "Where are the other two?"

Philip, extremely quiet until this point, added, "And what about Jesus? Where is he?"

Tad spoke up. "I have no idea where Brother is, but as for our South African gentleman, I'm not convinced Simon will show."

"Oh, I neglected to mention this,"said Pete, "but Jesus would prefer us to address him as Brother. He feels that this veiling of his name will keep outsiders from getting confused and perhaps even hysterical. As far as Simon is concerned, he probably has some doubts, but don't we all? I am confident that he will be here presently. Judas, on the other hand, has not made an appearance as yet, but perhaps we should not expect him to."

The climate in the room was relaxed, at least for the moment. It was clear the newcomers sensed that these men meant them no harm, but they still said nothing to confirm this feeling. James whispered to John, "These men are either telling the truth or are the most impressive liars the world had ever known.

A few quiet moments had passed when Andy said, "So as you can see, when I overheard you three introduce yourselves in the lounge, I knew, I mean, well, the names fit and...."

James interrupted. "Now I understand why you created this fisherman's tale."

John jokingly said, "You could have come up with a better lie than The-What-Do-You-Call-It Gourmet Club." This brought laughter to the group, which was certainly welcomed.

"On a serious note, gentlemen, this is quite a fascinating story,"said James. "I must inform you, I am a religious man, who is very active with various Christian charities in London. Despite my beliefs, what you have told me thus far seems more like a fairy tale than reality." He paused and looked around the room, then continued. "I too find the gathering of all of us with names matching the apostles more than a coincidence. But are you telling me that within a few minutes, I am to meet Jesus Christ -- excuse me, I mean Brother -- here and now?"

Pete nodded affirmatively. The reaction from John was hard to read, as he was keeping his emotions bottled up for the moment inside his churning stomach.

A concerned look on his face, Philip had many questions for which he, too, wanted answers. But he held all of them in, except for one. "I want to know if this mission you refer to, Pete, means I will have to be separated from my family?

"I don't know the answer to that question, Philip,"said Pete. "There are many questions which need to be answered by Brother, and that one is on the top of the list. Jim and Matt are compiling such a list at this very moment. Let me say again, that our meeting on the beach this afternoon was brief, and, at this time, you know about as much as we do."

John said to his brother, "I sense these men are telling the truth. Furthermore, if they wanted to do some dastardly deed to us, they needn't tell this incredible tale."

"Speaking for my brother John and myself,"James said aloud, "we accept your invitation to dinner. But I must add that we have our reservations regarding what you have told us. I trust that is understandable?"

Philip also smiled at Pete and offered him his approval.

Pete said, "Welcome to the group, gentlemen,"and he walked toward them and shook their hands.

This was followed by a spontaneous reaction by the rest of the group, as one by one they took Pete's lead and arose to shake hands with the new members.

Tom, in an effort to add some levity to the diminishing tension in the room, teasingly asked, "Is anyone interested in a vodka on the rocks?"

"Now, now, my Swedish friend,"replied Pete, a huge grin on his face, "how about a nice bottle of Beck's? Or perhaps you might choose to upscale your drinking habits and enjoy a glass of wine?"

"There, I knew I could get a smile out of you,"replied Tom.

"How about you gentlemen,"asked Andy. "Do you need a refill?" No one refused the offer, and everyone except for Matt and Jim Albright, who continued to write, arose and headed toward the portable bar.

Tad could not stop wondering about Simon. He informed Pete, "I'm going to call Simon's condo to see if he is still there."

"Good idea, Tad. See if you can locate him."

Andy made eye contact with his younger brother, marveling at how proficient he had been in handling an inflammatory situation. Pete just looked intently at his brother, sensing his best friend's emotions.

A few of the men chuckled as they joked about the menu for the "gourmet club."

Tad informed Pete of his inability to reach Simon. Although Pete was concerned about Simon not showing up yet, the whereabouts of Jesus was still paramount in his mind.

Philip's attention returned to his neighbor, Rudy. Was he still with Connie? Had the hostess informed him about the dinner? He considered calling the lounge to see if Rudy was there, but did not.

All heads turned as they heard a surprising sound from the corner of the room. The unexpected tones of an enchanting rendition of *Moonlight Sonata* came from the grand piano. This beautiful piece was being played by the talented Bart Kessler. For the next six and a half minutes no one spoke, as they gathered around to listen to the concert pianist do his thing. Bart was quite pleased and a little embarrassed by the ovation he received from his new friends. Moments later, Pete looked at his watch and noticed that it was now ten to nine and no sign of Jesus as yet. The concerned expression on his face did not escape Andy, or for that matter the rest of the group.

FIFTEEN

Rudy Romero maneuvered himself as close to Connie and this strange-sounding man as he possibly could without being seen -- so close, he could hear every word. It became obvious from the conversation that this man was her ex-husband -- the ill-tempered spouse who had left Connie when her daughter, Rosa, was just an infant. As far as Rudy knew, Eduardo Lopez had not only divorced Connie, but he had essentially been out of her life ever since. Why had he returned to see his ... no, my beautiful Connie, he thought? Why now?

A half hour passed and Rudy continued to listen as the ex-couple went on to discuss everything from her job to their little girl. Eventually, Rudy got his answer. Eduardo wanted money from her. His demands became stronger and Connie's refusal to meet them more pronounced. She walked around the corner toward an isolated part of the parking lot, shouting as she quickened her pace, explaining she barely made ends meet, providing for her daughter and mother. The ex-husband followed and told her to quiet down and asked her to talk to her rich boy friend, Rudy Romero. That Eduardo knew his name surprised and disturbed Rudy, while he positioned himself closer to them. He wanted to know how this low-life could have that information. So did Connie!

As her voice grew noticeably louder, Rudy turned around to see if anyone else could hear.

"How do you know his name? Are you following me" she asked. "Get out of my life and stay away from Rosa, too. Go back to your drug dealer friends."

"Quiet down,"said Eduardo. Rudy clenched his fists when he saw the ex-husband grab Connie's arms and began to shake her. "I don't want back in your life. I just need a few dollars until I get on my feet again. As far as your rich boyfriend is concerned ... well, let me just say that he is well acquainted with people who deal in the streets of Miami."

Rudy was overjoyed to see Connie break Eduardo's hold and slap him in the face. "He's been very good to Rosa and me. And he's an attorney, not one of your street junkies."

The ex-husband rubbed his cheek and said, "You can still use your hands pretty good. Ask him sometime who he associates with and how he makes his money. Won't you be surprised. Now how about the cash?"

"Not a dime, not one dime will I give you."

Rudy watched Eduardo grab her by the arms again, pinning them against her sides, this time with more force than the first time.

Connie yelled out, obviously in some pain, "Stop it, you are hurting me."

She began to cry, which got Rudy's already hot blood to its boiling point. Not only did he want to come to the rescue of his dear Connie, but he wanted to break the nose of this creep who defamed him. Rudy leaped into action, taking advantage of a surprise attack. First Rudy punched Eduardo on the side of his face, just below his right eye. A second blow to the chin dazed him. The assault from the rear brought the cowardly Eduardo to the ground. While Eduardo lay motionless, Rudy put his arms around Connie and asked, "Are you okay?"

She was shook up, but nodded yes.

"Go back into the lounge and stay there. I'll take care of this animal."

Connie kissed her hero on the cheek and walked gingerly toward the entrance of the Coral Reef.

As Rudy turned around to see what other parts of Eduardo he wished to punish next, he saw the glare of a switchblade before his eyes. The knife cut the left sleeve of Rudy's expensive red sports coat. He backed up to regroup and watched his assailant make his second attack. But this time, the knife was aimed at Rudy's face and it found its target. The sharp blade penetrated the skin an inch below his right ear, and blood began trickling down the side of his face. The cut stunned him briefly; moreover, in his attempt to avoid further injury, he fell back, losing his balance. As he lay stretched out on his back, the attorney was completely vulnerable, and his enemy, weapon in hand, sneered as he stood over him and quickly moved in on his prey.

"So you want to be a hero? I'll teach you to stay away from my wife."

But as Eduardo bent over for the final thrust, someone else, much stronger than Eduardo, grabbed his arm and twisted it, forcing the weapon to fall to the ground. Without looking around to see who this intruder was, Eduardo spun himself around, falling down in the process. He rolled several times, creating a distance of some twelve feet between himself and Rudy, who remained on the ground. This evasive action appeared effective, since whoever this interloper was chose not to pursue him. In a flash, Eduardo got to his feet and ran to the back of the parking lot, disappearing into the night. Rudy sat up, his eyes staring in the direction of the fleeing Eduardo. When the blackness of night absorbed any traces of the ex-husband, Rudy turned around to thank the man who had most likely saved his life.

Simon English, noticing the torn jacket where the knife had almost ended the attorney's life, asked, "Are you okay? "But when Rudy turned in the direction of Simon, the cut on his face came into view. Immediately, Simon reached for a handkerchief in his back pocket and placed it on Rudy's face, applying pressure directly below the right ear. Although blood quickly reddened the handkerchief, the cut did not appear to be deep. A few stitches or perhaps even a bandage properly applied, and all would be well, thought Simon.

Rudy, still sitting on the ground, stretched out his right hand to the man who had rescued him. "Thank you. How can I ever repay you for saving my life?"

Simon shook Rudy's hand and said, "I guess you are pretty fortunate that I happened to hear what was going on."

What the man from South Africa didn't say was that he had just arrived to have dinner with a group of men who believed that Jesus would be joining them. Simon thought to himself, how ironic -- two hours ago I was leaning toward not attending this dinner at all. If nothing else occurs tonight, at least my coming here was beneficial to this poor soul. "Here, hold this as best you can,"he said, placing Rudy's right hand on the makeshift compress. "I'll take you inside and get some medical assistance for your cut."

"I don't even know your name,"said Rudy. The men exchanged short introductions and the attorney again thanked this brave man for his heroic deed.

Simon helped Rudy to his feet and proceeded to walk toward the entrance of the Coral Reef. Rudy, still shaky from the assault, managed to start walking with Simon's help. But they were able to take only two or three steps, when out of the dark they heard Eduardo's voice. The ex-husband reappeared just a few yards in front of them, this time with a handgun, threatening both the boyfriend and the intruder.

"I'll show you who the boss is,"he grumbled, as he raised the gun.

But before he could squeeze the trigger, Simon and Rudy saw a hand reach out and grab Eduardo's wrist with such force that the gun slipped from his grip. Simon wasted no time in landing a right cross to Eduardo's face. Eduardo fell to the ground and Simon pounced on him like a lion on an impala. Not until the men heard the voice of the newcomer telling Simon to back off did the assault on tonight's two time loser stop. For Simon recognized this extraordinary voice. It was the man from the beach -- the man calling himself Jesus. He had saved both their lives.

"Take this man inside,"Jesus said to Simon, pointing to Rudy, "and have someone attend to him. I will deal with the other one. As soon as I conclude my business out here, I will join the two of you for dinner."

Simon walked towards the Coral Reef, Rudy followed closely behind, still holding the blood-soaked handkerchief to his face.

"Simon, what does he mean about joining us for dinner?"

"I'll explain that to you later,"responded Simon, no longer disbelieving that his personal savior was indeed who he claimed to be.

Jesus helped Eduardo to his feet, looked into his eyes, and admonished him. "I suggest you change your lifestyle or suffer the consequences."

Eduardo was hypnotized by the penetrating eyes staring into his, which further emphasized the words this stranger directed at him. He was stunned at the way the man ordered him to change his life -- more stunned than by the blows he had sustained at the hands of Simon. He did not know why, but the man's words had such an impact on him that he began to tremble and felt weak at the knees. Suddenly, the proud and tough Eduardo knelt on the ground in front of this man and began to cry for the first time since he had been a little boy.

"Your actions from now on are what is important, not your crying. Go now! Go forward and face life like a man, and perhaps we will see each other again."

Trembling, Eduardo bowed to this mysterious man half out of respect, the other half fright, and begged for forgiveness. "I do not know who you are, but I do believe in God. You, sir, surely are an emissary of God -- I just feel it. Please ask him to forgive me for all my sins."

Jesus put his hand on Eduardo's shoulder and said, "From this day forward you shall help those who need assistance. You will seek and find an honest occupation. And you will see to it your family is provided for. Now go, my son, and start your life over again. God will clean the slate if you do as he says."

Eduardo arose, straightened his shirt and looked toward this majestic individual, but he was gone. For some reason Eduardo wasn't surprised. Instead of heading for the back of the parking lot and into the dark as usual, he wiped the tears from his eyes and proceeded to walk toward the neon signs of South Beach a new man.

###

Connie had been standing inside the entrance to the Coral Reef. She had been tempted to call the police, but was reluctant to, for fear of getting both her ex-husband and boyfriend in trouble. She sensed that both of them had lived checkered pasts and didn't need the cops to mess up their lives any further. When Connie looked through the door's diamond-shaped window and saw Rudy holding his face, she opened the door quickly. "Are you okay?"

"It's just a small cut, thanks to Simon."Rudy gestured to his companion.

Connie took them to the manager's office and told them to stay there while she went to the kitchen to get a bandage and an antiseptic.

When she left, Rudy asked, "Simon, please explain what you said about the man who saved our lives. What did he mean about having dinner with us?"

Simon was careful not to reveal the identity of the man who had saved them, since Rudy's name suggested he was not intended to be part of the group. Even so, he was certain Jesus had said he would join both of them for dinner.

He told Rudy this man was someone special and left it at that. Connie's return enabled Simon to avoid answering any additional questions, at least for the moment.

Simon asked Connie, "Is there a group of men dining in a private room? I believe the host's name is Albano, Peter Albano."

"Yes, I believe the room was set up for a private party, but check with the hostess to find out who the host is."

Simon stopped by the hostess station, got directions to the room and made his way to the room. He chuckled at the thought of the people of South Beach thinking a party was actually going on within those four walls. At the door he was greeted by Tom, who immediately looked at Tad and smiled in a jauntily manner, as if to say, you non-believer.

"What's that look for?"asked Simon.

"Oh, the auto engineer didn't think you'd be making an appearance."

Tad quickly came to his own defense."I said it was fifty-fifty."

"You don't know how close you were to being right, my man,"said Simon. "But believe me, the reason I'm late has little to do with my indecision about coming tonight."

He looked around the room and noticed some new faces in the group. Since he now had the floor, Simon told the group that he had just seen Brother. This statement brought a handful of the men to the edge of their chairs. "We were in a scuffle together." This remark got the attention of the rest of them.

"Is he okay?"asked Pete.

"Oh yes, quite all right. Thanks to him there are no bullet holes in my midsection. "Simon proceeded to describe the events in the parking lot. No questions or comments until he finished this bizarre story.

"Simon, can I get you a beer or perhaps a glass of wine?"offered Tom.

"Is that all you have?"

"I'm afraid so."

"Too bad. I could sure use something stronger after what I've been through."

As the Swede made his way to the portable bar, Andy took the opportunity to introduce Simon to the newcomers. The man from South Africa was delighted to find a pair of Englishmen among the new arrivals. He commented that the people in this room represented almost the entire globe.

"A quick head count still leaves us one short. Perhaps that's all who will show,"said John.

Pete said, "Dinner was for thirteen and thirteen there will be."

But even Andy had his doubts about the man called Judas appearing.

Pete asked Simon, "Did Brother say he would be coming soon?"

"Yes he did." Simon noticed that his watch reflected nine-fifteen. "I'm confident he will be here before long."

The thought of him appearing shortly made most of the group edgy, especially those who had not see him that afternoon. Conversation slowed and the room grew quiet. Breaking the silence came a mellow sound from the corner of the room. The entire group, as if having practiced a routine, turned as one in the direction of the piano, where their resident concert pianist began playing the beautiful tones of a medley from Lerner and Loewe's *My Fair Lady*. Not only could Bart play the piano eloquently, but also his timing was exquisite. The music helped ease the tension in the room, which was as tight as an Olympic archer's bow string.

In the restaurant manager's office, Rudy received first aid from Connie in the form of a stinging medication, followed by a Band-Aid. The first aid stopped the bleeding, but Connie recommended he see a doctor as soon as possible. The best medical assistance he received was a big hug and kiss from her. He commented that perhaps she should become a nurse for her ability to dispense TLC.

She squeezed him tighter and for the first time in their relationship said, "I love you."

Elated, he echoed her words. Then Rudy briefly told Connie what had happened and how fortunate both he and Simon were.

Connie's boss entered the office to plead with the waitress to return to the lounge, which was packed with thirsty guests.

"Go ahead, Connie, I'll be fine." Rudy's thoughts finally returned to his new neighbor, Philip.

He walked into the lounge and looked around. The hostess spotted him.

"Hi Rudy. I hope you're okay."

"Yes, thank you, it's nothing."

She told him where to find his friend Philip and to meet him there. Funny, thought Rudy. That's the second invitation to dinner I've received in the last half hour. He wondered how the somewhat shy Philip had managed to get himself asked to a dinner.

But first, Rudy decided to walk outside the Coral Reef, perhaps to see if he could find the brave man who had saved his life. Dinner could wait, he thought, I want to thank this fellow. His intuition was correct, for as soon as he opened the door he saw this mysterious individual. Rudy was as humble as could be in showing his appreciation to this man. He told his hero his name and also mentioned he was an attorney, handed him a business card, and said, "Anything, anything you need, just...."

Before he could continue, Jesus said to him, "You can do something for me."

"Certainly, anything you want. How can I help you?"

"You can be honest and tell me what your real name is and where you are from."

"I told you my name, Rudy Romero."

Jesus paused and stared into Rudy's eyes, awaiting a different response. "You don't know who I am as yet, but before the evening is over I'm sure it will be clear to you that lying to me is a big mistake. If you so desire, for the moment I shall call you Rudy."

His surprising comments frightened Rudy. How does he know Rudy is not my real name? Has he been following me? Could he be a Narc or FBI? I've only represented drug dealers, not sold any drugs. The attorney sensed that he was being painted into a corner and didn't like the idea at all. He was beginning to lose patience with the man who had saved his life, but decided to maintain a calm and collected approach to this interrogation.

"I thank you for all you have done for me tonight, but I don't appreciate your prying into my private life. Besides, you have never gotten around to telling me who you are. If you are a cop or whatever, why don't you tell me? I've done nothing illegal, so why are you questioning me?"

Jesus did not respond. This riled Rudy to such an extent that he turned and started to walk back toward the entrance to the Coral Reef.

Finally, Jesus said, "Would you care to join me for dinner? I will be meeting with your friend Philip and the man who saved your life, Simon."

This invitation baffled Rudy. How did he know the name of my new neighbor? What goes on here, he thought to himself. "Listen,"he said to the man who knew more about him than he cared to let on, "you are starting to get to me. Unless you have been tailing me, there is no way you could possibly know Philip."

"Sure I can."

"But he just moved here from Chile!"

"Yes, I realize that. He came here from Santiago, correct?"

"That's right. But how, how in the world did you know that?"

"I know many things. I even know your true name, Rudy. And I also know where you were born and who your parents were."

This latest disclosure stunned the attorney. For the first time this evening, even though he had faced death at the hands of Eduardo, he felt vulnerable. There was no use trying to conceal his identity any more. This man, whoever he was, knew the truth. His shoulders slumped, and he conceded that all the devious tricks he had learned in law school were useless in defending his position. Then he straightened his back, wanting this meddling individual to realize he still had his pride, despite having been exposed. Regaining his composure, Rudy determined it was time to tell the truth to him.

"I was born in Morocco, my mother was from Spain, my father, Syria. Her family was in the olive oil export business and he was a weapons broker for ... I'd rather not say." After which he snickered. "You probably know for who. They moved to Colombia when I was sixteen and changed my name, so that I would fit in with the rest of the children at school. They sent me to my mother's uncle in Miami in order to attend college, after which I decided to stay." Rudy held the rest in as long as he possibly could, but after waiting a few seconds and swallowing hard, he said, "My real name is Serge Judas Karim." Sarcastically, he continued, "Are you satisfied now? You are the only person on the face of the earth who knows my true identity."

"Thanks for your honesty, Judas. I realize this revelation has been very difficult for you.

"Why did you call me by my middle name? No one ever called me Judas. Why did you?"

"You will find out shortly. Now let's join the others for dinner."

They walked into the Coral Reef, where Connie greeted her boyfriend and offered him a navy blue jacket the restaurant kept on hand to accommodate those guests in need of one. As they made the switch of apparel, she could not keep her eyes off the man with Rudy. He had a quality about him that entranced the beautiful waitress. He smiled at her as she thanked him for helping Rudy in the parking lot. His eyes were so warm and caring, she thought, he must be a very special man.

"Enjoy your dinner,"she said. "I will see you later, Rudy." She continued staring as they made their way to the private dining room and wondered who this man could be -- this hero who had saved her boyfriend's life. Her mind wondered about Eduardo; despite his actions tonight she still wished he could straighten out his life. He needed someone to help him get his act together. Connie did not know that Eduardo had been so fortunate as to receive guidance from the top of the mountain -- the highest possible source.

SIXTEEN

The beautiful music of Jerome Kern's *Old Man River* was filling the room when Tom opened the door for the last guests to enter. Tom greeted the new arrivals, bowing to the man he had seen on the beach earlier that afternoon. The man gently placed his hand on Tom's shoulder and proceeded to enter this room, which was overflowing with excitement and anticipation.

"Gentlemen, I'd like you to meet Judas Karim. Judas is from Morocco. He will be joining our group."

Those at the door greeted the newcomer as Thomas closed the room off to the rest of the world -- a room now occupied by thirteen men. Twelve of them came from various countries, the other man...?

In the corner, Thaddaeus was singing "He just keeps rollin, he just keeps rollin along...." Words that had endured the last three generations. Bartholomew's fingers on the well-tuned grand piano and Thaddaeus' scratchy voice stopped abruptly, as Brother and the other man came into view. Yes, there was no doubt in anyone's mind this man who wished to be called Brother was indeed Jesus Christ. All twelve men, even those who had not seen him earlier that day, stopped what they were doing and stood in reverence to the man who had sacrificed himself on the cross, some two thousand years ago. The sixty-four-thousand-dollar question going through their minds was -- why had he returned?

Brother was wearing a white sports jacket, white dress shirt and navy blue pants. Contemporary attire for a casual dinner with a few friends, thought Peter, watching from across the room. His clothing fit right in with that of most of the men in South Beach. He made his way to the piano and asked Bartholomew to continue playing, not asking Thaddaeus to continue singing.

"This is one of my favorite songs and your rendition of it is simply beautiful."

Bartholomew acknowledged the compliment and began to play once more, but he said nothing. Imagine, the Lord, Jesus Christ enjoying my music. He jokingly thought to himself, I'll also ask the conductor for a raise, based on the compliment I just received. An endorsement from the highest authority.

Peter made his way to the piano and greeted the new arrival, not forgetting to call him Brother. "Would you care for a glass of wine?"

"No,"replied Brother, "but one of those beers -- I think you called it Beck's -- sure is tempting."

This remark pleased Andrew, who reached into the ice bucket and handed him a cold beer.

"Now I owe you two beers,"he said to Andrew, smiled and raised two fingers in a "V."

"I apologize for being late. Please order dinner as soon as you can, Peter. These men must be famished."

Peter nodded and proceeded to follow instructions, taking stock of the beer and wine supply before calling.

Some of the men, including Andrew and Thomas, looked around at those who had not been on the beach earlier, as if to say, I hope you believe us now. There were no dissenters remaining in the room.

John and James Thompson, although with no doubts remaining, were still perplexed as to why this was happening.
Simon English, sensing this reaction from the financiers from London, decided to assist the two brothers in getting over their initial shock. "My feelings in the beginning were not too dissimilar from yours."

John thanked Simon for his thoughtful comments and asked, "Do you have any idea what is to happen next?"

"I'm as much in the dark as you."

"What could he possibly expect from us? "asked James.

"That's a good question, my friend. A darn good question."

Philip was pleased to see his friend Rudy and went over to greet him, surprised that Brother had introduced him as Judas Karim. So was Simon, who moments ago had saved this man's life. Judas told Philip what had happened in the parking lot and how both Simon and this man called Brother had saved his life.

Looking down in embarrassment, Judas apologized to Philip for not telling him his real name before."

"I understand, my friend. "He put his arm around Judas and said, "I'm happy to be with you, no matter what your name is. Let's get a beer."

"Sounds great." Judas pointed to Brother. "This guy actually knew my real name and where I was born. I don't know how he got all this information about me, but he is aware of my entire background. And another thing that puzzles me -- what is so special about this guy and why is everyone paying homage to him?"

"You mean you don't know who he is?"

"No, I don't." Judas scanned the room, looking for a clue. "Why don't you tell me?"

Philip informed his friend of who the people in the room were, assigning a name and a country to each. When he got to Jesus, whom he saved for last, he paused. "Judas, I hope you are a religious man -- for he is Jesus Christ."

"Who? What do you mean?"

Philip gazed directly into his friend's eyes and repeated his last comment. "Jesus has returned. Furthermore, all of us in this room tonight have the same first names as the men who were with him at the last supper."

"You expect me to believe that he is...."

"Yes, and he has asked us to have dinner with him. By the way, he wishes us to call him Brother."

"You mean to tell me, this is really happening, and you and I are a part of it?"

"Yes. I know it's difficult to believe. I've had many doubts myself. But Peter and a few of the other men met him on the beach this afternoon, and he asked them to come here tonight. Since then, others, like you and me, have somehow met one of that group and have been asked to attend tonight's dinner. For example, I met Andrew at the bar in the lounge. He invited me, and John and James Thompson, using some lame-brain excuse to get us in here. I think the others had a similar experience, although in your case, I must admit, the circumstances were a bit more complicated and dramatic."

"You can say that again. What happens next?"

"I don't have any idea, and if anyone else knows, they aren't saying. Let's see what happens, Rudy ... I mean, Judas."

"You might as well call me by my real name."

"Okay, Mister Karim."

Judas was momentarily stunned. It was the first time in his life he'd been called by his true last name.

"What I still can't figure out is, why me?" asked Judas. "I'm not very religious, and, I'm not even a Christian. I guess it would come as no great shock to you that there are some things in my past I'm not very proud of."

"I'm sure all of us in this room could make a similar statement, my friend. Would you mind telling me where you are really from and what your religious background is?"

"I was raised in Rabat." He paused sensing Philip might not be aware of where that was. "Rabat is the capital of Morocco, where I was born. I am a Muslim, as are most people who live in that area of the world. "He went on to explain about his family moving to Colombia when he was a boy. "When my father died, religion became less important to me. My mother was a Catholic, I believe, but she never practiced nor talked about religion, as best I can remember. I guess I still believe in Allah, but I have not said my five daily prayers nor gone to a mosque in years."

"That explains it."

"That explains what?" asked Judas.

"Brother wanted to make sure the three basic religions were covered, Christianity, Judaism, and Islam. That's why you were invited. You, my dear Judas, represent the Muslims."

"You mean to tell me he wanted to have people in the group, as you call it, who are not Christians?"

"Exactly. For some reason he wants a cross-section of religions represented."

"But what about the Hindus and Buddhists, and all the other religions practiced throughout the world?"

"That's a good question that I'm sure deserves a reply. By the way, Matthew and Jim are sitting at the table as we speak, compiling some of those very questions for him. If you have any questions, tell them to add it to their list."

"Would you mind if we talked about you for a minute?" asked Judas.

"Go ahead. What's on your mind?"

"What's your religious background?"

"I am a Catholic and you could probably say I am a true believer in my faith. Anna and I go to church every Sunday and all the holy days, and in Santiago, I was on the church council. Perhaps that places me at the very religious end of the spectrum. But as I said before, Brother must have a reason for inviting all of us here, regardless of what our beliefs are. If you look around the room, you will find men here from all over the world, and, for the most part, with different religious backgrounds. I think some of these men have no religious beliefs at all. I guess we just have to wait and see, Judas. Just wait and see."

Seated at the table, Matthew and Jim Albright had managed to compile a list of twenty-five questions, including input from a few of the other men. They determined that many of the paramount points would be covered within those twenty-five questions. Matthew's writing and interviewing skills kept the inquires short and concise. The flaw in asking too many questions, experience had taught him, was that the subject of an interview got fatigued and confused. Not that he expected Brother to react in that way, just that a thought-out interview, would give the group the best results. That is, of course, if Brother was willing to answer all their questions.

The music from the grand piano ended and those listening, including Brother, applauded the talented German.

"Dinner should be here shortly,"Peter announced.

"Would you please ask the men to take their places at the table so we can proceed?"

James asked, "Is there any special assigned seating arrangement?"

Brother assured him, "No, anywhere will be just fine."

When all twelve men were seated, Brother, who remained standing, began to speak to the group as a whole. He could understand that only a few in the group had believed who he was at first. "I trust all of you now recognize who I am. I know it has been difficult for you to believe not only that I have returned, but also that you twelve men from different cultures, with a variety of religious beliefs, have been selected to help me. Meeting me today must be incomprehensible."

James raised his hand, wishing to ask Brother a question.

He waved his right hand at James to acknowledge his request and said, "If you have a question, James, can we address it later?" He asked the men to continue to have some patience. "I'm sure you have many questions, which I will attempt to answer. I will be here for three days. I have no intention of speaking to you in parables or ancient religious passages. My conversation with you will be conducted simply, using contemporary language and phrases. Yes, gentlemen, I will be here on earth with you for three days!" Brother looked intensely at each man before he added: **"In which time the destiny of mankind will be decided."**

This profound revelation frightened each of the men, even those who had always been true believers. The men silent, thinking the end of time was surely not far off. This must be the reason he has returned, to announce to the entire population that Doomsday had finally arrived. Armageddon. The end. The final chapter of humankind.

Reading their minds, Brother paused for a few minutes before continuing. The expressions on their faces revealed both confusion and trepidation; in some cases, for the men with families, anxiety about the fate of their loved ones.

Brother calmed their fears by adding, "You men are going to assist me in making sure your most dreaded concerns don't come true. You, my dear friends, will see to it the entire world hears my message --

regardless of their religious beliefs or tribal spiritual customs and cults. Peter, I know you had some information that you wanted to share with the others. I think this would be a good time for them to hear what you have to say."

Peter, sitting at the opposite end of the table, stood. "Thank you, Brother." Still somewhat shocked and dazed from Brother's pronouncement, he said in a tone full of apprehension and anxiety, "I thought it would be appropriate to offer some opening remarks. My reasoning is to make sure everyone here is aware of how we met Brother this afternoon. In addition, I want all of the men who were not present today on the beach to know exactly what happened there. I just want everyone to be as knowledgeable and up to date as possible. For some unknown reason, I have been appointed the unofficial spokesman for the group. Perhaps Brother will address that point at a later time."

Brother nodded in agreement. Peter then proceeded to describe, chronologically, all the incredible events that had occurred that day. He summarized how each of the men who had not been on the beach had become part of the group. Then he asked Simon to describe once more the events of the parking lot.

When Peter continued, he said, "These meetings were not by chance, I believe. As I understand it, everything had all been pre-arranged."

Brother did not comment on whether that was true or not.

"This brings the entire group up to date, and now all of you know as much as I do. Speaking for the group, I think it's fair to say all of us firmly believe...." At this point Peter paused and looked directly at Brother, "to use your own words -- you are who you say you are."

This acknowledgment elicited a grin from Brother, who was remaining silent during Peter's dissertation.

"I don't quite understand your comment regarding the destiny of humankind, but I assure you this proclamation has captured my attention, and, I suspect, that of the others, as well. Please tell us more about...."

A knock on the door interrupted Peter. Two waiters had come to serve dinner. Thomas stopped them at the doorway, saying they would not be needed any further. He and Thaddaeus wheeled the serving carts to the side of the room where the portable bar was located. One by one the men walked over to the carts, served themselves, and returned to the table with their food and drink.

During dinner, few words were spoken, and none by Brother, who seemed to enjoy the broiled pompano as much as the rest of the group. The silence gave each of the men, especially those with families, time to reflect on the significance of what the next three days would have on their precious little ones at home. Even Simon's thoughts were focused on his son, Richard, whom he had not seen for almost two months. Bartholomew wished that Elsa and the children were close by. He had not mentioned to anyone in the group as yet that she would be flying to Miami in six days. Philip fantasized that his wife and son would be in their new apartment in Miami when he returned there tonight -- if he returned there tonight. Thaddaeus, who had not seen his children since Thanksgiving, wished he could be with them now. He even included his ex-wife in his thoughts and desperately wanted her by his side. John wanted to call his new love, Mary, despite her being less than an hour away.

When dinner was over and each man had cleared his place, they settled into their chairs, still uncertain as to what lay ahead of them. Silence prevailed. James looked at his watch and noticed that it was eleven o'clock. He was exhausted, and as he looked around the room it became obvious to him he was not alone. Peter sensed this fatigue and wanted to proceed as soon as possible, before many in the group became brain dead. He stood and attempted to continue where he had left off when dinner had arrived. Brother asked him to delay his questions and comments, for he wished to address the group. He wanted to explain why he had returned.

"Gentlemen, the Father of humankind has asked me to return. His reasons are elementary. As humanity approaches the new millennium, he wants you to look back at your achievements as well as your failures of the past thousand years. He is delighted at the progress you have made in some areas and extremely disappointed in others. Unfortunately, the latter far outweighs the former. I will go over these points in detail tomorrow.

"You might say I have returned to assist you in making your planet earth a better place to live. This includes seeing to it that people become more responsible for their actions. Also, to enhance their understanding of their fellow man's feelings, and changing their attitudes toward those who are of different races or colors.

"Yes, gentlemen, this is the task before you. It might appear monumental, and perhaps it is, though with proper planning and a lot of hard work you should be able to complete this mission. You must succeed! Please believe me, the alternative that Father has devised is not very pleasant." He looked around the room, with his penetrating eyes staring at each one of them. "Father means business, and you are the last line of defense for humankind. I am not going to go into details tonight, since many of you are tired and perhaps will not be able to absorb all I have to say. But believe me, before I leave you the day after tomorrow, your role will be clearly defined. With your guidance and leadership, you can assist humankind to survive and prosper in the new millennium.

"I also realize that Matthew and James Albright -- oh yes, let's continue to call him Jim, to keep the names straight -- have written some questions. I intend to give you some time tomorrow night, when I will attempt to answer them.

"Tomorrow, we will meet here for breakfast at nine o'clock. By the way, bring your swim suits, as I have planned a couple of hours of relaxation after our morning meeting. You may call your loved ones; but do not mention anything about the meeting or me. We don't want to alarm anyone, at least not for the moment.

"I have divided the agenda into three segments. Tomorrow morning I will give you the background as to why I am here. At dinner your questions will be addressed. And in the third segment, which I have scheduled to be discussed at breakfast the day after tomorrow, I will inform you about the mission that you have been chosen to carry out. I must leave you now. I suggest all of you return to your homes or hotel rooms and get a good night's rest."

The men obediently stood up and said their goodnights.

Brother placed his hand on Thaddaeus' shoulder and said, "Please, my dear friend, get some singing lessons."

This amusing statement to the off-key crooner got just the reaction that Brother had hoped for. It brought laughter to the entire room for the first time and -- he hoped -- not the last. The men left still smiling and teasing Thaddaeus about Brother's jovial comment. Only Peter stayed behind to ask Brother about tomorrow's breakfast and dinner.

"Thank you, Peter. Would you be so kind as to take care of the arrangements? Don't forget to take care of breakfast the following morning, too."

"Yes, Brother, I will see to everything before I leave."

The unofficial spokesman for the group and the official spokesman for God shook hands.

"Have a good night's sleep, Peter."

Brother departed leaving only Peter in the room to make arrangements for the following day.

Each man did precisely as Brother had requested. They returned to their hotel rooms or homes, and the married men called their wives. John called Mary and asked if they could postpone their date. Mary said politely that she understood -- business came before pleasure -- and she would take a rain check. He was delighted to hear her response but refrained from telling her his real reason for breaking their date. All the men staying in hotels picked up their copies of the Gideon *Bible* and read many pages before falling asleep. Philip reached into one of the packed boxes at his apartment after calling Anna and located his sacred book. Judas, went home to his apartment and stared at the ceiling for the better part of the night.

SEVENTEEN

Peter arrived at the White Sand Hotel at eight o'clock. He wanted to make sure everything Brother had requested was in place. He also wished to make sure breakfast would be served in the same manner as dinner had been the night before, with as little interruption from the waitstaff as possible. He met with the assistant manager of the Coral Reef, who assured him his instructions of the night before would be carried out. Coffee and juice were to be available at eight-forty-five and breakfast at nine-thirty. Everything appeared to be in order, and for the moment he could relax, but just for the moment. When his mind wandered to what would happen during the remainder of the day, he began to sense the stress associated with the unknown. Brother's comments of last night had not been taken lightly.

Peter's brother, Andrew, arrived shortly after eight o'clock carrying two styrofoam cups filled with coffee he had helped himself to in the lobby of the hotel.

"Thanks, Andrew, that hit the spot," Peter said, sipping his first taste of the freshly brewed coffee.

"Why do you think I made you my younger brother?"

"Ah, if Mama and Papa could see us now," Peter replied somberly. "Can you imagine what they would say if we told them we met...."

"Jesus," Andrew interrupted.

"Yes, Andrew. I hope the two of them have front row seats in heaven, so they can see what's going on here. By the way, can you recall what Brother looked like? I remember he was wearing a white sports coat, but for the love of me, I cannot describe his face. Not the color of his hair, nor his eyes." Sounding bewildered, he added, "For the love of me, I can't even tell you how tall he was."

"Come to think of it Peter, I can't either. I certainly would like to add this point about his features on our slate of questions. Don't you think?"

"No question about it. I'll be sure to tell Matthew to include it."

Each member of the group arrived before nine o'clock. They were casually attired for the most important meeting of their lives. Tension filled the room as they anticipated that what they would hear in the next few hours would change the world they lived in. Shortly, Brother would tell them what was to become of the human race.

James told his younger brother, John, "It reminds me of the moments before my final exams at Oxford."

Simon, who had joined the two Thompson brothers for coffee, agreed completely with John's analogy.

Thomas managed to lighten the conversations by asking Thaddaeus to refrain from singing today. "We sure as heck don't want to upset anyone like we did last night."

Everyone, including Thaddaeus, found some humor in the dressmaker's comments but deep down each of them had butterflies in his belly.

Matthew and Jim were prepared with their slate of questions. Although a few of the men had submitted ideas to Matthew and Jim, most of them didn't feel qualified to ask any religious questions.

Peter asked, "Are the two of you ready for tonight's session?"

Jim replied, "Yes, Peter, we are. Both Matthew and I think you should ask the questions." That was settled on, and it was also agreed that Matthew would act as secretary and write down Brother's replies.

Matthew suggested to Peter that he review the slate before tonight. "To familiarize yourself with the questions."

"I'm not sure which ones he will answer in what he tells us this morning,"said Jim, "and which he will have to be asked, but at least we have covered some basic points man has wanted to know for centuries."

"Yes, I agree,"replied Matthew. "Regardless of your religious background, Christian, Jew, or whatever, I believe the questions to be diverse and all-encompassing."

Peter nodded and said, "We will see, gentlemen. We will see."

At nine sharp, Thomas opened the door for Brother. Peter welcomed him and confirmed that everything was set up as he wished. Breakfast would be served at nine-thirty. He deliberately stared at Brother in an attempt to remember his features, since he had failed to recall them the first two times.

Brother helped himself to a cup of hot coffee. "How are you feeling, Judas? I hope you have recovered from last night's ordeal."

Judas replied, "Thank you for asking. I'm very grateful for your intervention last night."

"Have no fear, my dear friend, you will make it up to me in the near future."

Judas was momentarily dumb struck. "Brother, you sure have a way with words, shocking enough to scare the pants off a guy."

"And you, Mister Attorney, are not afraid to speak your mind, either." Brother smiled at the most controversial man in the group, who, in return, bowed to show a sign of respect.

Brother took Philip and Thaddaeus aside and asked, "Please identify which communications outlets with international capabilities we should employ. We will require the capability to reach all world leaders. This includes all the heads of governments and religious leaders. But I also want to reach out to as many people as possible, making them aware first hand of my return."

Philip and Thaddaeus looked at each other, speechless for a few seconds, honored by the confidence he had in them, but horrified by the responsibility that Brother had lain before them.

Thaddaeus, after careful deliberation, was the first to offer a suggestion.

"We could try videoconferencing. That's how the major corporations in America would proceed. It might be difficult to set this up by tomorrow morning, but it's worth a try."

Philip jumped on board, adding, "What about television? I mean, why not ask CNN to come here and set up their cameras, since their broadcasts are seen and heard internationally?"

Thaddaeus added, "That's a good idea, and we can also try to get time on the Today Show tomorrow morning." He said to Brother good-humoredly, "I doubt if we will have any difficulty at all getting some air time."

Brother responded, "Any method you think will reach those individuals that I wish to address is all right with me. But I wouldn't tell the telephone company that I am here, nor the reason why you want the hook-up. That could possibly delay them giving us the connection. You know, red tape and all that. Also, it would be wise to ask Matthew for his advice, since he is in the communications business."

Thaddaeus, his mind now focused on this project and sounding more sure of himself, said, "To reach the young people we could even use the Internet."

Brother responded. "Ah, yes, the young people, many of whom think that praying to Father is only for the sick and aged. That's a great idea, my friend."

Thaddaeus, giving serious thought to what he and Philip had said, gulped and retreated. "I hope you understand these are only ideas we have suggested. First of all, neither Philip nor I have an extensive background in computers. In addition, I'm not positive how we get to reach the rest of the world. I mean, those countries that are not hooked up to CNN or any of the networks will fail to hear what you have to say. And as far as a videoconference hook-up is concerned, we are at the mercy of the local telephone company."

Brother, sensing signs of trepidation, eased the anxiety of the two men. "I have a sense of your capabilities, and I realize it seems like an impossible assignment, but believe me, you can accomplish this task. For the right amount of money, you can get the local telephone company to hook up a videoconferencing system before the day is through. Television producers, I believe, will consider my return newsworthy and most likely will arrive within an hour after you contact them."

Philip looked at Thaddaeus and couldn't help but snicker at Brother's last comment.

Brother caught sight of grins on their faces and said, "All right, that's an understatement. Those countries who cannot pick up the signal of CNN or the other networks can be supplied with a videotape of the proceedings. As far as how we get on line with the computer to the Internet is concerned, well, I'm sure the two of you can wing it. That's the correct term, is it not?"

Thaddaeus smiled and said, "That's right Brother. Wing it. I hope you're right."

"Why don't we say for the everyone's sake, I pray that I am right."

Thaddaeus couldn't help but adding, "Brother, I don't know the proper way to put this, but would you consider one of your miracles to get this done?"

Philip almost dropped his cup of coffee when he heard his fellow engineer's comment. Brother laughed heartily and said, "You are a very funny fellow, Thaddaeus. But the answer is no." Still smiling, he added, "There will be no divine intervention to get this job accomplished. I want you to sit in on the breakfast meeting, after which you will purchase the necessary equipment to establish communications through the telephone company and the Internet. Don't worry about the money -- we are fortunate to have some men in this group who have, as you say, some very deep pockets. Also contact the production people at CNN and any of the other major radio and television stations and invite them to our meeting tomorrow." Brother looked at the two men with a reassuring expression and said, "I have the utmost confidence in you. Miracles -- who needs miracles when I have you two?"

Both Thaddaeus and Philip thanked him for his trust in them. If nothing else, his comments and charming smile lifted their spirits, for their task seemed impossible.

Philip knew exactly who Brother was referring to, James and John Thompson and Simon. Without wasting any time, he approached John, who understood completely. He would make sure they obtained the required equipment.

Philip decided he'd better tell John, "Neither Thaddaeus nor I are unfamiliar with computers, but we are not what you would call hackers. And as far as the telephone company's ability to deliver, well, that was nothing more than a guessing game."

John responded, "You two are probably the best candidates we have to get us up and running. I'm sure you'll get the job done." He put his arms around the two men to make them aware that they had his complete support.

Philip informed Matthew of what Brother was asking them to accomplish.

Matthew, his reporter's juices overflowing, said, "I'll cover the story for *Time*. The magazine has a distribution system that is nearly worldwide. I also suggest contacting the BBC in London. As far as other publications are concerned, I'll see to it that the print media around the world is notified and advised to send their reporters to South Beach." But deep down, Matthew Singer, reporter, wanted an exclusive on this, the story that would be talked about for the next two thousand years. He was not only reporting it, he was part of the story.

EIGHTEEN

The men were on their second cups of coffee when the waiter knocked on the door. Thomas, who acted as the Sergeant-at-Arms, opened the door, dismissed the waiter, and with the help of Andrew wheeled in the two carts carrying the food. Everyone helped himself to the miniature buffet Peter had ordered the night before. By a quarter to ten, breakfast was over, the tables cleared, and twelve men were waiting nervously for Brother to tell them the details of why he had returned. He did not disappoint them.

"Gentlemen, when Father asked me to return, I struggled with my approach to inform you of why. Initially, my thoughts were to give you a synopsis of the major events that occurred since I was here last and of the people who caused those events to happen. But after reviewing all that has happened in the last two thousand years, I sensed there was just too much to consider and too many events to talk about. Before we go any further, I'll answer the first of your questions. *No, I did not return at the end of the last millennium.* Although I must admit Father wished he had sent me, based on the results of humankind's progress over the last thousand years. Or shall I say, the lack of it?"

Matthew and Jim looked at each other, then proceeded to scratch that question off the slate of twenty-five that they had composed. The reporter from *Time* was careful to copy down Brother's exact words.

"While it is true your achievements in many areas were glorious, failures in some of the more important segments of your development were nothing short of a complete disaster. Not too many years ago, I recall an American western movie being made entitled *The Good, The Bad And The Ugly*. What a poetic and profound reference to humankind. A fitting description of man's successes and failures over the last thousand years, especially the last century.

"Let's begin with *The Good*. Without question, the greatest progress humans have achieved over the last thousand years is in their ability to comprehend and educate. You have erected thousands of preliminary schools, colleges, and universities, the latter serving as a giant fishbowl where students and professors can exchange ideas regarding the arts and sciences. These universities can be referred to as the quintessential laboratories for experiments and development of the human mind. The enormous accomplishments you have managed to achieve can be attributed to these classrooms, where men and women have come to expand their ability to think.

"Your inventors, scientists and engineers have managed to develop innovative means of transportation. From the steamship to the automobile to jet planes able to fly around the earth in a matter of hours. And your spacecraft, which can send people to the moon or soar hundreds of thousand of feet up in space for months at a time. A far cry from the donkey or wooden ships manned by slaves, who would oar vessels that were barely seaworthy, when I was here two thousand years ago. Electricity, the telephone, the cinema, computers, and television -- well, perhaps you haven't quite perfected that one as yet -- are inventions the human race should be proud of."

This last remark brought at least a little levity to this otherwise somber group, which was anxious but uneasy to hear the remainder of Brother's remarks.

"Your architects have also made extraordinary progress on the drafting tables, designing buildings to live and work in. And the construction engineers who erect these incredible structures have developed innovated methods to put up these neck-stretching skyscrapers. In recent years, these master builders have also seen fit to surround these magnificent structures with beautiful parks and, in some cases, even fish-filled ponds. You have learned to heat and cool these buildings, utilizing all types of energy sources, from fossil fuels to solar power and even nuclear. Yes, humanity has made great strides in its ability to erect these enormous structures you live and work in.

"For many centuries, humankind has continued to enhance its technique for manufacturing clothing. From hand-sewn frocks to the looms that make cotton fabrics. To the sewing machines that stitch anything from..."he looked at Thomas, the clothing manufacturer, and grinned, "expensive silk dresses to grubby sweatshirts that read Amalfi Fishing Co."

Brother's choice of apparel got a wide grin from Andrew and Peter. And had the circumstances been different, Thomas would have passed out his business cards.

"Your farmers have learned to increase the yield of their fields and groves. With the development of scientific research, the quality and quantity of poultry and cattle have been enhanced. Fruits, vegetables, grains, and dairy products have enabled much of the world's population to enjoy a well-balanced diet. The vineyards that produce the wines you drink are now strung all around the globe, and, may I add, produce a higher quality of grapes than ever before. And you now have the capability to restock the fish that you harvest in every ocean, sea, and lake."

"Although I cannot say many good things about how you have protected the environment, at least now your leaders understand that there must be some controls established to shelter it from abuse.

"One of the great gifts, and the most pleasing to the eye, have been the beautiful works of art that your sculptors and painters have created. To see the paintings of Monet, Renoir, Raphael, Van Gogh, and the sculptures of Michelangelo, just to name a few, is a pleasure to behold. One that each man and woman should experience. Or the exceptional writers and poets such as Shakespeare, Cervantes, Dickinson, and Shaw, that every person should get the opportunity to read. These talented men and women have surely left their mark on humankind for many, many generations. And I hope, with your help, many more in the future."

This last remark from Brother's lips jolted each of the twelve. Without question, his comment on the subject of future generations caught their attention, which was exactly the reaction he was looking for.

"Perhaps the most significant advancements have occurred in the medical profession. Your doctors and scientists have developed amazing procedures and medicines to treat and cure a variety of ailments. This has expanded life expectancy in what you refer to as industrialized countries to almost double what it was two hundred years ago. The medical field's research and dedication has almost totally eliminated fatal epidemics such as smallpox and polio, and have made some significant inroads into solving the causes of your most lethal afflictions such as heart disease and cancer. You now have sufficient expertise to deal with the aged and infirmed and have solved most of the problems associated with infant mortality.

"Yes, you have made some incredible progress in so many areas, but as you have surmised, I did not return to inform you only of your achievements. Unfortunately, your failures, or *The Bad*, is the reason I am here. Humankind has been guilty of many transgressions that have upset Father. Among those, a complete disregard for the fundamental values that men and women must adhere to if the human race is to survive. And, it is so unfortunate that humankind has seen fit to manufacture so many new weapons of destruction. Your armaments have escalated from a slingshot, to bow and arrow, to atomic bombs. Yes, I have left many gaps in your methods of culling the population, including the dreaded land mines that continue to kill innocent people for years after your wars end.

"Wars your leaders have started because of their greed and, more heinously, their need for power; all of them pointless, unnecessary, and totally reprehensible. Some of your historians prefer to call them conflicts of economics. The wars that are most incomprehensible are those begun because of religious differences. Religious differences." Brother paused and shook his head. "That's something I could never understand. Just think, if I were in Europe earlier in this century, I probably would have been executed in Auschwitz."

Over the last thousand years, there have been hundreds of battles between people of different cultures and religions. Conflicts that are the least understandable are those fought within the boundaries of the same country. Civil wars, as you refer to them, brother against brother, north versus south, east against west. These are extreme cases, I realize, but categorically, they are the most profound examples of humankind's failures on earth. They illustrate precisely how men and women have placed limitations on their ability to understand their neighbor simply because he or she is not of the same race or perhaps practices a different religion.

"Your advancements in education, as I mentioned earlier, have been significant. Although in many areas, both in developed and third world countries, little has been done to enhance the curriculum and in many cases, standards have been reduced, I think, for the most part, to accommodate teachers. Not that I desire to place the entire burden on them, mind you, but the profession of education requires a vast amount of passion and bravery -- reaching past the limits of the four walls of a classroom.

"I spoke earlier about your technological advancements and the inventions that have captivated humankind, especially over the last few decades. Despite these engineering wonders, far too many people must reside in huts or tenements that are not fit to live in. This does not include those poor individuals who are on the bottom of the ladder -- those poor souls who are considered nomads, who have no permanent abode and are dislocated, traveling from one third world country to another. What amazes me is that in this era of great scientific achievements, many men and women, and especially children, suffer from fundamental ailments such as cholera and dysentery, due, unquestionably, to the unsanitary conditions many people in these underdeveloped countries must live in.

"They wear clothes that are nothing more than rags sewn together. As far as nourishment is concerned, why, it is an outrage to see what some people in the lands of plenty throw away after feeding themselves and their families. If they could only see what the poor people of this planet must subsist on, I'm sure they would take a different view of how much food they consume. Why, the average family pet in America is better fed than some of these needy people. What really boggles one's mind are the crops that are destroyed annually in order to maintain some arbitrary price structure, while a good percentage of people aren't adequately nourished. It is inconceivable to me that the powers-that-be allow these conditions to exist. The need for the three basic necessities of life, food, shelter, and clothing, must be addressed by your leaders everywhere.

"One does not have to go very far to visit the house of horrors that people must survive in. Right here, in America, these despicable housing developments that blanket your major metropolitan areas serve to influence the lawless subcultures ruling these tenements. What never ceases to amaze me is that it is not the least bit unusual for these substandard living quarters to be in close proximity to the luxury towers topped by spacious penthouses the area's wealthiest people call home. And the new type of citizen who roams your city streets should not be omitted. You refer to them as bag ladies and men or street people. They walk your streets and alleys at night, pushing shopping carts that they have stolen from a local food chain and with all their belongings piled up inside their chariots, look for aluminum cans or returnable bottles to sell in order to survive. These indigent souls sleep in cardboard boxes and call any shelter under an overpass or alley their home."

Brother's voice had not wavered at all while describing what he referred to as *The Bad*. Thaddaeus and Matthew, who lived in metropolitan areas, knew exactly what he was referring to, while Simon, who had traveled to places such as Angola and Bangladesh, had seen with his own eyes what Brother was getting at. As for the rest of the men, they could all relate to the problems of poverty and destitution that existed in their own countries. Brother's speech was eloquent and the inflections in his voice spirited. His eyes, ever so caring, radiated concern as well as love for all of humankind and to everyone at the table.

"So much for *The Bad*; on to The *Ugly*." Brother paused before proceeding, as he could not help but notice the group's body language reflected signs of apprehension and trepidation.

Although silent, their gestures and the look in their eyes were a clear giveaway, exhibiting fear and anxiety over what they were about to hear.

"Yes, gentlemen, the worst is yet to come. While Father is deeply troubled by what I described earlier, it is what I will address now that has created this crossroads for humankind. You see, he is most concerned about the conduct and moral practices of humankind.

"The weapons you construct to engage in your frivolous wars are not as nearly as lethal and ominous as the attitude men and women exhibit on a daily basis for their neighbors. The transgressions you have been guilty of, from the lack of caring for one another, to the cynicism that is so prevalent in every nation, is quite disturbing, and Father will not tolerate it any more. The deterioration of morality and the lack of compassion for those who are in need typify the direction humanity has decided to take. The media throughout the world highlights and glorifies salacious conduct. The financial greed to promote this kind of conduct in the cinema, television, and in magazines has lined the pockets of these insensitive producers and publishers. What they don't seem to care about are the children of this planet, who are being desensitized to reality due to such exhibitions of violence and exploitive sexual behavior.

"In addition, the criminal element has been placed on a pedestal for the less fortunate and uneducated to look up to as some form of folk heroes. It is regrettable, the children who are exposed to these dastardly individuals cannot decipher right from wrong. This is but an example of some of the reprehensible trends that are helping to break down the moral fiber of your societies. Far too many of your celebrities, such as sports figures, movie stars, and politicians act like adolescents. Some of these adults are so juvenile, they are willing to participate in the most deadly game of chance -- drugs -- ranging from what many call a harmless social narcotic such as marijuana to the addictive drugs such as cocaine and heroin, which are the bane of existence for the weak and misguided.

"It is inconceivable to me why someone, who by your earthly measurements would be considered successful, would resort to these drugs in order to get a high or to find relaxation. These privileged few who participate in this detestable activity may be idolized and called successful by your earthly standards, but be assured, they will not enjoy the same status when the appropriate time comes. Conversely, those individuals in the public arena who maintain a balanced lifestyle, display the traits of a responsible adult, and are a credit to society, will enjoy what is to come of their virtue. Unfortunately this group of individuals is much too small and shrinking each day. Yes, the need for positive role models for your teenagers to look up to is at the crisis level.

"Perhaps the most corrupt transgression of all is that of greed. Those who would cheat their friends and neighbors to line their own coffers will surely be dealt with in an appropriate manner when they face judgment day. For their sins underscore the fundamental decline in values that is so pervasive in the world today. This is especially true of those who have prospered, amassed fortunes, and decided to withdraw from society. I believe you know some of these people yourself, those who think that their money should go to their graves with them. Needless to say, those who are successful and spend at least a portion of their time being philanthropic will enjoy the fruits of heaven. The old adage about the only true donation is the one that is given anonymously ... well, let's just say, this assertion does have some merit.

"I must also address the other side of the equation, those individuals who are healthy both physically and mentally but believe they can live off society for their entire lives. Work is not in their vocabulary and helping others is an action they would never consider. These parasites are as sinful as the most miserly millionaires who refuse to connect to those in need. Typically they do not relate to Father, nor do they make a conscientious effort to exist peacefully in their communities. These freeloaders who make no contributions to society are as useless as barnacles on the bottom of a shipwreck, and when the time comes will be dealt with accordingly.

"The bigots, who would deface or destroy a house of worship, lend truth to the fact that Satan, yes the devil himself, walks the face of the earth. He does so through humankind, with the venom and hatred that only he can fabricate. The animosity one person can show to another, simply because he is of another race or worships Father in a different fashion, is clearly the work of Satan. How humankind can accept all of this is beyond me. Without question this failure to be considerate and kind to each other is perhaps the most upsetting to Father.

"Those of you who have attained wealth through long hours of hard work and perhaps a bit of good fortune must assume the responsibility of assisting those others in your community -- and around the earth -- who are impoverished and without hope. These challenges can be accomplished not only with your money, but with the time, wisdom, business experience, and energy that helped make you a success.

"Surrounding yourself and your loved ones with material items is acceptable to Father. He gets great pleasure in watching those who have worked hard enjoy the fruits of their labor. But using these material items to build a wall around yourself is not acceptable. Keeping one's self at arms' length from the realities of life, such as ignoring the plight of the impoverished or turning your back on those in need of an education, undermines the fundamental values of society. Our good friend James Thompson so appropriately refers to his generosity as an investment, and an investment it surely is, in all of humankind."

The Englishman's face turned a deep shade of red, for which Brother apologized deeply.

"I trust you do not need to be reminded your material items -- be they works of art or your yachts and castles -- must be left behind at the doorstep of death. Moreover, those who have wealth and feel that because they are rich there is no need to believe in Father are in for a rude awakening.

"Inform everyone of the necessity to work together in harmony and to share the basic essentials of life with the less fortunate. And you must convince the religious leaders and heads of state to set aside their differences and to understand that a failure to do so will result in extreme consequences. Yes, gentlemen, this is your mission. To elevate humankind from the depths of hatred and greed to a new serene level of compassion and giving.

"My friends, this is what you will try to accomplish over the next few days and weeks. Your task will be to convince every man and woman, regardless of their race, religion, or status in society, to open up their hearts to their neighbors and become more understanding. To live in peace, to be compassionate, and to eliminate greed and cynicism. Let's talk about greed once again and discuss cynicism to some degree. I define greed as stepping over the ethical fence to attain success by deceit and deception, and the immoral ways selfish individuals treat their fellow workers, suppliers, and customers. Although the unscrupulous take a back seat to the cynics, who take great pleasure in watching someone fail, and, who attempt to find negative reasons why anyone should or could ever be so lucky as to enjoy a bit of success. I place the greedy and the cynical individuals in the same arena, for more often than not, their malicious traits are a common thread in each of them. Believe me, Father has very little tolerance for those individuals who spend their lives being corrupt and especially for those who gloat over the mistakes and failures of their friends and associates.

"Make a concerted effort to have faith in each other and above all have faith and trust in Father. All of you are on this earth for a very short time -- I believe one of your quips suggests five minutes. Make the most of it, both in your attitude toward your family and neighbors and in a spiritual way to Father. Inform everyone that their actions will greatly affect the quality and quantity of time they spend in what you call the afterlife. And perhaps that answers another one of the twenty-five questions on your slate.

"Yes, there is an afterlife!"

Each of the men felt a sense of euphoria, hearing this incredible proclamation directly from Brother's lips.They looked at each other with signs of exhilaration written all over their faces. Each man shifted in his chair as if someone had just told him he had won millions of dollars in a lottery, or perhaps had been chosen to captain a space shuttle to the moon. John grabbed his brother James by the hand, and James, in turn, reached for Bartholomew's hand, and so on until all the men were holding hands. The entire group stood as if on cue, and while still holding hands, raised them over their heads. This reaction created an incredible amount of electricity, probably enough to light up Times Square on New Year's Eve. And when Brother's hands completed the circuit, enough current was flowing to illuminate the entire earth on the darkest night of the year. The excitement lasted ten minutes or so, with little conversation, only looks of rejoicing and exultation.

When the men finally sat down, they tried to harness their excitement over Brother's remarks and get back to business. Still elated by the confirmation of an afterlife, their beaming eyes were focused on Brother. What would he tell them next? Shaking his head, Brother appeared somber, causing the smiles on the faces of the group to fall. He looked at each of them with a serious expression on his face and in his eyes -- yes those eyes, that were oh, so, penetrating -- and said, "Why are you surprised? Have you forgotten the Scriptures? Do those of you who call yourselves Christians not recall what I told my disciples? I can understand the reactions of Bartholomew, Judas, and Matthew, since they have perhaps not been aware of my prophecies, not being raised in the Christian faith. But the rest of you? Must I tell you again?"

Brother paused before proceeding and once again tension filled the room. He stood motionless for a few minutes, saying not a word. His arms extended out and his face reflected disappointment, as if to suggest to the men he was frustrated in their lack of belief in him and his teachings. Eyes filled with tears, Brother finally said, *"He will sit at the right hand of GOD, from whence he will come to judge the living and the dead."* He paused again for a few seconds before adding,"I promised I would not speak to you in parables." Then with a radiant beam returning to his enchanting face he said, "but even I can slip occasionally."

This jovial comment eased the tension in a room already full of mood swings that would from time to time reach each extreme end of the spectrum.

"Excuse me, Brother,"said Peter. "Please forgive us, not for being non-believers, but because hearing it from you directly has had a powerful impact on me and I'm sure on the rest of the group, Christian or not. I can tell you without reservation that Andrew and I have always believed in spending eternity with you and Father."

Brother looked around the room and saw a similar affirmation on the faces of the other men.

Jim rose and said, "Another question answered, that which pertained to judgment day." Shrugging his shoulders he added, "Not necessarily when, but for sure there was to be one. Brother, you have explained what is expected of us, and I am confident all of us in this room will try as hard as possible to see that it is carried out. But what if we...."

Brother raised his hands before Jim could finish his question, stating that the morning's session had ended. "Although I am sure you have given me your undivided attention, two hours of listening to anyone is plenty for one session. He told the group that as the meetings continued all of the questions they had prepared would be answered. He added, "I want to thank the group for its patience and I promise that tonight's meeting will be equally informative.

"I have one final thought for you." His sparkling eyes of an indescribable color scanned the room, focusing on Simon and James. "If I may use an analogy from this interesting as well as frustrating game you two gentlemen play, called golf. I believe you refer to the word 'par' to distinguish the standard, as to the score one should strive to shoot in each round. I will tell you here and now, this same word could be applied to religion. Let me explain what I mean. There are millions of people who attend religious services, praying and worshipping and even donating money to their respective religious orders. Some even make it a point to visit their church, mosque, or temple each day. They pray to Father, and some even seek me out for absolution or for the return of good health for their loved ones.

"Most of these frequent visitors to their places of worship consider themselves very religious. In their minds, they set the standard for who is religious and who is not, basing their rating system on how often one attends services, or how much money they contribute compared to their neighbor. Or how the young couple down the street from them chooses to conduct their life style." Holding his right hand to his heart, Brother said in a deep tone, "I am extremely disappointed at those who believe in me and pray for forgiveness and eternal life as they kneel in church and then, I'm sorry to say, once they descend the steps of my tabernacle, disregard the basic principles described in the *Bible*."

Extending his hands forward as if to reach out to each member of the group he added, "I will pontificate once again, although I assure you this is the last time. Going to church does not give one any particular benefits, unless he or she carries out the knowledge and wisdom it takes to be one of Father's soldiers. Teach them, in your travels, to treat their neighbors as they would their brothers and sisters. Ask them to help eliminate these rancorous sicknesses and the narrow-mindedness that poisons the minds of all too many people. Tell those who pray to Father that the responsibility is on their shoulders to rid the world of these malignant diseases called hatred, prejudice, and bigotry. And let no man or woman pass judgment on their neighbor or cast ill will on someone who worships to Father in a different fashion. There is only one that I know who determines what par is, as it pertains to religion. Lest we forget!"

Each of the men, regardless of his religious background, was able to relate to Brother's last comment. Even Bartholomew could understand what Brother had to say, despite his lack of religious credentials.

"Oh, before I forget,"Brother said as he looked at the group and chuckled, "all those humorous yarns regarding my golf swing will have to be shelved." Swinging his arms as if he were hitting a golf shot, he said, "I've never played the game."

Simon and James caught on immediately and laughed heartily. It took a few seconds for the others to catch on, and then they joined in on this welcomed pleasantry from Brother as well.

The only items he had left on the agenda were to inform the group about the meeting the following morning and to tell them that Philip and Thaddaeus were working on a communications hook-up to reach most, if not all, the leaders of every nation and as many people as possible. He asked for their help in reaching out to the masses in any conceivable fashion.

"Please inform either Philip or Thaddaeus of any method you believe can enable us to get our story out, be it television, magazines, newspapers, Internet, or whatever. The two of them, aided by the very generous financial assistance of John, will spend the remainder of the morning and this afternoon getting the necessary equipment in place for tomorrow's meeting."

Matthew was hesitant at first, but decided he'd better advise Brother as to how overzealous the press could be."I'd like to make a comment. Once the word leaks out to the various wire services that you are here, every tabloid newspaper as well as those infamous paparazzi will be at South Beach within a few hours. Honestly, it doesn't matter if these journalists truly believe you are here, just the fact that someone says he is you, Brother, is enough to attract every sleazy reporter in the western hemisphere, if not the entire planet."

Brother's response was pragmatic. "I guess we must accept the fact there are those who would sensationalize my being here, as well as those who are willing to assist us in getting our word out. In a sense, both the credible and the not-so-credible will work on our behalf. So take charge of the press, my dear Matthew, and handle them as you see fit. But do not restrict those who wish to cover the story."

Matthew nodded in agreement but remained apprehensive.

"If that is all, gentlemen,"Brother said, "the meeting is now over and those of you assigned to handle the communications link-up can proceed. As far as the rest of us are concerned, we will head to the beach and get some sun."

Brother smiled and stared at Andrew, each reading the other's mind, "Yes, and another Beck's beer or two."

Andrew raised three fingers in jest, indicating the third beer he would get for Brother, who knew exactly what he meant and nodded, signifying his approval.

"Let's set up headquarters at the same spot we were at yesterday,"suggested Brother. "Once there, the group, or those of you who are not working on the project for tomorrow's meeting, will assist me in developing a plan for addressing the subjects we spoke of this morning. We shall meet here tonight at eight to review what we have accomplished and determine how our communications experts have made out. Oh yes, and of course to address what's left of those twenty-five questions you have prepared for me. I wouldn't want to disappoint Matthew and Jim, who have worked so hard in compiling and organizing your inquiries. For those of you working on communications, have a fruitful day. With luck, we will see you later this afternoon at the beach."

With those words, Brother and the remainder of the group began the short walk to the beach. Matthew stayed behind along with John, Philip, and Thaddaeus to coordinate the contacting of the media. Being a little selfish, his initial phone call would be to the editor of *Time*. Matthew put his reporter's hat on -- a New York Yankee baseball cap he had brought along to keep the sun off his balding head. On a legal pad he began to design a plan as to how to relate this incredible story to his editor, Bob Edwards. How do you tell someone, even someone who is in the news business, that you have a scoop on the most historic, the most spectacular, story in the annals of humankind?

As Matthew was formulating his plan, John and Philip checked out the nearest Circuit City store in the phone book. Matthew informed the investor from England and the engineer from Chile that the giant computer outlet was sure to have on hand the necessary computer equipment that would enable the group to gain access to the Internet. While they were talking computers, Thaddaeus telephoned Bell South to determine who he would have to talk to in order to rent the appropriate equipment to conduct a videoconferencing meeting. After talking to several layers of management, he was finally connected with a vice president of marketing and informed him cost was not a concern, but time was of the essence. He was advised that although there were no guarantees, a representative and a technician from the local telephone company and from AT&T would be at the White Sand Hotel within the hour.

"That reminds me," said Thaddaeus, "it would be a good idea to tell the hotel manager what's going on. I mean, we don't have to tell him that Brother is here, only that we are having a press conference tomorrow morning and he should expect members of the press to be all over the place. Television crews, newspaper people and freelance photographers will be wandering in and out of the hotel all day. We should probably tell him about the computers and telephone hook-up as well, as we will need additional electrical outlets and telephone jacks."

"Good idea," responded Matthew. "I'll take care of that as soon as I deal with my editor."

John and Philip left for Circuit City -- via a white stretch limousine, of course -- to purchase the PCs and modems. Matthew continued writing his plan to his editor, while Thaddaeus was in the process of conducting a reality check, still unable to believe all of this was happening and that he was part of it.

#

It was a little less than a half-mile walk from the White Sand Hotel to the spot on the beach across the street from the Blue Crab, where the best bartender in all of South Beach was doing his thing. Can you imagine Speed's reaction to the goings-on the last two days, Thomas thought, smiling. Right under his meddlesome, prying nose, and yet he's not a part of the most important event in the history of humankind -- or at least since Brother appeared on earth two thousand years ago. When he finds out about this, he's liable to start drinking his own tropical concoctions. Thomas couldn't help but share his thoughts with Bartholomew as they began their walk to the beach. Bartholomew's laughter was so resounding, it compelled Thomas to share the story of the fastest and most inquisitive bartender on all of South Beach with the rest of the group.

Andrew added, "Wait till he finds out that one of the Beck's he served us yesterday was for Brother."

Bartholomew asked, "Should we tell him?"

"Of course,"replied Thomas. "Who's going to need a press conference after Speed finds out about Brother? All of South Beach will know within twenty minutes, the entire continent in an hour, and the rest of the world before the sun sets."

Robert Edwards was a twenty-five-year employee of *Time-Life*, having worked his way up from copy boy to managing editor of *Time*. He was well liked by his staff, in spite of the fact he was a hardnose, always a stickler for stories being accurate and authentic. Matthew had a very good relationship with his boss, both in the office and socially. There had been many long evenings of putting stories together, followed by a couple of hours of cocktails and dinner at P. J. Clarks. Matthew calculated he was going to have to call in all his markers with Bob in order for him to believe this story. Besides, even if he does believe what I tell him, is he going to allow me to cover this by myself, or is he going to get one of those young aggressive cubs to stick their two cents in? Well I can't worry about that right now. I'll just follow my game plan and see what happens.

Matthew cleared his throat while dialing the phone, understandably somewhat apprehensive, and said hello to his editor.

"How's the new Christopher Columbus from Australia doing?"

When Bob's chortling subsided, Matthew made his first attempt. "Bob, I'm sitting on perhaps the second greatest story ever told, if not the greatest."

This ended abruptly when Bob Edwards said,"Matt, you've downed too many piña coladas."He hung up before Matthew could respond.

A few seconds later Matthew called Bob again. After about twenty minutes of Matthew's describing the chain of events that had occurred over the last two days, he got the editor's attention. "I'm telling you that it's him,"repeated Matthew. "Jesus Christ! He's defined a mission for the twelve of us which we are to air to every living person via a videoconference and an Internet hook-up. I've been asked to coordinate the newspaper and magazine participation, as well as the major television networks and radio stations."

"What in heaven's name are you talking about? Do you expect me to believe...?"

"Yes I do! It's really him!"

Bob remained silent for a few moments, collected his thoughts, and said, "Matt, this man has persuaded you he is Jesus. Am I correct? But you don't expect me to believe he truly is...."

"I'm telling you he is! And furthermore, if you don't want to hear the rest of the story, I'll call one of our competitors."

Another minute of utter stillness as Bob contemplated his next move. "Okay, Matt, let's assume for the moment I accept this tale of yours. What is it you expect me to do?"

"I don't know exactly, but I have developed a plan for you to think about. Oh, before I forget, you're going to love this, Bob. Brother, as he has asked us to refer to him, is going to answer a slate of twenty-five questions tonight that we have prepared for him. He has already answered a few of them, and I want to tell you his responses are earth-shattering. Cover story revelations illustrating the fate of humankind. I'll tell you all about that later, but first consider the following scenario.

"With the resources you have at hand, I thought it would be easier for you to coordinate the task of getting the media here tomorrow morning from your office. Since we have a scoop on the story, I thought we could print an extra edition, giving us an exclusive on the story, certainly before the competition can react."

"Not so fast Matt."

Matthew spent the next ten minutes filling Bob in on more of the details, such as where and when. Despite his compelling describtion of this monumental happening in South Beach, Matthew realized no one, not even his best friend, Bob Edwards, was about to believe it. Taking notice of the lack of conversation from the editor, Matthew asked, "Are you getting all of this? I'm telling you it's true! You've got to believe me!"

"Yes,"responded his boss, who was formulating some unique ideas of his own. "With all sincerity, I do believe something unusual is going on in Miami. Don't get me wrong, I'm not completely sold on everything you've told me."

"Thanks, boss. Guess that's all I should expect from you at this point. Bob, I realize how difficult this must be for you and, by the way, just for the record, Jim Albright, you know, Australia's Christopher Columbus, well, he's one heck of a guy."

"Matt, my Uncle Bill is a good friend of Cardinal O'Connor, over at Saint Patrick's. What if I make a phone call to set up a meeting with him and a few of the other religious leaders from around New York?" Before Matthew could answer, Bob added, "Yes, I like the idea better and better, the more I think about it. And I'll have you hooked up on a conference call so you can tell them firsthand what's going on."

Matthew paused before responding to his boss's suggestion. "That seems like an interesting approach to get them and the other religious leaders around the globe primed for Brother's conference call tomorrow morning. There is plenty to do and the time line is critical. But more important, please keep a tight lip on this. I don't want those tabloids coming in here too soon and upsetting the apple cart."

"You're right, Matt, I'll just inform Max,"Bob said, referring to the managing editor, "before I phone Uncle Bill. Do you have to touch base with Brother before I proceed? That's what you call him, Brother, isn't it?"

"Yes -- he's asked us to call him that to avoid mass hysteria. And the answer to your question is no, you can get the ball rolling as soon as possible."

"Uh-h, where is he?"

"He's at the beach, probably drinking a cold beer."

"What?"

"You heard me right. Brother and most of the group are at the beach for the afternoon, and yes, he loves his beer."

"Come off it, Matt, you have flipped."

"No, no, that's the truth, he truly enjoys a cold brew. The entire group is at the beach, except for a few of us who are working on communications for tomorrow's meeting."

"You mean to tell me that the leader of my church is on the beach drinking a beer? Who's minding the store? Matt, I just have to ask you one thing before I go. Since you are not a Christian, how come you have been taken in by all of this? I mean, you never even participate in your own Jewish ceremonies."

"Believe me, Bob, if you were here to meet him and hear what he has to say, I don't care what your religious background is, even if you were an atheist, you would be taken in too. And don't forget, boss, Brother was born of Jewish parents, making him one of the tribe, just like me."

"Yes, remember to tell your mother when you talk to her next time. Make her aware of your instant affinity to the world of religion."

Matthew chuckled to himself, and said he didn't have time for this kind of bantering, suggesting that the editor didn't either. Bob got the point, called his reporter a spoilsport for not appreciating his humor, and added, "I'll call you back to tell you where and when I'm to meet with the cardinal."

Max Cohen's executive suite was situated two floors above Bob's office in *Time's* midtown Manhattan headquarters. Bob's call to the magazine's publisher reflected a sign of urgency and excitement, prompting his boss to invite him upstairs. Standard procedure for the hands-on management style of the publisher of one of the most read magazines throughout the world. Bob's face was flushed when he entered Max's lavish work space. This was an idiosyncrasy that his boss had seen on several occasions in the past, when Bob presented him with a questionable story he wanted to publish. Max thought, Boy, I wish I could get that guy in a poker game. "What's on your mind, Bob?"

Matthew's boss wasted few words informing Max about what was going on in South Beach. "It's just our good fortune that Matthew Singer was in South Beach on another assignment. And not only is he on the scene and on top of the story, he's one of the men breaking bread with this man calling himself Jesus."

Bob waited for a response from the publisher, who for a change had trouble finding the proper words to reply to his subordinate. Gaining his composure, Max said, "That boy has either been in the sun too long or has had too much rum to drink."

"That's exactly what I told him. Believe me, Max, he's completely in control of his faculties. If you'd like, you can talk to him yourself, but trust me, he believes all of this is happening."

Max pondered the response of his experienced editor and dedicated employee, then stood and faced the window in an attempt to hide his emotions. From a personal standpoint, this news was frightening as hell -- or should he say Gehenna, as he was taught in his early Hebrew lessons? But his reporter's desire and great determination to get a scoop on a story of such worldwide importance took over. "Okay Bob, let's assume he hasn't lost his mind. What next?"

"If you approve, Matt has asked me to assist him in the transmission of a videoconference with religious leaders and heads of state from every nation. I've already begun the process of setting up a meeting with Cardinal O'Connor. My uncle Bill is a good friend of his. And with your contacts in Washington, I thought you could start the ball rolling there."

"You mean you want me to get to the President?"

"That's precisely what I mean. Either we go the entire distance, or we drop the story completely. If you are even the least bit curious, or, and even more important, if you believe that God does exist, then I can't possibly see how you can walk away from this one."

Without hesitating, Max, who could sense a good story a thousand miles away, instructed Bob to start the machinery in motion, realizing that once things got started, there was no turning back. Once word leaked out -- and it always did -- pandemonium would reign whether the story was true or not. Without a doubt, once the media got hold of the story, it would change the world forever.

As the group approached the Blue Crab, Andrew looked at his watch, yawned, and said to his brother, "It's a few minutes to twelve, Peter. "Rubbing his hands together, he asked, "Shall we get a beer before we hit the beach?"

"Sure. Why not?"

Everyone, including Brother, echoed Peter's response.

"I'll have one!"

"Me too!"

"A nice cold one for me!"

"Okay! Okay, nine beers. "Somebody give me a hand. Is Beck's okay?" Andrew didn't wait for a response, as he started for the restaurant.

Thomas grabbed his arm and with an impish grin said, "I think it would be only appropriate for Brother to order the beers from Speed."

This stopped the men in their tracks, not knowing how Brother would react to Thomas' attempt to create a humorous situation, especially since Thomas was asking Brother to play the lead role in a plot to include, confuse, and confound South Beach's answer to Reuters, the Internet, and CNN, all rolled into one.

Brother, with a serious look on his face, turned in Thomas' direction, causing the Swede's chin to drop to his belt buckle. He placed his left hand on Thomas' shoulder and with his right hand raised over his head grinned, paused, and said, "How can I possibly resist?"

Brother's consent to this mischievous prank brought smiles to the men, which shortly grew into almost uncontrollable laughter. Even though he was still a bit unsure of himself or the situation at hand, Thomas needed no prompting to give Brother a high five. This set off a chain reaction, with high fives all around, as at this morning's meeting when they had heard Brother's revelation about the afterlife, but, without question, a lot more amusing.

The scene at the bar was what you might expect, with Brother ordering the beers from Speed and James paying the tab. The rest of the group stood in the background trying to control their emotions until they exited the Blue Crab, but with little success. Beginning with Thomas and Bartholomew and as contagious as chicken pox, the underhanded caper began at Speed's expense, but without his knowledge of what was going on. The street-smart bartender knew he was being had but couldn't put his finger on why. All Brother could do was shake his head, but as they left the bar, even he weakened and broke out in a smile.

"You, my friends, must come back here in the next few days to repair the damage we have done to this poor fellow."

Brother had his serious face on now, which convinced the men to do as he wished. They promised they would be sure to atone for their little prank at the appropriate time.

Cardinal O'Connor, although skeptical about any sightings of angels, crying Madonnas, and especially those over-zealous, devout Christians who constantly hear voices venerating Jesus, agreed to meet with *Time* magazine's Bob Edwards. He was receptive to hearing about this mysterious activity in Miami only because of his relationship with his old grammar school friend, Bill Edwards. Although Bill's telephone account of this so-called phenomenon at South Beach was vague, his eminence decided to listen to his old friend's nephew, the editor. He told his old friend he was busy for lunch, and that Bob should come to his office around two o'clock.

The cardinal took the liberty of inviting his lunch guests, Rabbi Marvin Silverman of Temple Beth El and Bishop John Parker, head of the Lutheran congregation in New York City, to sit in on the meeting. His eminence thought they might enjoy hearing about this miracle de jour.

It was 2 p.m. when Bob arrived at the cardinal's office, which was located next door to the imposing Saint Patrick's Cathedral. He was greeted by the three religious leaders, who agreed to stay and listen to what the editor had to say. After they exchanged pleasantries, Bob informed the bishop, the cardinal and the rabbi that he was aware of a historic religious occurrence in Miami Beach. "One of my staff is currently on the scene."

Bob went on to add, "The reporter, Matthew Singer, has informed me he is an active participant in what is transpiring. Therefore, I think it would be in our best interest to get the story firsthand from the man on the scene in Miami."

The cardinal responded, "By all means, call your man."

Matthew was in the meeting room finishing his plan for informing the media when the phone rang. "Hello Matt, I'm here with...." Bob went on to identify those who were at the meeting and their titles.

Matthew was surprised at how quickly his boss had responded to his request. On a personnal note, he was elated that the good rabbi was in attendance, representing him and his family and the twelve tribes of the Jewish faith.

Bob said, "Matt, we've got you on the speakerphone. Please reveal to the three religious leaders what has occurred at South Beach over the last two days."

Carefully selecting his words, Matthew spent the next fifteen minutes giving the clergy a full account of what had taken place, naming each of the men, Peter, Andrew, Thomas -- emphasizing the name and characterization of one of the thirteen men. The one who calls himself Brother. Naturally, the initial reaction of the three clerics in New York was of skepticism over some of Matthew's comments and total disbelief of the others.

"I realize it is difficult for anyone to comprehend that this is actually happening,"added Matthew. "Especially for you, gentlemen, who are men of the cloth, who I'm sure, see and hear your share of eccentrics, as well as religious fanatics, describing various sightings, miracles, and whatever. But it's true! Believe me! Everything I've told you has occurred, right here in South Beach. And, you are hearing this from a reporter, who up until this point in his life has not paid much attention to religion."

Bob wrote a note that Matthew was Jewish and passed it around for the three religious men to see, without interrupting his friend.

"I'd be happy to answer any questions you may have,"Matthew added.

Cardinal O'Connor, although quite apprehensive, considered the source of this information. The man on the scene was a reporter for one of the world's largest magazines, and his credentials appeared impeccable. He looked at the other religious leaders, listening carefully to this incredible account of the last two days, and decided to pursue the possibility, that yes, perhaps he had returned. Jesus, whom he had prayed to every day of his adult life. He removed his glasses, wiped his forehead, and began the examination of this, if true, most historical event in two thousand years.

"Matthew, please tell us, why did he select you men? Why not the Pope, or any of the other religious leaders?"

"I sense he thought it would be more believable if his epistle was delivered by laymen,"Matthew responded. "I'm only guessing at this, but a number of the men in the group suspect Brother thought that the average man and woman would be more apt to trust us, rather than any religious leader. We have spent the last two days with him, listening intently as he emphasized to us all the achievements and failures of humankind. But even when he speaks harshly about all of our wrongdoings, his great passion for the human race never diminishes. He has stressed that Father has many concerns about humankind's desire to live in harmony and peace. At this point, he has not told us what the alternatives would be if we don't comply with Father's wishes. I can only speculate that if we don't, the planet earth is not going to be the best place in the universe to reside."

Rabbi Silverman interrupted. "Matthew, please tell me. What does this man want us to do?"

Matthew went on to explain what Brother expected from them and his desire to conduct a conference call tomorrow morning with the religious and government leaders from around the world. Matthew's role was to convince the three men he was talking with to begin to inform the powers that be in their religious communities of the conference call with Brother and its significance to all.

Matthew said he needed the phone numbers and locations of each of the religious leaders they thought should be included. "You can fax that information to me at the White Sand Hotel in South Beach."

As Bob jotted down the fax number, he was aware of a silence in the room. Each of the holy men was reflecting on the possibility that what he had heard was true.

The Lutheran leader, Bishop Parker, broke the silence. "Matthew, would you mind if I put you on hold for a few minutes so we can discuss this amongst ourselves?"

Cardinal O'connor added, "Bob, please, I must ask you to step outside for obviously the same reason. Ask my secretary to get you a cup of coffee while you are waiting for us three old men to discuss this extraordinary occurrence."

When Bob left the office of New York's highest ranking Roman Catholic, Rabbi Silverman asked bluntly, "Well, where do we go from here?"

Bishop Parker, wanting to add some levity to this situation, said, "Why not start at the Stage Delicatessen for a pastrami on rye with hot mustard? It looks like we are going to share a few meals together over the next couple of days."

Cardinal O'Connor snickered. "Hold the hot mustard, my system can't handle it any more."

Despite their brief period of levity, the three men remain serious. Bishop Parker walked to the window facing Fifth Avenue and stared out for a minute before turning to his colleagues. "What do you gentlemen think? If this reporter is to be believed, what do we do next?"

"According to Bob, and I have no reason to discredit his integrity, responded the cardinal, this fellow Matthew is a middle-of-the-road type of guy, with no significant religious beliefs. Furthermore, the men in the group who have assembled thus far have names similar to those men,"and he paused, "whom Jesus, surrounded himself with before he made his sacrifice for humankind. Perhaps a coincidence, but it does add credibility to this story. By the way, I do believe Bob told us Matthew's parents were Jewish. What do you think, rabbi?"

"His story is very convincing,"the rabbi responded. "This man calling himself Jesus is probably an accomplished actor attempting to impersonate the leader of your churches. On the other hand, and the very thought of the idea makes my gray hair, or what's left of it, stand on edge, if it's true, why...." He rose from his chair and joined Bishop Parker near the window. "...Then I believe we must act and proceed with God's speed. First of all, I believe we should get some guidance from some of the religious authorities. Each of us should contact our respective theologians for guidance. Hopefully, these scholars can give us an idea as to what steps, if any, we should take next."

The three men agreed this was best before committing themselves further. Each knew it was not lack of courage that concerned them. No, it was the fear of how a hoax could cause significant damage to an already fragile religiously minded world.

Bishop Parker said, "Needless to say, the religions with the largest followings internationally are becoming more and more fragmented. Attendance at churches, synagogues, and temples is down dramatically. And the so-called X generation that's twenty-five and under in the United States barely understands the rudiments of the religious practices of their parents."

The rabbi added, "I think it would be a good idea to get in touch with a member of the local Muslim clergy and bring him in as soon as possible to participate in these discussions."

His reasoning was obvious to the others, since Muslims, Christians, and Jews are monotheistic.

Cardinal O'Connor agreed, even though he had long doubted that the people who call themselves Jewish, Muslims, and Christians did not all worship the same God. It goes without saying, he thought to himself, they could not possibly worship the same God I do. For if they did, there would be more understanding and empathy for one another, particularly, in the Middle East. But, he rationalized, this unfortunate lack of understanding was not too dissimilar from the insanity that prevailed in Northern Ireland, or Bosnia, Rwanda or even here in America.

Cardinal O'Connor went into his outer office to ask Bob to return to the meeting. Rabbi Silverman took the phone off hold and informed the reporter in Florida and the editor entering the cardinal's office of the decision, saying they would have an answer before five o'clock.

Matthew reminded them of the time constraints but agreed five o'clock would be fine.

Rabbi Silverman asked, "Matthew, do you know where Brother is this afternoon?"

The reporter's voice came over the speakerphone, "Sure. He's at the beach with the rest of the group. He's probably talking to Bartholomew about music or Thomas about the dress business. But most certainly he is enjoying the sunshine and without question drinking a Beck's beer."

The latter remark silenced the men of the cloth momentarily, lowering the doubt ratio below the fifty percent level.

Cardinal O'Connor looked at his friend the rabbi and said, "Aren't you glad you asked?"

The rabbi stretched his arms, looked up for guidance and responded, "On some occasions I have been guilty of asking one question too many."

The cardinal agreed. "Aren't we all?"

In the meantime, Bishop Parker had walked over to a second phone and contacted Imam Muhammad Abdul Qutb, one of the vanguard Muslim leaders in the New York area. The two holy men had represented their respective faiths the previous year on the Joint Council of Religious Understanding. This common council had been established to assist the communities in the Metropolitan New York area in becoming more sensitive to each other's religious beliefs. The two men had chaired a subcommittee and had maintained an engaging friendship ever since. The man representing the followers of Muhammad and Allah was understandably apprehensive when he heard what the bishop had to say, but he accepted the bishop's invitation to meet with the rabbi and the cardinal.

After Bob heard the clergymen's response, he opted to chat with Matthew in the outer office, where he could speak in private. "Matt at least they are on the same page as us. Now as far as believing what you have told them, well, that's a different story. Although funny as it seems, it appeared to me, by looking at their faces and hearing the inflection in their voices, I believe each of these men sincerely wishes that what you told them is really happening."

Matthew said, almost sheepishly, "I purposely omitted telling them about the questions that we have prepared for Brother. Perhaps this is a selfish approach on my part; but I imagine most of our group of twelve would like to take this occasion at dinner tonight to ask Brother about some of their most inner thoughts. If all goes according to schedule, the clergy will have ample opportunity tomorrow to ask him their own questions. I'm not really sure if he will address any of their inquiries, but he has promised us our questions would be answered tonight."

"Sounds okay to me, Matt. Let's keep it that way. Besides, having them get involved with a Q&A session will only complicate the matter." Bob shifted the phone to his right ear and adopted a corporate tone with his subordinate. "I trust you are keeping your reporter's hat on and taking copious notes of what is going on down there. I mean, at some point, we are going to be charged with the responsibility of publishing one heck of a story. Furthermore, it will be bylined with your name. It will be a blockbuster! Triple circulation for weeks and weeks! No, make that months and months. A career maker!"

"Yes, Bob, I understand,"said Matthew sarcastically. "This is probably going to result in great profitability for *Time* and, of course,"he added with a much more profound inflection, "a promotion for you."

The phone heated up on Bob's right ear as did his blood pressure, while Matthew continued to ramble in mock somberness. "Of course that all depends on your ability to handle this story properly." The voice from South Beach all at once perked up, almost to the degree of sounding cynical, full of mischief at the minimum. "Think of the possibilities. Well, let's see, triple circulation, wealth, notoriety, which all leads to the executive suite...."

"Come off it Matt. That was the furthest thing from my mind. You know darn well...."

Matthew cut his editor short. "I know, I know,"he said, laughing at his dear friend. "I was just getting even for that acrimonious comment you made earlier. I'll refresh your memory. Remember you were going to inform my mother about my new involvement in religion. My poor mother!"

"Touchè mon ami, touchè. I guess this ties the score."

"Yes, but the truth of the matter is, my mother really is going to be in a state of shock when she finds out about this."

The friends chuckled over the thought of Matthew's mother getting wind of this revival of spirituality on the part of her previously agnostic son.

"What next?" asked Bob.

"I honestly think the cardinal and his friends will do what's necessary to see to it tomorrow's press conference is well represented by religious leaders from around the globe."

"Including the Pope?"

"Well, even if the Pope isn't there himself, I'll bet dollars to doughnuts one of his high-ranking emissaries is on the scene."

This newfound confidence Matthew displayed surprised and even confounded his boss. He'd known Matthew for ten years, both of them having started working at the magazine about the same time. Through all these years, this was the first time Bob could remember his co-worker exhibiting a steel drum conviction on any issue. All the more reason to believe what was happening in South Beach.

"I'll handle the clergy, Bob. Meanwhile, you contact Max and bring our boss up to date."

As far as contacting the government officials was concerned, Matthew suggested Bob Edwards utilize *Time's* influence in Washington to get that part of the job accomplished. Bob did not comment, but his wheels were turning, trying to formulate his ideas as to how he could deliver this portion of his reporter's plan. Bob's silence concerned Matthew, prompting him to ask if his friend was in good health.

"I'm okay, good buddy, just thinking about my upcoming conversation with Max. But I'm in control. I won't let you down. Listen, it's probably a good idea if you and I remain in close contact. I'll most likely be on the road for the next few hours, but I'll call you every hour for an update. See if you can get a few more phone lines connected to the meeting room. I imagine that in the next twenty-four hours you're going to need them."

"Why don't you catch a plane and get down here?"

"I will, as soon as things are wrapped up in Washington, provided I can get Max to coordinate things on this end. Do you want me in South Beach to help you write the story? Is that why you want me there?"

"No, it's because I miss you, you stuffed shirt so-and-so. Talk to you soon."

NINETEEN

Another beautiful day in South Beach. Temperature in the high seventies, low humidity, and a glorious sun shining over one of the most popular beaches anywhere. The many tourists and the locals with a day off from work were tanning themselves, relaxing away from the office and the stress of everyday life. Nothing going on here in South Beach to get the blood pressure soaring. No, except that Jesus and a few hand-chosen men were within shouting range.

For the moment the sunbathers can take it easy in this serene, picturesque setting. A walk on the beach, a dip in the ocean, a piña colada or perhaps a good book to read, to occupy their time, at least for now. Because you never know who is sitting next to you on the beach. A group of men? They're probably just enjoying a few minutes away from a business meeting. Don't even give it a second thought. You ask yourself, this group of men has nothing to do with me, do they? How can these men possibly affect my life?

The men were sitting at surf's edge, the water rushing over their bare feet, watching the ocean's waves crest about twenty yards away. The Atlantic's warm water manifested a distinct dark brown shade to the otherwise lighter colored hot sand. Bartholomew suggested to the group that they go for a swim, and all but Peter and Brother did so. Led by Thomas, they got up and proceeded to push each other, like young boys would, to be first into the water. Brother beamed at the sight of his friends enjoying themselves diving into the oncoming waves.

Peter moved closer to Brother, his mind full of questions, trying to anticipate what needed to be accomplished at dinner tonight and especially at tomorrow morning's press conference. "Do you have any idea of the confusion and chaos that will be created when word of your being here reaches the media?"

Brother's response was direct, and under different circumstances it might even have been defined as amusing. "It's always entertaining to observe those so-called professional individuals salivate over an opportunity to make fools of themselves. From the attorney who chases an ambulance, to the doctor who overcharges the elderly patient, or the salesman who thinks only about his commission and not what he is selling. The media has its share of -- let's be kind -- overzealous characters. Do you get the picture, Peter?"

"What about fishermen?"Peter asked.

"Oh, those scoundrels,"Brother replied. "Let's not go into that." Jovially he added, "I don't have enough time to spend with you here on earth to tell you about the dastardly deeds of the fishermen." Smiling he said, "Perhaps at a later time we can discuss that issue."

The first thought that entered Peter's was, Much later, I hope. "Oh, excuse me Brother. I was just...."

"All in good time, my friend." Brother put his arm around him. "All in good time. For the moment, let's focus our attention on the task at hand. We have a busy agenda facing us tonight and tomorrow, after which time I will leave you."

"Will we see you again? What...?"

"I thought the question and answer period was tonight. Peter, I promise you, each of your questions will be addressed tonight. I'm not certain you will understand all of my answers, but believe me, tonight is dedicated to you men and your most inner thoughts. Now let's join the others for a few minutes, then back to see Speed for another Beck's."

Max Cohen's office had been the sight of numerous monumental decisions regarding important stories, including the Gulf War, scandals in Washington, and a certain murder of two people in Brentwood, California. But none of the decisions had been of this magnitude. Max even considered having an emergency Board of Director's meeting. He tabled his thoughts on that subject pending the meeting Bob had with the cardinal.

"Well, how did the clergy react to this saga?"he asked Bob."I honestly think they sense something unusual is going on in South Beach. But they won't commit themselves until they have had time to check out the consequences with their respective authorities on this type of occurrence. Not that there has ever been one such as this, mind you. Anyway, Matt presented his case in a most professional fashion. And may I add, there is no question in my mind after hearing Matt say it again for the third time, he actually believes this is all happening. But the clerics are no different than we are, trying to protect their rear ends."

"Tell me about it,"said Max, wiping the sweat off his forehead. "Do you believe this is happening, Bob?"

"I'm starting to believe, but more important, Matt does. To me, that is the essence of why we must proceed."

"Well, I don't. I'll give Matt the benefit of a doubt, and agree that something unusual is going on. But Jesus Christ in Miami Beach, Florida? Come on!"

Matt Singer is a straight-forward guy. He'd never fabricate a story. Never!"

"Suppose your reporter is involved with this story and it turns out by some odd twist of fate to be true, what do we do next?"

"I've thought it all out. First, you contact your friend at the State Department and ask for a meeting with the President."

"Come on, Bob, aren't we traveling too fast with this?"

"No, not at all. Remember, all the elements of this press conference have to be in place before tomorrow morning."

"Okay, okay. I get the idea. We'll leave right now. I'll call George Cooledge from the car and the two of us will catch the next shuttle to Washington. He'll tell us what steps to take next."

"How do you know he'll take your call?"

Sticking out his proud chin, Max replied, "My college roommate always takes my calls. Friends first and always. That was our motto for the four years we spent together and it will be, until one of us takes a taxi."

"Takes a taxi? To where?"

"Guess."

Max's limousine was waiting just outside *Time's* corporate office. He instructed his driver to get them to La Guardia Airport as soon as possible, after which he used the car phone to call his secretary to have her patch him into his friend at the State Department. Max asked Bob if he and Matt had established a procedure to communicate with one another.

"Let me explain to you first how Matt is handling the clergy. I'm confident -- and so is Matt -- that the men of the cloth are going to buy into this. They're to call him in South Beach as soon as they have any additional information for him."

Bob went on to explain that he was to call Matt every hour for an update. "I'll call him after you've finished your conversation with Cooledge to see if anything has changed."

Before the limousine reached the ramp to the East Side Drive, Max's secretary called to tell her boss that George Cooledge was on the line.

"Hello, roomie, what's up?"

"I'm going to need your help with perhaps the most fantastic story I've ever been involved with. I'm on my way to see you in Washington as we speak."

"What could be so important?"asked the Deputy Secretary of State facetiously. I haven't heard of any new conflicts or political fodder regarding the President or the Speaker of the House. Let's see, could it be Connecticut is withdrawing from the Union and you have been named king? Am I right? Did I hit the nail on the head? I've always liked kings. And I guess in my position, you can never know too many kings."

"Boy, are you full of yourself, roomie."

"Don't you call me boy, honkie."

"So you're the most powerful, underprivileged product of affirmative action in the State Department. Who cares?"

"You do, or you wouldn't be calling me."

The two friends of more then thirty years enjoyed the bantering and laughed heartily.

"Seriously, George, we have something brewing in Miami that we have to talk about."

"We being who?"

"Bob Edwards, one of my senior people, and me."

"What's going on?"

"Bob will give you an overview of what's happening. I might suggest that you consider alerting your boss and her boss. I'm sure they will most certainly want to hear this report, as soon as possible."

"Sounds serious."

"It is. Not catastrophic, but it will knock your socks off. Here's Bob."

On the limo's speakerphone, the editor began to describe the chain of events that had occurred in South Beach over the last two days. He was interrupted frequently by George Cooledge, who naturally was perplexed and astonished. He was even more taken aback when Max told him of the meeting with Cardinal O'Connor and the other clergy.

"You mean they believe all this?"

"It is Bob's opinion that they do, but we should contact them before arriving in Washington to get confirmation of their position."

"And now you want me to get to the Secretary of State and even get the President involved?"

"That's right, George. Wouldn't want to keep them in the dark, or have them find out about this in a special edition of *Time*."

"I get your point."

Max said in a more somber tone, "My friend, if this is true or even if it is some sort of a scam, they still better be on top of things. Because as soon as this leaks out and God knows, it will -- OOPS,"he looked over at Bob and continued, perhaps I best rephrase my last statement, wouldn't want to upset anyone -- well, anyway, when word gets out about this, all hell will break loose in South Beach. Not to mention the chaos that will encompass the Beltway, including the Capitol and the White House."

"Max, you really are of the opinion this is all happening?"

"All I know is that someone is stirring the pot down there. And if it isn't Jesus, then by God, he is one heck of a con artist. Because he's not only convinced twelve level-headed men that he is, but he's starting to make a believer out of me. Suffice it to say, you know me well enough to appreciate my participation in religion. I go to weddings and funerals. That's about the extent of it."

"Tell me, this press conference ... who is supposed to be involved?"asked George.

Bob replied, "I'm not sure of the details, but from what our reporter in South Beach tells me, it's expected that Jesus will make an address. As I understand it, he plans to comment on humankind's deficiencies and inform the world's religious and government leaders what he expects from them. Whether he fields any questions or not, well, I don't have the answer to that. And by the way, let's remember to refer to him as Brother, at least until this news breaks."

"I agree,"said George. "Even if this entire saga is a hoax, by heavens, we don't want the general public to know about what's going on until we are prepared for any possible situation in South Beach. I'll meet you at the airport. What time does your flight arrive?"

"I think we can still catch the four-thirty Delta shuttle to Reagan, which should get us to Washington by half past five."

"See you then, Max."

#

The conference room at the White Sand Hotel was bustling with telephone and computer technicians working feverishly. The room was cluttered with cables, PCs, boxes of laser paper for computer printers, cameras, telephones, and installation equipment. Additional phones and lines were being installed at a frenzied pace, and video-conferencing equipment, which was highly sophisticated, became operational in record time. Further crowding the room was the redundant backup equipment, which had been ordered just in case.

If John Thompson had one distinguishing business skill, it was how to organize projects and motivate people. Price and the amount of manpower were never part of the equation; only results mattered. Leave the numbers, as far as cost was concerned, to the accountants, and the effectiveness of personnel to the efficiency experts. Completing the project as quickly as possible and as close to specifications as any professional could hope to was his one and only concern.

Understandably, all the activity was driving the hotel manager to the brink of insanity. Her prized possession, as she liked to refer to the hotel she managed, was being invaded by a cadre of bearded men wearing blue jeans, with leather belts containing an array of screw drivers and pliers with pivot-like jaws. Dolores Quan, whose tenure with the White Sand Hotel was less than six months, had attempted to corner John for the last twenty minutes to determine what in God's name was going on at her establishment. She had worked so hard to attain her position, and was deeply concerned that these men conducting their meeting were up to no good. Dolores was the daughter of Chinese immigrants and the first in her family to graduate from college. "The first member of the family to work with the mind and not the back,"her father had always told her. She thought to herself, these bozos aren't going to change all of that.

She maneuvered around people and equipment and grabbed John by the arm, spinning him around. Stunned but not shaken, and employing all the self-control that one can expect from an Englishman, he greeted the irate manager.

Smiling, he said, "Seems like we've made quite a mess, but not to worry, things will be organized shortly."

"What's going on here? "I think you owe me an explanation."

John pondered over how he should address the issue raised by the young Asian proprietor. Brother and the others were at the beach and couldn't be reached. Thaddaeus and Philip were busy coordinating the efforts of the technicians, who were in the process of installing the equipment needed for the press conference. And Matthew was up to his eyeballs with notes and scenarios he had drawn up, trying to anticipate the decision of the New York clergy. John put his thoughts into action and decided that in fairness to the manager of the White Sand Hotel, she must be told what was happening right under the very roof of her domain.

"Miss Quan, can we speak privately? In your office, I believe would be best. I think you're in need of an explanation."

Still infuriated, but able to maintain the discipline of keeping her emotions concealed, she ordered a pot of tea when they reached her office. The modestly appointed office was located just to the left of the hotel's front desk. John smiled at Dolores as they sat across from her desk. For a moment his thoughts went back to Mary, whom he'd not seen for two days. It seemed like months had passed since the two of them were dancing their way across the Atlantic. When the waiter left the room after delivering the tea, she poured each of them a cup of tea and asked the smiling man with the English accent to explain to her exactly what was going on.

John did not hold back. It took him ten minutes to reveal to the incredulous manager what had happened over the last two days. After she got over the initial shock of John's unbelievable account of what had happened and -- even more important from her perspective -- what was to occur, Dolores contemplated her next step. Should she call her boss in Orlando? If she did, what would she tell him? Or should she just put a stop to this entire charade and kick these unwelcome guests out of the hotel?

She hesitated for a few moments and then said, "Mr. Thompson, you appear to be a man of the world; therefore, I could hardly describe you as being naive. How could you possibly believe this man? How could you be taken in by this scam?"

"It's easy," he responded. Staring into her deep brown eyes, he said, "Want to meet him?"

She paused once again, carefully choosing her words, "You sincerely believe this man, don't you?"

"I do and you will too, once you meet him."

"Who says I want to meet him?"

"Don't worry, you will. Miss Quan, are you a religious person?"

Seeming more mellow for the first time since they began their conversation, she responded, "Depends on your definition of religion. You see, I am Chinese, and like most of my fellow countrymen, I follow the teachings of Confucius."

"Please tell me about Confucius. I've always been curious about him."

"Well, if you comprehended and subscribed to his teachings, as I do, then you'd understand that we approach religion and prayer in a unique fashion. Obviously, dramatically different from the way you, who believe in Christianity, do. We truly believe that humankind is linked to everything in the universe. So we don't pray to a single God, as do Christians and Jews, and I think Muslims."

"That's correct, they are monotheistic also."

"Thank you. As I was saying, our prayers and periods of medita-
tion help us obtain a better understanding of our environment.
Confucius has provided us with a philosophy which enables all of us
to live together in peace and harmony. Not only with those around us,
but with all of the wildlife, waterways, vegetation, and inert objects
that we see each day. But what does that have to do with the mess you
are making in the meeting room?"the manager asked in a sharp and
business-like tone.

"Everything,"John responded. "Everything, Dolores. May I call
you Dolores?"

She nodded, although her eyes still reflected her unhappiness with
the entire situation. This point did not go unnoticed by John. He therefore wasted no time informing her, as tactfully as possible, about
tomorrow morning's press conference and the resulting consequences.
"The White Sand Hotel, in little old South Beach, is going to be looked
upon by the earth's population as the center of the universe. Religious
leaders and government officials from every country will be partici-
pating in a press conference transmitted from your hotel. People of all
religions, and even those who are not religious, from all around the
globe, will be tuned in to these historic proceedings.

"It goes without saying, the White Sand Hotel will be henceforth
looked upon as a shrine by all humankind. A temple of peace and tranquillity. A sanctuary from where the Son of God broke bread with
twelve men for three days. Where the Son of God presented his gospel
to all who could hear. Words describing his doctrine that we hope will
be embraced by everyone."

The words were flowing from the Englishman, as if from a musical score written by Cole Porter. The manager, mesmerized by his oration, imagined she was listening to a prominent playwright reciting
lines from his masterpiece on a Broadway stage.

He continued. "And you, my dear Dolores, yes you, are the
innkeeper of this shrine and will go down in history as such. As far as
I know, you are the only person on earth, other than the twelve of us,
to be aware of Brother's not only returning, but also the location from
which he will deliver his address tomorrow. For all concerned, I think
we best keep it that way. At least for the moment."

After completing his enchanting description of the magnitude of
the event to take place tomorrow, John arose from his chair, excused
himself, and departed for the meeting room. The unique way he

swaggered when he walked reflected a combination of pretentious-
ness and self-confidence. Irritating, yet demanding a certain respect.

What an interesting man you are John Thompson, thought Dolores
Quan.

When he had left the office, the confused and bewildered Asian
woman remained silently flipping her letter opener from hand to
hand. She searched for answers to her dilemma, remaining totally
aware of the need to take action. Dolores realized she would have to
contact her superior, at least at some point in time, to inform him of
what was taking place and ask for instructions on how to handle this
delicate situation. The question is, do I tell him now, or wait until
tomorrow morning, after the entire world knows about it? In other
words, should I close my eyes for now, as the Englishman has requested, or should I put a stop to the installation of all that equipment, at
least until touching base with my boss? Regardless of what her course
of action would be, she was sure of at least one thing. She was convinced that John Thompson believed all of this was true.

Having an overwhelming love for the theater, she tried to analyze
the situation as a critic in the theater district of New York would
review an opening night's production. If this man calling himself the
Son of God was an impostor, he certainly was a very talented actor. If
indeed this entire ordeal was a professionally choreographed production, it had been staged by a director with exceptional capability. And
if this was a charade orchestrated by a supporting cast of charlatans,
then the entire ensemble deserved a Tony award. It could be a colossal
scam, perhaps, but not in John Thompson's eyes. No, he really believes
this man is the Son of God, whoever he is. And, I imagine, so do the
others.

Giving the subject careful consideration, she made up her mind.
She realized the significance of her resolve and was willing to face the
consequences if she were wrong. It was a difficult decision for her to
make, but the only prudent one, for sure. Dolores decided to tell her
boss. Tell him about the equipment being installed in the meeting
room. Tell him about the thirteen men who had been meeting there for
the last two days. Tell him about the press conference. Tell him about
the man who says that he is the Son of God. Tell him about all those
things!

But -- she would delay the phone call until tomorrow morning!

TWENTY

Rabbi Silverman, Cardinal O'Connor, and Bishop Parker deliberated for forty minutes before making the difficult decision as to which religions should be represented in these historic proceedings. Having already contacted an Islamic leader, they thought it appropriate to diversify the group even further. They decided to ask both a Hindu and a Buddhist theologian, who would serve as spokesmen for their respective beliefs. Their faiths were considered to be primarily of a spiritual nature and, therefore, were not categorized as religions by most Christians, Muslims and Jews, who believed and prayed to a single God -- although it was quite obvious that God was sometimes seen in a different light, even by monotheists. In addition, four professors of religion from nearby universities were invited.

The theologians accepted the cardinal's invitation without knowing the complete story. The only information they received over the phone was that a sighting had occurred. By mutual consent, none of the religious historians was given any additional details until they arrived. They all appeared at the cardinal's office within forty-five minutes of his call. When they heard the account of what had taken place in South Beach, each of them was overwhelmed. It was their responsibility to examine cases such as this, but never before had any of them been part of an occurrence of this magnitude. Who had? Could it be? Could he have returned? The debate began.

These wise men spent the better part of two hours attempting to analyze the goings on in South Beach. They represented a large percentage of the earth's population and each of them was a teacher, a philosopher and a credible source of knowledge about all of the major religions. Each of them could recite various passages from the *Bible*, the *Koran*, or any of the other sacred books describing religious codes of conduct and history. The only commonality among the men was their living in the New York area. Together with the followers of Abraham, Jesus, and Muhammad, they would define and plot out a course of action which would deal with this complex situation.

Trying to digest what was happening in South Beach was tedious and understandably difficult. They were at least fortunate to have the detailed report provided by the seasoned veteran from *Time*. Typically, such sightings of icons, angels, spirits, satanic messengers, or weeping Madonnas were reported by individuals with less-than-acceptable credentials. Not that those reporting sightings were manufacturing their stories for either financial profit or political power in their community. It was just that most cases tended to be viewed or reported by overzealous individuals who were less than accurate about what they had seen or heard. More often than not, these events were checked out by the local clergy and disproved, and the community returned to reality. In the rare situation where an explanation could not be ascertained, typically it was put on the shelf in hopes the unusual occurrence would go away and never return. Rarely were they authenticated and considered true sightings. But comes this incident in South Beach.

They realized that even though the six of them represented different religions, essentially they were all in the same boat. Strangely enough, even the Hindu and Buddhist theologians sensed the importance of this event and its impact on their own true believers. They too must find their sea legs, for both of them knew they too were on the aforementioned boat. A boat for all of humankind, regardless of race, color, or ethnic background. And if what was happening in South Beach proved true, it would most likely be considered a ship constructed of wisdom, power, and glory, and would sail the seas of serenity through all eternity. A boat of more historical significance than Noah's Ark. A boat that would provide everyone everlasting salvation, regardless of what one's religious beliefs were. A boat, on the other hand, if proven to be captained by a fraudulent commander, would be unseaworthy, and would sink, taking all the men of the cloth in Cardinal O'Connor's office down with it.

A decision was finally reached, although the caveats and provisions of the document these distinguished gentlemen hastily created resembled a multicolored quilt with contrasting designs. There was total agreement regarding the press conference. All concurred that the proceedings should be aired to all religious leaders. Each of the theologians would provide Matthew with the names of individual leaders representing their respective religions and the locations to which the transmission should be broadcasted. But prior to the time this broadcast was to be aired, at least two of the men in the South Beach group in addition to Matthew must agree to meet with two members of this prestigious committee -- if not Brother himself. The clerics did not make the latter a prerequisite, heeding Matthew's assertion that

Brother did not want to meet with any men of the cloth.

Certainly there were concerns on the part of each of the theologians. For one, if this were a hoax, the effects could be devastating for the world's religions whose practitioners prayed to God or believed in Brother, not to mention the impact that a decision to proceed would have on each of their own reputations as historians of their individual faiths. Nevertheless, these men displayed courage, confidence, and decisiveness in developing a plan they hoped would address this historic occasion, knowing full well that there were concerns on the part of those who did not accept Jesus as their religious icon. The thought of his being the messenger of God and not Abraham, Muhammad, Buddha Prince Gotama, or -- through the grace of Brahman -- the Hindu Supreme Spirit, caused apprehension and caution for the well-respected theologians. If he is who he says he is, they wondered, will he undermine our way of thinking and attempt to sway those who listen to a life of Christianity? Needless to say, those who were not Christian had many reservations. Unfortunately, in some places on earth, issues such as this are not discussed; rather, religious differences are taken to the streets where young men and women use verbal abuse, as well as rocks and guns to contest their differing viewpoints.

But these men maintained their composure, determined to demonstrate to each other and all religious members of every denomination that they were capable of keeping open minds and accepting Brother as the messenger of God. Their decision demonstrated how people of different persuasions can reach an accord when a crisis or colossal issue occurs. These very talented, altruistic men arbitrarily concluded not what was best for them or their constituents, but what was best for all humankind.

Bishop Parker said, "Wouldn't we all be better served if people would just sit down and discuss their differences. At the conference table and ... not with demonstrations, conflict, or verbal abuse. Not with grotesque devices contrived to bomb one another. Not with a sniper's rifle, whose deadly rounds are fired from a dark rooftop. Not by a cold-blooded coward shooting into a village square full of innocent people. Not by over-enthusiastic supporters from faraway lands, supplying money, guns, and ammunition to promote conflicts. Not on the battlefield, where young men donate their precious lives to satisfy the ego of their leaders. No, none of these acts of aggression are solutions. Without question, it requires more courage, perseverance, and resolve to find a peaceful answer to the many problems that humankind is confronted with."

Rabbi Silverman added, "As diverse as our cultural and religious backgrounds are, if we battled with each other with our brains in the arena where wise men fight their wars -- the conference room -- facing each other around an oval wooden table, wouldn't we all be better off? What a unique approach -- discussion, deliberation, and determination, and not destruction, devastation, and death -- as a way to face and solve a problem."

Cardinal O'Connor concurred. Perhaps Brother's influence was already being felt!

The New York clergy's phone call to Matthew was placed at precisely five o'clock. On the speakerphone, Rabbi Silverman informed Matthew of the religious men's decision. The reporter was relieved to find out the clergy had accepted his story, but his relief was shortlived when he heard the rabbi give their conditions -- that representatives from the religious group in New York meet with the men in South Beach. Matthew replied he'd have to confer with others in the group to determine if this was acceptable. He put them on hold and met briefly with John, Thaddaeus, and Philip, who had just completed their job of transforming the conference room into a movie set.

Their initial reaction was to seek Brother's approval. But John spoke convincingly: "The time has come for the group to begin making decisions." He went on, "Don't forget, he will be with us for only one more day, at which point the twelve of us must take charge and carry out the task he has laid out for us." John took this occasion to tell the other three about his conversation with the hotel manager.

Matthew commended John for his leadership and forward thinking. At which point they all agreed the religious men should be permitted to come, but they should understand that meeting with Brother was not part of the arrangement. The conversation was brief. Two clergymen from New York would fly to Miami to meet with the men in South Beach. Matthew thanked Rabbi Silverman and the other religious leaders for their positive and decisive response.

When the telephone call ended, a decision was reached; Rabbi Silverman and Imam Muhammad Qutb would be delegated to meet with Matthew and his contemporaries. The meeting was ended by the cardinal, who invited all of the participants back to his office the next morning to attend the press conference. He would contact the mayor at the appropriate time to ask him to attend as well. His secretary had already made reservations for the two holy men representing the committee to fly to Miami on a seven-fifteen flight out of La Guardia. This gave each of them just enough time to pick up some personal things before heading for the airport.

The four monotheistic men of the cloth expressed their warm feelings and thanks to all of the theologians, but especially the Hindu and Buddhist spiritual leaders for their input and advice. Hugs and bows of respect served as the closing portion of this unique meeting of holy men.

The forty-five minute Delta flight to Washington's Reagan Airport was fortunately uneventful. The two publishing executives were relatively quiet. Although neither would admit it, they were reflecting on their own lives. Both men realized if the situation in South Beach was for real, not only would their lives be affected, but those of all humankind.

The chauffeur from the State Department met them at the gate holding a placard reading ROOMIE. Max shook his head and laughed at his friend's humorous greeting.

"Let's see how he reacts at the moment we put the squeeze on him,"Max snickered. "He'll probably squeal like a pig when I ask to see the President,"he murmured to Bob. He motioned to the smiling man with the card that he was Max Cohen, and the efficient but almost expressionless driver led them to a black car parked in front of the Delta terminal.

As the experienced driver opened the door to the State Department vehicle, George Cooledge waved from the back seat and greeted them warmly, smiling at the thought of his longtime friend's reaction to the whimsical welcome sign he had prepared for him. The two men hugged, reflecting a very strong bond of love and admiration. This sign of affection did not go unnoticed by Bob, who took the jump seat facing the two men. Bob had never seen this side of his boss before, but appreciated this extension of his personality.

After a few minutes of small talk about wives, children, and grandchildren, George became all business and asked Bob to give him a full account of what he knew about the goings on in South Beach. And that's exactly what the editor did, during the twenty-minute drive to the State Department. George Cooledge sat on the edge of his seat and remained completely silent, listening intently to this fascinating report.

"And you are sure of your man in South Beach?"

"Total confidence in him,"replied Max.

"I'd like to use your telephone to get an update on what's going on,"Bob said.

"By all means,"George responded, handing Bob the car phone.

Matthew informed his boss about the agreement with the cardinal and his committee in New York. He also told Bob that the preparation at his end for the conference call the next morning was completed.

He then asked, "How are things going in New York?"

"Max and I are in Washington, attempting to arrange a meeting with the Secretary of State and the President."

"Washington? You guys sure move fast."Pleased, but a bit shocked that things had reached this level, though he dared not reveal his emotions. Still, Matthew was in awe that this story he was part of was so close to reaching the desk of the President. But after considering the issue further, he came to his senses. Matthew said to himself, let me put things in perspective; I think in this story, the President, at best, has second billing.

Max and Bob convinced the government official to take this situation to his boss. It would be her charge to take it to the President. George Cooledge expressed some concern regarding security in the South Beach area. He told the two *Time* executives, "Once this gets out to the press, every nut job in the country will be there. They'll comb the beaches from Key West to Daytona in an effort to find this man calling himself Jesus."He paused for a moment. "I know, I'm supposed to refer to him as Brother. I wouldn't be surprised if thousands, if not hundreds of thousands of people show up, including the curious, those who are truly faithful, as well as religious fanatics."

"Let's not forget the lawless profit seekers and the petty pickpockets,"said Max.

George Cooledge added, "And as I said before, the flakes who want a piece of Brother and the other twelve men. Unfortunately, a few of them will be seeking their fifteen minutes of fame, and you know what that means. Imitators, copy cats, and worse yet, assassins, desiring to make the front page of the tabloids. I honestly believe the FBI should be informed at once. It's mandatory their agents have ample time to survey the area and draw up a game plan for crowd control. The more lead time we give them, the better opportunity they will have to curtail any riots. Not to mention totally securing the area to be able to deal with any potential crackpot who might double as a gun-toting sniper."

Looking concerned, Max told his friend, "Do whatever it takes to establish security in the area."

The car arrived at the State Department and the three men made their way directly to the Secretary of State's office. She was in the middle of a phone call to Tel Aviv with the United States Ambassador to Israel. It seems the Palestinians and Israelis were in the midst of a new crisis which might require her presence to act as arbitrator. Nothing new, another trip to the Middle East to offer advice tactfully. Yes, another plane ride halfway around the planet to help these two peoples with their distinct, but similarly ancient cultures, solve their most recent problem.

The Secretary of State's reaction to Bob's ten-minute dissertation amazed the three men. She said that Brother's return did not surprise her, and that she had been looking forward to this glorious day for many, many years. This surprisingly positive response to the greatest event in the last two-thousand years stunned her audience, composed of a not-so-religious Jew, an Irish Catholic who went to church only on Easter Sunday and Christmas, and an African-American Baptist who last went to services when his daughter got married two years before. They remained silent, while the first woman who had been appointed Secretary of State continued to digest this incredible story and attempted to determine all the consequences. Using all the tact and diplomacy she had acquired over the last three decades, the Secretary of State informed Max and Bob she was quite pleased with the manner in which they had handled this extraordinary situation thus far.

It was at that point she decided to toss them a curve ball, which is what the men had expected in the first place. She asked, "How do we authenticate that this man calling himself Brother is truly him, the anointed one? What signs, characteristics, symbols, or revelations have been made evident to confirm and validate his identity?"

Bob was amazed at her reaction. Obviously, the lady was very religious, a true believer in God and his son Jesus Christ. What he also admired about the Secretary of State was her presence and ability to absorb and dissect this complicated issue. The Secretary of State's propensity to be able to listen and comprehend was an outstanding attribute few individuals within the Beltway had acquired in their lives. Most of these cantankerous people within the inner circle of the nation's government believed they were above those living outside this imaginary waist line, or as many critics referred to it, waste line.

Not this charming and highly intelligent lady, who already was referring to Jesus as Brother. The Secretary of State was fully aware that life existed outside the capitol and kept in contact with what was going on beyond the District of Columbia. Before she could ask her next question, Bob told her about the two religious men on their way to Miami to attempt to confirm this was truly him.

She responded, "Again, my hat is off to you gentlemen for covering so many bases, if not all of them."

Max responded, "I'm flattered, but most of the credit should be extended to our investigative reporter in South Beach. Matthew Singer deserves high grades for his comprehensive report and for how this sensitive and complicated matter is being conducted."

The Secretary of State nodded, displaying her approval of Max Cohen's commendation. She continued with her questions, asking her most trusted assistant, "What are your thoughts, George?"

He shifted in his chair, almost embarrassed to answer her question. Despite her high regard for him, from time to time he worried about his performance -- a natural trait those who care about their jobs most certainly had. George had one distinguishing characteristic when put on the spot. His hands became clammy, indicating his tentative stance on an issue. But using all the tact he had learned in Diplomacy 101, George paused and collected his thoughts. He cleared his throat and responded, "I'm not the most religious man, and therefore I remain more than a bit skeptical. To be perfectly honest with you, Madam Secretary, if it were not for my long-term friendship with Max, I would have not brought this situation to your attention. I must admit, I have complete confidence in Max and his people, but remain mystified and perplexed about this entire saga."

What he didn't say was how shocked he was at the Secretary of State's reaction. He had never realized the scope and depth of her religious beliefs and the fact she honestly believed this event could actually happen.

He went on. "I cannot put any holes in Bob's story, at least not at this point. But I seriously think, regardless of whether there is any truth to this or not, pandemonium will break out in South Beach as soon as word leaks out. I would therefore like to suggest that the FBI be contacted as soon as possible, to prepare them for controlling the onslaught of people who will most certainly congregate in that area."

Max and Bob shook their heads in agreement.

"Good idea,"she responded. "Get on the horn with the Director at once. Inform him, the potential exists of a possible situation in South Beach, but do it without going into any details. Advise him it would be in the country's best interests to alert his men down there at once to be on their toes. But also make him aware, our national security is not at stake. This action is just to maintain law and order in the area for the next few days. Go so far as to inform him where he should deploy his men. The White Sand Hotel, correct?"

Bob was taken aback once more at the lady's retention capabilities.

"I'm sure his nose will be out of joint for not being told any of the details. Tell him, I have no intention or desire to jump into his area of responsibility. But since the situation fell into my lap, I thought it best if I handle this personally. Furthermore, inform him that within the next hour or so I will fill him in on the details regarding what is going on down there. Make him aware, I am presently on my way to the White House to meet with the President regarding the situation occurring in South Beach. Once I receive his approval to move ahead, I'm sure the Director will be consulted to develop an action plan to handle security."

As she got up from her desk to begin the short trip to the White House, the Secretary of State once again thanked the two men for their efforts, telling them to stay in touch with George. He would serve as point man for the department. All matters concerning the government's response to this issue would be communicated to the press by George Cooledge. She told the three men, "If this tale of epic proportions is in fact true, we are on the threshold of a dramatic renaissance for all of humankind."

Max and Bob stood up and shook hands with her. Their enthusiastic facial exprssions suggested how pleased they were with the proceedings. They had been expecting a much more difficult time of it, both of them realizing the job was not done as yet, and hoping Madam Secretary of State could convince the man residing at 1600 Pennsylvania Avenue.

But before the Secretary of State opened the door to her conservatively appointed office, she paused and looked at each of the three men. That's when the lady threw a change of pace, saying, "Let's go." Gesturing with her hands for them to arise, she continued, "Come on, let's go, everybody up. I've made a management decision -- we're all going to see the President."

Bob was flabbergasted. The President himself. Even Max, who had met the man a few times, was pleasantly surprised. Not to mention George Cooledge, who snapped to attention at just the thought of being in the Oval Office. And so the foursome departed the Department of State to meet with the Chief Executive.

TWENTY ONE

Ahmad Thair, a waiter at the White Sand Hotel, realized something unusual was taking place within the walls of the meeting room. The twenty-four-year-old college student from Turkey couldn't put his finger on exactly what, but he knew that all this equipment being installed in there was definitely out of the ordinary. His sister's husband, who was his sponsor for his getting into the United States, worked as a cameraman for CNN. The waiter's phone call to his brother-in-law got a swift and enthusiastic reaction. There were some rumors of a happening in the Miami area circulating around the local news bureaus, but where and what was going on and who was involved had not yet surfaced. Could the White Sand Hotel be where it was occurring? The ten-year employee of the all-news channel went to see his team reporter to inform her of Ahmad's tip.

Pauline Demitri listened intently to what her cameraman had to say. It's what every rookie reporter dreams about. An exclusive! Hearing information about a potential story from a third party and from a variety of individuals were normal occurrences in newsrooms everywhere. Deciding which ones were for real -- well, that took a true professional reporter to decipher. Chasing dead dogs down blind alleys cost many cub reporters their careers. This tyro reporter, only ten months on the job with CNN, had several attributes, not the least of which was the ability to smell out a juicy story.

Pauline was the youngest daughter of Greek immigrants, an absolute natural in the busy, seemingly disjointed society of reporting the news. Her counterparts respected her ability to unearth and develop a story. They also considered her extremely lucky in finding, or perhaps even bumping into hot stories. Some of the cynics in the newsroom went so far as to suggest that many of the sizzling stories had been thrown her way by the executives in the white tower. Those men in the dark blue suits and paisley ties, who knew nothing about news and cared only about ratings, enjoyed watching Pauline's presentation on the tube.

And so did the CNN viewers, who found this twenty-eight year-old with the black hair and brown eyes a refreshing alternative to the blue-eyed blondes who dominated the news broadcasts on the twenty-four inch TV screens in their homes.

Pauline felt an odd sensation on hearing the South Beach story, telling her boss she was on her way to the White Sand Hotel to check it out. Although apprehensive, the editor permitted his relatively new hand to follow up on this rumor.

Along with her experienced cameraman and driver/producer, Pauline Demitri began the short ride from CNN's Miami newsroom to the White Sand Hotel. She could smell a story of great magnitude developing there, but had no idea what the subject matter might be. How she acquired this capacity was a mystery to Pauline and her associates at CNN. There was no question she had an uncanny ability to not only find a penetrating, hard hitting story, but to effectively deliver it, when the camera got rolling. Little did anyone realize that Pauline would not only report the story but also become part of it!

If one rumored account of a potential story was out there, you can be sure many others would be on the street. It was no different with this one. Word had gotten to the tabloids as well *The Star*, *Enquirer* and *The Globe*. Their reporters and freelance paparazzi were on their way to the hotel to check out next week's potential scandal or human interest headline story. In addition, it was rumored some of the participants involved were possibly at the beach, not too far from the Blue Crab restaurant. Even though dusk had darkened the white sandy beach, this did not prevent the aggressive group of cameramen and reporters -- whose motto was, all the dirt that's fit to print -- from combing the area in search of next week's edition.

The media found nothing but sea gulls and over-fed pigeons searching for a final morsel of food on the beach before these scavengers called it a day, hoping something of substance might have been discarded by an untidy sun worshiper. Since no humans remained on the beach, pictures and interviews with the feathered inhabitants were discussed by the newspapermen, who resorted to a bit of humor as this particular lead appeared to be at a dead end. Perhaps the White Sand Hotel would supply them with a story, since that was the other venue described by the tipsters. Though before heading there, a few of these thirsty reporters made a pit stop at the Blue Crab for a couple of beers.

Little did they know how close they were to finding the cast of characters involved in this news story of epic proportions. They missed by mere minutes running into some of the principals in the story they were searching for, on the beach and again in the bar across the street, where they, too, had stopped for a beer before returning to their respective hotels and apartments. Unfortunately for these pundits of the press, they even missed the main character and leading man in this most important saga.

All the networks, NBC, CBS, ABC, and Fox, also had their sources. Their newsrooms were informed of the unusual activities in and around South Beach, and most particularly at the White Sand Hotel. Each of them, in an effort to outdo the competition, immediately sent crews to cover whatever was going on in South Beach. Of course, the local newspaper reporters, representing the *Miami Herald* and Fort Lauderdale's *Sun Sentinel* were on their way too.

What none of these assignment editors realized was that this story was not only of local and national interest, but would also play to every man and woman on the face of the earth. It would have an audience of millions glued to their television sets. An audience larger than the Super Bowl and World Cup combined. In addition, millions more would read about what Brother had to say in newspapers and on the Internet.

###

The scene at the White Sand Hotel reminded one of a misdirected, under-budgeted Class B movie whose cast was not familiar with the script. Reporters, local police and members of the sheriffs' department, numbering close to one hundred, were all over the facility, at times bumping into each other with a look of uncertainty and suspicion on their faces. The federal agents on the scene kept a low profile, awaiting further instructions from their superiors in Washington. While walking in a remote section of the parking lot, two men bumped into each other. A reporter asked himself, could this be one of the men involved with whatever this story is? Answering his own question, this old salt of the news business realized he had just run into one of Miami's finest. This character had to be a cop, he thought, just check out those shoes and dead-giveaway flat feet. The law officer had his own ideas about the old tug he had just passed, shaking his head at the sight of the well-known newspaperman, who still chain-smoked unfiltered ships of the desert and whose weight was, perhaps, the equivalent of two Xtra cargo containers.

What appeared obvious to the old-time reporters and well-trained law enforcement officers was that something of significance was going on. Although none of the men or women congregating at the hotel knew exactly what, it was apparent they were there to cover a very important story. All those informants couldn't possibly be wrong! Could they? What was going on? Any situation which kept these professional guardians of law and order in the dark was obviously frustrating and created an atmosphere filled with tension. Keeping their cool and maintaining their composure during one of these stakeouts was what they were trained to do. The large number of members of the press loitering around this facility was enough to get on one's nerves, asking questions no one seemed to have an answer to. The avid photographers snapping pictures of no one in particular was enough to test one's patience.

Within minutes of their arrival at the hotel, Pauline Demitri and her crew watched as other news vans with their satellite dishes perched on top filled the front section of the parking lot. Some scoop, she sarcastically told her cameraman and driver/producer. And now the sham of being polite to her colleagues/competitors began. The regulars were all anxious to greet the young reporter. The veteran, Nat Kramer, CBS; the oriental beauty, Kim Luke, ABC; the proverbial blue-eyed blonde, Barbara Barnabas, NBC; and the new heartthrob of the air waves at Fox, Tim Collins. The latter even bought coffee and sweet rolls for his new friends. They were all present at the scene of this event, but none of them knew as yet what was happening.

The likely source of information for these darlings of the afternoon and evening television news shows was the public relations officer of the Miami police department. He was the usual source of leaks in the department and, hence, received more than his share of Miami Heat and Dolphins tickets throughout the year. But not even the man who knew most everything about the goings on in Miami was aware of what was taking place in the hotel's meeting room or who was there.

The commotion in and around the hotel was driving its ordinarily placid manager ballistic. First the meeting room being converted into a television studio. At least that was confined to the meeting room and easily controlled, she thought. But now the assault on her hotel, which she managed with a passion, by a slew of reporters and policemen! Dolores Quan was in a quandary, questioning her decision to permit John Thompson and the others to continue their activities, not to mention the religious icon, the central figure in this saga.

She realized deep down the significance of what was going on and for the first time visualized what was about to occur. She could sense the potential of hundreds, or thousands, if not hundreds of thousands of people, swarming around the hotel, trying to get a glimpse of him.

What was to follow? Perhaps chaos, destruction, mass hysteria -- at the minimum irritated guests and complaints, complaints, and more complaints! Dolores also knew neither she nor the hotel were of importance, if this man really was the messiah. Is he who he says he is -- the revered, loved, and worshipped leader of the Christian community? History being made, right here in my hotel, she thought, but now having second thoughts, wished she had informed her boss first. For he was certain to find out soon enough. Perhaps she should call him now, before he put his television set on to listen to the late news.

The meeting at the White House was held in the Oval Office, with the President, Vice President, his Chief of Staff, the Secretary of State, her deputy, and the two men from *Time*. A very persuasive dissertation, presented jointly by Bob Edwards and the Secretary of State, convinced the Chief Executive to take immediate action. He contacted members of his Cabinet, as well as the leaders of each party and prominent politicians from the Senate and the House, representing both sides of the aisle. The President-Elect was on vacation after a hard fought campaign; within the hour, he too would be brought up to date.

At the meeting, these men and women of a variety of religious beliefs were informed of what was happening in South Beach. The evidence presented to these political and diplomatic servants, although sketchy, was convincing enough to gain a unanimous decision to proceed with the press conference. In an unprecedented action, United States ambassadors from around the globe would begin contacting heads of state from every nation to have them join in as well. Security in the South Beach area was, at least for the moment, under control; but more needed to be done to secure the safety of the citizens of the community and the cast of characters involved with this momentous event. As far as the man calling himself Brother was concerned, his safety was of extreme interest to this body of lawmakers. Heaven forbid that something unimaginable would happen to this *man of all men* on American soil. All care and prudent protection must be put in place immediately to see that nothing of this nature could occur.

This able body of statesmen and politicians also agreed that if he had returned, the dimension of his influence on people of all religious backgrounds would be overwhelming. They were concerned about the possibility for total disregard of government. Although they all sensed Brother's return was for the good of humankind, the thought of this potentiality was of deep concern to these powerful men and women.

The meeting ended with the congressional representatives and members of the Cabinet scurrying back to their offices to make calls to their loved ones, prominent constituents, and hometown newspapers, to inform them of what was happening in South Beach. Keep a secret? In Washington?

The President thanked both Max Cohen and Bob Edwards for their conscientious report. He asked, "Are either of you men flying to South Beach to see for yourself what's going on?"

Max replied, "I feel we're well represented there."

Bob asked the Chief Executive, "Would you like an updated report through the eyes of Matthew Singer?"

He nodded, "Most assuredly."

Bob reached Matthew at the hotel after only one ring, which suggested the reporter on the scene was awaiting his call. Matthew said that other than the army of reporters, cameramen, and law enforcement agents mulling around outside, there was nothing new to report. "Although you could sense the tension and excitement building,"he added.

At that point, Bob informed Matthew that the President was listening in on the call and wished to say a few words.

"Hello, Matt."

Standing up, Matthew replied, "Hello, Mister President."

"You've got yourself one heck of a story down there."

"I sure do, sir."

"Tell me, has he given you a list of demands -- or perhaps that's too harsh? I mean, has he asked you gentlemen what it is he wishes us to accomplish?"

"Essentially, he has informed the twelve of us to proceed with an assignment designed to enhance life for all of humankind."

"Why did he select you men? Why didn't he choose to speak to religious leaders or heads of state?"

As diplomatic as he possibly could, Matthew replied, "Present company excluded, I'm sure, he was of the belief the average person might take more kindly to us than to the people in power."

The President was pleasantly surprised at the tactfulness of the reporter. "Well stated, Matt. If you ever decide on a career change, we could use a person with your tact in the State Department."

Max and Bob both enjoyed the President's candor and told their associate in South Beach they would call him later that night.

#

The imam and the rabbi discussed many issues during their ride to La Guardia. The tension in the Middle East caused by yet another bombing attack in Jerusalem was the focus of most of their conversation. Unnecessary and unmerciful killing of innocent civilians continued to be an all-too-common occurrence in that region. Both Rabbi Silverman and his Muslim counterpart, Imam Muhammad Abdul Qutb, were considered moderates in their respective religious communities. They each realized the conditions in and around the Holy Land were once again sensitive, a hotbed of irrational people, with access to deadly explosives, desiring to blow up one another. This sacred land was where the man calling himself Brother had been born, had performed many acts considered miracles, was hung to die on a cross and, the most important revelation, had been resurrected.

They talked briefly about the virtues, righteousness, and significance of the upcoming holy days. Ramadan, the Muslim holy days, was just about a month away, and Passover not too many weeks after. The holy men discussed how this latest explosive confrontation in Jerusalem would affect their respective religions' most important and certainly most sacrosanct periods of the year. They also knew, no matter what words and signs of friendship each of them might express to one another, little could be done to prevent these cowardly acts in the future.

The scope and content of their conversation altered course as soon as the two-and-a-half-hour Delta flight began. Both religious leaders realized the meaningfulness of their impending meeting in South Beach with representatives from the group led by this man referring to himself as Brother. They were both determined to keep an open mind to all they would hear and see, despite the fact that the Muslim and Jewish religions and their millions of followers might be affected to a great degree, positively or adversely. Perhaps, however, this was all a sham. Who could tell? Before the moon set in the west and the sun rose once again in the east, perhaps they would know.

Imam Qutb wrestled with a thought that had been on his mind since this saga began. He could not resist the temptation to ask his traveling companion, "Could you perhaps rethink your position on the life, miracles, and resurrection of Jesus Christ?"

Rabbi Silverman, ever so diplomatic and tactful, responded evasively. "Interesting fellow. Interesting fellow."

The imam just grinned at his new friend's response as he closed his eyes searching for a few minutes of rest before they landed.

###

By seven thirty the activity in and around the pastel pink hotel intensified. More reporters appeared on the scene from every imaginable magazine and television and radio station, and correspondents from all the major wire services were also in attendance. But why were they there? A good question. A hot story for sure was taking place within the walls of the White Sand Hotel. But no one seemed to know what it was, or if they did, they weren't saying.

These providers of the news were not only outside the hotel, they had managed to gain access to almost every nook and cranny of the beautifully appointed interior as well. Their unrelenting desire to report a major breaking story before the competition did had no boundaries, no ground rules, no code of ethics. Just get the story, with as much glitter and sizzle as possible.

Guests of the small hotel and those patrons who arrived to have dinner or cocktails were inconvenienced by the growing number of aggressive reporters. The paparazzi pointed their expensive cameras at everyone and anyone who entered the establishment. Flash attachments intermittently lighting the parking lot resembled a gala Hollywood movie preview. The only element missing were the superstars to fill a giant screen. But there were no actors performing in the hotel's meeting room. These special men, chosen by Brother, were about to congregate for dinner and to ask him profound questions regarding the history of humankind and its future course.

On the third floor where his suite was located, James opted for a seldom used back stairway to return to the meeting room. The rest of the twelve men filtered into the hotel, trying to maintain a low profile as they squeezed their way through the hordes of reporters to join John, Matthew, Philip, and Thaddaeus, who had remained in the meeting room with the doors locked most of the day. When Peter and Andrew arrived, they were amazed at the amount of equipment installed since morning. What appeared to be thousands of feet of cable and wire were spread out along the perimeter of the room. Computers, television cameras, and technical equipment were prominent throughout the room. As the men entered the facility they were asked questions, had pictures taken of them, and were hassled by the aggressive reporters.

They were all there now, with the exception of Brother. They hoped his entrance would be uneventful. What with all the over-zealous characters inside and outside the hotel, the men showed great concern over his safety. Peter and the others realized there was virtually nothing they could do to prevent any idiot from badgering the principal member of their group, or, for that matter, physically abusing him. As they waited for his entrance with trepidation and anxiety, the talented German musician from the quaint city of Heidelberg played the piano for the enjoyment of his new friends. The beautiful and soothing music Bartholomew's fingers produced on the well-tuned piano relaxed the group for the moment; though to a man, the safety and well being of Brother was paramount in their thoughts.

Matthew informed those who had not been there during the day what was taking place that would enable Brother to proceed with tomorrow's press conference. He brought them up-to-date on the meetings both in New York at the cardinal's office at Saint Patrick's, and in Washington within the President's Oval Office. The men were pleasantly surprised at the significant progress made by Matthew's associates at *Time*, considering the brief period they'd had to work with. The visit by the rabbi and the imam to authenticate what was taking place was also received favorably by the group, which determined that Peter, Thomas, and Matthew would serve as their spokesmen to talk to the religious men flying in from New York. They all agreed that Brother would probably not want to get into a direct dialogue with the two religious men.

Jim and Matthew reviewed each of the questions the group had prepared for Brother, who had already answered some of them. The diverse list of inquiries covered many areas, from the beginning of life as we know it, to the end of it. A variety of other questions regarded the many religions and cults, some believing in Father, others not. But these were not profound questions attempting to dissect specific areas of religion, such as a group of theologians would ask, just basic ones you would expect a panel of common men and women to ask.

Would the twelve men hear any new revelations from Brother? Or would he just reinforce passages describing the Scriptures and prophecies from the *Bible*? Would he give them his thoughts and his code of ethics regarding some of the controversial subjects the human race is struggling with today? These twelve chosen men hoped and prayed they were worthy of delivering their assignment from Father to everyone on the face of the earth.

TWENTY TWO

It took no longer than a half hour for the State Department to inform every embassy to be prepared for a major conference call the next morning. The communiquè read as follows:

December 18, 1999 ... From, The Secretary of State ... Urgent ... Ambassador, or second in command ... The President requests you inform heads of state in your respective countries to make themselves available at their official headquarters or at the American Embassy at eight-thirty tomorrow morning ... Make every effort to inform and invite country's religious leaders of all denominations and faiths as well ... Important religious figure will conduct a worldwide conference call at that time ... Recommend an English translator be on hand ... The President has complete control over the situation and is most graciously requesting all be in attendance ... Make every effort to contact appropriate parties as soon as possible ... Operator, inform Ambassador ASAP ... Details as to how conference call to be conducted later ... Reply and confirm ... Urgent....

Along with the above communiquè, the Secretary of State personally made telephone calls to the United Nations ambassadors of Iran, Iraq, and those other nations without diplomatic ties, explaining the importance of the conference call. She cordially invited them to participate in this historic event and suggested they contact their heads of state. They wasted little time communicating with their respective leaders and advised the Secretary of State of the positive reply. She informed the ambassadors that staff members would contact them regarding the details of the conference call.

Less than an hour after their meeting in the Oval Office, the Secretary of State telephoned the President in his private quarters and brought him up to date. She advised him of the enthusiastic responses to the communiquè and of the phone calls and positive replies from the United Nations ambassadors of both Iran and Iraq. The President requested a list of all the cities to be included in the conference call. She said George Cooledge would have one delivered to the Oval Office in thirty minutes.

She also advised the President that a special hook-up was being established for the Dalai Lama outside of New Delhi, India. Since his forced departure from Tibet, his safety had been of the utmost importance to his followers. Hence, for security reasons, the information regarding the whereabouts of this exiled Holy Man would not appear on the list of cities.

It took less than twenty minutes for George Cooledge to reach the White House and give the President copies of the list he had compiled of more than thirty cities.

"So far so good,"said the President.

George Cooledge added, "We've decided on the A list plus an additional number of countries with large Christian populations."

"That's good thinking on your part,"the President replied. His voice befit his title when he said, "The Secretary of State informed me Baghdad, Tehran, and Havana were receptive as well. I trust they will not attempt to put a fly in the ointment."

"What are you getting at, Mr. President?"asked his trustworthy Chief of Staff.

"If they don't know already, they will shortly, as to where this call is to emanate from and who the principal speaker is."

"I see your point,"replied his top aide, nodding his head. "Shall we increase security in the area?"

"Not a bad idea, considering the circumstances. Whatever is happening at South Beach must go off without a hitch. Advise both the CIA and the FBI to send some additional agents there as soon as possible. Above all, please keep me advised of any problems."

The President waited until he retired to his private quarters before telephoning his confidante and every other President's ambassador to God for the last forty-plus years. Reverend Billy Graham was not at home, but that was no big surprise. Although he had just completed another heartwarming tour through South America in front of thousands of people, the tireless and energetic evangelist was in New York for an interview on CNN with Larry King. This pious man had not only advised each of these chief executives on matters of state, he had counseled most of them when it came to their personal religious beliefs. The call from the President reached the fundamentalist preacher during the last segment of the show hosted by the Brooklyn-born, braces-clad journalist.

He was naturally elated, but not nearly as surprised by this his toric event as was the President. It was as if he expected this eventuality to occur during his lifetime. Reverend Graham was pleased the President sought his counsel and expressed his gratitude. A decision was reached for this unpretentious, humble minister of God to proceed to Washington, DC, as soon as possible. From the preacher's perspective, Jesus Christ returning was the essence of what he had been teaching his followers about for much, if not all, of his adult life. To be in the nation's capital, standing on the steps of the White House as the Chief Executive verified this event of the faithful would please him very much, as it would have an incredible impact on the country and the entire world. From the President's position, both religious and political, who better to have standing at your side than the revered and admired Reverend Billy Graham.

The plane carrying Max Cohen and Bob Edwards back to New York was in its final approach for landing. It was then that the junior of the two had an idea.

"Max, we've already told our readers that the Teacher was our man/woman of the year -- and a great selection I might add. But what do you think about publishing a second Man of the Year special edition? With you-know-who-on the cover."

It took little time for his boss to respond. "Fabulous idea, Bob. I can envision the cover quite vividly, with,"and he cleared his throat, "Brother in the center and his group of twelve in oval frames surrounding him. That's it! I can see circulation going through the roof. Why it would be more popular than *The New Yorker* poster of the city."

"Yes, Max, framed and hung by every mother in every religious home in the country, if not the world."

The two men were noticeably quiet as the Delta shuttle touched down at La Guardia, each wondering if he was guilty of something sacrilegious for thinking about circulation and profits and not the religious significance of this historic event. They said nothing to each other about the subject.

"Call Matt from my car, after which I'll contact my secretary at home to set up a meeting with the executive staff to discuss your idea."

Max's reliable driver always found a way to park his boss's lavish black limousine close to any arrival terminal at the airport. Bob wasted no time getting Matthew on the phone.

"Hello, my good friend. How are things going down there?"

"We are all prepared for the conference call, if that's what you're referring to, although the main speaker has not made an appearance as yet."

"What's the matter with you, Matt? I mean, your response leads me to believe there's a problem. What's up?"

"To be perfectly honest with you, Bob, it's turning into a zoo down here. There are reporters from every corner of the planet in South Beach, as well as enough cops to handle a Macy's Thanksgiving Day Parade. Television crews, with antennas raised high, ready to broadcast something, I'm not sure they even know about what. But when the news hits around the country, South Beach will resemble a Barnum and Bailey three-ring circus. With lots of live animals out of their cages, the human variety. Some seeking absolution. Some forgiveness. Some, a piece of anything that moves. Some idiots will even want blood. Anybody's blood. The situation in South Beach could get awful nasty before the night is through."

"Keep the faith, Matt,"Bob replied, adding, "I'm sorry for the pun. Do you want me to come down there? I mean to help you with the story."

"No, that's okay, I'm sure I can handle things, and as far as the pun is concerned, all I can say is bad timing on your part. But I'll excuse you."

Bob went on to share his unique idea of a special Man of the Year edition. "What do you think, Matt?"

The reporter didn't say anything at first, pausing to collect his thoughts. Altering the pitch in his voice to reflect uncertainty, he said, "I'm not sure we can get a photograph of Brother. I don't believe I could describe enough of him to one of our artists to even draw a picture of him. I'm not sure anyone else in the group can tell you what he looks like either. Other than his clothing, which blends in smartly with the rest of the guys in South Beach, I'm not sure I can give you any details about his features. Not his complexion, nor his hair, how much he weighs or how tall he is. And yet when you are in his presence, you're sure it's him. No question about it. It's him. The Son of God."

His comments stunned both Bob and Max, listening on the limousine's speakerphone. Although he didn't let his feelings be known, Bob sensed his idea was fizzling out, but Max realized this was a special situation -- one that required not only aggressive leadership, but also a vivid imagination. And with his mind working overtime, he surely would find a way to produce a likeness of Brother. Even if it meant going with the accepted version of what most Christians already assumed he looked like.

Max knew it was time for him to play executive, taking over the situation and making the crucial decisions that had elevated him to the top of the corporate ladder. "Gentlemen, we'll work around Brother. But as soon as possible, I want a photographer to take a picture of the entire group." Sarcastically he added, "Of course, if that's still a possibility."

Bob smirked at Max's comments. Matthew didn't. For the first time since this journey to the unknown had begun, Matthew lost his composure. And he wasted little time informing both of the men in New York that he saw little humor in Max's comment.

"Max, I wish I could find some humor in your last remark and perhaps later on, I just might. But you have to understand, this is not your basic feature article that's going to raise its head up for a few days or weeks and then go away. Or let me say it another way -- this story does not have the characteristics of a one-night stand. The scope and profoundness of this entire situation is overwhelming. And I hope you understand by now, I'm not only reporting this incredible story, I'm a part of the cast of characters!" Like a volcano ready to erupt, Matthew went on to say, "Let me explain my position again."

He paused for a few seconds, gained some sense of calmness, and added, "Brother's plans appear to have not only a wide-reaching and everlasting effect on the world, they also include the group's direct involvement. For how long, I can't tell. But believe me, the thought has crossed my mind, this mission he's asked the group to carry out may be a life-long job. Changing all of our lives. All twelve of us, for as long as we are still breathing, for the rest of our lives!"

There was no response for a few seconds. Just two men squirming in the plush seats of the extravagant limousine. In a much softer tone, Max said, "I'm sorry, Matt, I guess I'm just having a hard time understanding exactly what you are going through. Let me promise you, neither Bob nor I will ever lose sight of that again."

Max could feel the perspiration dampening his Brooks Brothers shirt as he waited for his reporter's response.

"Apology accepted. Let me make this clear, as long as I'm on the payroll, my reporter's hat sits squarely on my head. I'll make every effort to deliver an accurate account, with all the bells and whistles associated with it, of what has, is, and will happen in South Beach. A story of epic proportions of Brother's return."

Feeling relieved at his associate's comments, Max said, "Thank you, Matt. Spoken like a true professional. We're all very proud of you. If you need anything, I mean anything at all, please get in touch with either one of us. Bob will call you in an hour or so, and just remember, we are with you all the way. Good luck!"

"Thanks Max."

TWENTY THREE

The noise level outside of this newly ordained shrine resembled the high pitched fanfare of a Friday evening rally before a college football game. The cacophony and hullabaloo lacked only cheerleaders and pompon girls, as the number of law enforcement officers grew. Amazingly, the media coverage continued to expand too.

Nine-fifteen at night and Brother was yet to make an appearance. Naturally, concern for his safety as well as their own continued to magnify. To maintain some sense of calmness, the men gathered into small discussion groups, one of which was concerned with the different qualities and comparisons of soccer to the game of choice in the United States, American football. Peter, James, and Thomas did not participate in the small talk, but instead took this opportunity to discuss some of the issues at hand as well as the problems they could foresee over the next few days. The three men spoke of devising a plan as to how to handle the press after Brother departed. It was obvious to each of them that a briefing would have to be made to the ever-growing number of reporters waiting outside, some of whom waited patiently, some restlessly, for this story to unfold.

After his conversation with James and Thomas, Peter approached the bands of men huddled together in twos and threes, joining in briefly with them in their light conversations. At the appropriate time, he placed his arms affectionately around each man and praised them for maintaining their composure and patience while awaiting Brother's appearance. The serious nature of Peter's comments and the warmth and fervent inflections in his delivery returned the entire group to the realities of the moment. All of their most profound inner thoughts had come to the surface once again. Their ears and eyes became more focused. Indeed, their minds were cleared of anything and everything other than the task at hand. And if there was any doubt before as to who the leader of this hand-chosen group was -- besides Brother -- that point was once and for all put to rest. The captain of the Amalfi fishing vessel from San Francisco was, without question, in command, the individual they would look up to for guidance and direction after Brother returned to his heavenly abode.

Three computers were situated against the far wall, just to the right of the piano, the videoconferencing equipment on the opposite side of the room. Peter could not explain his reason for asking John Thompson to check to see if there was any e-mail. The fisherman was not what you would call a computer hacker. He considered himself a blooming idiot when it came to new technology, although he and Andrew had installed a modest system for bookkeeping purposes. Still, he had a burning sensation that was unexplainable. A feeling someone was trying to communicate with him.

Peter said, "I'm sure glad you're here, John. I'd have trouble turning the blasted thing on."

John smiled as he continued, entering his password, then getting on line with the fanfare of music welcoming him. He took a few seconds in an attempt to explain to Peter what he was doing. The fisherman acknowledged what was said, but truly had no comprehension of how John had actually established contact with the electronic universe.

The uncharacteristic excitement in John's voice captured everyone's attention. "Peter, you were right, there is an e-mail for you!"

As John proceeded, the screen displayed what seemed to be a lengthy text. Peter, leaning intently over the English financier's shoulder, wasn't surprised that this mail was for him. In fact, he acted as though this is what he expected.

"What's going on?"asked Andrew.

Thomas, Philip, and Jim echoed Andrew's inquiry with their own inquisitive questions. Now all the men chimed in, wanting to know what was on the screen.

"Oh nothing special,"answered John in a nonchalant tone, just a letter for Peter and the rest of us." John paused briefly as he turned around to face Peter and the others, adding, "A letter from Brother."

The room was abuzz with joy and exhilaration.

"Finally some word from Brother."

"Is he coming?"

"Where is he?"

"What did he say?"

"Patience, my friends,"the fisherman requested. "Patience."

John couldn't help but bellow when he told them, "You will all get a kick out of this. His e-mail address is ritehanman."

Simon said, "What an appropriate address."

Peter placed his hand on John's shoulder, thanked him for his efforts and for maintaining his poise. He asked, "John, could you please print this? You can, can't you?"as Peter backed away from the certainty of his request.

"I see no reason why this can't be printed, unless Brother does not want it so."

The thought of not being able to recall what Brother's physical features were went through John's head as he requested the printer to begin doing its job. The microprocessor began to click as the command function to print was executed. The men waited patiently to see if the words of the Son of God could be reproduced on paper. Shouldn't be a difficult task for the new Hewlett-Packard laser printer, John thought, although not even the computer whiz was totally optimistic.

All eyes turned in the direction of the printer and to their delight, Brother's letter was being printed. They were captivated by Brother's choosing to communicate with them over the Internet.

Thaddaeus pushed his elbow into Philip's ribs and quietly said "Well, at least we contributed something of value to tonight's proceedings."

"Yes,"Philip responded,"but no more than a twelve-year-old could have accomplished." Philip suggested that John stay on line on all three computers just in case another e-mail was posted by you-know-who. No one reached for the printed sheets, leaving that chore to Peter, who waited patiently for the printing process to end.

Peter picked up the twelve sheets of paper, clutched them to his chest for a few seconds, then began to read the holy epistle. He examined only the first two or three lines of Brother's e-mail, looked up to face the rest of the group, and smiled. Then he began to laugh, albeit not as one would react from reading or hearing a humorous story. Peter, shaking his head, simply said, "Brother,"then he paused for a few seconds. "Brother requests that we first have dinner. I'm sorry to say, he will not be joining us tonight. I am to share the remainder of the details of the letter with you after we finish dinner.

The entire group was stilled by the initial contents of Brother's electronic as well as electrifying letter. Only Peter managed to maintain his composure as the others scurried around, seeking comfort and support from one another. Peter used his outspread arms to shepherd the men to their chairs, flicking his fingers and shaking his head in an effort to give them some reassurance that all was well; taking their seats for dinner without anyone uttering even a single comment about Brother not appearing. Disappointed, words of conversation were tough to come by. Moreover, the unhappiness of this emotional let down was evident by the saddened expressions on their drawn faces.

Now the thought of not seeing him ever again was a distinct likelihood. Could it be he had just given up on the human race? Perhaps after sizing up the initial reaction to his reappearance he sensed a feeling of apathy or too many disbelievers -- not on the part of these twelve men, but those in Washington and the religious leaders in New York. Possibly he felt the international community was not receptive to this incredible news. Or could it be the *Time* executives hadn't delivered Matthew's story correctly? Maybe Brother had decided to select another approach to communicate with the masses.

All of these possibilities went through their minds, although no one made reference to them. Peter led the men in a brief prayer before they began, asking Brother for guidance and understanding as well as offering a special thanks for the food they were about to eat. Other than this short prayer, silence was the predominant accompaniment to dinner. It was apparent that whatever his reasons for not showing tonight, the group as a whole accepted his decision. Nonetheless, the feeling of frustration was obvious, since each of these men had a burning desire to see him once again. There was no question, tonight's dinner would not be as captivating or engaging as last night's. His letter was here, but Brother was not.

There was little that could be done to ease the emotional pain and disappointment of Brother's not being with them. Fifteen or twenty minutes passed, with only the chime of a water glass being accidentally tuned by a fork cracking the silence. At last, a break in the absolute quiet occurred by Philip's remarking on how interesting he thought it was for Brother to select e-mail as the mode to reach them. And how unique it was for him to utilize this most modern form of communication. Andrew then commented on how thoughtful Brother was for sending them this letter and not keeping them in the dark, the contents of which was on everyone's mind. Needless to say, the anticipation of hearing what Brother had to say in it created a very hastily consumed dinner.

All eyes turned in Peter's direction to see if he had anything to add to Andrew's or Philip's comments. Controlling his emotions, he said nothing. Peter had not even so much as glanced at any of the twelve printed sheets of paper, although his curiosity level was at least as high as the others. Peter pointed to the entrance to the room, then placed his hands over his ears, suggesting what was apparent on the other side of the doors.

The noise level outside of the meeting room had escalated to an alarming pitch; with those outside waiting for some sensational news to be disseminated. John could only imagine how Dolores Quan was handling all this. John asked Peter if he should question Dolores to determine how bad the conditions were out there, since the situation appeared to be almost out of control.

Peter agreed. "It's in our best interest to size up the situation and determine what exactly is going on,"adding, "we might be secluded in here overnight and best be prepared for it."

The men arose from their seats. Thomas and Andrew took this opportunity to clear the table, leaving only coffee cups and what was left of the dessert plate, consisting primarily of small chocolate tarts and butter cookies.

When John finally reached Dolores in her office, it was obvious to him that her patience was running thin. She complained vehemently to John, reminding him constantly of all the trouble he and his friends were causing her. He just shook his head and grimaced, while holding the telephone a distance from his ear. Interesting and entertaining, even though she was angry, John thought to himself, with her exotic Chinese-American accent.

With his finest English articulation, John replied, "Now, now, Ms. Quan, you do realize what is taking place here, don't you?"

"I certainly do! All you have to do is to look at the hundreds of people swarming around my hotel. When is this..."and she paused, searching for the proper words, "how much longer are you gentlemen going to be here?"

"We shall be gone by tomorrow afternoon."

"Not a moment too soon,"she retorted. "But that doesn't solve the current problem of getting all these people out of here. Especially those reporters, what with all their questions and hassling of the guests. What a bunch of parasites. Not to mention the number of policemen walking around, scaring the guests half to death. Many of whom would find another hotel to stay at, if rooms were available. And my staff, why, half of them have threatened to quit if these conditions persist. Including my own cousin Deng, who's the sous chef in our kitchen."

John waited a few seconds for the steam to cool off before replying. "My dear Ms. Quan, although my friends and I will be departing tomorrow, I'm afraid things may never return to normal at this establishment."

"What do you mean by that?" The rage noticeably reappeared in her voice.

"Whether you believe what has happened here or not, I must inform you the mere fact the Son of God has chosen this place for this historic meeting has transformed the White Sand Hotel into a sacred shrine. A sacred shrine for humankind to worship at for all eternity. Millions of people from every continent will visit here each year to pray to God, the Father of all humankind, the Almighty One. Pray to him, for their salvation. Pray to him, for his forgiveness of all their sins. Pray to him for the health and well-being of their family members. Pray to him for eternal peace."

Although Dolores was not a Christian, John Thompson's eloquent description of what he perceived would be happening caused her to become very emotional. The innkeeper did all she could to hold back her tears after listening to his carefully chosen words. She acknowledged the importance of this event taking place right under her nose, despite her being a non-believer of this man calling himself Jesus and not even subscribing to the theory there was a God.

Dolores felt as if someone had given her an overdose of caffeine. "Mr. Thompson,"she cleared her throat, "John, how bad is it going to get around here?"

"I should think pretty awful,"he replied. "It's fair to say South Beach as we know it now will never be the same, and, as I said before, the hotel will most likely be converted into a shrine."

It was at this point Peter motioned to John that he wished to say something to Dolores before she hung up, for Peter had begun to read the e-mail from Brother. And to his surprise, in the first paragraph Brother had requested Peter to invite a reporter to sit in on the meeting -- a reporter from CNN by the name of Pauline Demitri. All Peter could think was that she too had been hand-picked by Brother. Pauline, he thought to himself; the name certainly fits, although the gender is a bit off.

Before John handed him the phone, he covered the mouth-piece and said to Peter, "She's not a very happy person at the moment. For obvious reasons, I might mention."

Peter shook his head, as if to say he understood what the poor young lady must be going through. He introduced himself, offering her only his first name, and expressed his apologies. "We appreciate your putting up with all the turmoil and commotion currently taking place at the hotel. Hopefully, by this time tomorrow night most of the pandemonium will have subsided." Before she could respond, Peter asked, "I wonder if you would do me a favor? There is a reporter by the name of Pauline Demitri somewhere outside the hotel. Could you please locate Ms. Demitri and ask her if she wouldn't mind joining us in the meeting room? And could you please escort her here? We certainly would appreciate your help. I trust you understand why we cannot accomplish this task ourselves?"

"Mr. Albano, isn't it?"

"Yes, thanks for all of your help,"replied Peter.

"After all you and your friends have put me and my staff through, you expect me to help you?"

"Why yes, if that's not too much trouble. Brother has requested Ms. Demitri be asked to sit in on the meeting. You have been advised who Brother is, Ms. Quan? Am I correct?"

"I know. I know who he claims to be. I realize why no one from your group should search for her. That would only lead to more of a disturbance at the moment. But even if I wanted to help you, Mr. Albano, do you realize how many people are wandering around the hotel? Many of them are reporters and most of them are the major source of all the chaos. You're asking me to find one reporter amongst the hundreds that are out there, Mr. Albano?"

"I recognize the problems you're having, putting up with all of those people in and around the hotel. But I plead with you, please help us locate Ms. Demitri. If it would help,"he added, "I'm informed she's employed by CNN. And by the way, Ms. Quan, please call me Peter."

Dolores hesitated before replying to Peter's request, but came to the conclusion she really had no choice but to find the reporter. Delaying this would only keep this unwanted group locked up in the meeting room longer. "Okay, Peter. And just call me Dolores."

She couldn't help but present what she perceived as a fitting innuendo before parting and acting on his request. "Next time we speak, Peter,"she hesitated for a moment, then continued, "you probably will be referring to me as the ex-manager of the White Sand Hotel. But be that as it may, I'll try to find this reporter and bring her to you as soon as possible."

"Thank you, Dolores. Thank you very much."

#

Finding the CNN van and its occupants was easy. Getting Pauline Demitri inside the hotel was another story. Dolores sought and received the assistance of one of the local police lieutenants she knew. Together, they walked along the edge of the roped-off area until the CNN van came into view. Pauline was naturally shocked by the innkeeper's request, but wasted little time in accepting her invitation, much to the dismay of Pauline's associates, who were leery about her getting personally involved.

"Be careful,"her cameraman pleaded as the two women walked back to the doorway of the hotel.

Peter waited for the men to be seated before informing them of Brother's first request regarding Pauline Demitri. "Brother wishes us to wait until this reporter is located. She's to sit in with the group while I read his letter." He then turned to John and asked, "Is it all right if I refer to this e-mail as a letter? Okay, John?"

The Englishman offered no verbal reply, just a nod of the head and a smile, followed by a laugh he failed to conceal. The rest of the group joined in the brief frolic, which at least cut through the frustration of Brother's not appearing tonight.

Dolores Quan opened the door to the meeting room accompanied by several members of the FBI. Keeping the unruly reporters at bay, the well-dressed agents in suits and ties created a passageway for the two women to walk through. Dolores' newfound friends and body-guards were a blessing in disguise, as they led her and the other young lady inside. John rushed to the entrance and thanked Dolores for locating the newest member of the group. As Thomas escorted the beautiful young reporter to the table, a knock on the door got everyone's attention once again.

Dolores opened the door from the outside and ushered in a waiter carting a fresh supply of beverages. The thoughtful innkeeper put her hands on her hips, smirked, and said, "I would imagine this is going to be a long evening."

All the men, as if on cue, arose from their chairs and thanked the innkeeper. She in turn waved her hand and faked a second chance to smile, backtracked to the doorway, and returned to her office.

Pauline introduced herself to each of the men, feeling somewhat vulnerable without the rest of her television crew. Peter informed the new arrival as straightforwardly as could be expected about Brother and the role he had outlined for the group. She, predictably, was over-whelmed.

Very religious and an active parishioner at the Greek Orthodox Church of the Annunciation in Miami, Pauline believed deeply in Jesus and his teachings. But at the moment she was in total awe of the possibility that he actually had returned. Pauline remained silent as Peter finished with his description of tomorrow's conference call. She thought to herself, so this is the reason why every reporter this side of Alligator Alley is here tonight. And little old me is right in the middle of it.

Peter asked her if she understood and believed what he had told her. "I do! I most sincerely do," she replied.

Peter placed his hand on her shoulder and welcomed her to the group, saying to Pauline he had no idea of what her role was to be, but further explaining to her, as he pointed to the e-mail, "Brother most likely has defined your role right here."

She nodded and thanked him for sharing this fascinating story with her. As they walked to the table where the others were patiently waiting, Pauline informed Peter that regardless of what role Brother had planned for her, she would carry out his charge with every bit of energy in her body, with every ounce of intelligence in her brain, and with all the love in her heart.

Regardless of her spiritual beliefs and complete devotion to God, she still couldn't help wondering why she, Pauline Demitri, had been selected to sit in with this group of twelve men. Understandably excited, she managed to conceal her emotions.

Thomas, playing the role of the perfect gentleman, offered her a chair next to his. He poured a cup of coffee, placed what was left of the dessert plate in front of her, and then began a light conversation with Pauline to make her feel a bit more comfortable. One could say that perhaps her remarkable beauty may have been responsible for the dressmaker's actions.

This fact did not go unnoticed by Peter and Andrew, whose friendship with Thomas predated their meeting Brother. The two men smiled at each other as Andrew contrived an attention-getter by knocking over an almost-empty glass of water. Thomas looked up, his focus on the lovely reporter interrupted, and knew instantly, in spite of the solemnity of the situation before them, he had been had by the two fishermen. All he could do to get even was return the warm smiles and ask if he might be of any assistance in cleaning up the mess. Under different circumstances, Andrew and Peter would be rolling on the floor in pain from uncontrollable laughter. But that would have to wait for another day.

Getting back to reality and the task at hand, Peter called for order to proceed with the reading. Before he could begin, the phone rang. Could it be Brother had decided to communicate with them once again? Perhaps he wished to reinforce the contents of his e-mail? Simon was nearest the phone; taking it off its cradle, he tentatively greeted the caller, anticipating it might be him, but it was only Bob Anderson, seeking an update from his colleague.

"Has it been an hour since the last time we spoke?"asked Matthew, taking the receiver from Simon. The rest of the group sat quietly listening to Matthew's side of the conversation.

"Oh, let's see, it's ten o'clock now, about forty-five minutes, I'd say."

The reporter informed his boss about the e-mail, as well as Brother's creative electronic address, ritehanman.

"Enchanting, illuminating, and descriptive as one could be," remarked Bob.

"We all feel the same." Matthew continued, telling his boss, "Brother will not be putting in a personal appearance tonight."

"Did he give you a reason why?"

"No, but you can imagine the frustration and disappointment we are feeling."

"I'm sorry, Matt. What else did he have to say?"

"There is a new addition to the group. A reporter from CNN by the name of Pauline Demitri."

"He's added a woman? ...From CNN?"responded Bob. "What else?"

"We haven't read the entire letter as yet, but personally, I find it a bit amusing he selected an e-mail to communicate with us."

"I'll say,"echoed Bob. "He unquestionably is up to date on computers and what modern technology has brought upon us."

"Yes,"replied Matthew, "he most likely has a superior vantage point to observe what's taking place down here."

Bob wished he hadn't said what he did. Nevertheless, he chuckled at his thoughtless remark and Matthew's amusing retort.

Bob said, "I'm glad you have still maintained your sense of humor, my friend."

"I believe the entire group is going to need a sense of humor over the next few days,"Matthew responded.

"Things starting to get sticky?"

"It's not so much that. I believe each of us has absorbed the initial shock of what has occurred thus far and are willing and able to face the future and carry out Brother's will."

"What's the problem, then?"

"It's just the concern we have over the responsibility that has been placed on our shoulders and the thought of failing to live up to Brother's expectations. It's especially frightening when you think of the potential consequences."

"Hang in there, Matt. I'm sure things will work out. Should you need anything, don't hesitate to call."

"Thanks, Bob. If there are any other dramatic developments, I'll contact you. Where will you be?"

"Matt, I intend to camp out here at the office all night. I'll call you about eleven. Okay?"

"Fine, Bob, talk to you later."

TWENTY FOUR

The Delta flight from La Guardia touched down early, thanks to the modest tailwinds. The two holy men deplaned and began their trek through the mass of humanity at Miami International, quite normal for this time of year. As the vast number of travelers made their way to their awaiting planes or to pick up their luggage at the baggage claim area, they appeared to be marching to a Caribbean beat from the song playing over the public address system, leaving little room for walking. Rabbi Marvin Silverman was accustomed to this, having been to Miami Beach just about every year since he was a small child.

It was Imam Muhammad Abdul Qutb's first visit to this vacation paradise where hundreds of thousands retired and well-to-do individuals from the northeast and Canada, whom the locals referred to as snowbirds, spent most of their winters. The imam expressed his amazement to his new friend, Rabbi Silverman, regarding the many different languages one could hear while attempting to walk through this maze of people, unquestionably an international melting pot.

Minutes after they began their taxi ride to the White Sand Hotel, the two men of the cloth were stunned at the Haitian cab driver's comments regarding the commotion in South Beach. In his Creole accent, the driver continued by telling his passengers that some great and powerful religious man was said to be there, and apologized to them, adding that there might be some delays in getting to South Beach. He told them the man on the radio reported many people were on their way to see him, but when Rabbi Silverman asked, the cab driver did not know who this man was.

The rabbi was curious and asked, "What religion do you practice, my dear friend?"

"Voodoo," the cab driver proudly responded.

Imam Abdul Qutb and Rabbi Silverman were surprised not only by what he said, but also by the conviction in the tone of his voice. The two men in the back seat just shook their heads over this primitive belief, in which natural phenomena and objects sometimes resembling well-crafted look-alike dolls, were utilized to possess an individual's soul.

"Animism, I believe that's what the Greeks referred to it as,"said the imam. "It amazes me how these cultures and customs have continued to survive through all these many generations. And what's more inconceivable is the fact it is still practiced so overtly in many parts of Haiti."

Rabbi Silverman remarked, "And isn't it interesting, the Haitian immigrants have brought this ancient ideology with them and continue to perform these rituals."

"How did you find out about this news?" the imam asked.

"One of the drivers said he just heard the man on the news speak of this on his radio."

"Would you mind turning your radio on so we could hear about this too?"requested the imam.

The remainder of the ride to South Beach was void of any further conversation between the driver and his passengers. The over-enthusiastic commentator on the radio did all the talking.

The air waves were now filled with reports that someone claiming to be Jesus Christ had been seen sometime this afternoon somewhere in South Beach. Media crews from the metropolitan Miami area as well as Fort Lauderdale were airing on-the-spot taped reports from all over this artsy community -- reports indicating the inconceivable and incredible rumor of the return of Jesus Christ. Interviews with local residents ranged from historical to hysterical, from believers to non-believers, from the very religious to the cautious and circumspect.

Helicopters, mostly used for informing motorists about rush-hour traffic conditions, were now offering live telecasts of the situation, flying just above the rooftops from Alton Road to the beach, informing their viewers of the thousands of people headed toward South Beach. From the ocean to the intracoastal waterway, multi-colored vans with satellite dishes on their roofs and distinguishing corporate logos on their sides scurried about, seeking additional information regarding this extraordinary story. From Hallandale Beach, ten miles north of South Beach, to South Point Park, its southern boundary, these television crews roamed, looking for anyone who could substantiate this story.

Information regarding Brother's whereabouts came from an unnamed government official in Washington. Those reporters already on the scene at the hotel were brought up to date by their news departments regarding the subject matter of why they were sent there earlier in the evening. Initial reactions to this unbelievable development did not slow these aggressive reporters down at all. Many of them worked through the emotional trauma, which is certainly understandable. Even the very religious among them sensed the awareness that news comes first. They managed to table their emotions and proceeded to manifest the greatest story of the last two millennia.

The camera lights around the hotel were turned on as each network began to prepare its impromptu telecast beginning at ten o'clock and again on the half hour until the late news shows were normally aired. Decisions were already approved by the networks to telecast the story nationally. Of course, CNN's Atlanta headquarters would air the story internationally. The only difference between CNN and the other networks was that Mr. Turner's reporter was now a part of the story. Each reporter, with one hand holding a microphone, the other hand pushing back windswept hair, gave his or her sketchy account of the story, with the unambiguous promise and allurement of further details at eleven.

Traffic on the main drag was normally bumper to bumper this time of year, what with tourists seeking an almost impossible-to-get parking space circling the area between Third and Tenth streets, and teenage drivers, against the wishes of the authorities, out for a night of cruising, sitting behind the steering wheels of their convertibles on Ocean Drive, with their radios blasting some forgettable sounds.

"Now this,"grumbled a policeman to his partner, as they slowly peddled their bicycles through the line of stagnant automobiles. The two officers, both veterans of the force, had never seen anything like this crowd before. But who had? Traffic was at a complete standstill in South Beach, as well as the city of Miami and all of the surrounding communities. As thousands of cars from every main road and secondary artery tried to make their way up and down the Florida Turnpike, Interstate 95, or south on Federal Highway One (Biscayne Boulevard), A1A (Collins Avenue), or from west to east on the Dolphin Expressway and every side street imaginable. All were seeking to converge on the various causeways connecting Miami Beach to the mainland.

Initial reports indicated even eastbound traffic on Interstate 75 (Alligator Alley) was bumper to bumper, as thousands of cars occupied by people of all faiths crossed the Everglades from Naples and the surrounding areas. Tour bus companies added additional vehicles and Amtrak tacked on extra cars to accommodate the curious and faithful. Reservations for seating on these land carriers was virtually impossible to come by for the foreseeable future. Airlines, both domestic and international, destined to Miami and Fort Lauderdale were completely booked, with thousands more waiting on standby at airports around the globe. Cities hundreds of miles away from Miami, such as Orlando and Tampa already at the height of their own tourist season, and as far north as Atlanta, were feeling the impact of the tens of thousands wishing to come to South Beach. Car rental companies had simply run out of automobiles to meet the demands of the travelers to the world's newest shrine.

Thousands of people proceeded to make their way on foot across the crowded causeways connecting Miami to Miami Beach. Many of them were praying, weeping, chanting, and praising God every step of the way. Others, curious to see what was happening, just couldn't resist the urge to come. It was a procession never before seen. Each person was embarked on a pilgrimage to a small hotel in South Beach where he or she expected to see and hear this man called Jesus Christ, the Son of God.

Rabbi Marvin Silverman and Imam Muhammad Abdul Qutb were fortunate. They managed to miss most of the onslaught of people and automobiles passing over the Julia Tuttle causeway, but their smooth and uninterrupted ride was about to reach an impasse. When the black and yellow taxi reached the intersection of Alton and Arthur Godfrey Roads, traffic came to a complete halt. They waited for twenty minutes, in which time the overheated cab did not move one inch. It was then the rabbi and imam decided to continue the remainder of their fact-finding expedition south to the White Sand Hotel on foot. Joining the thousands of people already on their way there, they began the rest of their journey to the shrine in South Beach. The two holy men would not arrive there until quarter past eleven.

TWENTY FIVE

The phone rang again, once more interrupting Peter before he could proceed with the reading of Brother's letter. He tightened his grip on the twelve pages, shook his head in frustration and motioned to John, seated nearest the phone, to answer it. This time it was the innkeeper, who said, "The news of your religious leader's return was reported on television. I just received a call from my boss in Orlando." Then, holding back tears, her voice cracked. "They even mentioned the hotel. Hundreds of thousands of people were said to be on their way here. Do you hear me? Hundreds of thousands! What am I supposed to do now?"

"Take it easy, Dolores. Trust me, these people come in peace. They just want to see if Brother is actually here. I'm sure they will do no harm to you or the hotel," John replied. "And in a day or two, most of them will return to their homes." Though he didn't truly believe all of what he said, John hoped he could ease the pain and anguish Dolores was encountering. "The law enforcement officers will maintain security around the building. I'm certain of that. There shouldn't be any problems."

When John put down the phone, Peter began to read the e-mail, starting at the top, repeating Brother's wishes to include Pauline Demitri in the group. As he referred to that specific paragraph of the letter, Peter bowed in her direction as a gesture to once more welcome her to the group. Pauline's eyes were filled with enthusiasm and a burning desire to be a part of this momentous event. Peter glanced at Thomas to capture his reaction. The serious look and intensity on the dressmaker's face was an indication of the significant business at hand. The manner in which Thomas stared at him reinforced the meaningfulness and the gravity of the task before them.

Peter scanned the room before proceeding, noticing a similar look on each of the men's faces. He read further, expressing Brother's explanation for not attending tonight's dinner. "I do not wish to have my presence here on earth become the major focus. Although I am the true Son of God, you must understand I did not come back to be glorified or venerated. Father looks upon each and every man and woman as his son and daughter. All of us are his children. All of us are part of his family.

"Believe me, the only reason for my return was to convey to you Father's wishes. This above all must remain the primary objective for you, Peter, and for the entire group to concentrate on. Each of you in this room tonight must be recognized as the deliverer of Father's proclamation."

Although difficult for them to comprehend, it became apparent that this was the paramount reason for Brother not appearing. They were astonished by his humility and humbleness, considering this son, this member of the family, exhibited his devotion to Father, and the love he had for his brothers and sisters by being crucified on a cross two thousand years ago.

Furthermore, Brother wrote, he was quite certain Peter could successfully conduct the press conference tomorrow morning, prevailing on his newly acquired profound faith and wisdom, which had been enhanced considerably over the last two days. Brother stated that these were the key elements, and along with the energized enthusiasm and forcefulness, were the essential ingredients required to convince the earth's population to heed what Father had requested. The end of the paragraph reflected Brother's utmost confidence and assurance that Peter would deliver this presentation as well as he could.

Obviously the last comment he read stunned Peter. This emotional reaction now affected him physically and did not go unnoticed by the group. The fisherman's face turned pale, his hands trembled, and his knees weakened. Bartholomew and Thaddaeus, sitting on either side of him, jumped out of their chairs to attend to Peter. A few sips of water and a couple of supportive pats on the back stabilized the man who had suddenly become responsible for airing tomorrow's conference call ... the man who would attempt to convince those listening that Jesus Christ returned three days ago ... the man who had been chosen by the Son of God to stand behind the podium to deliver his Father's tenet.

Peter perceived he was not capable of what he had been asked to do. He considered himself unpolished as a speaker completely unworthy to be placed in this esteemed position. He told the group this momentous occasion should be conducted by a prominent religious leader, such as a cardinal or a bishop, or perhaps even the Pope. Moreover, people wanted to see and hear Brother, not Peter Albano. How could he possibly be accepted as a substitute? Why should they believe anything he would have to say? Why didn't Brother ask one of the others to be the speech maker? Peter was searching for excuses and knew it. It was extremely difficult for him to rationalize Brother's motives; however, after several minutes of deliberation, the fisherman accepted this significant challenge. Brother had chosen him over all the others, and that should be enough of an incentive. He looked around the room for some type of reaction, some assistance in making his decision or, at minimum, his colleagues' support. His eyes pleaded for some response. But each man looked bewildered, no doubt as surprised as he was. The news had distressed and confused each of them. They realized Brother's mere presence at the press conference would captivate and enthrall every human being on the planet. It was incongruous to think that any mortal man could hope to duplicate the sound of his voice, the inflections when he spoke, and his mannerisms when he raised his hands during his proclamations.

James Thompson, passionate, understanding, and considerate, finally spoke up, telling Peter he had performed admirably, conducting himself as a true leader would. In spite of the delicate issues at hand and with all the uncertainty and stress, Peter had done a remarkable job of holding the group together thus far. James went on to add that he for one would be at Peter's side tomorrow, not only to give him moral support, but to back him up in the event he needed assistance with the presentation. Simon stood up and seconded the Englishman's comments, followed by each of the others, including the newcomer, Pauline.

Peter's reaction to this sign of unity and support restored his confidence in both his ability to continue and in the group's determination to proceed. The color returned to his face, the nerves stopped twitching around his hands, and the muscular legs became as strong as California redwoods once again. His brother, Andrew, sitting at the opposite end of the table with an enthusiastic expression on his handsome face, stated proudly, "Peter, I can't think of a better man for the job."

Thomas added, "I agree, the best darn fisherman in America."

Peter acknowledged the accolades as he made eye contact with everyone at the table. He then proceeded with the reading of the second page, carefully placing page one in a manila folder.

"Last night, I spent most of the evening informing you about Father's thoughts regarding the state of the world. The next seven pages summarize what we talked about last night. You'll notice I have expanded on some of what I said, specifying the details of what Father wants accomplished. He also has provided you with his time frame -

- the 'when' in the equation -- or the target date Father expects society to begin the process to make the necessary changes. Father recognizes these changes cannot be made in a few days or even a few months. He does expect each country to develop a plan of action and implement it before the defined deadlines. And he also envisions that the so-called super powers will assist the underdeveloped countries along the way, providing them with the necessary strategies, planning, resources, and manpower to help them with the implementation of their plans."

Peter sat down and continued reading. "Let me make this clear to you: the fact that one country or even a majority of countries sub-scribes to Father's request will not be enough to satisfy his demands. For many countries which heretofore have been believers in spiritual leaders and their teachings, the task will be more difficult. The follow-ers of these spiritual beings will tend to be inflexible; but they must be informed Father is the creator of humankind and all of Heaven and Earth. He is transcendent, with unequaled wisdom and unapproach-able power, and he will always be.

"Father has no desire to alter the philosophy and teachings of the likes of Buddha or Confucius. They, along with the many true spiritu-al teachers through the centuries, were wise, judicious, and sensible leaders. Their followers can continue to follow the practices and codes of law these sage and sagacious men taught. But they must also be made to understand that Father is the ultimate source and consum-mate being of all that is seen and unseen. To live their lives to the fullest, despite the various idiosyncrasies in the innumerable unique cultures throughout the world -- live their lives to the fullest, under one God, the Father, the Almighty.

"Father understands humankind's shortcomings. The allurement of greed, the weakness of envy, and the temptation of the salacious enticements of the promiscuous, will unfortunately be actions and thoughts men and women must encounter and experience. Humankind was created with all of these flaws and many, many more, but it must learn to live and endure, praying to Father for his forgive-ness of these transgressions. The perfect human has not been born, nor will ever be. Of this, I am sure. However, Father is forgiving, willing to accept humankind's frailties, provided each man and woman makes every effort to reform themselves and pray for absolution."

Peter stopped speaking at this point, giving everyone, including himself, a chance to digest and reflect on what Brother had written. He searched ahead for the date Father had given as his deadline. He found it toward the end of page eight. To his amazement, Father had not been overly generous with his time horizon. He expected this renaissance to be planned, structured, and put into action before the end of the year 2000. That left a little more than a year to convey his thoughts to everyone on earth -- to convince them that Brother had actually returned. And if that were not enough, to have them develop a plan to work together to straighten out the problems in each country -- something no one had been able to accomplish since humans were first placed on this planet. All of this in one year! Impossible, Peter thought to himself, shaking his head in frustration and wishing Brother were here so he could describe to him his feelings. Peter's silence created an air of uncertainty, another emotional swing not really needed at this time.

"What's wrong, Peter?" asked Jim.

Without hesitating, Peter responded, "Father, in his infinite wisdom, believes the world can be changed by the end of next year."

"You mean to tell me he expects all of this to be accomplished within the span of one year?" asked Judas.

"It's taken thousands of years to screw up and he expects humankind to mend its fences and change its ways in one year,"yelled Bartholomew.

"Impossible! I'll say,"Philip chimed in. "He should see the smog in Santiago."

Thomas couldn't help but add a bit of levity to this serious discussion by adding, "I think he knows about the smog in Santiago, Philip."

This comment would ordinarily have brought a few chuckles, but no one showed even the slightest hint of humor. Their eyes reflected a combination of anger, fear, and seriousness as they contemplated the extent and gravity of Father's plan.

"There are just too many evil people on earth to achieve this goal,"said Judas, as if he knew this for a fact. And he most likely did, based on the number of drug dealers he had defended.

Jim said, "For centuries men and women have fought with their neighbors because of different religious beliefs, or over a parcel of land or the rights of a waterway. Even in lands which tend to be tranquil and serene, you will observe these bitter conflicts taking place from time to time."

"Brother against brother have cheated or even killed one another for nothing more than to improve their financial wealth or enhance their status in the family,"said John. "I'm usually a very positive thinker, feeling humankind can overcome any obstacle placed before him. The word 'no' is generally not in my vocabulary. But this!

Perhaps given enough time,"as he shook his head and paused. "Even then, darn near impossible. This is a monumental task that goes beyond the boundaries of probability."

Thaddaeus took his turn, venting his frustration. "I realize Father is aware of the horrid conditions of the inner cities in America. It's not because people choose to live this way. Not being educated, they can't help themselves find the proper path to get out of these deteriorated sections of their cities. They take turns being the bad guy, robbing the people next door for a few dollars so they can shoot themselves up with cocaine or heroin. They have little perception of right from wrong. How does Father expect them to comprehend that every man and woman should live in harmony with their neighbors or else? I guess we could include all poverty-stricken areas where similar conditions are so prevalent. The numerous backward regions of Africa, South America and Central America, just to name a few." The African-American engineer from Detroit added, "When do we get to the 'or else' portion of Brother's letter?"

This exact thought, had been on everyone's mind. Each of them was relieved that somebody else was courageous enough to bring the subject to the table.

Matthew said, "Thanks, Thaddaeus, I'm glad someone had the guts to bring up this provocative subject, which I will call, 'what if they don't succeed.'"

"Perhaps the ultimate subject matter, not as yet defined by Brother,"said Judas.

"Exactly,"Matthew continued, "although I'm reasonably sure he reserved a page or two for that very thought, my dear friend. You are all correct in your observations and commentary, but we must as a group try to maintain our focus. Diminishing the importance of the responsibilities before us would serve no purpose."

Andrew entered the conversation. "You are right on the money, Matthew. It's almost as if we are being tested to see how strong and perhaps how durable our faith is. To see if we honestly and truly believe Brother has indeed returned. That we had dinner with him, right here in this very room. And now, the most profound test of all. Informing the rest of the world about all of this, and even more important, having them believe us. I think we all agree, this portion of the agenda will be the most difficult. The most taxing for us, and also the most critical, based on what Brother has told us. I think we are all subject to the possibility of being harassed, tormented, ridiculed, and maligned for preaching the word of the Lord. Few will side with us.

Many will wish us ill fate. The more radical, perhaps even worse. I guess you could say we are not too dissimilar from the martyrs who were persecuted because they subscribed to the new belief during those early days of Christianity. Not that our lives are on the line -- at least I hope they aren't."

Simon couldn't help attempting to add a small degree of levity to the speaker's intense comments. "Andrew, you know I live in Africa, which, by the way, has the largest contingent of carnivorous beasts anywhere." Trying to hold back a smile, but unable to, he added, "As I'm led to believe, lions just abhor the taste of fishermen's meat."

The South African's amusing comments were received with grins and then laughter, especially from Peter, who obviously was the object of Simon's humor.

As for Andrew, his face turned red, but then he joined in. "Okay! Okay, but think about it, we have a lot of convincing to do, beginning with tomorrow morning's conference call."Andrew's laughter was short lived. His facial expression turned to dead seriousness as he said, "I hope my remarks did not come across as being overly melo-dramatic. And perhaps I've used a bad analogy,"his eyes focusing in Simon's direction, "about the martyrs, I mean. It's just...."

Andrew paused, tears filled his eyes and his mind wondered for the moment as he focused on his deceased wife, Ellen, and his daughter, Diana. He was speechless while trying to gain his composure. Directing his thoughts to the subject at hand, he wiped away the tears trickling down his cheeks and said, "It's just that we must move ahead, as Brother has asked us to do. Persevere, regardless of the deadlines that have been set for us or the obstacles which may be in our path. Not to mention the large number of nonbelievers we will encounter along the way. And Peter, my dear brother, Peter you will lead us. You undoubtedly are the right man for the job."

Thomas was the first to get to his feet and praise his friend, Andrew, whose brief, albeit articulate speech, would serve as a rally-ing point for the remainder of the evening. It took less than ten sec-onds for the entire group to join in, each of them standing and echoing the dressmaker's accolades for the elder of the Albano brothers. They complimented him for what he said and for the passion in which he delivered his short and to-the-point oration. Of course, Andrew's sen-sitive reaction came from recollections of his dear wife and child, which the others were not aware of, except for Peter, who had con-soled Andrew many times since the tragic car accident. But beyond his personal grief, Andrew had spoken with love for his fellow man.

Thomas added, "Andrew, you just might want to consider giving up that foul-smelling boat and becoming a professional speaker. Yes, off the boat and onto the stage. What do you think?"

The elder Albano brother could only smile at Thomas's remarks, but was appreciative of the support the entire group displayed for Peter. These signs of affection and heartwarming gestures strengthened the newly formed friendships. Friendships created out of necessity, perhaps, but based on a solid foundation. Friendships established with a singleness of purpose in mind. Nevertheless, friendships which would have to endure many curves in the serpentine road ahead.

Next it was Matthew's turn to take the floor. "Each of our newfound friendships could unknowingly be characterized by an outsider as fragile, untested, unsound, and potentially brittle enough to snap with the first encounter of adversity. Any pragmatic thinker would never in his right mind believe these relationships could persevere over any extended period of time, especially with the monumental task lying ahead of this diversified group. We've different ethnic backgrounds, each with his or her own unique culture -- not to mention distinct differences in our financial status. Although, even the richest of men and women might forget about their wealth, at least for the moment.

"And the most critical barrier, the vast divergence in religions that this group, now thirteen strong, believes in. No. No one would expect this unproved, blended congregation to survive intact. The odds makers in Las Vegas, who make point spreads on just about any form of gambling, wouldn't touch this bet with a ten-foot pole.

James Thompson said, "All of us must understand instinctively that our survival as a group and ability to fulfill this colossal assignment depends on the trust and faith we have in one another. Over the next few days, and perhaps for years to come, this group will be tried and tested by religious leaders on every continent. The media will be reporting and printing every word we speak, and possibly, if not probably, many words we don't say. The public, on the other hand, will be following our every move from day to day, from city to city, from country to country. All of us must understand, we will have to lean on each other's shoulders for support, in addition to seeking one another's counsel."

Fifteen minutes had passed since Peter last spoke. Fifteen minutes devoted to reassuring themselves about their ability to carry out the mission Brother had asked them to perform. Fifteen minutes to reassert themselves as an inseparable group and to confirm and assure

Peter he was their leader. And so, after this seemingly long diversion, Peter picked up the remaining pages and continued with Brother's e-mail.

Brother had put in writing what he had discussed with them the night before: essentially, his description of the progress mankind had made over the past two thousand years. Peter's initial thought was to just highlight what Brother had already told them. But for Pauline's benefit, he decided to read the entire eight pages, word for word. He explained to the others this was necessary to bring Pauline up to date, and asked that they be patient. All the men were as attentive as they had been when Brother had spoken to them the night before; and they felt as much in awe of Brother's words, even though they were hearing them for the second time. Hearing Brother's every well-chosen word describing man's virtues, deficiencies, and failures captivated the entire group. As for Pauline, little doubt remained in her mind that the author of this text was Jesus Christ. She committed herself completely to him and waited on the edge of her chair, anxious to hear the balance of his letter.

Peter's articulation and eloquence as he spoke Brother's words elevated him to a new position of eminence, but not by design, for that was the last thing he wanted to see happen. Peter accepted the leadership role though his wish was to be treated no differently than anyone else in the group. He read the last paragraph of this segment of Brother's e-mail out loud to this fervent group already filled with anxiety.

"You now know Father's thoughts on the state of the world. Peter, I would think these points should be conveyed during tomorrow morning's conference call. I trust these issues do not intimidate the newcomer to the group."

Pauline blushed ever so slightly but assured Peter, with a nod of her head and an infectious smile, that she was up to accepting the challenge.

Peter read further. "Your charge, my dear friends, is to go out and deliver Father's message. Convince the leadership of each nation as well as the preeminent religious leaders of every faith to heed his advice. Inform them to enlist the support and the financial aid of the haves, and the time and attention of the have-nots. Tell them to monitor the efforts of their administrators and see to it that appropriate progress is achieved. Time is of the essence! As I told you earlier, Father expects these changes to be implemented before the end of the first year of the new millennium. The fine tuning can be installed at a later date."

Peter choked back as he read Brother's next comment. "But hear me now and hear me well, if Father does not see any significant improvements, he will inject his rage and fury throughout every corner of the earth. Not with the forces of nature, such as earthquakes, fire, or floods, which humankind is anticipating will destroy his planet. Oh no, examples demonstrating his anger should the masses not respond to his requests will be of a much greater magnitude than the destructive natural disasters predicted by your prophets and soothsayers, whose unfounded and groundless revelations are more often than not without merit.

"Father's wrath will be revealed in a very subtle fashion. It will attack and torment the most sensitive and very core of mankind's existence. His vanity! The most susceptible and arguably the most cherished part of each individual's emotional stream. Be assured, the outcome will be deteriorating, degenerating, disheartening, degrading, and debilitating."

At this, the entire group was confused and unsettled. The thought on each of their minds was what could Father possibly mean by this? The five D words, as they would be referred to later, certainly struck a chord in each of their minds and hearts.

Some of the men got up from their chairs and began pacing around the room, pondering why Father, who was thought to be so forgiving, had come up with this morbid plan to punish humankind.

Jim Albright said, "And I always believed fire, floods, and earthquakes would destroy humankind."

"When will he tell us what he has contrived?"asked John. "Perhaps there will be more details regarding his plan at the end of Brother's letter."

"Yes! That's it! He surely will inform us what he means by all this at the end of the letter,"added his brother, James.

Thomas and Andrew pleaded with the others to return to their seats so Peter could continue with the reading. Pauline remained in her chair, more positive than ever she was hearing the words of Father. It took about ten minutes for the group to return to some sense of normalcy. In spite of having failed to understand Father's grand scheme if society declined to adhere to his doctrine, each of them realized that they quite possibly were the only hope humankind had.

Thaddaeus wanted so desperately to retract his earlier thoughts regarding the "what if." For a moment, he felt responsible for bringing up the issue in the first place, and his chin sunk to his chest. Only a friendly nudge in the ribs and a heartwarming grunt from Philip sitting next to him returned Thaddaeus to reality. The Chilean engineer set the American engineer's mind at ease when he placed his arm around his shoulder. Although Philip said nothing, the compassionate look on his face was all that was required to assure Thaddaeus that the consequences of "what if" were no fault of his.

Peter, sensing the members of the group had regained control of their emotions, raised his hand, holding up the last few pages to signify he was ready to continue reading.

"What is to happen will not take place overnight. Instead, each day will bring more grief and suffering for society to agonize over. I can understand your desire to know what Father has planned. But as I have stated before, his wishes are not to reveal his intentions to you at this time."

As Peter finished reading the ninth page, Matthew, with contempt in his eyes for what he had been hearing over the last few minutes, interrupted him. The *Time* reporter arose once again from his chair and pounded his fist on the table. He asked with a tinge of sarcasm, which was completely out of character for him, "As upset as I am regarding Father's punitive course of action if we fail, I would appreciate knowing if Brother took the time to answer our questions."

Jim chimed in, supporting his co-writer. Although the Australian was much more in control of his emotions than Matthew, he too realized there were only three pages left to be read. He said, "Peter, I am and forever will be a believer in Brother; but he did promise to give us a response to the slate of questions we prepared. Before you read any further, could you see if there is any reference to them?"

Even though he still felt in control, Peter reasoned he'd best look ahead to see if Brother had in fact addressed the questions Matthew and Jim had written, sensing the last few pages of Brother's e-mail had taken its toll on the group. Scanning the pages before reading their contents out loud, he assured the entire group Brother had indeed responded to the slate of questions. The tension and strain on Peter's face did not go unnoticed by his brother, Andrew, who mentioned this to Thomas. Before his younger brother had an opportunity to continue, Andrew suggested the group take a short break. Thomas seconded the idea. Peter nodded his head in agreement.

In no more than ten seconds, the members of the group arose from the table and dispersed throughout the room. In twos and threes, they gathered to discuss all they had heard. As one might imagine, some of the conversations were calmly discussed, a few developed into loud debates, while others grew into shouting matches.

TWENTY SIX

The religious, the curious, and those vacationers caught up in this saga soon numbered in the hundreds of thousands. They lined the streets of South Beach, causing traffic to come to a complete stop throughout the entire Miami Beach area. Police closed the causeways and actually began the process of turning traffic around, which was currently in a gridlock on all the access roads to the beach. All the major streets in South Beach, including Alton Road, Washington Avenue, Collins Avenue, and Ocean Drive, capitulated to the thousands of vehicles going nowhere. People left their cars in traffic and began to walk. Sidewalks and streets were inundated, as the crowds inched their way to the White Sand Hotel, where the Son of God was reported to be.

Tens of thousands trudged their way on the unlit sandy beach, as well. This is the route two bare-footed elderly gentlemen decided to take, one a Jew, the other a Muslim, both dressed smartly in contemporary clothing and each with a light garment bag strapped over his right shoulder. Shoes in hand, they walked arm in arm, holding one another for support. Now just a hundred yards east of this newest of shrines, though with the multitude of people surrounding the hotel it seemed like a hundred miles.

"How are we going to get in there?" asked Imam Muhammad Qutb.

"I'm not sure,"responded Rabbi Silverman. "But get in there we must."

The two holy men managed to make their way to the white stone retaining wall, where they sat for a moment to wipe the sand off their feet and put their shoes on. Then they worked their way through the boisterous crowd to the brightly lit hotel parking lot. There they were stopped by several law enforcement agents, who numbered well into the hundreds and had been assigned the difficult task of keeping control of the swarm of people lining the hotel's perimeter. The distinguished-looking gentleman with a gray beard informed a pleasant-looking officer who he and his associate were and pleaded with him to grant them entrance to the hotel. Rabbi Silverman explained that he and his associate were here for an important meeting and were expected.

Not being able to accommodate them, the officer raised his hands and apologized.

"May I talk to one of your supervisors, please?" the rabbi asked. The overworked and underpaid public servant turned away in hopes this kind-looking gentleman and his friend would disappear.

Rabbi Silverman said with a more authoritative tone, "It is of the utmost urgency that I talk to him."

Completely out of character, Imam Qutb yelled over the noise of the crowd, "At once."

The uniformed state policeman, stunned by the demands of these two slightly built men, spent little time deliberating about his next move.

"Captain Bryant," he petitioned on the radio strapped to his shoulder, "this is Officer Redman. Your presence is required at the south east end of the parking lot, at position number seven."

Within seconds, the captain responded, "Richard, is that you?"

"Yes, Captain."

"What seems to be the trouble?"

He explained to his superior the details of his problem, and he added for emphasis that he sensed the two men in question were on the level.

"Okay, Richard. But I'm currently up to my elbows in alligators at position number three. It will take me about ten minutes to get over there. Tell them to keep their shirts on."

"I copy, Captain."

Brother was totally aware of the slate of questions Matthew and Jim had prepared. For as Peter began reading to himself the last of the three remaining pages, it was quite obvious the principal member of the group, although not in attendance, was familiar with the subject matter of each one. True to his word, he had devoted the remainder of his e-mail to these profound inquiries. Not that all the answers would be appreciated or understood.

As Peter prepared to speak the words of Brother, Pauline and the men sat on the edge of their chairs, focused, one and all, without distraction, to listen to Peter's narration. Their ears were primed to absorb every word and capture any inflection in his voice. Their hearts, filled with passion and adoration, were open to accept the love and tenderness they anticipated in Brother's responses.

Peter glanced at each of them before he began to read further. "Oh yes, your questions. I've given your questions a lot of thought. And although my responses could be construed as somewhat ambiguous, trust me, the answers -- or what you might think is avoidance -- is for the benefit of mankind."

Peter continued reading. "First, let's talk about some of truths and myths reflected in the scriptures written in the *Bible*. Father is the Creator. He and he alone is responsible for all living things. He gave man life, and through the holy of the holiest, presented the human race with a code of laws to live by. Beginning with Abraham and again with Moses at Mount Sinai, Father made known his covenant with the Jewish people, and through them, humanity. An agreement designed to assist each man and woman in their everyday conduct. When you think about the commandments, they're rather simplistic. Just a few dos and don'ts to govern your thoughts and actions. Easy to read, elementary to comprehend, sometimes difficult to carry out. Hence we have transgressions.

"We pray to Father for the forgiveness of our sins, to clear our conscience of the wrongdoings we are guilty of. We pray for absolution to prepare ourselves for entrance into his eternal Kingdom of Heaven. Those who choose to live their lives in sin will unfortunately be subject to places less desirable. I trust this answers your questions regarding Heaven and Hell, as well as what I told you last night about the After Life and Judgment Day. Very simply, follow the rules in the good book, pray to Father for the forgiveness of your sins, and maintain a consistent life style, being kind to your fellow man and above all, keeping evil far removed from your every thought.

"As far as the accounts of my deeds while here on earth, believe what you will about what is written in the scriptures. Just understand, I received the power and might from Father which enable me to perform these acts of kindness and benevolence. Some refer to these acts as miracles, others perceive them as unexplainable phenomena. Again, believe what you will. For it is your acts and deeds that are important, not mine.

"The quest for the Holy Grail and the authentication of the Shroud of Turin continue to challenge the experienced archaeologists. The whereabouts of the cup I drank wine from with your namesakes two thousand years ago still baffles those who search for it. For ages, men have pursued this elusive chalice. In Turin, scientists have attempted many types of sophisticated tests over the years to prove or disprove whether or not this was my burial cloth. The answers to these mysteries perplex even the most astute theologians, but for me to respond to these questions would be breaching the ground rules of even the most tyro adventurer. Let them keep testing and searching for these so-called historic relics of the past. You, my dear friends, are only to remember I was born and died for the sake of mankind. If you believe in me, then fulfill your mission with the zeal and determination of those who search for the cup and examine the cloth."

Brother's approach to answering the questions thus far did not surprise Jim, certainly the most accomplished and experienced authority on Christianity in the group. To some of the others, especially Thomas and Bartholomew, it appeared Brother was avoiding answering their questions. Jim sensed the reaction of some of the less informed and explained to them, "The mystery of faith is what you believe but do not see. We, with the exception of Pauline, that is, have at least met with Brother and broken bread with him. Being religious requires unqualified belief and on occasion a vivid imagination."

Peter resumed reading. "There is only one true way. Father's way! To give credence to any other ideology is blasphemy. That is not to say some of the ancient spiritual philosophies practiced are considered an act of irreverence, because the majority of these peoples, who have little or no knowledge at all about Father, tend to live within the codes of law he expects all mankind to adhere to. You must make them understand that they can continue their spiritual lives, but they must be educated to learn about and venerate Father. This most demanding assignment also is your charge.

"The philosophical portion of the slate of inquires I will answer next. You've asked the following questions, which I will address collectively. What is the meaning of our existence? What is our purpose in life? Why does Father allow evil to exist? Why are there so many inequities in life? Why do so many of the good die young? Why are so many young children inflicted with terminal diseases and lifelong disfigurements? I commingled these questions since they all are answerable by mankind. The human race has the capability and capacity to address each and every one of these issues.

"Those with the talent and time to assemble with one another to address these profound issues have not dedicated themselves to finding the solutions to these subjects. Think tanks are created every day to deal with business or economic problems and political opportunities. But each of you should ask yourself this question: When did man last sit down with his neighbor to talk about the philosophy of life? Think about it! And mind you, don't wait for divine intervention, for none is forthcoming.

"Should the human race ever decide to select representatives to convene and sincerely discuss these issues, life in general would improve dramatically. Debate and discussion would replace conflicts and wars. Future battlefields would instead become beautiful parks for your senior citizens to stroll through and those precious little children to play in. And famine and poverty would be virtually eliminated in every corner of the earth. You can add your own thoughts to these.

"Yes, many are called at a very young age to await their time to enter the Gates of Heaven. No one has ever said this is a perfect world. Even Father in his infinite wisdom will attest to that. Birth defects related to genetic diseases continue to plague the innocent. In spite of the marvels of your scientists, the number of birth defects remains a universal problem. If only a single mother suffers because her infant child is afflicted with an incurable disease, it's one too many. Again, man can find a remedy to cure these sicknesses. It is quite apparent your researchers have developed the required technology to eliminate or at least reduce a number of these. All that is needed is to devote the necessary resources and manpower to come up with a solution to wipe out these afflictions. I wish that I could give you a better answer to this most difficult and complex question."

James Thompson, cognizant of the unusual and paradoxical answers to their questions, interrupted Peter before he continued. He sensed most of the group, if not all, were somewhat overwhelmed by the responses thus far. Certainly he was. A few of Brother's answers placed most of the onus on mankind to solve its own problems. These answers appeared ambiguous, but stimulated one's thought process. His answers were provoking, but in a strange sense inspiring. With a tone of reverence in his voice he said to Peter, "It seems Brother wants us to understand mankind truly is in control of his own destiny."

Simon added, "But don't you agree he has avoided responding to some of the questions?"

"On the contrary," James replied. "I believe his responses reflect the need for the human race to mature to a point where we will have the ability to answer most of these questions ourselves. Expand our minds to overcome the issues which malign and segregate society. Issues such as religion -- well, I believe that will be a harder sell. Especially to those who do not believe in Father."

"Thank you for your wisdom and simple explanation," Peter told James. "If no one has any other comments, I'll continue." Peter read from the next-to-last page.

"Science covers a broad range of topics, from medicine to exploring outer space. I touched on medicine earlier. Your question regarding euthanasia is a complex subject that the human race is currently faced with. My response to you is, let no man play the role of God. Taking a human life is not an acceptable means to an end. Yes, I can understand the position of relatives wishing to ease the pain of the terminally ill by turning off the life support system of those loved ones in death's doorway. This is an area which is quite perplexing, where science and religion cross paths. Each of you faced with this difficult decision must do so with the help of your doctor and clergyman. But as I said before, let no man take the life of another indiscriminately.

"Which leads me to your very serious and timely question regarding abortion. This subject has divided men and women everywhere into two distinct camps, those who are totally against this procedure and those who support it. I unequivocally am opposed to this medical procedure. But I'll qualify my statement by adding that the medical profession as well as the clergy should create a simple formula to a very complex problem -- one that permits abortions be performed on only the rarest of occasions. A woman who has conceived a child does not have the right to snuff out the very breath of the unborn simply because she does not want it. No one should have the right to arbitrarily take the life of an unborn child.

"You've surprised me with the next one. As you so cleverly stated, destiny! Is the future in our hands or Father's? I'll respond to this perceptive question as clearly as possible. I wouldn't wait to the end of your life before making peace with Father. Fate is in your hands while you are here; but there is no question, he has the final word when you pass on. Do you get my point?

"The scientists studying early cultures and those seeking life in other galaxies spend many years and in some cases a lifetime searching for the unquestionable evidence to prove their positions. First, I'll address the subject of evolution. All I can say about those who subscribe to the theory of evolution is, everything changes. Including mankind, over the many centuries. Nonetheless, man is man and always has been. Perhaps he doesn't look the same as those who preceded him, but man he was and man he will always be! As far as life on other planets is concerned, exploring for it is not only intriguing, it's fascinating. And why should I spoil these space travelers' fun by telling them anything further. Let these astronauts continue to travel to the outer reaches of your solar system and beyond to see what they can find.

"As I informed you last night, I did not return to earth at the last millennium. Nor do I believe I'll be returning again, unless Father has other plans. Will you see me again? Quite possibly, though I can't say when; but you, my friends, are aware that some fine day you will all be standing before me. The day of judgment passes no one by. Retribution for your actions and deeds will be examined at that time."

Peter took a sip of coffee and a deep breath before continuing. All eyes continued to be focused on him as he began to read the last page.

"So, my friends, this brings us to my final thoughts. The task before you is a difficult one. Convincing leaders around the globe as well the religious hierarchy that I have returned will consume all your time over the next year. It will require each of you to travel to foreign lands to inform the populations of many countries what is expected of them. Most likely you will be ridiculed, taunted, and even castigated for your beliefs. But you must march on. You must persevere, regardless of the consequences. Time is of the essence!

"Try to make them understand that their perception of the apocalyptic revelations they have been led to believe, which foretell the destruction of life here on earth, are child's play compared to what Father has in store. As I said
earlier, if they fail to alter their life styles and significantly change the way they treat their fellow man, Father's wrath will be unrelenting. His rage will encompass the globe. There will be no hiding from his anger.

"Those of you who are married will accept this challenge with your spouses, sharing with your loved ones the adventures ahead of you, as well as the roadblocks which accompany them. Those of you who are single will abstain from joining together with a mate until the year has passed. Your sacrifices and devotion to Father will be rewarded in his eternal kingdom of heaven. Yes Andrew, with your loved ones! Bless you, my friends, and may each day bring success and glory for the good of mankind.

"Finally, every group needs to be commissioned with a fitting title. From this day forward, you shall be known as THE STEWARDS OF SOUTH BEACH."

Tears and smiles signified the mixed emotions at the conclusion of Brother's letter. Peter walked over to where Andrew was seated and placed both his hands on his brother's shoulders. This set off a true sign of friendship on the part of all the group, and they shook hands or hugged each other. Thomas shook Pauline's hand. She in turn embraced him, causing the somewhat shy Swedish dressmaker to blush and the two fishermen to grin. This aside, the aura emanating throughout the room captivated the imaginations of everyone at the table. They all realized their calling from Brother had changed their lives, perhaps forever; as would the seemingly impossible responsibility he had given them to convert billions of people within the matter of one year.

Philip asked, "Could someone please define the term 'steward'?"

Jim replied, "I believe Brother is asking us to take charge of his as well as Father's affairs here on earth."

"Yes, that would seem proper,"added John. "A steward could be categorized as one who acts as a manager for an absentee owner."

Philip said, "That certainly fits the bill."

The musical but normally quiet Bartholomew chimed in. "Now that you two gentlemen have been kind enough to give your definition of a steward, tell me what in God's name do we do next?"

"Yes,"echoed Judas, "what is our plan of action?"

James, always the businessman, stood up and said, "I've got things all worked out. First, all of us will sleep here at the hotel tonight. I believe we should keep away from the crowd outside as much as possible. Should anyone out there have any inkling that one of us is involved, there's a good chance he or she will be ... well, let's just say we are better off out of harm's way. Obviously, we must avoid the potential of injury or even controversy at this time, at all cost. With a few extra folding beds, we can probably accommodate four or five of you in our suite upstairs. As far as the rest of you are concerned, you can sack out right here in the meeting room. Oh, I forgot about you, Pauline. Perhaps our quick-thinking innkeeper can find a room for you."

"That's fine -- you worked out plans for sleeping, but what about tomorrow morning?"asked Bartholomew.

"What about tomorrow morning? We conduct the conference call exactly as Brother has asked us to do,"James replied.

The tones of voice displayed by the men raising the questions were an indication of how apprehensive and unsure some members of the group were. That's not to say they didn't believe Brother or were unwilling to proceed with the task ahead of them. They were understandably skeptical of their own ability to enact this monumental deed, not unlike Peter's reaction when asked to lead this group.

"And after that?"asked Judas.

Jim, whose inner strength appeared inexhaustible, stood up to respond to the last question. "I'll tell you what we'll do. First of all, we spend the next few days here in South Beach, reviewing each and every segment of Brother's letter. Second, a subcommittee within the group will arrange a schedule, including travel plans for us to visit every major city on the face of the earth, a plan so contrived to enable us to cover the entire globe within a six-month period. We will then proceed to meet with every religious leader and every head of state in every country on the planet. Sometimes alone, occasionally in small groups. The six months following we'll reserve to retrace our steps in order to validate our action plan. Whatever it may take to get the job done. If necessary, we'll go out again and again until we convince every man and woman that Father in his infinite wisdom wishes for mankind to change his ways."

"And may I ask," said Judas, "who is going to finance this globe trotting? The cost of all this traveling could easily run into hundreds of thousand of dollars."

Without any hesitation, Simon spoke up. "Well, I guess I can spare a diamond or two to pay for things."

John added, "I ..., I mean, my brother and I will most assuredly match Simon's generosity."

Thomas, wishing to provide his usual humor observed, "Of course we could always sail across the seven seas on the fishermen's boat, if worse comes to worse."

Peter picked up the debate once again. "Thank you for your comments, James, and for your generosity, Simon. As for you, dressmaker, just wait until I get you on board the Amalfi. I'll have you swabbing the decks from bow to stern."

Thomas reacted by smiling and saluting the first mate of the fishing boat.

"I apologize to those of you who don't know; Amalfi is the name of our boat," Peter added.

Andrew turned to his brother and whispered kiddingly, "Isn't it amazing, it's almost as if Thomas has somehow absorbed your sense of humor."

Peter responded, "That's just fine, brother. We're going to need all of his humor, as bizarre as it is, to help ease the tension over the next few days."

Andrew nodded in agreement but added, "Perhaps even longer than a few days, Peter."

"Suppose we can't get the religious and governmental leaders to listen to us," said Philip. "Or for that matter, let's assume they just take us for granted."

"What do you mean?"asked Andrew.

"Well, the way I see things, it's very possible some of these leaders will be gracious enough to give us an audience and then continue on their merry ways. They'll accommodate us, just so they don't lose face with the other world leaders. You can see what I mean, can't you?"

James responded to Philip's question by telling the group,"Point well taken. I agree completely with Philip. They'll most likely agree to extend an invitation for us to visit them, even spend time with us, per-haps at an elaborate state dinner. But the issue is, will they listen to what we have to say and implement the necessary programs to pro-duce the desired results Brother is seeking?"

Peter raised his hands to quiet the across-the-table conversations sparked by Philip's comments. "Okay, okay, I understand Philip's position, and thank you, James, for your added advice. The fact remains, lady and gentlemen, we must not let these issues distract us. Certainly there will be setbacks. There will be many obstacles in our path. Furthermore, there are unknowns that will test our strength as we proceed. Test our fortitude. Examine our faith and trust in Brother. And attempt to wear down our stamina as we strive to complete our assignment.

"There is no room for the weak as we move on to the next phase of this incredible challenge that Brother has hand-picked us for. A chal-lenge that will require each and every one in this group to leave self-doubt and the fear of the unknown behind. I will ask all of you only once. If you have any mistrust or are hesitant to proceed, I suggest you leave now. Don't wait until after we have formulated our plans. No one, I repeat, no one will think any less of anyone at this table if he or she backs out now and decides the task is too extreme. Or for that mat-ter, if you have any reason at all which you believe will prohibit you from fulfilling Brother's mission."

Andrew was stunned by his brother's comments. Not so much at what he said but how he delivered it. Peter, who before the meeting on the beach was a fun-loving guy with a "what me worry"attitude about life had made a one-hundred-and-eighty-degree turn. Even Thomas was taken aback at the extraordinary authority in his friend's voice. What neither of them knew was that the speaker himself was sur-prised by his own remarks. If Peter's desire was to get their attention, he hit the bull's eye. For the umpteenth time, the group needed emo-tional reinforcement, and that's exactly what Peter gave them. On this particular occasion, it felt like a kick in the shins and not the pat on the back they had grown accustomed to.

Moments later, the phone rang. It was Bob Anderson checking in with Matthew once again. "Nothing new up here, Matt, how about down there?"

"We just finished listening to Peter read Brother's e-mail."

"Anything new?"

"He answered our questions."

"Any revelations to make your hair stand on end?"

"Not something I would want to discuss over the phone with you."

"I understand. Can you secure a copy?"

"I don't see any reason why I shouldn't. Why, do you want the magazine to publish the answers?" Matthew continued, "I think we best tread slowly, at least until the group has an opportunity to reveal the answers to the clergy for their review."

Bob responded, "I'll talk to Max and get his stand on the subject."

"Okay, Bob, call me in the morning. Before eight o'clock. We'll be sleeping right here in the meeting room."

"Why there?"

"To avoid the mass of humanity outside the hotel."

"I see. There have been accounts of hundreds of thousands flocking to South Beach."

"That's what we've been told, Bob."

"Oh, before I sign off, Matt, have the two religious leaders from New York made it down there as yet?"

"You know, Bob, I completely forgot about them."

Before he hung up, Bob's advice to his friend and coworker, was to send out a search party for the two men.

Once more Dolores Quan received a call in her office from John.

"The only two things I can be sure of when you're on the other end of the phone is, one you want something and, two, whatever it is, it will cause me more grief and aggravation."

"Right on both accounts again, my dearest Dolores."

"Don't sweettalk me, John Thompson! What do you want?"

John described the sleeping arrangements the group had planned, emphasizing the special need for accommodations for Pauline.

"No problem with the beds. I'll have the bedding over within the hour. As far as Pauline, that's the television reporter, right? Well, she can bunk in my office with me. I'm sure not leaving here tonight! And as far as sleeping, you've got to be kidding. What else?"

"There are these two clergymen who flew to Miami from New York to see us. One is a rabbi, the other a muslim holy man. Chances are, the two of them are amongst the crowd outside. Could you...."

She stopped him and asked John their names before he could continue. "I'll see what I can do."

Captain Bryant and Officer Redman led the procession through the entrance to the hotel. Two additional uniformed officers, all six feet or taller, with nightsticks in hands, accompanied them. In the middle of this caravan were two slightly built elderly gentlemen, and Dolores Quan. Through the crowded lobby filled with reporters, local police, and federal agents, they made their way to the meeting room. Television cameras were turned on. Flash attachments illuminated the softly lit lobby, and overzealous reporters asked innumerable questions of the two holy men. Neither of them had ever been exposed to a scene like this before.

As for Dolores, she was getting used to this display of aggressive journalism -- which didn't mean she was enjoying it. The door opened to the meeting room, meaning the innkeeper had delivered once again. John thanked her and proceeded to usher Rabbi Marvin Silverman and Imam Muhammad Abdul Qutb to the table. After a round of introductions, Thaddaeus approached them.

"Would you care for a soft drink, coffee, wine or..."he paused for effect, "...Brother's favorite, Beck's beer."

"Coffee would be just fine,"responded the imam.

Surprised by the unusual manner in which Thaddaeus presented the menu of alternatives, the rabbi requested a soft drink.

Peter thanked the clergymen for joining them and requested they proceed without delay. He added, "It's almost midnight and surely the two of you are fatigued from the plane trip. As you can imagine, the last two days have been filled with an incredible amount of excitement. We have learned so much from Brother and have much to do ourselves, beginning with the conference call tomorrow morning, which I hope you gentlemen will stay for."

Rabbi Silverman responded, "With the crowds outside, I don't believe we have much choice but to stay."

"Okay then,"continued Peter. "We have many plans to consider as yet, which will require numerous hours of meetings. Therefore, I will ask Matthew and Jim to bring you up to date on what has transpired thus far. They will also attempt to answer any questions you may have. I hope this meets with your approval?"

Rabbi Silverman thanked Peter and indicated that the arrangements were fine.

"Good,"responded Peter. "Matthew, I think you and Jim should take our two new associates upstairs to James Thompson's suite. Answer any questions they may have, after which the four of you can sack out there. But before you go, I have a question for the rabbi. We've heard there are thousands of people outside the hotel. Is this true?"

"Perhaps hundreds of thousands,"he responded. "And possibly millions more on the way."

It shouldn't have shocked the men and woman at the table, but it did.

"Millions you say?"inquired Pauline.

Although she said no more, her eyes glistened at the thought of the scope and impact of this epic story. Pauline was extremely honored to be asked to be a part of Brother's group, but the reporter in her wished she could be broadcasting what was happening, to probably the largest audience ever to listen to a news story.

"I have a question for you, Peter,"asked the rabbi. "What did Thaddaeus mean?"

"As far as what?"

"This thing about Beck's beer?"

Peter smiled but held back from laughing out loud. "Matthew can fill you in on one of the more amusing events we've enjoyed over the last two days."

The two religious men were noticeably tired. The imam clutched Jim's arm for support as he and Matthew, with the rabbi on his arm made their way to the Thompsons' suite.

When they reached the privacy of the suite, Rabbi Silverman asked, "Do you honestly believe this man is really Jesus?"

Matthew replied, "Yes, rabbi, I do. I realize it is especially difficult for you men of the cloth to accept the fact that he has returned, particularly since,"as he looked directly at Rabbi Silverman and continued, "our faith never accepted him when he was here two thousand years ago!"

Rabbi Silverman asked, "Matthew, please tell us the entire story once again, from the beginning. Please, Jim, add any comments you'd like to make as well."

Both Jim and Matthew spent the next twenty minutes describing the events that had occurred, never wavering in their belief that all of it was true.

"And now you have accepted him as Jesus Christ?"asked Imam Qutb. Jim said, "Yes, we do. But honestly, all of us to a man have had our reservations. What he said to the group and the manner in which he did so has eliminated any doubt in my mind that he is truly Jesus."

"But surely you have heard great orators before. Couldn't this man just be an unusually gifted speaker or an accomplished stage actor?"asked Rabbi Silverman.

Matthew replied, "I've seen my share of Broadway plays, and God knows, a number of eloquent speakers, but this man is so much more persuasive and powerful when he talks, more so than anyone else I've ever listened to. More important, when he talks to us, his voice is full of such passion and warmth, a spiritual quality that can only come from someone close to God."

Jim added, "Who else could have orchestrated the gathering of all of these men from different countries with the same names as his apostles? Or speak in the manner that Matthew has described? Perhaps you can debate or discount portions of what has occurred in South Beach over the last two days, but placed together, it's impossible to undermine its authenticity."

Imam Qutb said, "Rabbi Silverman, Matthew and Jim most certainly believe they have been with Jesus."

"I believe you're right, imam. They most assuredly do, and their compelling story is beginning to make me a believer also."

Until three-thirty in the morning, the group pondered over the format for the conference call. Eventually it was decided that Pauline, with all of her television experience, would serve as emcee. Precisely at nine a.m. she would give an overview of what had occurred here in South Beach the last two days. Then Pauline would introduce Peter, who would reveal to those on the conference call, as well as the television audience, Father's message, after which Pauline would give a brief recap of Peter's presentation. She would then inform the world's leaders that Brother's stewards would be visiting them in person before long, and then close the meeting.

Dolores Quan, true to her word, had taken care of the sleeping arrangements. Not that it was very complex to handle, since many ofthe guests scheduled to check in either couldn't make it to South Beach or decided to find accommodations elsewhere. She instructed the hotel's housekeeper to make up rooms facing the rear section of the parking lot, since the noise level out front would keep even the soundest of sleepers awake. The ever-thoughtful innkeeper carted into the meeting room razors, toothbrushes, and two boxes of tee shirts and jogging pants in various sizes. Peter thanked her for all she had done for them. Thaddaeus chuckled when he picked up a shirt with a pink and blue logo on it entitled White Sand Hotel.

"Well,"Dolores replied, "I might as well get some free advertising out of all this."

"And that you will,"responded Peter.

Dolores and Pauline scurried through the maze of reporters and law enforcement agents to a second floor suite. On the way, Pauline commented to a few of the reporters she knew, "Doesn't the press ever go to sleep?"

They filled her head with questions, ranging from the obvious to the ridiculous.

"Tomorrow at nine a.m.,"Pauline responded. "Nine sharp,"she repeated, as she walked rapidly past her ever-aggressive media colleagues.

When they arrived at their room, the two women tried to get some sleep, but each felt as if she had consumed an overdose of caffeine. They talked for forty-five minutes before finally giving in to what was to be less than a three-hour sleep.

TWENTY SEVEN

Matthew and Jim stopped by the lobby to pick up a newspaper before heading for the meeting room. They had spent an hour and a half late last night with Rabbi Silverman and Imam Qutb, and Matthew sensed that both men had been satisfied with the responses he and Jim made. Imam Qutb desired to see a copy of Brother's e-mail and suggested the two holy men sit in as Peter conducted the conference call. Rabbi Silverman agreed, but first he wanted to telephone Cardinal O'Connor to inform him of what he and the imam had seen and been told. Jim looked at his watch as he and Matthew entered the meeting room, noticed it was seven-thirty, and was a bit surprised the others weren't there.

The room was cluttered with papers, and unfinished coffee cups lined the table like pawns on a chess board.

"It must have been a late night," Matthew remarked.

"Jim, trying to find a clear spot on the table. "Just look at that headline!"

The *Miami Herald* had reported in one-inch type:

"CHRIST ON THE BEACH
TO ADDRESS THE WORLD"

Jim continued reading Florida's largest newspaper, which related the sketchy details of what was occurring in South Beach. The paper even mentioned the hotel and speculated on the contents of this morning's conference call.

"A fairly accurate report," Jim said.

Matthew replied cynically, "Just wait until the tabloids put out their editions."

Newspapers virtually everywhere printed similar stories, although the media in countries composed mainly of spiritual worshippers, such as Japan, India, and China, gave less emphasis to this account of Brother's return or of his upcoming speech. Naturally, those countries still under the rule of tyrants and dictators who still maintained control over the press managed to suppress any news regarding Brother entirely.

Two by two the rest of the group appeared, eyes with red streaks and faces drawn from the lack of sleep.

Matthew asked, "I thought you guys were going to sleep in here?"

Andrew replied, "We were. But the snoring was so loud we ended up pleading our case to Dolores, who managed to find us some vacated rooms. Seems the noise in and around the hotel disturbed some of their guests."

Small talk centered on the reporters, who appeared to be in a trance from staying awake most of the night. Dolores Quan escorted Pauline to the room, who chuckled when she entered. The men's uniform of the day seem to be pink shirts and white jogging pants. She commented to Peter, "All we need is a Nike contract to complement our wardrobe."

Peter smiled but was obviously preoccupied by the enormous responsibility that lay ahead of him.

Waiters entered to deliver food, along with their assistants to clean up the remains of last night's dinner. They were followed by technicians and the sales representative from the telephone company, all there to assist in the hook-up of the conference call. How all these loyal and dedicated employees managed to make their way to the hotel was quite an achievement and would take hours to explain. The crowded room was abuzz with activity as the critical hour approached.

The imam and the rabbi were the next to make an appearance. Their bloodshot eyes matched those of the others. The only difference in appearance were the shirts and slacks worn by the holy men, in disregard for the group's uniform-of-the-day. Helping themselves to a cup of coffee, the holy men were surprised by all the goings-on.

Peter asked, "I hope you slept well? More important, I trust all of your questions were answered by Matthew and Jim?"

Imam Qutb assured Peter, "Your two associates answered our questions in detail. Mind you," the Muslim teacher added, "that's not to say either of us fully understand why Brother has chosen this path to deliver Allah's tenet."

"Nor do we," responded Peter.

Pauline, coffee cup in hand, walked with the ever-present federal agents to the front door of the hotel. She was searching for the CNN television crew that had been assigned to cover this story with her yesterday. It had been decided early this morning, at Pauline's suggestion, to have Peter's presentation televised worldwide to the public. To the right of the front entrance Pauline located her trustworthy troop taking footage of the massive crowd. The CNN van doubled as the place where Pauline's coworkers had spent the night.

In an authoritative tone to her voice, she petitioned the police captain to permit her colleagues entrance to the hotel.

"What's going on?" her producer asked.

"Get the equipment, I'll tell you inside."

As they made their way through the mob, the catcalls from the other network camera crews bordered on the obscene. Although she told the competition nothing, Pauline realized she was compelled to share the feed for this historic event with the networks. Yet this young woman, who was to become the principal speaker for Brother's stewards, knew deep down her first responsibility was to Brother and not CNN.

Around the globe, heads of state and religious leaders waited patiently, albeit with great trepidation, to hear Brother speak. Interpreters were on hand to translate the oration from English to the language of their respective countries. Even in those countries that were predominately non-believers in Father, anticipation was felt. In the Vatican, his holiness the Pope was surrounded by his immediate staff as well as by prominent theologians from every corner of Rome, all waiting anxiously. The United Nations General Assembly convened to listen to what was described as a speech for all mankind.

Television audiences everywhere, regardless of the time of day, sat motionless in front of their sets, some praying for absolution, expecting Brother to announce the end of world. Some viewers were simply curious about all the goings-on in the southeast peninsula of the United States, while millions of others tuned in to see and hear the anointed one. What could he want to tell them?

The cameras focused in on an empty lectern with block letters prominently located on its facing, reading:

The White Sand Hotel
South Beach, Florida

Precisely at nine o'clock eastern standard time, a young lady appeared, much to the surprise of the millions viewing as well as those state leaders watching via videoconferencing. Off to the side, out of camera range, sat two distinguished religious leaders -- one a Jew, the other a Muslim -- along with Brother's twenty-first-century disciples. Thomas, who was totally captivated by the beautiful Pauline, sat on the edge of his chair, joining the others who watched intently as she projected a beam of self-confidence.

Pauline's meticulous description of the events leading to the conference call was impressive. She possessed the natural ability to illustrate a simple chronological account of what had occurred, and to transmit in reverence, without pontificating, the fact she and twelve men had been selected by Brother. It was apparent to the rest of the group that Pauline would play a significant role in the scheme of things from here on in.

Peter, on the other hand, possessed a minimal amount of that natural talent to speak to an audience. Instead, he relied on a newfound inner strength, which projected passion and fervor. The warmth in his voice depicted an expression of Peter's true belief and devotion to Brother. He addressed the obvious question, why had Brother not conveyed Father's message in person? "Brother spent the better part of two days with most of us,"said Peter. "He sat on the beach with us, had breakfast and dinner with us. In the simplest form imaginable, he explained in detail why he had returned and what it was he expects us to achieve."

Peter was as candid as one could be, adding, "I believe there is a valid explanation for promoting one of us to speak for him. I sense he wishes for us to solve our own problems. To change our life styles and, most important, to face up to the challenges before us."Peter, whose voice had somehow acquired a distinctive quality displayed by only the greatest of orators, said, "We are certainly capable of addressing the issues, solving the problems, and paying homage to the Lord, God."

Andrew, listening to his younger brother, was full of emotion as tears of joy and pride rolled down his cheeks. Of course, of prime concern to all those involved was -- what did the rest of the world believe? That, only time would tell. But for now, standing before the cameras, Peter Albano was charged with the responsibility of convincing those listening that the Son of God had indeed returned.

He ended as he began, stressing the importance of heeding Father's words and reiterating the "what if"with the same intensity as Brother had. Without attempting to duplicate it, Peter emphasized the gravity in Brother's voice when he informed the audience of his concern for mankind; his fear of what would happen in the event people didn't conform to Father's demands; and the belief that Father's rage was waiting in the wings if mankind failed to listen.

He closed his speech by adding, "Our mission is unparalleled, our travels will be arduous, and as I stated before, the time frame we have been given is extremely brief. We will need the cooperation of all of you."

Peter thanked those viewing, relieved that his segment of the conference was completed. He froze in place, exhibiting his nervousness by perspiring through his new pink tee shirt. At the same time, he clumsily shuffled Brother's letter in front of him. The television camera scanned the meeting room where the iman, the rabbi, and the other stewards where sitting. Pauline, with her great stage presence, was on the scene to conduct the remainder of the conference call. She literally had to physically push the fisherman-turned-speaker away from the lectern to continue the presentation. Pauline was smooth and at ease as she recapped Peter's presentation. It was almost as if she were born to be in front of a camera. Thomas watched in awe of the young Greek-American as she confidently highlighted the critical points of Peter's address.

"Members of the group will be visiting governmental and religious leaders throughout the world within the next few weeks. We will not be taking any questions at this time; but if you like, you can communicate with us...." She went on to advise those listening of the stewards' fax number and e-mail address:

ritehanman@stew.com

She concluded by asking everyone to keep an open mind. Furthermore, Pauline suggested in an unrehearsed comment, "I think it would be wise of those of you in power to begin enacting whatever it may take to change things for the better in your respective countries." Pauline raised her hands, and with a visible look of apprehension on her face she said, "Take the initiative. Heed Father's warning. Let us not wait to sample his rage. Time is of the essence." She paused for a few seconds, sincerity gleaming in her eyes as she concluded, "Thank you for listening."

The cameras and their glaring lights were turned off. Pauline was embraced by her CNN co-workers. She thanked them as they left the meeting room. They suspected their friend and associate would probably never work with them again. Their seasoned producer and highly skilled cameraman knew at a glance that this young lady, still inexperienced, was on the ride of her life, one that would elevate her to untold heights. The telephone crew, still in a state of shock from being a part of this historic event, began the laborious task of breaking down the videoconferencing equipment.

Each of the stewards was quick to display his sincere congratulations to Peter and Pauline. The forty-five-minute presentation had been concise and to the point, and it had been delivered in a manner all who were listening could comprehend.

"Brother, wherever he is, has to be elated,"said John aloud.

"I agree,"said Philip."Peter, you and Pauline delivered his thoughts extremely well. I hope you don't misunderstand me when I say I do wish Brother had stayed on to speak. They were expecting Brother and he didn't appear. Just his presence would have been enough to convince even the most profound skeptic. Do you see what I mean?" Before anyone could respond to his question, Philip went on to say, "The fact he didn't speak places a suspicion on this entire saga. Furthermore, I'm just not sure people will take to heart anything we have told them today, or for that matter, what we try to tell them in the future. Especially when we visit them in their home countries."

"It won't be easy,"observed James.

"Please,"said Peter, "let us sit at the table and discuss this point further."Coffee was poured, and when the men finally settled down, Peter added, "No one ever said it would be easy. But on we must proceed, as he has asked us to. We'll go from country to country. Religious leaders and heads of state will hear what we have to say. We'll tell them over and over again until we convince each of them that Brother had indeed returned. And for their good and the welfare of all their people, they best adhere to his demands."

Rabbi Silverman asked, "May I say a few words?"

"Please,"responded Peter. "Speaking for the group, we would sincerely appreciate your comments."

"Thank you, Peter. I, like the teacher you refer to as Brother, can understand why he has entrusted the group to speak for him. Imam Qutb and I both concur, he has chosen this approach to test mankind. We believe he wishes for mankind to lift itself off the desecrated soil of our planet, a land tarnished with hate, bigotry, cynicism, and envy, to name just a few of our transgressions. We have placed ourselves in this unfortunate position. It is now up to us to cleanse the earth of our sinful ways."

Imam Qutb added,"In spite of the differences in our religious backgrounds, the one common denominator flowing through them is, of course, Allah, regardless of how we address him or whether it is through the eyes of Muhammad, Abraham, or the teacher who calls himself Brother. These great men, who symbolize our three unique religions, are all faithful to and revere the same God. Rabbi Silverman and I want you to know, we will be honored to assist you in any way possible. Even to the extent of accompanying you stewards in your travels to talk to people who have religious beliefs similar to the rabbi's and mine. Also, we intend to inform the cardinal and the rest of the religious leaders on his eminence's committee that we believe you did see and meet with Brother."

Rabbi Silverman added, "We will also recommend that the cardinal and the others follow our lead and escort you through every country with religions akin to theirs."

Imam Qutb said, "Even those countries where Allah is not worshipped will be traveled to, in hopes of informing the people of these spiritual countries of what has occurred. I for one would be most obliged to escort you to Mecca and the countless countries whose people worship Allah."

Peter thanked the two holy men for their comments and their willingness to escort the stewards on their incredible journey, one that would most likely take them around the planet many times, visiting people of all races and religions, believers and non-believers. The presence of clergymen would unquestionably enhance the steward's chances of convincing the many skeptics they would encounter.

Judas asked, "I wonder if they believe us?"

"Who precisely are you referring to?" asked James.

"Those hundreds of government and religious leaders whom we spoke to. After all," he continued, "if we can't convince them ... why I guess we will have...."

Pauline, the newly appointed spokesperson for the group interrupted and confidently asserted, "Gentlemen, we will convince them. Peter was correct when he stated it would not be easy. We must have confidence in each other and trust the wisdom and faith of Brother. Self-doubt at this juncture will cause this group to fade into oblivion. The roads to achieving our goal will possess many pitfalls. My intuition tells me we will encounter many failures before we accomplish our objective. Perhaps we may even sample a bit of Father's wrath before succeeding. But succeed we must, for this is the mission Brother has asked us to carry out. We dare not fail."

Judas, in a more demanding tone, asked again, "You have yet to answer my question. How do we know if the many leaders who were listening believe what you and Peter have told them?"

"Take it easy, Judas," Peter responded. "I'm sure we'd all like to know the answer to that question."

Matthew added, "I think it's about time to contact Bob Anderson to see if the State Department has had any feedback."

John intervened. "Let's see if we have any idea of just how people are reacting. I'll check to see if there are any faxes or e-mail."

Philip, Thaddaeus, and John walked rapidly toward the tables housing the computers. The four fax machines were chiming like a carillon, and a peal of bells blended together to play a most enchanting tune. The amount of e-mail was overwhelming, numbering in the thousands. The numerous quantity of questions and comments to ritehanman, was tying up traffic on the entire Internet.

Printers were hard at work, producing hard copies of the incoming e-mail. Stacks of paper began to overburden the cradles. James was first to reach for a pile and began reading the comments. "This is from someone calling herself 42atis jane. Very creative name," he announced. "She says, 'I have always been a true believer in God. Your speech only serves to strengthen my faith in him.'" He continued but dispensed with the reading of the other senders' names. "Brother has returned, I'm on my way to South Beach to see him." And the next one: "I have not been a religious person up until today and now I realize why, you bunch of cornballs." And from a priest in Canada, "How can I help you with your important work?"

Andrew and Peter, along with John, took turns reading the diversified reactions to the television broadcast. The emotional swings covered the entire spectrum. Many were very supportive, a few wished for more information. As they read on, thousands of messages contained prayers in a variety of languages and represented many religious preferences. Still others asked questions as to why Brother did not choose to meet with the Pope. If the end of life as we know it was near, why did he come to South Beach and not Jerusalem? What does he look like? Does he resemble the portraits and statues displayed in churches?

Some with terminally ill relatives wrote that they were on the way to the White Sand Hotel in South Beach to see him at his newest shrine. As you can imagine, the number of non-believers reveled in the fact that Brother did not conduct the presentation. Calling the entire situation a sham. Jokesters, wannabes, and cynics had a field day, using the Internet to defame the Son of God and his twenty-first-century disciples.

But for the most part, the reaction was extremely positive. Well-wishers from all across the globe sent e-mails supporting the efforts of the stewards. They even received comments from Buddhists, Hindus, and those practicing Shinto, who desired to know more about Father. Pauline and the men, including the rabbi and the imam, spent a half hour reading through stacks of e-mail and faxes. They would still be sifting through the mounds of paper three days later.

The reaction warmed the hearts of Peter and the rest of Brother's hand-picked group. His STEWARDS. The words of encouragement helped to build confidence in each of them, so much so that they could even laugh at a few of the humorous comments, including one which wanted to know if Brother would be available to speak at a ladies tea.

Rabbi Silverman's phone call to Cardinal O'Connor was brief. The rabbi explained to his friend and contemporary that both he and Imam Qutb believed this man who appeared in South Beach was truly Jesus Christ. The stewards, as he referred to them, had a very ambitious task facing them, and he and Imam Qutb would be traveling alongside these individuals to any destination where they could be of help. They would travel anywhere as often as they were needed and he advised his eminence and the Lutheran bishop to do the same. Both he and the imam had every intention of staying in South Beach for the next few days to collaborate and help guide the stewards.

Matthew finally got through to Bob Anderson, who had spent the night at *Time* magazine's headquarters. "Have you heard from the State Department as yet?"

"As a matter of fact, Matt, I just got off the phone with Max. He spoke with George Cooledge just a few minutes ago."

"Well, what's the reaction?"

"Just as you'd expect from a bunch of politicians. The majority of wires coming in are quite favorable, while a few are apprehensive, but open minded. I understand the Pope would like to meet with Peter. Of course, they'd all like to deal with Brother directly."

"That's not possible," replied Matthew. "I'm not certain he plans to reappear."

"I gathered that when I saw Peter and Pauline on the screen this morning."

"You won't believe the amount of e-mail we've received."

"I can imagine. How has the public responded?"

"Mostly positive, I'd say, but there are a number of negative comments as well. The concern I have is the number of people who plan to visit South Beach wanting to see Brother. I think you'd best pass on to George Cooledge the need for additional security, based on what we've seen thus far."

"Good idea. I'll bet they have already planned on that."

"I hope so. When you talk to George, ask him if the State Department would be kind enough to assist us with our travel schedule."

"What do you need?"

"Well, I'm sure some members of the group will need passports, although I believe mine is still current."

"I think he can handle that. What else?"

"I realize this is a laborious task, but could you ask him if he would be willing to set up meetings with the heads of state. We have worked out a travel plan which I'll fax to you. Tell George, anything he can do to facilitate our trek around the planet would be greatly appreciated."

"I'll see what I can do."

"By the way Bob, how did the President react to the call?"

"From what Max has told me, he was extremely enthusiastic. But he also remarked that he had great reservations about Peter's ability to convince a few leaders who are inflexible on most topics, let alone one so profound as this."

"That doesn't surprise me at all. We'll have to meet with those disagreeable individuals over and over again until they do heed Father's words."

"The Secretary of State was more explicit. She sensed most of the heads of state would be compelled to make revisions in their social programs because of the pressure placed on them by their citizens. Besides, the religious leaders will more than likely exert an incredible amount of pressure on them, but Madam Secretary was also realistic, citing a number of instances in which certain leaders would just as soon start a conflict before making any positive modifications. When do you plan to begin your road show?"

"We intend to visit the first of our targeted cities right after the first of the year. Or shall I say, the first of the century?"

"I'll call you as soon as I hear back from George Cooledge."Bob continued, "Oh, I meant to tell you, we are putting a special edition together. I trust you will supply us with the details from South Beach for the story."

"Certainly, Bob. By the way, doesn't Brother's e-mail address have an eternal ring to it?

Bob replied, "Very original. Perhaps I should ask him to write the story?"

"Sure, Bob. Talk to you later."

TWENTY EIGHT

Seventy-two hours had passed since the masses were told about Brother's return. The headlines were no longer making reference to South Beach, Brother, or of his return. The news coverage of this historic event shifted instead to the C section of the dailies, where religion and feature stories were typically found. Of course, that wasn't the case with the tabloids. The front page captions on these widely read weekly editions ranged anywhere from: **THE END IS NEAR** to **AN EXCLUSIVE INTERVIEW WITH JESUS**. Doctored pictures showing Brother standing, arms extended, some hundred yards out in the Atlantic Ocean.

Television news anchors continued to make mention of what had occurred but they did not dwell on the subject, which had been so newsworthy just a mere three days before. Although the likes of *Dateline, Sixty Minutes,* and *Prime Time* continued to present feature stories. Weekly magazines made the most of things, with glossy covers picturing South Beach and the masses gathered there.

Time magazine cashed in too, with a special man-of-the-year edition. The cover depicted a painting of Brother as most Christians have perceived him to look like for all two thousand years, surrounded by colored sketches of the twelve men, as reported by Matthew, in oval-shaped inserts. On the bottom right-hand corner appeared a square with a likeness of Pauline Demitri. The caption heading the cover was entitled

THE MAN OF THE AGES
AND HIS STEWARDS

Circulation at *Time* broke all records. This was consistent with circulation of all the other major publications, which surpassed their high-water marks as well. Retailers' magazine racks were barren. Customers pleaded with unhappy vendors for a copy of any of the week's magazines. But it was the *Time* issue with its unique cover that was sought after most. True to form, this cover would be framed and placed in a prominent place in millions of homes in every country.

Media from across the globe were actively seeking an interview with the stewards. From the *Today Show* to *Oprah*, to England's BBC, producers called, pleading for a representative of the group to appear on their shows. Halfway around the globe, agents for *The People's Daily*, Taiwan's daily newspaper, faxed requests soliciting an interview. There would be time for interviews, but not at the moment.

Three days of ironing out details of the steward's travel plans proved a tedious and exhausting exercise. Decisions about who would visit where were spelled out with workmanlike precision. George Cooledge was given the responsibility of overseeing the State Department's involvement, which consisted of coordinating each meeting between heads of state and members of the group. A very demanding schedule, with little time for rest, faced these dedicated stewards.

Brother's failure to appear had reduced the human pressure in South Beach. The crowds began to dissipate almost as quickly as they had emerged. That's not to say things returned to normal on this late December day. Many of the faithful, and those who were just curious in case he might return, managed to extend the area's population to double its usual winter size. Traffic was moving once again, although at a snail's pace. The city did a commendable job in providing all the fundamental services required to keep the area functioning, maintaining security, and upholding sanitary conditions.

The beaches were being cleared of the tons of litter from the makeshift housing that had sprung up quickly. On the beach where all of this had begun, sun bathers soon replaced many of the curious and religious. Imam Qutb and Rabbi Silverman had returned to New York to meet with Cardinal O'Connor and Bishop Parker, pledging their unqualified support for the stewards in their travels before they departed.

In the all-too-familiar confines of the meeting room at the White Sand Hotel, the stewards were in need of a few hours of diversion. Peter suggested a day off, including an afternoon at the beach, to stretch their legs and absorb some sunshine. It seemed like an ideal manner in which to ease the stewards' tension and fill their lungs with some fresh air. One stipulation -- no discussion about what had occurred or the plans for the future.

Elsa Kessler arrived from Germany to join her husband, Bartholomew. Anna Silva would fly from Santiago to Miami later that afternoon to be reunited with Philip. Both men were perplexed as to how to explain to their wives what had happened. Of greater concern was how to tell Elsa and Anna that they would be traveling with their husbands to spread the word of the Lord. Bartholomew and Philip agreed to inform their wives together, for Brother's wishes were very specific -- the married men would have their wives accompany them. Both couples would first enjoy a brief vacation on the beautiful beaches of Miami, before proceeding on their demanding journey.

John was finally able to reach Mary Dellany by phone. The two met for breakfast at the hotel's coffee shop. In spite of what he had experienced over the last few days, his feelings toward Mary had not receded. Warm hellos were followed by a pointed question by the perceptive lady. Without any explanation, Mary asked her new heartthrob if he was one of those men.

"How did you know?" John asked.

"Just call it female intuition," she responded.

John spent the better part of an hour telling her about Brother and the other stewards. He had desperately wished for Mary to go with him as he traveled to his scheduled destinations. He mentioned this to Mary, although he realized it was an impossibility. She on the other hand did not feel worthy of accepting his invitation. Mary's tainted past, which she had decided not to tell him about yet, was still a stumbling block for her. John promised her they would reunite as soon as time allowed.

Southwesterly breezes were unusual for this time of year. Not a cloud could be seen. Only the high humidity kept the day from being classified as a perfect weather day. With the assistance of the ever-present Dolores Quan, the stewards managed to evade the few remaining members of the press corps who were still searching for more to this story, and the hundreds of faithful praying outside this South Beach shrine. Making their their way to the beach in small groups, the stewards settled on their customary location across the street from the Blue Crab restaurant.

Peter regained some of his prior flair and vitality, for as soon as he saw the captivating waters of the Atlantic, he raced to its edge and dived in. Andrew was pleased by this, and surmised his brother was finally getting an opportunity to release some of the mental pressure he had labored under the last few days.

Thomas accompanied Pauline, who was attired in a modest one-piece bathing suit; they spent time finding out what each other's likes and dislikes were.

Philip yearned for the hours to fly by so he could be once more with his adoring wife, Anna. Thaddaeus and Simon spoke openly about their ex-wives and children. Jim and Matthew's conversation centered on the literary world; both being prolific readers and on occasion frustrated authors. Judas thought back to last week's dinner with Connie, hoping somehow he could right all the wrongs in his life and convince her to marry him. James waded in the temperate shallow water. He needed this time of solitude to do some serious thinking, not only about his role as one of the stewards, but also about his personal life as well. Around noon, Bartholomew and John appeared, having had prior commitments; one with his wife, the other with a likely candidate for that position, Mary Dellany.

The ever-thoughtful Dolores Quan had overseen the preparation of a picnic lunch for the group. All that was required was a beer run. Andrew enlisted the services of Bartholomew and John, the two late arrivals, to assist him. As the three men waited for traffic on Ocean Drive to pass, they were startled by an engaging voice coming from behind the beaches' white stone retaining wall. An all-too familiar voice, full of kindness and warmth, which they had become accustomed to hearing some days before.

"No need to turn around, Andrew. I said, don't forget mine,"the voice repeated.

Andrew was elated! His face beamed with excitement. He knew exactly who it was and precisely what he wanted. Before the other two men could comment on what they had heard, traffic thinned out, allowing them to cross the busy street. As he made his way to the Blue Crab, Andrew's thoughts focused on Peter and the others. How surprised they would be to see him once more. Especially Peter. Understandably, he was curious as to just why Brother had returned. Had we stewards done something wrong? Perhaps he was not happy with the manner in which the conference call was conducted? Did we misrepresent him?

His concerns were interrupted by John. "Was that Brother?"

"It sounded just like him,"added Bartholomew.

His voice sparkling as Andrew responded, "He's with us once again."

Other than ordering the beverages, including the extra Beck's, the men asked no further questions or made any additional comments. With their hands holding trays of cups full of beer and soft drinks, they made their way back to the beach. The anticipation of seeing him once again lengthened their strides.

There, under a flowing palm tree bowed by years of gale force winds, Brother waited for them. Their faces radiated with exhilaration when they saw him. Brother greeted them with his ever-enchanting smile as he reached to help carry one of the two trays John had been juggling. He cut short Andrew's attempt to welcome him, making it clear with an obvious facial expression that he wished to wait until they reached the others before conversing with them. It was only a short walk in the tepid sand to where the remainder of the stewards had set up camp, blending in with the unsuspecting crowd on the beach.

The stewards were naturally surprised and did all they could to suppress their elation. The group gathered around him, sitting on their colorful beach towels -- all but Peter, who continued to swim the warm blue waters of the Atlantic, reaching the limits established by the observant lifeguard, who at that moment whistled for Peter to swim toward shore.

Thomas took little time introducing Pauline to Brother.

"My dear Pauline, you are a welcome addition to my distinguished stewards."

Although in awe of meeting Brother, Pauline maintained her composure and responded, "I am deeply honored you have chosen me and look forward to the challenge before us."

Brother assured her his selection was most appropriate.

Peter sensed something unusual was happening when he exited the water. Losing concentration momentarily, he was almost knocked to the wet sand by an exceptionally strong wave. Making his way to where the others were located, he heard the lifeguard blow three long blasts on her whistle, indicating some sort of trouble. Looking up at the stand housing the deeply sun-tanned young woman, Peter heard her warn of a waterspout approaching. She advised everyone to leave the beach at once.

When Peter turned to the southeast he saw this rare phenomenon gyrating directly toward the beach. All around him, bathers and sun worshippers alike picked up their belongings and raced for shelter across the street from the beach. Peter ran to where his brother, Andrew, and the others were sitting, only to notice they either hadn't heard or chose to disregard the lifeguard's warning.

"Let's get out of here,"Peter shouted, as he neared his friends. "Don't you see the waterspout out there?"

It was then he discovered Brother holding court with the others.

"Hello, Peter."

Peter's emotional capacity had been exhausted, what with a dangerous weather condition lurking over the ocean less than a mile from the beach, and the return of a man he had met there a few days ago.

"Brother, we must leave here at once,"Peter said. "A waterspout is headed in this direction."

All heads turned to view the spinning cyclone, seemingly stretching from the ocean to what appeared to be a clear blue sky above.

With little concern in his voice, Brother responded, "I know, Peter. There is no need to worry. It will not present a problem."

Peter's concerns were partially addressed, but even Brother could not put him completely at ease.

Ships anchored off the coast had already taken action to avoid the potentially deadly force of the waterspout. Seagulls took shelter on the roof tops of the hotels and restaurants on the other side of Ocean Drive. In either direction, north or south, one could see an empty beach that only a few minutes before had been filled with sunbathers. The sole small congregation that had not dislodged itself was made up of Brother and his stewards.

Sitting close together facing the twister, the stewards were both fascinated and understandably overwhelmed.

"Don't worry, it will dissipate before hitting shore,"Brother assured them. "Have faith, my friends, and just enjoy one of Mother Nature's majestic performances."

He looked at Peter with his penetrating eyes, comforting him that all would be okay. Thomas held Pauline's hand very tightly to lessen her fears and concern, frightened yet confident that their leader, who had reappeared, was in charge of the situation.

They could feel the gale force winds as the meteorological spectacle approached the shoreline. The orange and white rental umbrellas spun through the air like children's tops. Blowing sand tried unsuccessfully to work its way through their closed eyelids, but did sting the pores of their skin. Lying face down on their towels they endured the effects of the storm's rage. A suddenly darkened sky, the results of swirling sand rather than the abbreviated cloud cover above, cast an eerie pall over them, and the whipped up ocean water sprayed them until they were soaking wet. They lost track of time as they waited anxiously for things to return to normal. What appeared to them to last an hour was over in less than five minutes.

Brother's sanguine voice contained a playful tone to it as he told his stewards the worst was over. The waterspout had indeed dissipated, just as he had predicted. They arose and attempted to brush the uncomfortable mixture of sand and salt water from their clothing and their skin. Their hair took on the characteristics of a peculiar spiked look, resembling one of the current teenage fads. Not even Brother escaped nature's onslaught. He grinned as the stewards looked at the mixture of sand and water riveted to his skin and hair.

Up until this time, his facial features had been impossible to recall. But for a reason only he could explain, his stewards would remember him this way for all of eternity. Days later, James would offer this profound explanation to the others: "Perhaps he wanted us to remember him this way, full of humility, subjected to the elements as we were. Remembering him as the Son of God would not have the same meaning or represent who he truly is. Just a man!"

Peter, feeling somewhat sheepish for his lack of confidence in Brother's prophecy, apologized for giving in to his human frailty.

Combing his hair back with his hand, Brother replied, "I understand." He smiled as he added, "You might want to change your hair styles before you take to the road." When he said, "I know I'll have to rework mine also,"his stewards smiled too. "Now I'd like to say a few words. I wish to thank you for the manner in which you have all conducted yourselves thus far. Your action plan has been well conceived and you have managed to captivate millions of people in every corner of the earth."

"With a little help from you, Brother,"remarked Matthew.

"On the contrary,"he replied. "Perhaps I planted the seed, but it has been you gentlemen,"he paused as he bowed to Pauline, "and lady, who are responsible for taking things this far. You, my stewards, must take significant credit for all that has occurred. Without you, there is nothing but a void. Nothing but a continuation of the ever-present envy and evil, as well as the endless excesses that Father wants eliminated. Your conference call was delivered with enthusiasm and passion. I hope you have convinced many of the world leaders to at least meet with you. My experience and wisdom tells me the road ahead of you will be most difficult, full of adversity and complicated by numerous hurdles you will have to overcome."

Brother's plastic cup filled with beer had strangely escaped the high winds and the blowing sand. He paused to take a sip of his favorite beverage, then continued in a more serious tone. "Your schedule is demanding, as it must be. Without question, your travels will contain many emotional highs and lows. Maintain your focus and composure and be sure to keep your innermost thoughts to yourselves. Don't get sidetracked, and above all refrain from displaying any signs of overconfidence. Speak the truth, but don't pontificate. Inform those whom you speak to of my visit with you, but abstain from embellishing anything you've seen or heard. Communicate with each other as you travel from city to city. Coordinate your efforts, making sure to utilize every possible means to accomplish the task at hand. The rabbi and imam whom you have met with are but a few of those who will be willing to travel and assist you. I realize the time constraints are limited. Do what you must to meet Father's demands. I have the utmost confidence in all of you."

They had heard this speech before. But for some reason, this time his words had the essence of finality to them.

Philip asked him, "Brother, you are leaving us now, aren't you?"

"Yes, Philip. My time here on earth is brief. You shall not see me here again. But down the road I look forward to seeing you in my home."

He gazed into the eyes of the newest member of his stewards and said, "As for you, young lady, from this day forward you shall represent the stewards as their official spokesperson. Speak to the masses. Convince them Father's way is the only path to gain salvation. You represent millions of your gender who have become leaders in every station of life, rising in the ranks to attain positions of power as well as responsibility.

"I have one final thought I'd like to share with you. The swirling sand reminds me of one of the catchwords of the twentieth century. Velocity! It seems as though everything happens at such an accelerated pace these days, what with the new technological advances in industry and science, as well as the incredible speed one can travel." He shook his head and motioned with his hands in a gyrating motion. "Things just seem to occur so swiftly. It's a way of life most of you living in industrialized countries choose to live. I bring up this word 'velocity' to you, but not to alter your thinking as it pertains to advancements in technology. Let us just make sure mankind does not program its time praying and worshipping Father in a similar manner. Enough said. Now, before I depart, let us walk to the water's edge."

He placed his hands on their shoulders and baptized his stewards by submerging them in the shallow water. He baptized Peter last, impressing on him to serve as the shepherd of this flock and guide these stewards in their travels. Peter felt Brother release his grip on his shoulders and turned around to assure him that he would try his best. But Brother was nowhere to be seen.

TWENTY NINE

The beginning of the third millennium was celebrated in all four corners of the earth with the obvious fanfare. Religious ceremonies, at least in Christian churches, took on more than the normal symbolic meaning this new year, commemorating not only the two thousand years of Christianity, but the reports of the return of the man whom people had worshipped all these centuries. Parties ringing in the New Century lasted for days. However, the thought occurred to many millions that if he truly had returned, this could be the year life on earth as we knew it was to come to an end.

Even in South Beach, despite the incredible task before them, the stewards took time out to join in the revelry. Aware that their lives had changed forever, they knew they would never return to their normal routines. Those who were employed arranged to obtain a one-year sabbatical. The deep pockets of the Thompson brothers and Simon English were footing the expenses for the group.

Peter and John appointed Dolores Quan an advisor to the stewards. She hosted a New Year's Eve party at the hotel for them and their spouses. John recalled Brother's instuctions regarding romantic attachments for the following year or until the steward's task was completed. Still, he invited Mary to the party, hoping she would accept his proposal of matrimony, realizing they would have to keep on hold exchanging vows. She came to the party but turned down his proposal. Nevertheless, they danced the night away, although the festivities were short-lived, as they went back to work on New Year's Day. They spent the first two days of the year 2000 in intense planning sessions and finalizing travel arrangements.

###

The Alitalia 747 arrived on time, touching down at 9:50 a.m. at Rome's Fumicino Airport. It was the fifth of January, the date of the first meeting scheduled by the stewards. Cardinal O'Connor, Bishop Parker, Pauline Demitri, and Peter Albano were greeted by one of the Pope's emissaries. Two white Mercedes were waiting to transport them to the Hassler Hotel overlooking the Spanish Steps. After freshening up, they were to proceed to the Vatican.

The trip to the hotel was a sightseer's delight, taking in the breathtaking historic structures the Eternal City was noted for, such as the Colosseum. So impressive were these ancient ruins, Pauline and Peter were mesmerized to the extent they almost forgot the purpose of their visit. Even the American clergymen, who had been to Rome on numerous occasions, were caught up in the mystique of this enchanting city.

The Pontiff sat next to Italy's prime minister and three of the Vatican's most noteworthy scholars, as the stewards and their eminent advisors entered his private chambers. After introductions and cups of espresso had been passed around, Cardinal Fiori, the Pope's principal advisor, spoke in English to request details of what Brother had told them. The response, delivered equally by Pauline and Peter, took the better part of an hour and was punctuated by numerous interruptions. Question after question led the two stewards to sense the Catholic hierarchy did not believe one word they had said. Pauline's thoughts wandered to the images of the Inquisition. Cardinal O'Connor and Bishop Parker took turns attempting to persuade the Catholic hierarchy, but to no avail, and the anxiety and stress in the ornately decorated room intensified.

Frustrated and disappointed, Peter looked at the Pope, who up until this time had said not a word. "Please, your Holiness, you must believe us."

The leader of millions of Catholics offered no response, other than asking Pauline and Peter, "Would you care for another cup of espresso?"

They declined and the conversation came to a standstill. Fifteen minutes passed while the Pontiff appeared to be meditating. The silence was deafening.

Finally, the Pope gestured to Cardinal Fiori to help him to his feet. The bishop of Rome reached out to take Peter's hands in his, firmly gripping the strong hands of the fisherman. He was most charming as he smiled and said, "I have but just one question for you, Peter. How can I help you deliver Father's message?"

Peter kissed the pontiff's ring and replied, "You already have, your Holiness. You already have."

Elated, the stewards returned to their hotel, with the understanding that Cardinal Fiori would join them in their travels throughout Italy, starting right here in Rome, and journeying wherever their help was needed, church to church, in every Roman Catholic diocese, until each cardinal, bishop, priest, nun, and parishioner had heard this monumental account of Brother's return.

Sunday masses would include the church's position on Brother's return, acknowledging the fact that he, without any doubt, had returned. The Pontiff stressed the point that the Vatican would endorse the stewards with all the resources of the Roman Catholic Church. Catholic newsletters in every country would sanction the story, which would be written by Jim Albright and Matthew Singer. The Italian prime minister proposed a national day of recognition celebrating this colossal event.

The Pope's chief writers prepared an urgent communication to the hundreds of cardinals located around the globe, explaining the Vatican's position on the subject. Most paramount of all the actions taken by the Pope was the mass scheduled for the following Sunday at Saint Peter's Basillica celebrating the observance of Brother's return. This would give the Pope the opportunity to express his thoughts and wishes to all people, regardless of their religious preference. On Christians of all denominations, he placed the extra burden of embracing Father's requests and helping the stewards complete their work.

Before returning to New York, Bishop Parker and Cardinal O'Connor took on the added responsibility of meeting with a Protestant leadership council in Augsburg, Germany. Their presentation mirrored the efforts of Pauline and Peter in Rome, familiarizing this influential panel with the events in South Beach. The Lutheran bishop informed the twenty-two clergymen, who represented various Protestant denominations from all across Europe, of his position on the authenticity of Brother's return and the epistle given to his stewards. Cardinal O'Connor clarified the Vatican's views on this historic event and what the Pope's intentions were.

It was one thing to have watched the astounding press conference on television delivered by two unknown twenty-first-century disciples of this man calling himself Jesus, but to hear the same accounts from two of the most respected and revered religious leaders in the United States was downright shocking. Their unequivocal support of the disciples and unwavering position that Jesus had indeed returned added credibility to what occurred in South Baech and magnified its importance.

The ad hoc council of clergymen spent less than an hour in coming to an agreement to take the appropriate actions to inform their parishioners. Like the Vatican, the Protestant leadership counil stated that they too would celebrate a special service the following Sunday to pronounce the return of the leader of their church.

In Tel Aviv, a conclave of holy men and the Israeli prime minister met with Matthew Singer and their counterpart from New York, Rabbi Marvin Silverman. Without question, a significantly tougher selling program was expected here than in Rome. It was understandably difficult for the Jewish leadership to hear one of their own describe and adhere to the actions of the religious icon they had chosen to disregard for the last two thousand years.

Rabbi Silverman, speaking in Hebrew, was very persuasive in presenting his case. Directing his attention to the prime minister, he expressed Brother's views on the need for lasting peace and tranquillity in the region, and he described as many of the pertinent details of what had occurred in South Beach as was necessary to convince the perplexed representatives of the holy land.

"Brother has no desire for us to alter our religious beliefs. He only wishes us to validate our worship and adoration of Father. Besides,"he concluded with a glow on his face, "Brother is a Jew himself as you know, born in Israel to Jewish parents and, therefore, will always be considered one of the tribe."

Because agreeing to the actuality of the events occurring in South Beach was tantamount to believing in Jesus Christ and all his acts and miracles, the leadership council decided to discuss Rabbi Silverman's oration in private. They would be most happy to meet with him and Matthew tomorrow at which time the holy men of Israel would give their response.

The Israeli prime minister reacted positively to what Matthew and Rabbi Silverman had to say. At an early morning meeting the following day, a statement was read by a member of his staff agreeing to promote the very ideals stipulated in Father's covenant. It stated, "The entire Israeli government will do everything in its power to proceed with peace talks with its neighbors." The prime minister would also conduct a press conference to explain his views on the subject. "As far as the religious aspects of your requests are concerned, these will remain in the hands of our religious leaders as to whether or not to accept what you have told us. If the decision is yes, it will be up to them to develop a concentrated and concise plan to suit all religious groups in Israel."

The questions the holy men of Israel asked were well thought out but contained no great surprises, including, why did this man calling himself Jesus decide to return to South Beach and not the holy city of Jerusalem? Brother had supplied each of his stewards with sufficient information to respond to most areas of concern, and Matthew and Rabbi Silverman were well prepared and able to address each one. Except for the question reserved for last.

A rabbi sitting at the head of the table asked, "We do take exception on one issue. The one dealing with the Messiah. As you know, those practicing Judaism have been expecting the anointed one to appear for centuries. When will he come forth?"

This unexpected question was like so many others asked that deserved a response, if not a definitive answer. Rabbi Silverman nodded his head to express his understanding of the extreme nature of the inquiry. These wise and deep-thinking teachers had to protect the integrity of the very foundation of their religion.

The New York rabbi told them, "I have taken your concerns to heart. I advise you and all of our flock in every nation to continue to look for the Messiah's return. I, as a professed and determined member of our faith, will be looking for him as well."Pausing for a moment, Rabbi Silverman recalled Brother's ultimate warning to avoid embellishing any particular issue. Gesturing with his arms and shoulders, he suggested "On the other hand, it is possible this man referring to himself as Brother just may be the Messiah."

This remark stunned his fellow holy men, who up until this time had been reasonably patient and composed. But this last statement created a significant amount of clamor among some of the more radical members of the group, many of whom threatened to walk out. The eldest and most moderate of the Jewish ministers and teachers attempted to take control of the meeting. After a few heated exchanges, he was finally able to reason with his peers, returning a sense of order and tranquillity, at least for the moment, to the meeting.

Matthew waited for the commotion to die down, adding, "Well stated, Rabbi Silverman." Matthew's demeanor was commanding and determined, more so than at any time in his thirty-five years, he realized, wondering where this newfound strength had come from. Addressing the skeptical religious leaders, he continued. "As you know, although I too am a Jew, up until a few days ago I would not have been considered a very religious person." The reporter, expressing himself with unreserved emotion candidly but forcefully informed them, "I have broken bread with Brother."Pausing, he added, "I have listened to him speak."And with passion he had never displayed before said, "I've spoken with him. You must believe me, he truly is the Messiah. He has finally appeared, not just for the followers of Christianity, but for all humankind.

Without any further comments or questions, the local holy men understood Matthew and Rabbi Silverman's justification. That's not to say they accepted either of the American's responses as factual. They simply saw themselves in a no-win position. They had determined after careful deliberation the night before that this man who appeared in South Beach might have indeed been the reincarnation of Jesus Christ. And while his return might not be in tune with their theologian's prognostication, to deny that this event had been witnessed by thirteen people would be unwise. The session ended on a positive note. They, the religious hierarchy of Israel, had decided to join the ranks of those willing to assist the stewards in their work.

Medina, Saudi Arabia, was selected as the city for the Muslim leaders to convene with Judas Karim and Imam Qutb. The Mosque of the Prophet, one of Islam's most holy sites, was selected as the meeting place. Members of Islam's hierarchy from every Arab nation, including Iraq and Iran, attended. Even representatives from the out-of-favor Shiites were present. Although heads of state from several nations declined the invitation for security reasons, they all dispatched high-ranking officials to sit in for them.

Judas, working through an interpreter, and Imam Qutb, speaking fluently his native language of Arabic, made their position on the events in South Beach clear. They wasted few words describing the details of Brother's return and the mission he had asked his stewards to carry out. Their compelling dissertation captivated the religious leaders and government dignitaries. Both Judas and Imam Qutb's affirmation of Brother's understanding and compassion of all religious groups, including Islam, eased the minds of the devoted followers of Muhammad in a region where politics, ancient cultures, and religion, all seem to be intertwined.

Nevertheless, the look on the faces of the listeners reflected disbelief. This did not surprise either speaker, who knew their selling job would be extensive. The distrust between east and west was still at an uncomfortable level. Could this be another ploy on the part of the United States and the other western nations to suppress the spread of Islam? Or a mechanism contrived to stir the pot once more between Israel and the Palestinians? And what did the Israelis think about all this? What was their position on Brother? Why should we believe in anyone but Muhammad?

For many long, tedious hours, these and many more pointed questions were asked of Imam Qutb and Judas. Fortunately, the stewards were well prepared to respond to this esteemed body of clergymen and government representatives. Imam Qutb made clear that he was first and foremost a Muslim, with the well-being and integrity of his religion and congregation ever present in his thoughts. He continued by stressing one fact. "Last month, Jesus Christ returned to earth. His mission is well defined and requires all of us, especially the clergy, to carry out Allah's demands."

The expressionless faces of the Muslim holy men indicated to both Imam Qutb and Judas that there were still many skeptics in the room. "Brother made it quite clear,"Imam Qutb added in a more commanding tone, "failure to do so will result in devastating consequences for all. By the power and wisdom of Muhammad, we must subscribe to the wishes of Brother. Allah has given him this revelation. We must comply with his demands."

The religious leaders met privately while Imam Qutb and Judas took in the sights of the intriguing city of Medina. Two hours later, the call on the guide's cellular phone beckoned them back to the mosque. The temple of Muhammad was unusually chilly, but not as frigid as the men sitting in on the conference. Although they agreed in principle on what they had been told, it was obvious something was amiss.

Imam Qutb was pleased by their conclusions but somewhat concerned at the lack of sincerity with which it was stated. He sensed it was his duty to clarify. "Does this include a reshaping of the peace process with Israel? And will you also agree to have a better understanding with those who are not of the Muslim faith in your region?"

The imam representing the Shiites welcomed this request.

"Of course,"responded the smiling government official from Iraq. "On all accounts."

Imam Qutb felt uncomfortable with the way his proposal was accepted. With an obvious tone in his voice of trepidation, he continued, "I must stress the issue once again with you my friends, it is not the government of any nation requesting this, but Allah himself."

Judas could sense the transparent reaction of the Iraqi. He had hoped the imam from New York would be able to convince the representatives, but after the superficial response they received, his concerns deepened. They obviously didn't believe what Imam Qutb had told them, or else they chose to disregard the magnitude of what was said.

Frustrated by the lip service he received, Judas decided to activate his attorney's license. For some strange reason he pictured himself standing in front of a triad of justices in an old English courtroom, complete with the traditional solicitor's garb of robe and wig, as he defended an outstanding citizen against the state who faced charges of deceit and misrepresentation. The eloquent words that followed would endear him to every barrister ever presenting a case in the halls of justice. He began his closing argument by describing how Brother had saved his life and finished it with the waterspout scene on the beach.

His choice of words mesmerized the interpreter, who carefully conveyed Judas's every word. Imam Qutb vigilantly tracked not only the Arabic translation, but supplied the necessary inflections when the multilingual aide omitted them, either deliberately or unintentionally.

Judas concluded by saying, "You, the holy men representing most of the Islamic world, must promote Allah's requests. Let us Muslims stand up tall with our Christian and Jewish brothers." He bowed to the religious leaders and exited the mosque, leaving Imam Qutb behind to answer any further questions.

On his way back to the hotel, Judas stopped for a cup of coffee at an outdoor cafe. No sooner had he sat down than he was joined at the small table by two men. Dressed in business suits, these two strangers could have blended in quite easily with a group of advertising executives on Madison Avenue. They sat on either side of him, pinning Judas against their shoulders. One of the men made his point without any frivolous words. The people he represented were prepared to make Judas a wealthy man if he would make a statement to the local newspaper discrediting Brother.

Judas sipped his coffee, pushed the man to his left away, and arose from his chair. Leaving more than enough riyals to pay the bill, he told the two men that he was glad to have met them but had no interest in their proposition. As he walked toward the hotel, Judas wondered if Brother was testing him to see if he would betray him, as the apostle Judas had done two thousand years ago.

###

It took three days for Judas and Imam Qutb to receive a response from the Muslim council. They returned to the sacred mosque and recited one of the five daily prayers, after which the meeting with the Muslim holy men began. Judas made no mention of his encounter in the local coffee shop.

The leader of this esteemed group of clergymen stood, and his words were translated. "We have reached a decision and have agreed to work with you. The government of each of the Arab states and their religious leadership council will prepare a joint newsletter explaining our position. We will communicate our doctrine to people of all religions living in this region. In essence, we support your efforts, and with the guidance of Muhammad we will do everything in our power to convince his many followers in every nation to do the same. And I add,"he continued, "we invite both of you and the rest of your fellow stewards to join us during the holy month of Ramadan."

Imam Qutb was encouraged by the invitation. At last, he thought, we have finally convinced them.

Judas was not so sure he and Imam Qutb had persuaded them, although he kept his suspicions under wraps. The two questions troubling him were age-old problems. One, they agreed to our terms, but for how long? And two, can they possibly find it in their hearts to make a lasting peace with their neighbors? Only time would tell.

###

Cardinal O'Connor and Bishop Parker had returned to New York to work on plans for their own congregations, including interfaith rites at both Catholic and Protestant churches throughout the New York City area. These were to be celebrated on consecutive Sundays, commencing the last week in January. They had also planned a meeting to be attended by Christian leaders from around the United States and Canada to expand on the interfaith services. Not stopping there, a commission of Muslim, Jewish, and Christian representatives was established to bring the three religious groups together to discuss how to promote Father's message.

###

It was the last week in January. Those who had been on the road were glad to be back in the familiar surroundings of the White Sand Hotel. Now that the three primary religious groups had been briefed, it was time for the more difficult task, addressing those who were not as well versed about Jesus. First, Peter, Matthew, and Judas gave a synopsis of their meetings with the Jewish, Muslim, and Roman Catholic leaders. Peter also conveyed Bishop Parker's report from meeting with the leaders of the Protestant council in Augsburg, Germany.

The initial reports of cooperation were encouraging in each city visited, but Peter emphasized,"There is a lot more work still to be done." He was quick to add, "I wish I was as confident regarding the long-term attitude and position on the part of some of the religious and state leaders. Without question, we will have to establish follow-up meetings throughout the course of the year. Father was not overly generous in the time he allotted us, and January is rapidly coming to a close, leaving us eleven months to complete our work. We must make every day count, if we are to keep on schedule. Let us use the successes we have enjoyed in our initial meetings to bolster our campaign to glory."

Peter's leadership and passion permeated the meeting room, warming the hearts and stimulating the minds of the other stewards. Jim and John had hired ten young men and women to update the web pages each day in an attempt to respond to the questions asked most often.

John commented, "The number of faxes we have received and hits on our web site over the last few weeks has reached well into the millions. Many of the responses confirmed that the public was totally captivated by Brother's return."

Peter said, "We may need the people to force their leaders to listen to what Brother has said. In your travels, inform the leaders of the world of the enthusiastic interest and support we have received from their citizens. Assure them we have no intention of subverting either their governments or the religion of choice of their populace. With one exception that is! Every man and woman must be made aware that there truly is a Supreme Being. Tell them he is the Father of all humankind. Try to make them understand they can still believe what they will about the prophets and religious icons who preceded them, but assure each of them they were born under one God who is their Father. Inform them of the compelling story of Brother's return." Peter rethought his last comment and added, "I guess you might have to refer to Brother's life here two thousand years ago for those who never heard of him. Or for those who, perhaps, don't believe what they have read or heard."

The second phase of travel would commence tomorrow, with plans to cover the entire globe over the next five months. John, James, and Thomas had prepared an itinerary which would take the stewards to virtually every country. In units of two and three, they were assigned countries to visit. With the aid of the State Department, and particularly George Cooledge, passports and visas were obtained as required. George was also responsible for establishing meeting dates between individual government officials worldwide and the stewards.

Pauline was asked to make a special presentation to the General Assembly of the United Nations. In addition, at the request of the incoming President of the United States, she was to address both houses of Congress before the State of the Union speech next week. Her upcoming speech, to be broadcast nationwide, was not without controversy. Skeptics claimed it would destroy the keystone of the country's doctrine, separation of church and state. The leadership of both political parties, as well as the newly elected President, burned the midnight oil in an attempt to convince the concerned congressmen. Although those skeptical senators and members of the house vowed to maintain their silence during Pauline's speech, they would be permitted to speak to the nation afterward to explain their viewpoint.

The stewards were informed of this rebuttal by the White House Chief of Staff. Some of them were shocked and dismayed at this action to undermine their efforts, sensing, if we cannot convince the government officials of a free country like the United States, how are we to persuade those still under a dictatorship?

Andrew addressed this question to those stewards living outside the United States, explaining, "This is how our congressmen approach issues. Regardless of the significance of the matter, there is always another side to it." He went on to say, "They have a need to be heard and they always appear to be watching their political behinds."

Pauline Demitri's speech before the American public would serve as a model for all future presentations. It would be the first time a country and its government's officials had sponsored the stewards: therefore, her address would have to be easy to comprehend but convincing, without contradicting the Constitution, the foundation on which the United States was built.

Peter and the other stewards realized that as significant as their task was, in no way should they compromise the laws and culture that people had learned to live with. For only anarchy and turmoil would follow. Each step Brother had asked them to take would have to be thought out with care and executed with precision, realizing the odds of convincing mankind were a long shot at best. The importance of

Pauline's discourse was therefore magnified dramatically. She, on the other hand, was as cool as could be, maintaining her composure and completely prepared to face this complex challenge.

If that wasn't enough, this talented young lady would follow up her speech with a trip to Greece, her parents' homeland. Along with the Vatican's representative, Cardinal Fiore, she would meet with the patriarchs of the Orthodox Church. These twenty-four autocephalous prelates would travel to Greece from all over Europe, the Middle East, as well as the United States, and from as far away as Australia.

Pauline's position as spokesperson for the stewards placed her in the forefront whenever a major speech was to be made or a religious sect to be addressed. In spite of her elevation to this esteemed level, she remained humble and dutiful to the cause, always understanding that Peter was selected by Brother to manage and direct the stewards; and she was only his spokesperson. Pauline's humility and loyalty did not go unnoticed by the other stewards, who had the utmost respect for her, especially Thomas, who made no attempt to conceal his fondness toward her.

###

Once again, Cardinal O'Connor, Bishop Parker, Rabbi Silverman and Imam Qutb were to accompany the stewards, traveling with them to the far reaches of the earth. The clergymen's knowledge of the innumerable spiritual cults practiced in the underdeveloped countries in particular, would be invaluable in assisting the stewards with their charge.

They also engaged the services of one Dolores Quan, who contrived to take a leave of absence from her post as manager of the hotel for six months. Dolores agreed to join the contingent of stewards traveling to Asia, Australia, and New Zealand. She spoke both Chinese and Japanese fluently, enabling her to serve as interpreter for the stewards. She was also well aware of many of the spiritual practices in the region. Dolores was a devoted follower of the teachings of Confucius; so she realized informing the millions of people of Asia about what had happened in South Beach would be a difficult task. But she believed Brother represented someone with unlimited authority and more influence than even her sacred idol, and the people of this great continent had to be told about him.

The stewards assigned to the region were Jim Albright and James Thompson, with Bishop Parker serving as their religious authority.

Along with Dolores Quan, they had a wide area to cover. Although Christianity is firmly entrenched in parts of the region, especially in China and South Korea, with over a billion people living within these lands and as complicated and fragmented belief systems in this part of the world were, they knew their task would not be easy.

Simon and Thaddaeus were assigned the countries of Africa. Judas and Imam Qutb would return once again to the Middle East, then on to India, where they would be joined by Pauline. Not only would they speak to the government and religious leaders in the Hindu nation, but a special session was also scheduled with the exiled religious icon, the Dalai Lama. Bartholomew, his wife Elsa, and Thomas were scheduled to travel to eastern Europe. Cardinal O'Connor, along with John, would work both Ireland and England before crossing the Atlantic once again to Canada. Philip, his wife Anna, and Matthew were scheduled to go to South America, and Andrew and Peter were to cover the United States, Mexico, and Central America. There would be frequent crisscrossing of the globe to reach as many people as possible, working the press in each country visited in an attempt to continue to keep the news of Brother's return on the front pages.

South Beach, specifically the White Sand Hotel, would remain their headquarters. Almost a month had passed since word of Brother's return was made known to the public. The enormous crowds that had originally gathered had dwindled to just a few hundred -- those who still wished to gain a glimpse of him, or, perchance, plead with him to heal their bodies or perhaps their souls. The months flew by, with various degrees of success and pockets of extreme failure. It was obvious to the stewards that second and third trips to certain isolated areas would have to be undertaken to further educate the people and their leaders. A three-by-eight-foot colored map of the earth graced the far wall of the meeting room in the hotel. It illustrated the numerous countries the stewards had visited, the successes shaded in green and the areas of concern in red. It was frustrating to visualize the countries with no markings at all, indicating those not yet visited.

Back to the drawing board they went to plan and put into effect phase two. A plan to intensify the media coverage internationally was agreed on. Matthew was charged with this important responsibility. Pauline again would serve as spokesperson, using all the experience she had attained at her ex-employer, CNN, to present the steward's case in front of the television cameras and when talking to the print media. They would go so far as to produce a videotape with Bishop Parker serving as narrator to define and clarify their mission.

Three more grueling months of globetrotting provided the stewards with more accomplishments, although the disappointments were still evident. But at least the number of conflicts and skirmishes in the usual hot spots subsided. In some regions, particularly in the Middle East, what appeared to be a lasting peace accord was finally taking shape. Nevertheless, much work remained.

Their dossier of countries visited soon included even the smaller island nations, those appearing as mere dots on the large map. Peaceful people lived on these remote atolls and, for the most part, knew little about Father, but they were intrigued by the possibility of his presence.

It was the middle of September, and a week of rest and relaxation in South Beach was greatly appreciated and well deserved. Peter sensed his fellow stewards were reaching the point of exhaustion. Not only had physical fatigue set in, but also it was quite clear they were beginning to lose their edge mentally. Having been on the road since January, traveling tens of thousands of miles from country to country, had taken its toll. Peter recommended a few days of relaxation on the beach to get the cobwebs out. It was obvious to him that delivering the last phase of Brother's epistle would probably be the most intense. Therefore, they would all need to be physically strong and intellectually sound. Time was running short, with only a little over three months remaining.

The red-shaded spots on the map, such as China and North Korea, were definitely on their agenda for a return engagement. Northern Ireland, Bosnia-Herzegovina, and Israel were also programmed for another visit, as well as those nations within Africa and Asia still faced with political turmoil. On prior visits to these countries, the stewards had been greeted cordially, but it wasn't uncommon to hear the sounds of automatic gunfire in the streets of some of the pain-racked capital cities.

Although they did not particularly look forward to a return visit to these divided nations, they realized how imperative these trips were. Political systems had continued to break down, despite the stewards' efforts, with many of these countries still in a state of anarchy and their citizens still faced with bloodshed and despair. To the stewards it grew even clearer why Brother had returned.

The time spent with the leaders of these troubled nations was very trying, the accomplishments minimal at best. But all they could do at this point was to spread Father's message to the people of these unstable countries, attempting to develop a foundation of ideals and principles for them to live by. In countless languages through a legion of translators, and with unyielding faith in Brother, they worked sixteen-hour days.

Bartholomew and Elsa traveled to the war-torn country of Bosnia. Fifty miles outside Sarajevo, the German couple held a meeting with Croats and Serbs in a bomb-riddled church. The outskirts of town still contained several minefields which every so often produced their share of casualties. Elsa's delivery was smooth as she told the hundreds of local residents about Brother's return, although the sad faces of those in attendance gave her and Bartholomew little hope of any success. What neither Elsa nor Bartholomew realized was that the horrifying battle scars that had transformed the once happy and spirited townsfolks made it almost impossible for them to smile.

Elsa worked many hours with the women of the town in an attempt to develop a dialogue of mutual trust and understanding. For a week she undertook the difficult task of uniting this divided population, while at the same time telling them about Brother's return. Though they appeared to believe what she was telling them, Elsa could not brighten the sullen faces of the widows and mothers who had buried their loved ones.

The stewards preached in the fields of Somalia, where the natives tended to their livestock, then traveled to the overcrowded, problem-laden country of Rwanda. There, forty miles from the capital city of Kigali, Simon and Thaddaeus conducted a session with local tribal leaders. Through a translator supplied by the government, the two stewards described what had occurred in South Beach. The Bantu-speaking translator, himself a Protestant, conveyed the incredible story of Brother's return to this group of men, whose religious beliefs varied from Christianity to Islam to ceremonial rituals handed down from generation to generation over thousands of years.

Thaddaeus was delighted at the progress he and Simon had made with the many tribes throughout Rwanda. The majority of the meetings were conducted in open fields with hundreds, and sometimes thousands, of members of the Hutu and Tutsi tribes -- longtime enemies -- standing alongside each other to hear the stewards define Brother's wishes.

In a rain forest in Paraguay, dining on mangos, guava, and figs with Native Americans called Guarani, Anna and Philip Silva spent an evening in a small village, informing the forty or so people who lived there about Brother's return. All the people of the village were Catholic and were captivated by Anna, as she told them of Brother and the stewards. Philip sat across from Anna on the damp ground and grinned as he listened to her presentation, which he concluded was far better than his.

Anna had vivid recollections of her visit to the village: a frightening experience with a fifty-plus-pound capybara, who stood eye-to-eye with her as she washed her hair in a nearby stream, and a much more pleasant memento presented to her by one of the woman in the village, a beautiful handcrafted copper bracelet.

In the monsoon-drenched country of Bangladesh, dining on herring and prawns, Dolores Quan, Bishop Parker, Jim Albright, and James Thompson spoke with the people of a small fishing village. The unappetizing odor of decaying fish permeated everything. Through a local imam, who spoke English with an unmistakable British accent, they informed the hundreds of people who gathered about the events in South Beach. The religiously blended population was for some inexplicable reason quick to accept Brother's return.

As they prepared to depart the following day, John mentioned to his traveling companions how fascinated he was with the response of their audience. Bishop Parker commented that he was not surprised, for those who work the soil and fish the waters would typically be more receptive to God and his Son.

The mud and offensive stench remained on their gear for the remainder of their tour. But the fond memories that would stay with Dolores and the others forever were of the hugs and gifts showered on them before they returned to the small vessel taking them down-river to the next village.

###

Christmas decorations adorned the brightly painted buildings along Ocean Drive. The holiday celebrated by millions of people regardless of their religious preference was only two weeks away. Simon and Thaddaeus, having spent the last three months in central and northern Africa, were the last of the stewards to return to South Beach. There, they met once again with the others to spend their second Christmas together.

Dolores Quan, back from her sabbatical -- having been reinstated as manager, had her executive chef prepare a simple meal to celebrate the reunion. She felt it was fitting to serve the identical meal the stewards had shared with Brother the previous year. After dinner, Peter took the opportunity to praise the group, which now included Elsa Kessler and Anna Silva. He applauded them for their efforts and devotion, adding that although their travels were not concluded, the strategy called for them to revisit only the remaining trouble spots.

For the most part, they were amazed at the success they had achieved. Each of the stewards related their travel experiences, confident they had done what Brother had asked them to. They were filled with optimism and hope that Father would be satisfied. Peter reasoned with them to remain positive, but cautioned that their enthusiasm should be tempered and their optimistic outlook guarded. He commented apologetically that their lives most likely would never return to normal. However, should things go well in the foreseeable future, they would all be able to return to their homes. That is, all but Pauline and himself, who would continue the crusade. The stewards were all very dedicated and committed to Brother, but they knew it was up to the people of the world to change their ways.

The first year of the new millennium was fast coming to a close. The deadline Father had given them was just days away. Had they done all they could do? What other avenues could they have taken? And what would Father do if they hadn't? In a matter of weeks or months, they were sure to know.

Or were they?

THIRTY

Church bells rang in the New Year, a New Year filled with hope and newfound energy. Yes, the prospects for the state of the world in 2001 were optimistic. Most people were confident the first year of the new millennium would produce a lasting peace and harmony, from Northern Ireland to the Middle East, to the complicated disputes that had destroyed the very essence of the social structure in many parts of Africa. The gunfire and bombing ceased in these volatile regions, followed by an increasing number of treaties of peace. Significant signs of agreement and reconciliation were apparent in areas normally known as hotbeds of violence. Even in countries where basic spiritual beliefs up until this time did not recognize Father, a wave of understanding and freedom of worship to this new ideology was not only accepted, but encouraged.

Churches, mosques, synagogues, and temples of all faiths and denominations were filled with parishioners. Worldwide, services were added to accommodate the overflow of new members praying to Father. More important, they took the word of Father home with them to live their lives by, treating their family members and neighbors with compassion and understanding in the truest sense of His doctrine.

Over the past year there was a noticeable increase in the number of men and women of all faiths enrolling in universities, seminaries, and religious preparatory schools, breaking a long-term spiraling trend downward the last few decades, especially in the Roman Catholic Church. All faiths planned to reopen or build new places to worship. Pilgrimages to the holy cities of Mecca, Jerusalem, and the newest of them all, South Beach, were planned by millions of people. Missionaries established to aid and educate people from underdeveloped countries were overwhelmed by the number of applications to join their ranks.

Politicians in virtually every country implemented comprehensive plans to deal with the devastating issue of hunger and famine in needy countries. Poverty levels in the inner cities of developed nations were approached with meaningful education and work programs. Even the members of the press became proactive, toning down the bizarre and sensational stories which had often headlined their papers, magazines, and newscasts, almost totally eliminating the cynical nature of their reports, with a broader account of the issues and less emphasis on the personal lives of those in the limelight.

Crime rates declined, especially in the inner cities of the United States. Arrests for the distribution and use of illegal drugs fell to their lowest level in twenty years, and the backlog of court cases was reduced for the first time in the memory of anyone connected with the criminal justice system.

Contributions to worthy causes increased significantly, not only in monetary terms, but also in terms of the time and experience brought to the table by those more fortunate who wished to help the underprivileged and to donate their time and energy to worthwhile causes. A network of vocational opportunities created a noticeable decline in unemployment rates worldwide.

Life in the holiday-decorated homes seemed to have been altered as well, affecting deeply rooted daily habits that have been splitting families apart for years. Many allocated time every day to bond with others instead of spending countless hours of solitude in front of their hypnotic television sets or captivating computer screens. Attitudes seemed more reasonable when families addressed problem areas between parents and their teenaged children. Discussing issues replaced arguing or slamming doors behind them, followed by the uneasy silences which ultimately divide families.

It was evident to Peter and the other stewards that what they were doing was having an impact. Finally, after numerous centuries, Father had managed to reach out to man to unify this planet we live on. And they, the messengers of his mission, were at least partly responsible for the positive results. On the surface, the entire world appeared to profit from their unselfish labor. The contacts they had made in each country they visited produced refreshing reports of the visible enhancements instituted over the last year. Yet the stewards realized all these modifications that society had made could be superficial. Man was known to be a very fragile creature. He might split at the seams at the first sign of pressure. The test of time must still be endured.

###

The weather was particularly pleasant the last week of January in southern Florida. Hundreds of thousands of tourists and snowbirds flocked to Miami Beach. And thousands of others, continuing to add to the millions before them, made their pilgrimage to the newest shrine, the White Sand Hotel. The glistening rays of the sun drew like a magnet, attracting many visitors to the hot sandy beach. The stewards arrived at their usual location, across from the Blue Crab Restaurant. They gathered in small groups to enjoy the last few days together before heading home.

Andrew and James were in the middle of a conversation regarding the current state of affairs when Peter showed up. The focus of their discussion was not centered on what they had done, but on how long the results would last.

"Why do you feel this way?" asked Peter.

James answered directly, "We were debating how long these serene and tranquil conditions would last."

"And what are your conclusions?"

Andrew replied, "James believes people will revert back to their usual belligerent selves before the end of the year."

"And how do you feel, my older brother?"

"I say no more than six months."

"It appears you're both getting cynical. Have you no faith in humankind?"

Neither Andrew nor James responded.They wished to be more positive, but elected not to answer Peter's question. The three of them sat in silence for more than ten minutes, looking up at the sky as a dark cloud worked its way above them, blocking the rays of the sun. Surprising both Andrew and James, Peter revealed he had similar concerns. And more than that, he was worried what Father might have in store when and if things reversed themselves. His comments were as bleak as the rain cloud overhead. For the moment, they would enjoy the remainder of the week here in South Beach before heading to their respective homes. The onerous-looking cloud drifted out over the Atlantic, as the radiant sun commanded the sky once again.

Peter wished Brother would reappear to give him and the others some guidance, advise them of what to do next, and, more important, how to avert Father's anger if Andrew and James were correct. Unfortunately, he believed deep down it might require a sign from above to convince the masses once and for all to live in peace and unity. After traveling around the planet several times this past year, he sensed it would be only a question of time for all the good the stewards attempted to manifest to go up in flames.

They gathered together in a man-made ring of colorful beach towels and reminisced about their adventures. Before they departed,

Peter wished to express his concerns to the entire group. "Most of you will be going home soon. I hope you don't misunderstand me when I say, be prepared to return."He added, "Satan, or whatever you want to call him, unfortunately is firmly entrenched in the minds and souls of too many people, and for some unknown reason, in too many of those in powerful positions. There will come a time, much likely sooner than later, when the deliverer of hate and evil will reveal his depraved and despicable head, causing the dreaded repudiation of Brother and us, his stewards, ultimately facing Father's understandable cataclysmic rebuttal."

Expressing his views and those of Andrew and James, he added, "I hope we are wrong and just going through a phase of paranoia, or perhaps it's only a case of skepticism. What we have accomplished thus far pleases me no end. I'm sure Brother is ever so thankful for the impact our efforts have had. But the question is, have we really made a lasting impression on mankind? Have we convinced them that the changes they have made in their life styles and the way they respect their neighbors must endure the ages?"

Pauline asked, "What else can we do?"

"That's just the point,"responded Peter. "I wish I knew. Perhaps spending another year retracing the paths we traveled might be fruitful."

James was quick to mention, "We delivered Father's directive just as Brother told us to. I'm not sure telling those that choose not to listen will do any good. But if you think it will help, Peter, I'm positive you have the complete support of all of us. We'll go back on the road again for another year if that's what it takes."

The stewards all chimed in with similar words of encouragement to verify James's position.

Peter thanked James and the others, telling them, "No, it's time for you to return home. After all, you have your own lives to live. Some of you have wives, and you have children to raise. James is right, though; we've done all we can. We fulfilled Brother's mission, just as he asked us to. Now we must wait and see if mankind will heed Father's appeal. This does not imply our work has come to a standstill. Pauline and I will continue to speak to religious and government leaders. Although they are returning to their homes, Matthew and Jim will continue to support our efforts in the print media and John will see to it that the web page on the Internet is updated on a weekly basis. But I leave you with this thought. If necessary, I will travel anywhere to reaffirm our mission."

"And we'll all be right there beside you, Peter,"said Philip.

"That's right,"added Judas.

A unanimous display of support followed, reinforcing the single-ness of purpose and unity of the stewards of South Beach.

The following night, the meeting room was the scene of consider-able emotion, and eyes filled with tears. The next day the stewards would be heading for home.

"Home in body,"Simon suggested, "but in South Beach, our spirit will always be."

Good-byes were tabled; only goodnights could be heard, as the meeting room emptied out, most likely for the last time.

The planet earth seemed to be at peace, and with the exception of a couple of minor incidents over the last few months, all was well. Pauline was in New York speaking to a graduating class at Rochester University. It was early June, and Peter was on his way to San Francisco to visit his brother Andrew, where he would perhaps spend a day or two on their fishing boat.

When he arrived in the City by the Bay, Peter heard the first horri-fying bulletin on Andrew's car radio, which blurted out the sketchy details of a deadly bombing in the Gaza Strip, killing at least forty-two Israelis and injuring hundreds more. Naturally, retaliation was already in progress in Lebanon, meaning more killings would occur. After which, the newscaster told his listening audience of a riot that had bro-ken out between Protestant and Catholics during a soccer game in Northern Ireland, with unconfirmed reports of deaths and injuries.

If that were not catastrophic enough, China had taken part in a military exercise in the waters north of Taiwan, during which a com-mercial Japanese airline with two hundred and four people aboard was shot down. The flight had been on its way to Tokyo from Taipei. There were no survivors. Accusations by Japanese officials, charging China with the inexplicable infringement of air space were fired off via diplomatic channels. Beijing responded coldly that the Japanese plane had been sent there purposely to spy on Chinese naval forces. Tension in the area replaced the short-lived harmonious attitudes that had pre-vailed for the better part of a year. More important, it resulted in dis-patching armies everywhere and placing the far east on alert.

"Can you imagine that, all in one day?"asked Andrew as he read the following morning's newspaper.

"You, my brother, are somewhat of a prophet."

"What do you mean, Peter?"

"You said it would take less than six months for things to change. Your time frame was right on the money."

"I wish I were wrong, Peter. Dead wrong. What do we do now?"

"Never mind what we do. What Father intends to do concerns me even more. But you're right, we must act without delay. The other stewards must be consulted to see how we can possibly help settle these disputes. It will probably require the aid of Cardinal O'Connor, too. He and John have represented the stewards in Ireland."

"And Imam Qutb, Judas, Matthew, and Rabbi Silverman to deal with the predicament in the Middle East?"

"Exactly, Andrew. Would you please get the ball rolling and contact them? As far as the situation in China and Japan is concerned, I intend to fly there as soon as possible. We will have to call on all our resources, beginning with George Cooledge at the State Department, to handle this one."

Andrew asked, "Don't you think they're on top of this?"

"Of course, Andrew. I'm not that naive. The President probably has already contacted the Chinese leaders protesting their actions."

"Then what more can we offer?"

"We can tell them once again that Father's retaliation will be much more severe than any man-made weapon, and it's time to stop their belligerent acts of aggression or suffer his rage. We must continue to do battle under the banner Brother has provided."

"Do you want me to go with you, Peter?"

"No. I'd like you to fly to Washington, contact George Cooledge, and keep me informed of the mood there."

"I don't think it's wise to go to China by yourself. How about taking James and Bishop Parker? I believe they were with you the first go around."

"Good thinking, Andrew. I'll ask Dolores Quan if she can free up to join us as well. We must get to the bottom of this and find out exactly what happened. Perhaps we'll be accused of interfering with politics and national -- or, shall I say, international -- security. But that's the risk we have to take. Our charge supersedes any government's agenda, and I believe this is exactly what Brother would want us to do."

"Newspapers in every country will run these stories for weeks to come,"Andrew said. "No question about it. Unfortunately these events will produce enough venom to filter down to the street level, affecting the sympathizers or opponents of these dastardly acts and giving those misguided individuals an excuse to perform acts of violence and sponsor the prejudices which erode the very foundation of society."

Whether these acts of violence were the catalyst for triggering a reversal of mankind's pathetic behavior, no one will ever know. Before the year was over, it was obvious many people had forgotten why Father was so enraged and why he had asked his Son to return. What appeared to be isolated acts of aggression and an age-old repetition of misdeeds, including hate and violence, spread like cancer around the globe, from the vicious acts of the militant, so-called religious groups to the petty street crimes, drug dealings, and decadent acts of promiscuity in the cities and suburbs of the United States.

That's not to say that the stewards' work was entirely unsuccessful. For millions of people had placed themselves at the mercy of Father, having enhanced their life styles while fighting off the evil of Satan and his deplorable followers. It was the millions of others who had not heeded the warning Brother's mission had defined that concerned the stewards.

###

Pauline was the last to arrive at the hotel. She had been in Moscow, speaking to a joint council of religious leaders from Eastern Europe. The mood in the meeting room was solemn. The somber classical selection Bartholomew was playing accentuated the mood of the stewards. Dismay and disbelief saddened what should have been a joyous reunion.

"What more can we do?" she asked Peter.

"I believe the stewards have done all they can. Father must now show us if he is content with the modest progress we have managed to make, or, and heaven forbid, he is not satisfied. Pity mankind if he is not, for his wrath will certainly be felt by all."

"Even those who have joined the ranks of his faithful?"asked Philip.

"I'm afraid so,"replied Jim. "His wrath will have no boundaries until all of humankind joins the ranks, as you have suggested."

"That doesn't seem fair,"replied Philip.

"Do we just sit here and wait until his acts of anger are visible?"asked Judas.

"No, Judas,"responded Peter. "We must go amongst the people once again. Talk to their leaders. Work with them, until they are finally convinced His way is the only path to eternal salvation. We must try to convert these sinners to the road of glory and redemption."

###

The new road show was not greeted with the same enthusiasm as before. The streets were filled with protesters. In the Middle East, for example, complaints were heard regarding everything from the United States involvement in the region to Brother's complete disregard for Muhammad in the Muslim sections. The situation was no better from the Jewish perspective. People bewailed the fact that Abraham and their entire ancient religion had been adversely affected. American flags were the usual targets, as burning of the stars and stripes was performed with regularity. Crosses were desecrated and Christian artifacts and churches were targeted by both religious groups.

The religious and political leaders in the Middle East were once again caught up in the cataclysmic division that had besieged the region for thousands of years. The stewards realized the chance of a lasting reconciliation in the area was virtually impossible, at least in the immediate future. Time would be needed to heal the wounds of conflict and hate so prevalent in this divided land. Both Imam Qutb and Rabbi Silverman couldn't believe the reversal the leaders of Israel and the Arab countries had made. More important was the negative attitude of the people of this land.

"What has happened in the last six months to lead to this?"asked the imam.

"Sometimes I sense the hate and animosity are too deeply ingrained to lead to lasting peace,"responded the rabbi. "Generations of distrust and bitterness unfortunately cannot be altered in such a short period of time. Perhaps if Father would just give us a few more years to implement programs to bridge the cultural gaps in the region we might see some significant changes."

"I believe you're right, rabbi. We will require more time to assist these people to work through their differences. I honestly think we can achieve a fair amount of success, but we need more time."

Rabbi Silverman replied, "My friend, I hope Allah understands our plight."

###

John Thompson had a difficult time understanding the rationale behind the sudden outburst of violence. As they walked the rain-soaked streets of Belfast, he told Cardinal O'Connor, "It is inconceivable to me why these radicals in Northern Ireland are hard at work plotting to bomb their neighbors. When one attempts to reason why they try to kill one another, it is difficult to identify the underlying problem. First, both sects claim to believe in Father and Brother. They pray in similar places of worship and raise their children to do the same. Another unfortunate similarity is that both groups have no boundaries when it comes to killing. Many children are caught in this crossfire of misguided extremism. Can you figure this out, your eminence?"

Cardinal O'Connor stared at the destruction caused by the most recent fanatic's attack on a corner pub. The bomb's force had blown out the front window, killing three of the patrons and two young children on their way home from their grandmother's house. The leader of New York City's Roman Catholics just shook his head in disgust, as the two men climbed into a taxi for their trip back to the airport.

On the plane returning to Miami, Cardinal O'Connor asked John, "When will these people learn to live in peace?"

"Your eminence, I wish the answer to that question could easily be found. Perhaps Father has a solution to their problem."

"Based on what Brother has told you, John, I hope they resolve their differences before he decides to enter the picture."

Peter and the others found the Asian situation more volatile than even the media had reported. Tension in the area could be visibly seen by the extraordinary number of armed soldiers at the Tokyo airport. Extensive customs evaluations and luggage checks detained weary travelers for hours. The same was true when they arrived in Beijing. Another issue both countries had in common was their unwillingness to alter their views of Father. All signs of cooperation in educating the people of these two great counries about Father had been tabled. All the efforts of the stewards had been set aside. The other common denominator for these far eastern nations was the subject of retaliation and counter attacks. Not if, but when.

A reporter representing CNN asked Pauline to comment on the current events undermining the groundwork of the stewards' mission. The reporter asked, "Could you explain to our viewers what has caused the fundamental deterioration in the world today?"

She replied, "The one-hundred-and-eighty-degree turn seen in the usual explosive regions reflects mankind's belligerent nature. It also displays his lack of trust in his neighbor and unwillingness to compromise. More important, he has revealed his lack of faith and veneration for the Almighty. Amazing how little time it has taken for mankind to revert back to his sinful ways. Aggression between neighboring countries has surfaced once again, resulting in death and destruction. On a micro basis, signs of regression are obvious, with street crimes on the rise in the overcrowded cities. Why, in the city of Los Angeles alone, crime rates have returned to levels not seen for over a year. Even the manner in which people treat one another seems to have eroded. And for some unimaginable reason, attendance at places of worship has declined."

The reporter asked, "What can be done to reinstate the guidelines in Brother's mission that the stewards have worked so hard to implement?"

"I can't say for sure. For the last few weeks I have asked myself, how could thoughtful attitudes and compassionate behavior be replaced by indifference and insensitivity? How could the words of Brother be placed aside in such a short span of time? Are men and women that shallow and naive as to believe their thoughts and actions are invisible? What does Father have to do to convince mankind of his anger?"

The interviewer was apprehensive about the possibilities in Pauline's last comment and thanked her for candid responses.

###

The meeting room at the hotel was filled with the stewards and their advisors. All were disappointed at the state of the world -- disappointed at the failures they felt responsible for.

"It reminds one of the losing team of the Super Bowl,"Thaddaeus said. "To get so far and then fail is akin to not winning any of the games played during the regular season. Furthermore, no one remembers the team that lost to the Super Bowl winner, or how good a year their team had."

Peter thanked him for his unique analogy, adding, "The only difference is, there is another football season the following year. I'm afraid if Father enacts his anger on us, there might not be another year."

Peter's profound comments gave thought to when Father would show his ultimate power. When would he strike at mankind's inability to live in peace? How would he punish mankind for his failures? These questions circulated the room -- a room which less than two years ago was filled with hope and excitement. Where the ultimate experience of dining with Brother occurred. Where he spoke of his love and passion for every man and woman. Where he named them his stewards. And only two years later, the room was full of apprehensive world travelers, dismayed at the thought of the consequences of man's failure to obey.

Thomas asked Peter, "Are you suggesting the only question is how Father plans to deal with us?"

"Precisely, my friend. In the near future, I am sure we will begin to see the evidence of his wrath."

"The sign of the end, Peter?"asked Bartholomew.

"I don't know. I just don't know."

THIRTY ONE

Peter spent the balance of the year 2001 on the road. He and Pauline had continued the crusade of speaking engagements in hopes that they could create a new cadre of supporters to spread Brother's word. They were pleasantly surprised at the interest and willingness of the thousands of new recruits they had enlisted.

With the newspapers and television screens full of conflicts and reprisals, doubt and apprehension remained in Peter's mind. He and Philip had just concluded an emotional speech in Rio de Janeiro when he called to explain his concerns to Pauline. She was in Oslo, accompanied by Thomas, in the final city of a northern European tour. "Two steps forward and one step back,"Peter said. "With all the positive signs we receive, there is still an abundance of those who do not believe. We convince thousands, sometimes millions, at least for a while, then they go back to their sinful ways. It's like climbing up Mount Everest filled with potholes donated by New York City and detours compliments of Italy's autostrada."

Convincingly, Pauline warned Peter, "Don't believe all the newspaper stories, especially the headlines. They will only make you cynical and cause you to lose your objectivity. And you, of all people, must maintain your focus. I'll see you back in South Beach tomorrow."

The other stewards had returned home; however, they too continued to spend many hours dedicated to the wishes of Brother. Each communicated with Peter weekly to discuss their successes and failures. The conversations with Thomas contained a few barbs about the Swede's relationship with Pauline. Otherwise the talks were serious. All asked Peter if any signs of Father's wrath had been experienced.

But there were none. No major earthquakes, volcanic action, fires, or floods to report. Not that Mother Nature had been totally silent during the first six months of the year; it was just that nothing was out of the ordinary. An earthquake in the scenic valley of Puerto Montt, Chile. A flood in the picturesque setting of Saint Mark's Square in Venice, Italy. A destructive brush fire in the rolling hills of Ojai, California. A few volcanoes erupted along the Ring Of Fire in the Pacific. Nothing new -- these were to be expected.

Rabbi Silverman told Peter in his weekly phone call, "It's like living in the fifties and sixties, waiting for the big one to fall."

Imam Qutb informed Peter, "The last few weeks I've heard from Muslim leaders all over. Each of them is showing signs of apprehension and trepidation waiting for Allah's anger to become visible."

Cardinal O'Connor's and Bishop Parker's phone calls were no different. They both reported having received numerous calls from bishops and church pastors reflecting the uneasiness of their parishioners. Even Dolores Quan brought to his attention an article on the front page in a Taipei newspaper speculating on the potential impact of Father's fury.

But Father's wrath was still under wraps. Could it be that he was content with the way humanity received and acted on his demands? After all, there had been some new believers, and many millions more had at least partially altered their life styles. This conclusion was reached by theologians of each of the major religions. They made their feelings known by sending letters to Peter, who subsequently passed the information on to the other stewards and advisors.

Peter was gratified at the response of the theologians and the comments he had received from the stewards' advisors, but he also felt he was on the planet's largest roller coaster. The emotional swings reflected in recent telephone conversations gave him some hope that perhaps humankind was coming around. But he also sensed deep down that tomorrow's newscast, portraying crime, violence and dictatorial repression, would reveal the uphill climb still facing the stewards. Peter selfishly wished for the open waters of the Pacific and a great day of fishing on the good ship Amalfi.

By all accounts they should have died days ago. Their brains continued functioning although their low blood pressure indicated that the patients should be in shock and subsequently in a coma. Doctor Alan DeLong, chief of staff at Johns Hopkins Hospital in Baltimore, listened intently to the veteran doctors affiliated with this prestigious facility explain their incredible dilemma. He called a staff meeting to get to the bottom of this bizarre incident.

The medical staff was perplexed at the sheer number of similar cases throughout the hospital. Thirty-six in all, suffering from the usual debilitating conditions such as cancer, heart disease, and AIDS. Twenty-five of them, at the request of their families, had been taken off life-support ventilators more then seventy-two hours before.

Intravenous fluids were ceased in an attempt to not prolong the inevitable. Many of these cases endured what the intensive care unit so humanely refers to as the friend of the elderly, pneumonia. One veteran physician commented, "The pain and agony these poor souls are experiencing is creating a stir throughout the entire ICU, the likes of which I've not seen in my thirty years of practicing medicine."

Another doctor said, "I can't explain why they're still alive. It's a wonder their brains are functioning at all. When they speak, signs of insanity and uncontrollable emotional stress are evident. They've crossed over the line of the disturbed and now can be classified as in a state of madness. What's more, we have no prescription for this condition."

The head nurse of fourteen years also mentioned, "Our supply of morphine is as low as it's been since I've been at the hospital. And don't ask me about obtaining any new supplies of it, either. Every drug company in the area is on back order. We are at our wit's end as to how to ease the pain of these hopeless people. And my nurses are threatening to quit unless something is done, and soon."

"What's your opinion of this?"Doctor DeLong asked of his chief neurosurgeon.

"I've examined several of them and by all signs, they should have passed away days ago. At the very least,"he added, "the reduced blood flow should have affected their brain stem functions, subsequently causing a stroke and eventually leaving them brain dead. But none of them, I repeat none of them, shows any indication on the e.e.g. As I've often said,"the perplexed neurosurgeon continued, scratching his balding head, "what I think will happen doesn't always happen, leaving me and the poor grieving family members without an answer. Something or someone is keeping them alive, and whatever it is, it's beyond my scope of medicine."

"What do you mean by that?"asked the chief of staff.

"I don't actually know, but it sure is eerie."

After two and a half hours of deliberation and an examination of six of the patients by the chief of staff himself, a decision was reached to take this situation to another level.

There were reports of victims surviving shootings at point blank range. What would ordinarily have caused fatalities from head-on automobile crashes resulted in over-filled hospitals of mutilated victims, when by all that is understood of physiology, they should have expired on inpact.

A bombing in Palestine that would have killed twenty bus passengers resulted in severe injuries, but no deaths. Astonished medical people on the scene couldn't explain why any of the victims survived after suffering such incredible mutilation.

The newscaster on the radio cited similar occurrences at hospitals in Chicago and New York, as the black Mercedes took Doctor DeLong and two of his associates to the National Institutes of Health in Bethesda. The data that had been collected there was consistent with what others were experiencing. Reports from Madrid, Berlin, and Tokyo revealed hundreds of cases with identical characteristics.

World health organizations around the globe were at a loss to explain this phenomenon. As the days went by, thousands of patients in every country were being attended to by doctors who could not rationalize why these poor souls remained living. The pain and suffering was felt not only by these pathetic individuals near death, but by their grieving relatives as well. This situation also had its effects on the thousands of frustrated doctors and nurses who had taught themselves to be immune to the sounds of discomfort and suffering which had now reached its saturation point. Not only did they have to cope with the sounds of pain, they had to deal with the frustration of a situation out of reach of the medical journals and research laboratories.

Patients were crowding hallways, foyers, and administrative offices in hospitals all over the world. The dilemma did not end there! Incoming cases of the usual illnesses, as well as the day-to-day accidents requiring emergency room assistance, were hastily administered antibiotics or first aid and sent on their way. Surgery cases that were not life-threatening were being delayed, and elective procedures were out of the question.

Trauma cases received appropriate attention, but even they were not being accorded adequate care. Physicians in ERs were sensing they were not in control of the fate of their many heart attack and accident victims, who lay partially covered with white sheets. The professionals knew full well some of these patients should probably be covered with sheets from head to toe. Hospital staffs were working twenty-hour shifts, to try to cope with the overcrowded facilities. The morale of doctors, nurses, and the many voluntteers who are required to make hospitals function had deteriorated to the depths of desperation and disillusionment. Hospital administrators feared it would be only a matter of days or weeks before the entire culture within these facilities and the medical society as a whole would come tumbling down.

At first, news accounts of unusual events appeared in the middle pages of the medical and science sections of the daily newspapers. Television reports were sketchy at best, with just the customary twenty-second blips dedicated to mentioning what was occurring. Before the week was out, the number of cases swelled to tens of thousands. And it wasn't restricted to any country, region, or continent. Headlines in the tabloids read "The Living Dead,"with pictures and interviews from family members. The rest of the media compelled to run the stories, did not know how to tone down this horrific phenomenon.

In the North Atlantic, a supertanker filled with oil sliced through a Norwegian freighter, cutting the cargo ship in two. Twenty-two seamen on the vessel were tossed overboard into the Atlantic's frigid waters. Almost completely submerged in the ice cold ocean for more than fifteen minutes, their lowered body temperatures caused severe hypothermia. Before the tanker's crew was able to rescue them, they lapsed into shock. Their limp torsos were placed side by side in the galley and examined by the ship's captain. These men should be dead, he stated, but they are still breathing, although their other vital signs suggest that they should have expired.

In New Zealand, a crowded passenger train from Auckland to Wellington derailed, leaving more than seventy people in critical condition. Emergency crews found it difficult to respond when asked by the media if there were any casualties. A spokesman for the paramedics on the scene described the various injuries, which normally would have been fatal, but said none of these victims had expired. They survived, despite receiving what one of the paramedics called, "the most severe injuries I have ever seen."

An inmate on death-row in Florida continued to plead for his release as he sat in the infamous electric chair, claiming his innocence right up to the moment the two-thousand volts passed through the electrodes on his scalp and calf, and shook his body like a rubber doll. The coroner examined the seemingly lifeless body, but to his surprise the three-time loser had survived. Shouting out in pain and shaking from the jolt of electricity to his body, the condemned man was taken to the prison infirmary.

###

An avalanche in the Salzburg Alps in Austria buried thirty-two people in a ski chalet. Forty feet of snow buried the luxury resort. Officials had little hope of finding any survivors. Rescuers drilled several holes in the tightly packed snow, then inserted pipes to deliver oxygen to the trapped survivors. For three days, hundreds of volunteers and emergency crews used plows, shovels, and barehands to rescue those trapped. What they found when the chalet was finally uncovered were thirty-two poor souls, near death, but still hanging on. The screams and the sight of the horrific injuries caused even the most seasoned rescue worker's stomachs to turn, as they wondered how and why all of these people could still be alive.

###

Even several ill-fated aircraft, which could be expected to account for devastating losses of passengers and crew, produced screaming, barely living survivors who endured the pain and agony of life without hope, wishing to have, but not being able to find, eternal rest. From patients experiencing heart failure, who should have been straight-lined, to AIDS patients taken off life-support systems, the results were similar.

No one died!

These reports did not go unnoticed in South Beach. There, Peter and the others had gathered for the engagement party for Pauline Demitri and Thomas Olson. Andrew acted as emcee, explaining to the others the only reason Pauline accepted his proposal of marriage was that the dressmaker knew how to sew. Although no one allowed the spreading accounts of these eerie occurrences to spoil the party, Peter asked the stewards to set aside some time the following morning to discuss these strange events the following morning.

James asked, "Could this be what Brother meant when he told us about the consequences? Is this how Father intends to exhibit his wrath?"

Jim's question was more direct. "Does he plan to condemn all of mankind to a prolonged life of suffering and pain?"

"Is this the Father you told me about, Peter, who was all-loving and forgiving?"asked Bartholomew.

"Why has Brother permitted this to happen?" questioned Simon.

"We have converted millions through our work. Why doesn't he give us more time to complete our job?"asked Judas.

Peter was taking it all in. The heated questions from the others burned his ears. He held up his hands in an attempt to quiet his associates, while at the same time searching for the proper words to defend Father's actions. But, Peter realized, he would have to yield to the concerns and observations of the other stewards. For almost fifty minutes, the group continued its sizzling debate.

Finally, Pauline said, "What did you expect Father to do? Tell the world everything was okay? Just watch things continue to regress until humankind finally went over the edge? If it hasn't already. If it is his wrath causing these poor suffering people to hang on to the very threads of life, then I, too, am surprised Father has decided to show humankind his anger in this fashion. If this is indeed his work, then we have to accept it and do what we have to do to reverse course. We must now move more forcefully than ever, retrace our steps to convince the masses once and for all that Father must be reckoned with. Plead with the leadership of each country and every congregation in all religious circles to change their ways. And for those who don't believe, let them visit the hospitals and clinics to see for themselves God's anger. Let them see firsthand what our children and all generations to come will be faced with."

"Well stated, Pauline,"said Peter. "We must now face a ravaged world on the steps of iniquity. Tell them, this may indeed be their last opportunity to mend the fences with their creator. Perhaps another chance, if he is so gracious and compassionate as to give us one more opportunity to alter the way we live. We must have faith that Father is truly all-loving, and, more important, inclined to forgive. Let us proceed with our plan, a blueprint to convert those many sinners to a life of understanding and conciliation, willing to atone for their transgressions, while at the same time working for the betterment of all mankind. Keeping one thought in our minds at all times: Father is the true God of all of mankind."

THIRTY TWO

It reminded oldtimers who had been around since World War II of the horrifying pictures and eyewitness accounts of the holocaust, or a soldier's chronicle revealing his buddy close to death in an adjacent fox hole or crippled yards away in a mine field. The sounds of those near death lingered in their minds for more than fifty years. All those reminders of the destruction of war and violence returned to their minds.

Two months had elapsed since the first sign of prolonged existence had been reported. Uncontrollable screams and the repulsive stench of decay permeated hospitals all around the globe. Hundreds of thousands lay on gurneys, makeshift stretchers, and cots, or were wrapped in blankets on the cold marble or earthen floors of these institutes of health.

Even in the most sophisticated sanctuaries in the United States, it was obvious an unnerving crisis was in full swing. Hospital hallways and cafeterias were needed to house the increasing number of patients who under normal circumstances would have died. They were jammed together, shoulder to shoulder, in a manner resembling the inadequate facilities in impoverished and overpopulated countries such as India.

People had to step over the mass of humanity lying beneath them as they made their way around the ever-narrowing passageways. With nothing to ease their pain, the victims' penetrating tones of torment and distress reverberated throughout each hospital floor. On many occasions in the past, physicians have told loved ones a patient's fate was out of their hands. Never before had this been so true.

There was no space for distinctions in class, affluence, or social status. Aging Hollywood stars were placed next to street urchins. Wall Street executives were screeching just as loudly as the Bowery indigents lying beside them. The penniless and the millionaires, clad in the clothes they arrived in, moaned together, suffered together, and by some strange force hung on to life together. The unmerciful sounds and stomach-turning odors prevailed throughout each facility.

But no one died!

#

Peter and Pauline visited hospitals in southern Florida to examine what appeared to them to be the consequences of Father's fury.

"Why else would this be happening?" Peter asked. "Brother said things would not be very pretty on earth. But this!"

"You're right, Peter. How could Father possibly do this to us if he is all-loving, as he says he is?"

"Good question, Pauline. We must take this opportunity to restate our case. Explain to the world leaders the Almighty has decided to play hard ball, and we best alter our thinking toward him."

#

It took the better part of a year for the stewards to revisit each metropolis. At their request, meetings with heads of state and the various religious leaders were conducted not in plush government offices, but in the repellant surroundings of over-filled hospitals.

The mighty and powerful bureaucrats pleaded with the stewards for assistance in ending this unbelievable problem. The stewards responded by reiterating Brother's message, walking throughout the hospitals to baptize each of the poor souls near death, as Brother had taught them to do.

As a result of the stewards' visits and the acceptance of Father, and his covenant, many thousands of sufferers ended their misery and died in merciful peace. This time around humanity got the message. Within weeks, the renaissance that the stewards had worked so hard to achieve was beginning to take shape. Even in regions not familiar with all of his goodness, people began to worship Father. Shrines and temples were erected worldwide to pray to him, including a very unassuming one in South Beach, Florida. A sacred holiday asking for his forgiveness and tolerance was established, to be celebrated the seventeenth of December, the date Brother had returned.

Although burials were backed up, they were conducted with all the dignity and self-respect due those who had finally been allowed to pass on. Hospital staffs were able to deal with the living and assist those near death with the necessary doses of medication to make their last days on earth less painful. The medical profession could at last proceed with the task of saving the lives of the infirm.

Father's warnings had finally been taken to heart through the profound words told to this small group by his Son in a small hotel in South Beach, in a doctrine set forth by the man who wished to be called Brother. He had stressed that humankind must remember to maintain these ideals, principles, and ethics in their everyday lives and to live under man's laws, but above all, under GOD's commandments.

###

The steward's reunion was a joyous one. Thousands gathered outside the White Sand Hotel to join in on this festive occasion, the first commemoration of the holiday that was called by many Salvation Day. It was a day the redeemer was to be glorified and worshipped by people from all walks of life.

The private party celebrated by the stewards recalled their first day on the beach when they met Brother. They recalled the subsequent encounters which forged the newcomers into the group. Reminiscing about the meals they had shared with Brother and the interactions with Speed, the bartender at the Blue Crab restaurant, brought laughter and merriment to all. But the most jubilant portion of the day was reserved for Pauline and Thomas, who were wed by the combined religious triad of Cardinal O'Connor, Rabbi Silverman, and Imam Qutb.

Their meeting lasted two days and was understandably filled with joy. Peter asked for a volunteer to stay behind with him to answer the correspondence from a few of the world's religious leaders. It was an easy decision for the younger Thompson brother, who would take the opportunity to resume his relationship with Mary Dellany. The parting of friends filled many an eye with tears, as one by one the stewards headed for home. The days ahead for them would be filled with the satisfaction that they had played a role in changing the planet we live on for the better.

THIRTY THREE

The New Year was celebrated in South Beach by Peter and John. The following week, on January sixth, Peter asked John to fly to New York to chair a meeting with Cardinal O'Connor, Bishop Parker, Rabbi Silverman, and Imam Qutb. The purpose of the meeting was to arrange a series of seminars for theologians representing more than thirty different religious orders. In addition, John was to make them aware of the numerous reports of unconditional cooperation the stewards had received from every country. Without question, Father's doctrine was finally understood. Even the persistent skeptics appeared to comprehend the preeminent power and everlasting love the Almighty had for them.

It meant John had once again to break an appointment with Mary Dellany, a date that had been postponed for months because of his travel schedule. He searched for the appropriate words as he dialed her number, hoping once again she would forgive him for this sudden change of plans. Not that she wasn't used to the emotional let-downs caused by his untimely trips. Over the last two or more years, these experiences had come to be considered normal.

He was thankful the girl of his dreams did not pick up the phone, because he could use the extra time to figure out how he could make up for his bowing out at the last minute. Instead, the house sitter explained that Mary was on her way to New York.

"Seems there was an emergency in the family," she said, "and Mary is enroute as we speak to be with her sister. Mary instructed me to tell you, John, she tried to get in touch with you, but since she was unable to, gave me these two telephone numbers and locations. One is Mary's sister's apartment, the other, Sloan Kettering Hospital in midtown, Manhattan."

The first hour of Mary's flight was uneventful. The man sitting next to her wasn't very talkative. The only words she heard from him were "thank you" as she played the role of middleman when the flight attendant delivered his beverage. He passed her the cash for the beverage as she handed him a plastic glass and a Beck's beer.

However, as the Delta flight reached the metropolitan New York area, he spoke. "Is this your final destination, or are you commuting to another city?"

Mary informed the casually dressed gentleman, "I'm here to visit my sister in Manhattan." She added sadly, "My nephew is seriously ill."

"I'm sorry to hear that. You must be very close to your sister."

"Yes, I am. It appears she is going to need someone to lean on over the next few weeks. You see, her husband passed away about five years ago and she has no one else but me. She has another son, but he's just a teenager."

The man nodded but said nothing further as the plane landed.

Mary tipped the sky cap as he placed her luggage in an accessible spot at the taxi stand. To Mary's surprise, standing in front of her was the man who had sat next to her on the plane.

He smiled and asked, "I'm going to Manhattan too. Do you wish to share a taxi?"

Mary hesitated and looked at his kind and enchanting eyes before answering. "Okay. Do you live in Manhattan?"

"No, I'll be here for only a few hours."

Mary entered the yellow cab, a bit confused at his last comment, but she thought it best not to pursue the point further.

The driver asked, "Where in Manhattan are you going?"

Mary looked at the man sitting next to her and was surprised to hear him say, "Sloan Kettering Hospital. That's on...."

But the driver interrupted and arrogantly replied, "I know where it is, Mack."

Mary held her hand to her mouth to prevent a silly giggle from bursting through. Yet at the same time she was puzzled over the gentleman's destination. She wanted to find out more about this man but was reluctant to probe. Wondering why he was going to the same hospital, she tactfully said, "You realize we have spent the better part of three hours together, and I don't even know your name. Mine's Mary. Mary Dellany. What's yours?"

"My friends call me Brother. I would like you to do the same."

"Okay, Brother, and you can call me Mary." She asked agreeably, "Are you visiting someone at the hospital?"

"As a matter of fact I am."

"A relative?" she pried further.

"Why, yes, he sure is."

The remainder of the thirty-five minute ride to the hospital was spent looking at and commenting about the spectacular sights and skyline of the city.

"Can you please tell me the room number of Robert Gordon?" Mary asked the middle-aged woman at the information desk. She looked toward the bank of elevators left of the foyer and noticed her traveling companion had gotten on one. Mary wondered how he knew which room his relative was in.

"It's room number 1207. You take the elevators to your left."

"Thank you," Mary replied, and she walked in that direction.

Outside the room, the two sisters, who had not seen one another for almost a year, embraced, tears slid down their cheeks, reflecting both love and admiration as well as worry and fear.

"How's he doing?" Mary asked her older sister.

"Not so good." Linda sobbed softly. "The doctors are at a loss as to what to do next, and it seems each day he gets weaker and weaker. I'm really worried, Mary, he's not going to pull through."

"Now, now, Linda, let's think positive. You told me on the phone, but tell me again, what exactly is his condition called?"

"It's a very rare disease known as 'mastocytosis.'" Through her tears she added, "All of this is very confusing, Mary."

"What does it affect?" Mary asked.

"The type of mastocytosis he has is systemic, meaning it affects some of his major organs, especially the liver."

"What do the doctors say?"

"They tell me that little is known about this condition. A lot of research has been done, but the experts have very few answers. They know Robert's blood levels are not normal, but they can't seem to find the proper medication or treatment to correct the balance."

Mary hugged her sister once again, adding, "We'll fight this together, Linda. I'm not leaving your side until he's back on his feet."

Linda held her sister's hand tightly as they made their way to the cafeteria for a cup of coffee, which led to a bowl of chili after Mary admitted to being famished. After nearly three hours of catching up on each other's lives, their conversation got around to the enchanting man Mary had traveled with.

"A pleasant man," Mary said, "but there was something very unusual about him."

An aide at the twelfth floor nurse's station gave Mary the message that John Thompson would be there within the hour. Mary couldn't believe her eyes when she read the scribbled note, having been unaware that her "date"was in New York for a meeting. She elaborated on her relationship with the Englishman as the two women walked to Robert's private room. The boy was still sound asleep when Mary and Linda entered the darkened room.

Linda first saw the silhouetted figure of a man standing over her youngest son.

"Is that you, Doctor Freeman?"she asked.

"No, Linda,"he responded.

She was concerned about who it could be and turned on the lights. She was still mystified when she saw the man was not dressed in hospital attire. She asked him, "Well, who are you?"

But before he could respond, Mary interrupted, "I know this man. He's the man I traveled here with from Fort Lauderdale. What in heaven's name are you doing here?"

"I thought I might be able to help."

Linda asked, "Are you a doctor?" Expecting a negative response, she walked toward the door to seek hospital security.

"No wait,"Mary said to her sister. She thought for a second as to how to address him and then gave in to his interesting nickname. "Brother, why are you here? I thought you implied to me that you were here to see an ailing relative."

"That's right, Mary. That's precisely why I am here."

"Then what are you doing in Robert's room?"

"To visit one of my relatives."

"But he's not one of your...." Before she could finish her sentence, Mary was astounded by the strange and enchanting aura surrounding this man. The glow in his eyes and the warmth and tenderness of his voice stopped her from interrogating him further.

Now it was Linda's turn to ask, "Haven't we met before?"

"Yes, a couple of years ago. I believe we met at the airport."

It was him. The man she had not been able to get out of her mind, ever since that chaotic winter day. "You were on your way to Miami, if I'm not mistaken."

"That's right."

"But that still doesn't answer the question as to why you are here."

"That's also right."

Mary finally sensed who this extraordinary individual might be, and although she wasn't totally convinced, had to ask the question anyway. "Are you the same Brother who has been sending my friend

John around the world over the last couple of years?"

"Oh, you mean my English friend, John, the younger of the Thompson brothers."

Her body slumped, revealing a measure of astonishment and shock. "You mean you are...."

"Yes, Mary, I am."

"And you are here to help Robert overcome this dreaded disease?"

Brother placed his hands on the boy's forehead and replied, "Yes, ladies, I am."

Linda did not quite understand as she looked at her sister for clarification and guidance.

"I'll tell you later." Mary beamed happily.

Robert awoke at the touch of Brother's hands on his head. His face revealed a smile for the first time in weeks, and he moved his arms and legs back and forth to ease the cramping he had endured.

"Aunt Mary! What are you doing here? So nice to see you," he said with a sparkle in his eyes.

Mary bent to kiss her godson, telling him how much she loved him. She was joined by Linda, and the three embraced. Exhilarated by the very thought of Robert being healed, Mary turned to thank Brother, but he had already left the room. She raced past the nurses' station to the elevators, but he was gone. Smiling and sobbing at the same time, she returned to her sister and nephew.

###

John Thompson waited patiently for the elevator to descend, browsing through the most recent edition of *Time*. When the blue elevator door opened, he stood aside to allow the passengers to exit.

"Hello, John."

Surprised, John looked up, but stood motionless as Brother placed a firm and reassuring hand on his shoulder.

Pointing up, Brother smiled and said warmly, "Take care of Mary and her family. And by the way, please give my best to Peter and the other STEWARDS OF SOUTH BEACH!"